The Vineyards of Calanetti

Saying 'I do' under the Tuscan sun. . .

Deep in the Tuscan countryside nestles the
cturesque village of Monte Calanetti. Famed
its world-renowned vineyards, the village is
al home to the crumbling but beautiful Palazzo
Comparino. It's been empty for months, but
rumours of a new owner are spreading like
v ldfire. . .and that's before the village is chosen
the setting for the royal wedding of the year!

I going to be a rollercoaster of a year, but will
edding bells ring out in Monte Calanetti for
anyone else?

Find out in this fabulously heart-warming,
u fting and thrillingly romantic new eight-book
continuity from Mills & Boon Romance!

Bride for the Italian Boss by Susan Meier

turn of the Italian Tycoon by Jennifer Faye

nited by a Baby Secret by Michelle Douglas

oldier, Hero. . .Husband? by Cara Colter

s Lost and-Found Bride by Scarlet Wilson

The Best Man & the Wedding Planner

Hi: nters

HIS
LOST-AND-FOUND
BRIDE

BY
SCARLET WILSON

Published in Great Britain 2015
by Mills & Boon, an imprint of Harlequin (UK) Limited,
Eton House, 18-24 Paradise Road, Richmond, Surrey, TW9 1SR

© 2015 Harlequin Books S.A.

Special thanks and acknowledgement are given to Scarlet Wilson for her contribution to The Vineyards of Calanetti series.

ISBN: 978-0-263-25181-4

23-1115

Harlequin (UK) Limited's policy is to use papers that are natural, renewable and recyclable products and made from wood grown in sustainable forests. The logging and manufacturing processes conform to the legal environmental regulations of the country of origin.

Printed and bound in Spain
by CPI, Barcelona

Scarlet Wilson writes for both Mills & Boon Romance and Medical Romance. She lives on the west coast of Scotland with her fiancé and their two sons. She loves to hear from readers and can be reached via her website: www.scarlet-wilson.com.

This book is dedicated to my fellow authors
Susan Meier, Jennifer Faye,
Michelle Douglas, Cara Colter, Teresa Carpenter,
Rebecca Winters and Barbara Wallace.
It has been so much fun creating this series with you!

PROLOGUE

'Signor! Signor, venga ora!'

Logan Cascini was on his feet in an instant. As an architect who specialised in restoring old Italian buildings, to get the call to help transform the Palazzo di Comparino's chapel for a royal wedding was a dream come true.

The property at the vineyard was sprawling and over the years areas had fallen into disrepair. His work was painstaking, but he only employed the most specialised of builders, those who could truly re-create the past beauty of the historic chapel in the grounds and the main *palazzo*. Most of the buildings he worked on were listed and only traditional building methods could be used to restore them to their former glory.

Timescales were tight in order to try and get the chapel restored for the royal wedding of Prince Antonio of Halencia and his bride-to-be, Christina Rose. No expense was being spared—which was just as well considering he had twenty different master builders on-site.

'Signor! Signor, venga ora!'

He left his desk in the main *palazzo* and rushed outside to the site of the chapel. His stomach was twisting. *Please don't let them have found anything that would hold up the build.* The last thing he needed was some unexpected hundred-year-old bones or a hoard of Roman crockery or coins.

This was Italy. It wouldn't be the first time something unexpected had turned up on a restoration project.

He reached the entrance to the ancient chapel and the first thing that struck him was the fact there was no noise. For the last few weeks the sound of hammers on stone and the chatter of Italian voices had been constant. Now every builder stood silently, all looking towards one of the walls.

The interior of the chapel had been redecorated over the years. Much of the original details and façade had been hidden. The walls had been covered first in dark, inlaid wood and then—strangely—painted over with a variety of paints. Every time Logan came across such 'improvements' he cringed. Some were just trends of the time—others were individual owners' ideas of what made the building better. In restoration terms that usually meant that original wood and stone had been ripped away and replaced with poorer, less durable materials. Sometimes the damage done was irreparable.

His eyes widened as he strode forward into the chapel. Light was streaming through the side windows and main door behind him. The small stained-glass windows behind the altar were muted and in shadow. But that didn't stop the explosion of riotous colour on the far wall.

A few of the builders had been tasked with pulling down the painted wooden panelling to expose the original walls underneath.

There had been no indication at all that this was what would be found.

Now he understood the shouts. Now he understood the silence.

Beneath the roughly pulled-back wood emerged a beautiful fresco. So vibrant, the colours so fresh it looked as if it had just been painted.

Logan's heart rate quickened as he reached the fresco. He started shaking his head as a smile became fixed on his face.

This was amazing. It was one of the most traditional of frescoes, depicting the Madonna and Child. Through his historical work Logan had seen hundreds of frescoes, even attending a private viewing of the most famous of all at the Sistine Chapel.

But the detail in this fresco was stunning and being able to see it so close was a gift. He could see every line, every brushstroke. The single hairs on Mary's head, baby Jesus's eyelashes, the downy hair on his skin, the tiny lines around Mary's eyes.

Both heads in the fresco were turned upwards to the heavens, where the clouds were parted, a beam of light illuminating their faces.

Part of the fresco was still obscured. Logan grabbed the nearest tool and pulled back the final pieces of broken wood, being careful not to touch the wall. Finally the whole fresco was revealed to the viewers in the chapel.

It was the colour that was most spectacular. It seemed that the years behind the wood had been kind to the fresco. Most that he'd seen before had been dulled with age, eroded by touch and a variety of other elements. There had even been scientific studies about the effects of carbon dioxide on frescoes. 'Breathing out' could cause harm.

But this fresco hadn't had any of that kind of exposure. It looked as fresh as the day it had been painted.

His hand reached out to touch the wall and he immediately pulled it back. It was almost magnetic—the pull of the fresco, the desire to touch it. He'd never seen one so vibrant, from the colour of Mary's dark blue robe to the white and yellow of the brilliant beam of light. The greens of the surrounding countryside, the pink tones of Jesus's skin, the ochre of the small stool on which Mary sat and the bright orange and red flowers depicted around them. It took his breath away.

He'd hoped to restore this chapel to its former glory—but he'd never expected to find something that would surpass all his expectations.

'*Signor? Signor?* What will we do?' Vito, one of the builders, appeared at his elbow. His eyes were wide, his face smeared with dirt.

'Take the rest of the day off,' Logan said quickly. 'All of you.' He turned to face the rest of the staff. 'Let me decide how to proceed. Come back tomorrow.'

There were a few nods. Most eyes were still transfixed on the wall.

There was a flurry at the entranceway and Louisa, the new owner of the *palazzo*, appeared. 'Logan? What's going on? I heard shouts. Is something…?' Her voice tailed off and her legs automatically propelled her forward.

Louisa Harrison was the American who'd inherited Palazzo di Comparino and hired him to renovate both it and the chapel back to their former beauty. She was hard to gauge. Tall and slim, her long blond hair was tied up in a ponytail and she was wearing yoga pants and a loose-fitting top. Her brow was furrowed as she looked at the fresco and shook her head. 'This was here?' She looked around at the debris on the floor. 'Behind the panelling?'

He nodded while his brain tried to process his thoughts. Louisa would have no idea what the implications of this could be.

She turned back to face him, her face beaming. 'This is wonderful. It's amazing. The colours are so fresh it's as if the painter just put down his paintbrush today. I've never seen anything like this. Have you?'

He took a deep breath and chose his words carefully. 'I've seen a few.' He gave a nod to the wall. 'But none as spectacular as this.'

She was still smiling. It was the most animated he'd seen her since he'd got here. Louisa rarely talked to the tradesmen or contractors and when she did it was all business. No personal stuff. He'd learned quickly that she was a woman with secrets and he still had no idea how she'd managed to inherit such a wonderful part of Italian history.

But her intentions seemed honourable. She'd hired him after going along with the request for a wedding venue from Prince Antonio. And with his growing reputation, thriving architecture business and natural curiosity there had been no way he'd turn down the opportunity to do these renovations.

'It will be the perfect backdrop for the wedding,' Louisa said quietly, her eyes still fixed on the fresco. 'Won't it?'

He swallowed. Exactly how could he put this?

'It could be. I'll need to make some calls.'

'To whom?'

'Any new piece of art has to be reported and examined.'

She wrinkled her nose. 'And a fresco falls under that category?'

He nodded. 'A fresco, any uncovered relics, a mosaic, a tiled floor…' He waved his hand and gave a little smile. 'We Italians like to keep our heritage safe. So much of it has already been lost.'

'And you know who to call? You can sort this all out?' He could almost hear her brain ticking over.

He gave a quick nod.

'Then I'll leave it to you. Let me know if there are any problems.' She spun away and walked to the door.

Logan turned back to the wall and stood very still as he heard the quiet, retreating footsteps. The enormity of the discovery was beginning to unfurl within his brain.

He could almost see the millions of euros' worth of plans for the prince to marry here floating off down the nearby Chiana River.

In his wildest dreams the prince might get to marry his bride with this in the background. But Italian bureaucracy could be difficult. And when it came to listed buildings and historic discoveries, things were usually painstakingly slow.

He sucked in a deep breath. The air in the chapel was still but every little hair stood up on his arms as if a cool breeze had just fluttered over his skin. He knew exactly what this fresco would mean.

He knew exactly who he would have to contact. Who would have the expertise and credentials to say what should happen next. Italy's Arts Heritage Board had a fresco expert who would be able to deal with this.

Lucia Moretti. His ex.

CHAPTER ONE

LUCIA STARED OUT of the window, sipped her coffee and licked the chocolate from her fingers.

If her desk hadn't been on some priceless antiques list somewhere she would lift her aching legs and put them on it. She'd just completed a major piece of work for Italy's Art Heritage Board. Months of negotiations with frazzled artefact owners, restorers and suppliers. Her patience had been stretched to breaking point, but the final agreement over who was going to fund the project had taken longest. Finally, with grants secured and papers signed, she could take a deep breath and relax.

She pushed her window open a little wider. Venice was hot, even for a woman who'd stayed there for the last twelve years, and the small-paned leaded-glass window obstructed her view out over the Grand Canal. A cruise ship was floating past her window right now —in a few months these larger ships wouldn't be allowed along here any more. The huge currents they unleashed threatened the delicate foundations of the world-famous city. So much of Venice had been lost already—it was up to the present generation to protect the beauty that remained.

Her boss, Alessio Orsini, put his head around the

door. His eyes were gleaming and she straightened immediately in her chair. Alessio had seen just about every wonder of the world. There wasn't much left that could make his eyes twinkle like that.

'I've just had the most interesting call.' She waved her hand to gesture him into her room, but even though he was in his late seventies he would rarely sit down.

'What is it?'

He gave a little nod. 'There's been a discovery. A new fresco—or rather an old one. Just been discovered in Tuscany during a chapel restoration. I've given him your number.' He glanced at her desk. 'Seems like perfect timing for you.'

She smiled. Alessio expected everyone around him to have the boundless energy he had. But her interest was piqued already. An undiscovered fresco could be a huge coup for the heritage board—particularly if they could identify the artist. So many frescoes had been lost already.

It seemed as though the whole of Italy was rich with frescoes. From the famous Sistine Chapel to the ancient Roman frescoes in Pompeii.

The phone on her desk rang and she picked it up straight away. This could be the most exciting thing she'd worked on in a while.

'*Ciao*, Lucia.'

It was the voice. Instantly recognisable. Italian words with a Scottish burr. Unmistakable.

Her legs gave a wobble and she thumped down into her chair.

'Logan.' It was all she could say. She could barely get a breath. His was the last voice in the world she'd expected to hear.

Logan Cascini. The one true love of her life. Meeting him in Florence had been like a dream come true. Normally conservative, studying art history at Florence University had brought Lucia out of her shell. Meeting Logan Cascini had made it seem as though she'd never had a shell in the first place.

He'd shared her passion—hers for art, his for architecture. From the moment they'd met when he'd spilled an espresso all down her pale pink dress and she'd heard his soft burr of Scottish Italian she'd been hooked.

She'd never had a serious relationship. Three days after meeting they'd moved in together. Life had been perfect. *He* had been perfect.

They'd complemented each other beautifully. He'd made her blossom and she'd taught him some reserve. He'd been brought up in a bohemian Italian/Scots family and had often spoken first and thought later.

She'd had dreams about them growing old together until it had all come to a tragic end. Getting the job in Venice had been her lifeline—her way out. And although she'd always expected to come across him at some point in her professional life she hadn't realised the effect it would have.

Twelve years. Twelve years since she'd walked away from Logan Cascini. Why did she suddenly feel twenty years old again?

Why on earth was he calling her after all this time?

He spoke slowly. 'I hope you are well. Alessio Orsini suggested you were the most appropriate person to deal with. I'm working in Tuscany at the Palazzo di Comparino in Monte Calanetti. I'm renovating the chapel for the upcoming wedding of Prince Antonio of Halencia and Christina Rose, and yesterday we made the most amazing discovery. A fresco of the Madonna and Child. It's exquisite, Lucia. It must have been covered up for years because the colours of the paint are so fresh.'

His voice washed over her like treacle as her heart sank to the bottom of her stomach. How stupid. Of course. Alessio had just told her he'd given someone her number. He just hadn't told her *who*.

Logan Cascini was calling for purely professional reasons—nothing else. So why was she so disappointed?

It wasn't as if she'd spent the last twelve years pining for him. There was a connection between them that would last for ever. But she'd chosen to leave before they'd just disintegrated around each other. Some relationships weren't built to withstand tragedy.

She tried to concentrate on his words. Once she'd got over the initial shock of who was calling, her professionalism slipped back into place.

This was work. This was only about work. Nothing else.

Being involved in the discovery and identification of a new fresco would be amazing. She couldn't believe the timing. If she'd still been caught up in negotiations, Alessio could have directed this call to someone else on the team. Even though frescoes were her speciality, the Italian Heritage Board expected all their staff to be able to cover a whole range of specialities.

She drew in a deep breath. Her brain was still spinning, still processing. This was the man she'd lived with, breathed with. What had he been doing these last few years?

Her heart twisted in her chest. Was he married? Did he have children?

'Lucia?'

His voice had been brisk before, but now it was soft. The way it had been when he'd tried to cajole or placate her. Just the tone sent a little tremor down her spine.

She cleared her throat, getting her mind back on the job. She had to take Logan out of this equation. This discovery could be career-changing. It was time to put her business head on her shoulders.

'What can you tell me about the fresco?'

He hesitated. 'I almost don't know where to start.' His voice was echoing. He must be standing in the chapel now. She squeezed her eyes shut. She didn't need to imagine Logan—his broad shoulders, thick dark hair and oh-so-sexy green eyes. He was already there. Permanently imprinted from the last time she'd seen him.

After all the emotion, all the pent-up frustration and anger, all the tears, she'd been left with his face on her mind. A picture of resolve. One that knew there was no point continuing. One that knew walking away was the only way they would both heal.

She'd known he wouldn't come after her. They had been past that point. He might not have agreed but he'd realised how much they'd both been damaging each other.

The vision of him standing in the stairwell of their apartment, running his hand through his just-too-long hair, his impeccable suit rumpled beyond all repair and his eyelids heavy with regret had burned a hole in her mind.

'Just tell me what you see.' She spoke quickly, giving her head a shake and trying to push him from her mind.

He sighed. 'I can't, Lucia. I just can't. It's just too… too…magnificent. You have to see it for yourself. You have to see it in the flesh.'

Flesh. Every tiny hair on her arms stood on end. Seeing it in the flesh would mean seeing *him* in the flesh.
Could she really go there again?

'Wait,' he said. She could hear him fumbling and
for a second it made her smile. Logan wasn't prone to
fumbling. 'What's your email address?'

'What?'

'Your email. Give me your email address. I've just
taken a photo.'

She recited off her email address. It was odd. She
didn't even want to give that little part of herself away to
him again. She wanted to keep herself, and everything
about her, sealed away. Almost in an invisible bubble.

That would keep her safe.

Being around Logan again—just hearing his voice—
made her feel vulnerable. Emotionally vulnerable. No
one else had ever evoked the same passion in her that
Logan had. Maybe it was what they'd gone through together, what they'd shared that made the connection run
so deep. But whatever it was she didn't ever want to re-
create it. She'd come out the other side once before. She
didn't think she'd ever have the strength to do it again.

Ping. The email landed in her inbox and she clicked
to open it.

As soon as the photo opened she jerked back in her
seat. Wow.

'Have you got it?'

'Oh, I've got it,' she breathed. She'd spent her life
studying frescoes. Most of the ones she'd encountered
were remnants of their former selves. Time, age, environment had all caused damage. Few were in the con-
dition of the one she was looking at now. It was an
explosion of radiant colour. So vivid, so detailed that

her breath caught in her throat. She expanded the photo. It was so clear she could almost see the brushstrokes. What she could definitely see was every hair on the baby Jesus's head and every tiny line around Mary's eyes.

'Now you get it,' said the voice, so soft it almost stroked her skin.

'Now I get it,' she repeated without hesitation.

There was silence for a few seconds as her eyes swept from one part of the fresco to another. There was so much to see. So much to relish. The palm of her hand itched to actually reach out and touch it.

'So, what now?'

The million-dollar question. What now indeed? 'Who owns the property?' she asked quickly.

'Louisa Harrison—she's an American and inherited the property from a distant Italian relative. She hired me to renovate the *palazzo* and chapel for the upcoming royal wedding.'

Lucia frowned. 'What royal wedding?'

Logan let out a laugh. 'Oh, Lucia, I forget that you don't keep up with the news. Prince Antonio of Halencia and Christina Rose. It's only a few short weeks away.'

'And you're still renovating?' She couldn't keep the surprise from her voice. All the Italian renovation projects that Logan had been involved with before had taken months to complete. Months of negotiation for the correct materials sourced from original suppliers and then the inevitable wait for available master craftsmen.

This time he didn't laugh. This time there was an edge to his voice. 'Yes. I have around forty men working for me right now. This fresco—it was more than a little surprise. There was wood panelling covering all the walls. Every other wall we've uncovered has been bare. We expected this one to be the same.' He sighed. 'I expected just to use original plaster on the walls. It should only have taken a few days.'

Now she understood. This discovery was amazing— but it could also cause huge hold-ups in Logan's work. She'd known him long enough to know that would be worrying him sick.

Logan never missed a deadline. Never reneged on a deal. And although she hadn't heard about this wedding she was sure it must be all over the media. If Logan couldn't finish the renovations of the church in time the whole wedding would be up in the air and his reputation would be ruined.

Not to mention his bank balance. She'd no idea who the owner was, but there was every chance she'd put a clause in the contract about delayed completion— particularly when it was so vital.

'I'll come.' The words were out before she really thought about it. She grabbed a notebook and pen. 'Give me the address and I'll make travel arrangements today.' As her pen was poised above the paper her brain was screaming at her. *No. What are you doing?*

She waited. And waited.

'You'll come here?' He sounded stunned—almost disbelieving.

Her stomach recoiled. Logan obviously had the same reservations about seeing her as she had about him. But why—after twelve years—did that hurt?

But he recovered quickly, reciting the address, the nearest airport and recommending an airline. 'If you let me know your flight details I'll have someone pick you up.'

His voice was still as smooth as silk but she didn't miss the implication—Logan hadn't offered to pick her up himself.

It didn't matter that she was alone in her office, she could almost feel her mask slipping into place. The one that she'd used on several occasions over the years when people had started to get too close and ask personal questions. When past boyfriends had started to make little noises about moving to the next stage of their relationship.

Self-preservation. That was the only way to get through this.

'I'll email you,' she said briskly, and replaced the receiver. She ignored the fact her hands were trembling slightly and quickly made arrangements on her computer. Alessio would be delighted at the prospect of a new fresco. As long as it wasn't a complete fake and a wasted journey.

But it didn't sound like a fake—hidden for years behind wood panelling in a now-abandoned private chapel. It sounded like a hidden treasure. And even though she didn't want to admit it, Logan was so experienced in Italian architecture and art he would have enough background knowledge to spot an obvious fake.

She sent a few final emails and went through to give the secretary she shared with five other members of staff her itinerary for the next few days. It was five o'clock and her flight was early next morning. She needed to pick up a few things and get packed.

She turned and closed her window. Venice. She'd felt secure here these last few years. She'd built a life here on her own. She had a good job and her own fashionable apartment. There was security in looking out her window every day and watching the traffic and tourists on the Grand Canal. The thought of heading to Tuscany to see Logan again was unsettling her. She felt like a teenager.

She picked up her jacket and briefcase, opening her filing cabinets to grab a few books. She had detailed illustrations of just about every fresco ever found. There were a few artists who'd lived in Tuscany who could have painted the fresco. It made sense to take examples of their work for comparison.

She switched on her answering-machine and headed for the door. She needed to be confident. She needed to be professional. Logan would find this situation every bit as awkward as she would.

She was an expert in her field—that's why she'd been called. And if she could just hold on to the *career-defining* thought and keep it close, it could get her through the next few days.

Because if that didn't, she wasn't sure what would.

CHAPTER TWO

Lucia stepped down from the chartered flight with her compact red suitcase in her hand. She'd spent most of the flight going over notes, trying to determine who the likely artist of the fresco would be.

The style was vaguely familiar. But there were a huge number of fresco artists spanning hundreds of years. Often the date of the building helped with the determination of the artist, but it seemed that Palazzo di Comparino had existed, in some state, for hundreds of years. The chapel even longer. There were a number of possibilities.

The airport in Tuscany was private—owned by some local multi-millionaire—so she was practically able to walk down the steps into the waiting car.

She gave a nod to the driver. '*Grazie*, I will be staying at Hotel di Stelle.'

He lifted her case in the trunk of the black car. 'No, *signorina*. A room has been prepared for you at Palazzo di Comparino.'

Her stomach clenched. She'd been definite about booking her own accommodation. Working with Logan was one thing, living under the same roof—even for a few days—was too much.

'No, I insist. I must stay at the hotel. Can you drop my bag there, please?'

He gave a little smile and climbed into the driver's seat. The Tuscan countryside flew past. The roads in the area were winding, climbing lush green hills, passing hectares of olive groves and vineyards, filling the air with the aroma of Mediterranean vegetation. Tuscany was known for its rolling hills, vineyards and fine wines and olive oil.

It was also unique in its representation of class. Every kind of person stayed in these hills. They passed a huge array of houses and tiny cottages dotted over the countryside. Medieval villages, castles—some ruins, some renovated—and old farmhouses crowning hilltops.

After thirty minutes the car passed an old crumbling wall and turned onto a narrow road lined with cypress trees, then rolled into the picturesque village of Monte Calanetti. Lucia put down her window for a better view. The village had two bell towers that were ringing out the hour as they arrived. There was also a piazza surrounded by small shops and businesses, cobblestoned walkways going up and down the narrow streets and a fountain where a few children were walking around the small wall surrounding it and splashing water at each other.

There was an old well on one side next to red-brick houses with gorgeous flower boxes and laundry strung overhead.

A few blue and red scooters whizzed past, ridden by young men with their trousers rolled up at their ankles and their hair flapping in the wind. Helmets didn't seem to be a priority.

She smiled. It was gorgeous. It was quaint. It could

be a setting for a film. Every character that was needed was there—the small wizened woman hanging her washing from a window, the young mother hurrying past with her child, a shopkeeper standing in a doorway and a couple of young girls whispering and watching the guys zipping past on their scooters.

The car turned onto another winding road, again lined with cypress trees. It only took a few moments for the *palazzo* to come into sight.

It was a sprawling, grand building with lots of little scattered buildings around. Lucia twisted in her seat, but it wasn't until the car pulled up outside the sweeping entrance of the *palazzo* that she finally saw the building she was after on the other side of the courtyard.

An old traditional chapel. Dark stonework, arched windows and door. It had two stained-glass windows, which had obviously been added at a later date than the original build.

But before she had a chance to focus on the beauty of the building something else took her breath away.

Logan, emerging from the entrance of the chapel. It had been twelve years since she'd seen him and she hadn't quite expected the jolt that was running through her body.

He ran his fingers through his dark hair, which was still a little too long. Logan had always been stylish, had always dressed as if the clothes had been made personally for him. Today he had on cream suit trousers and a pale blue shirt, open at the throat with the sleeves pushed up. Only Italian men could get away with cream suits. She imagined his cream jacket would have been discarded somewhere inside the chapel.

It wasn't just that he'd aged well. He'd aged *movie*

star well. He was still lean, but there was a little more muscle to his frame. His shoulders a bit wider, his shape more sculpted. He lifted his head and his footsteps faltered. He'd noticed her at the same time she'd noticed him, but she could bet his body wasn't doing the same things that hers was.

The car halted and the driver opened her door. There was no retreat. There was nowhere to hide.

She stared down at her Italian pumps for the briefest of seconds, sucking in a breath and trying to still the erratic pitter-patter of her heart. Thank goodness she'd taken off the stilettos. She'd never have survived the cobbled streets of Monte Calanetti.

She accepted the extended hand of the driver and stepped out of the car, pulling down her dress a little and adjusting her suit jacket. The cool interior of the car had kept the heat of Tuscany out well. It was like stepping into a piping-hot bath. This situation was hot enough without the sun's intense rays to contend with.

Logan walked over. His faltering footsteps had recovered quickly. He reached out his hand towards her. 'Lucia, welcome.'

For the briefest of seconds she hesitated. This was business. *This was business.* She tried to appear calm and composed, even though the first little rivulet of sweat was snaking down her back.

She grasped his hand confidently. 'Logan, I hope you've been well. I take it that is the chapel?' She gestured to the building from which he'd emerged.

Straight to the point. It was the only way to be. She had to ignore the way his warm hand enveloped hers. She definitely had to ignore the tiny sparks in her palm and the tingling shooting up her arm. She pulled her hand back sharply.

If he was surprised at her direct response he didn't show it. His voice was as smooth as silk. 'Why don't we go into the main house? I'll show you to your room and introduce you to Louisa, the owner.'

He waved his hand, gesturing her towards the *palazzo*, and she could instantly feel the hackles rise at the back of her neck.

'That won't be necessary. I'm not staying. I've booked a hotel nearby.'

Logan exchanged a glance with the driver, who was already disappearing into the *palazzo* with her red case. 'Why don't you have some refreshments in the meantime? I'd still like to introduce you to Louisa and I'm sure you'd like to see around the *palazzo*—we've already renovated some parts of it, including the room Louisa has set aside for you.'

He was so confident, so assured. It grated because she wished she felt that way too. She was trying her best to mimic the effect, but it was all just a charade. Her stomach was churning so wildly she could have thrown up on the spot. It wasn't just the intense heat that was causing little rivulets of sweat to run down her back, it was Logan. Being in his presence again after all these years and the two of them standing here, exchanging pleasantries, as if what had happened between them hadn't changed their lives for ever, just couldn't compute in her brain.

Business. She kept repeating the word in her head. She was probably going to have to keep doing this for the next few days. Whatever it took to get through them. She had to be professional. She had to be polite. The

Italian Heritage Board would expect her to discuss her findings and proposals with the owner directly—not through a third party. Maybe this way she could take Logan out the equation?

She gave a nod and walked over the courtyard towards the *palazzo*. The first thing she noticed as she walked into the wide entrance hall was the instantly cool air. The *palazzo* may be hundreds of years old but it seemed as though the amenities had been updated. She gently pulled her jacket from her back to let some air circulate.

Logan showed her through to a wide open-plan sitting area. Glass doors gave a wide, spectacular view over the vineyards. She was instantly drawn to the greenery outside.

'Wow. I've never really seen a working vineyard before. This is amazing.'

A beautiful slim blonde emerged from another doorway, her hair tied in a high ponytail, wearing capri pants and a white top. She smiled broadly and held out her hand. 'Welcome. You must be Lucia. Logan told me to expect you. I'm Louisa.' She nodded to the view outside. 'And I knew nothing about vineyards either before I arrived here.'

Lucia shook her hand easily. Should she be cautious? What exactly had Logan told her?

Her eyes flitted from one to the other. Was there a relationship between Logan and Louisa? She watched for a few seconds. Logan had his hands in his pockets and was waiting in the background. He wouldn't do that if he were in a relationship with Louisa and this was their home.

Louisa nodded towards the doorway that must lead

towards the kitchen. 'Can I get you coffee, tea, water or…' she gave a smile '…some wine?'

Of course. She was in a vineyard. Would it be rude to say no? She was Italian, she loved wine. But she was here for business, not pleasure. 'Just some water would be lovely, thank you.'

There was a few seconds of uncomfortable silence as she was left alone with Logan again. He moved over next to her, keeping his hands firmly in his pockets.

'How is your job at the heritage board? Do you like it?'

She gave a brief nod but kept her eyes firmly on the vineyard outside. 'It was always the kind of job that I wanted to do.' She left everything else unsaid. If things had turned out differently there was a good chance that she would never have taken the job in Venice. It would have been too far away from the life they had planned together in Florence.

Something inside her cringed. It was almost as if she'd wanted things to turn out this way and that just wasn't what she'd meant at all.

But Logan didn't seem to notice. He just seemed more concerned with filling the silent space between them. 'And how do you like living in Venice, compared to Florence?' It was his first acknowledgement of anything between them. They'd lived together in Florence for just over a year.

Louisa came back out of the kitchen holding a glass of water. 'You've lived in Florence and now Venice? How wonderful. What's it like?'

Lucia took the water gratefully. Her throat was achingly dry. For the first time since she'd got here she felt on comfortable ground—questions about Venice were always easy to answer. 'Venice is amazing. It's such a welcoming city and it absolutely feels like home to me now. It is, of course, permanently full of tourists, but I don't really mind that. My apartment is on the Grand Canal so at night I can just open my doors and enjoy the world passing by on the water. Some nights it's calming and peaceful—other nights it's complete chaos. But I wouldn't have it any other way.'

Louisa gave a visible shudder. 'Too many people for me. Too much of everything.' She looked out over the vineyards. 'I can't imagine what this place will be like when the royal wedding takes place. There will be people everywhere.' She gave a shake of her head. 'All the farmhouses and outbuildings are being renovated too. Logan's the only person staying in one right now while we still have some quiet about the place.'

Lucia didn't smile. Didn't react. But her body was practically trembling with relief to know she wouldn't be under the same roof as Logan.

Now she might consider staying in the *palazzo* for the next couple of days.

Louisa gave her a smile. 'I intend to stay out of the way as much possible. Now, about the fresco. What happens next? You do understand that we are under an obligation to get the rest of the restoration work finished as soon as possible?'

Lucia could hear the edge in her voice. The same strong hint that had come from Logan. She chose her words carefully. 'It all depends on the fresco itself. Or, more importantly, the artist who created it.'

'Will you know as soon as you look at it?'

She held out her hands. 'It would be wonderful if we could just look at something and say, "Oh, that's by this artist…" But the heritage board requires authentication of any piece of work. Sometimes it's by detailed comparison of brushstrokes, which can be as good an identifier as a signature—we have a specialised computer program for that. Sometimes it's age-related by carbon dating. Sometimes we have to rely on the actual date of the construction of the building to allow us to agree a starting point for the fresco.'

Louisa smiled and glanced over at Logan, who looked lost in his own thoughts. 'Well, that's easy, then. Logan has already been able to date the construction of the *palazzo* and chapel from the stone used and the building methods used. Isn't that right, Logan?'

He turned his head at the sound of his name, obviously only catching the tail end of the conversation. He took a few steps towards Lucia. 'The buildings were constructed around 1500, towards the end of the Italian Renaissance period. The fresco could have appeared at any point from then onwards.'

It didn't matter how tired she was, how uncomfortable she felt around Logan—it was all she could do not to throw off her shoes and dash across the entrance courtyard right now to get in and start examining it.

She gave a polite, cautious nod. 'I'm keen to start work with you as soon as possible, Louisa.'

Louisa's eyes widened and she let out a laugh. 'Oh, you won't be working with me.' She gestured towards Logan. 'You'll be working with Logan. I have absolutely no expertise on any of these things. I've started to call him Mr Restoration. Anything to do with the work has to be agreed with him.'

Lucia eyes fell to the empty glass on the table. Where

was more water when she needed it? This was the last thing she wanted to hear.

She smiled politely once again. 'But, as the owner, I need to agree access with you and have you sign any paperwork the heritage board may require. I also need to be able to come to and from the *palazzo* at my leisure. I will be staying at a nearby hotel.'

'What? Oh, no. You're staying here. Come, and I'll show you to your room.' She was on her feet in an instant. 'We have renovated some parts of the *palazzo*, you know.' She waved her hand. 'And it will all be finished before the wedding.' As she reached the door she turned, waiting for Lucia to follow her.

The corners of Logan's lips were turning upwards.

'Ms Harrison, I really don't want to put you to any trouble. I'm more than happy to stay in a hotel and just travel to and from the *palazzo*. It will only be for a few days. I don't expect my research to take any longer than that.'

Louisa shook her head. 'Nonsense. You'll stay here. I insist. As for the paperwork, Logan will need to read that first and explain it to me. My Italian is still very rusty.'

Louisa had already started up a flight of stairs, obviously expecting Lucia to follow her. 'You're going to have a beautiful view over the vineyard. And you're welcome to use the kitchen if you want.' She paused. 'But there's a really nice restaurant in Monte Calanetti you should try.'

She wanted to object. She wanted to get away from here. But it was important that she have some sort of relationship with the owner. And because of that the words were sticking in the back of her throat. Louisa hadn't stopped talking. She was already halfway up the stairs. It obviously didn't occur to her that Lucia might continue with her objections. 'I'm sure you'll love the room.'

Lucia sucked in a breath. She wasn't even going to look in Logan's direction. If she saw him smile smugly she might just take off one of her shoes and throw it at him in frustration. At least she had the assurance that he wouldn't actually be under the same roof as her.

Just achingly close.

'I'll be back in five minutes. I want to see the fresco,' she shot at him as she left the room.

She walked up the stairs after Louisa and along a corridor. This *palazzo* had three floors—it was unusual, and had obviously survived throughout the ages. The person who'd built this had obviously had plenty of money to build such a large home in the Tuscan hills. Even transporting the stones here must have been difficult. What with the land, and the vineyard, along with all the outbuildings she'd spotted and the chapel, at one time this must have been a thriving little community.

Louisa took her into a medium-sized room with a double bed and wooden-framed glass windows overlooking the vineyard. Everything about the room was fresh and clean. There was white linen on the bed and a small table and chair next to the window, with a classic baroque chair in the corner. A wooden wardrobe, bedside table and mirror on the wall completed the furnishings.

A gentle breeze made the white drapes at the window flap, bringing the scents of the rich greenery, grapes and lavender inside. Her red case was presumptuously sitting next to the doorway.

'I'll bring you up a jug of water, a glass and some wine for later,' said Louisa as she headed out the door. 'Oh, and we don't quite have an en suite, but the bathroom is right next door. You'll be the only person that's using it.'

She disappeared quickly down the hall, leaving Lucia looking around the room. She sank down onto the bed. It felt instantly comfortable. Instantly inviting. The temperature of the room was cool, even though the breeze drifting in was warm, and she could hear the sounds of the workers in the vineyard.

She closed her eyes for a few seconds. She could do this. Two days tops then she could be out of here again. *Logan.* Seeing him again was hard. So hard. The familiar sight of Logan, the scent of Logan was tough. She couldn't let him invade her senses. She couldn't let him into her brain, because if she did a whole host of other memories would come flooding back—ones that she couldn't face again.

This is business. She repeated her mantra once more.

The smell of the Tuscan hills was wrapping itself around her. Welcoming her to the area. Her stomach grumbled. She was hungry, but food would have to wait. She wanted to see the fresco.

She walked over and grabbed her case, putting it on the bed and throwing it open.

It was time to get to work.

Logan had finished pacing and was waiting for Lucia to appear. He'd walked back out to the courtyard and was leaning against the side of the doorway to the chapel with his arms folded across his chest.

It was much warmer out here, but he thrived in the Italian sun.

Seeing Lucia had been a shock to the system. His first glance had been at her left hand but there had been no wedding ring, no glittering diamond of promise. He was surprised. He'd always imagined that after twelve years Lucia would have been married with children. The fact she wasn't bothered him—in more ways than one.

She'd been hurt, she'd been wounded when they'd split. Even though it had been by mutual agreement. But he'd always hoped she'd healed and moved on. When he'd heard she was working for the Italian Heritage Board he'd assumed she'd pulled things together and was focusing on her career. Now he was suspicious she'd *only* focused on her career.

Lucia had aged beautifully. She was still petite and elegant. Her pale pink suit jacket and matching dress hugged her curves, leaving a view of her shapely calves.

And she'd kept her long hair. It was maybe only a few inches shorter than it had been the last time he'd seen her. He liked it that way. Had liked it when her hair had brushed against his face—liked it even more when her long eyelashes had tickled his cheek as she'd moved closer.

It was odd. Even though there were lots of parts of his body that could have responded to the first sight of her, it had been his lips that had reacted first. One sight of her had been enough to remember the feel of her soft lips against his, remember the *taste* of her. And as she'd stepped closer he'd been swamped by her smell. Distinctive. Delicious. In any other set of circumstances…hot.

But not in these circumstances. Not when delays on this project could result in a late completion penalty that could bankrupt his company. Louisa was serious about this place being ready for the royal wedding. She was depending on it.

He straightened as Lucia appeared, walking briskly across the courtyard. She'd changed and was now wearing flat shoes, slim-fitting navy trousers, a pale cream top with lace inserts on the shoulders and a dark silk scarf knotted at her neck. She had a digital camera in her hand.

He was disappointed that her legs were no longer on display.

She stopped in front of him, meeting his gaze straight on. She'd changed a little over the years. There were a few tiny lines around her eyes, but the rest of her skin was smooth. She, like him, had naturally olive Italian skin. Her dark brown gaze was uncompromising. 'Show me your fresco, Logan.'

It was the most direct he'd ever heard her. He tried not to smile. Twelve years had instilled a new-found courage in her. He liked it.

But something else swamped him for a few seconds. There had been a time in his life that Lucia had encompassed everything for him. She'd been the centre of his universe. He shifted self-consciously on his feet. He'd never felt that way again—he'd never *allowed* himself to feel that way again.

It was too much. Too much to have so much invested in one person when your life could change in an instant and everything come tumbling down around you both.

It didn't matter that seeing Lucia again after all these years was swamping him with a host of memories. It was time to put all those feelings back in a box. A place where they were best left.

He gestured towards the entranceway. 'It's all yours. Let's go.'

She walked ahead of him, her tight bottom right in his line of vision. He lifted his eyes to look straight in front of him and smiled as her footsteps faltered as she saw the fresco.

'Oh…whoa.'

He smiled as he stepped alongside her. 'Pretty much what I said too.'

She lifted her camera then put it back down and walked right up to the wall. She lifted her hand but didn't actually touch it. 'It's been covered for…how long?'

Logan shook his head, his hands on his hips. 'I couldn't say for sure.' He pointed to the corner of the room where debris was stacked. 'The wood panelling could be between three and four hundred years old.'

She glanced at the wood and turned back to the fresco. This time she did lift her camera and started snapping, first capturing the full work then systematically snapping detailed sections. Images that she could take time to pore over later.

When she finished she placed the camera on the floor then picked up some tiny fragments of clay that were on the floor—obvious remnants from the uncovering of the fresco. She gathered them in little plastic bags, labelled them, then put them in her bag. Once she'd finished she moved so close to the fresco that her nose was only inches away.

She lifted her fingers. It was obvious she was itching to touch it, but, she was resisting the temptation. 'I can see the movement,' she said quietly. 'I can see the brushstrokes. What kind of brush do you use to paint individual hairs? This is amazing.'

Logan waited, watching her relish her first viewing of the fresco. It was strangely exhilarating. He could see the wonder on her face, see the excitement in her eyes. Just watching her sent a little buzz through his body. Memories were sparking. This was part of the Lucia he'd loved. The wonderful, passionate girl who'd embraced life to the full. When they'd first met she'd been quiet, reserved as a result of her upbringing. But studying in Florence had made her blossom into the beautiful woman he'd quickly grown to love. The buzz, culture and bright lights had been a nurturing environment for the young artistic woman. And the two of them meeting had seemed to spark her even further. All his first memories of Lucia had been about their drive, their passion and their instant connection.

He could feel it even now—twelve years on. The palms of his hands were actually itching to reach out and touch her—just the way hers were obviously itching to touch the fresco. Parts of Lucia had been so easy to read.

Other parts she'd kept tightly locked up and tucked away. Those had been the parts that had sealed the end of their relationship. Every person grieved differently. But Logan just couldn't understand why she'd been unable to talk to *him*, why she'd been unable to share with *him*. After all, he'd been going through exactly the same thing.

He took a deep breath. 'What do you think?'

'The fresco was prepared in sections. *Giornate*— done on a daily basis with small sections of plaster laid at a time to be painted—much in the same way that Michelangelo carried out the work at the Sistine Chapel.'

Logan was incredulous. 'You think this was done by Michelangelo?'

She laughed. 'Oh, no. Of course not. The artist of the time just used the same techniques. Michelangelo used different skin tones from those used here.' She leaned back critically. 'Different draping of the clothes. This definitely isn't his work.'

She finished snapping a few more shots with the camera and turned to face him again. 'I have a program on my computer that I can upload these pictures to. It finds similarities between frescoes and gives the most likely artists.'

He shook his head. 'Why do I feel as if you don't really need it? What's your gut instinct?'

She shook her head. 'I'm not sure. It could be one of a few possibilities.'

He pressed her again. 'But you think…' He let his answer tail off.

She brushed her hair off her shoulder. 'I think there's a chance it's a lesser-known Renaissance painter. His name was Burano.' She gave a wry smile. 'The same as one of the islands in the Venetian lagoon.'

Logan's brow creased. 'He was from Venice, then?'

She nodded.

'So what was he doing in Tuscany?'

She turned back to face the fresco. 'That's my question too. That's why I'm hesitant. I could be wrong. Journeying between Venice and Tuscany in Renaissance times wasn't easy, but we both know the European Renaissance started in Tuscany and centred in Florence and Siena.' She raised her eyebrows. 'Venice was the late starter.'

She walked back to the entranceway. 'Give me some time to run the program and see what it comes up with.'

Logan held out his hand as she made to leave. 'And in the meantime?' He spun around. 'Time is marching on, we've still got work to do in the chapel—even if we aren't anywhere near the fresco.'

She looked around and gave a little nod. 'Let me give you some recommendations on the best way to protect it in the meantime from dust, plaster and paint.' Her gaze connected with his. 'This could be a really amazing discovery, Logan.'

It was the way she'd said his name. Her accent, her lilt. He'd heard it on so many occasions. Last thing at night, first thing in the morning. In the heat of passion and in the depths of despair.

He just hadn't admitted how much he actually missed it.

His feet were rooted to the spot. But Lucia's weren't. She was headed out the door. She was leaving. Who knew how long she would actually stay here. He could get up tomorrow morning and discover her gone.

'Have dinner with me?'

'What?' She stopped. She looked shocked.

'Have dinner with me,' he repeated, stepping closer to her. The words had come out of nowhere. He couldn't take them back. He didn't *want* to take them back.

'We have things we need to discuss.' He saw a wave of panic flit across her eyes. '*Business* we need to discuss.'

'Oh, of course.' She glanced down at her digital camera. 'My program will take a few hours to run.' She was stalling. Of course she was. The last thing she'd want to do was have dinner with him.

'Then you'll have a few hours to kill,' he said quickly. This was embarrassing. Logan Cascini wasn't used to women saying no to him. But Lucia wasn't just any woman. Lucia was the woman he'd once loved. Sure, it felt awkward. Sure, this wasn't an ideal situation.

But this was the first time he'd seen her in twelve years. If this fresco turned out to be important, it could have significant repercussions for his business. He had to keep on top of this.

He almost laughed out loud. His mind was giving him all the rational, professional reasons for having dinner with Lucia. But his heart was giving him a whole host of completely irrational, emotional reasons for having dinner with Lucia.

None of them professional. All of them personal.

His mouth kept talking. 'We can discuss any paperwork that will need to be completed. I'll need to translate everything for Louisa, and if there's going to be any extra expenses we'll need to discuss those too. There's a nice restaurant in Monte Calanetti. It will give you a chance to see the village.'

She was hesitating, looking for a reason to say no, and he wasn't prepared to accept that.

He walked around her in long strides. 'Leave the arrangements to me.'

'Well, I… I…' She was still murmuring while he left.

CHAPTER THREE

FOUR DIFFERENT OUTFITS. That's how many she'd tried on. She hadn't brought that many clothes as she'd only expected to be here a few days and hadn't expected to be socialising at all, let alone socialising with the man she used to live with. Two suits, one pair of trousers, one extra skirt and a variety of tops were all that her trusty red case held.

A white shirt, a pale pink shirt and a bright blue one were currently lying on her bed. She was wearing a flared white skirt and red shirt. And against all her better judgement a bright red pair of stilettos.

The shoes gave some height to her diminutive stature. Right now she was praying that the restaurant wasn't in the middle of the cobbled streets of Monte Calanetti.

Logan was waiting outside for her in an idling car. She'd expected him to drive something black and sleek but instead he was in a four-wheel drive.

He gave her a nod as she opened the door and climbed in. Catching sight of her shoes, a glimmer of a smile appeared on his face. 'We're going to the local restaurant—Mancini's. I hope you like traditional food.' His eyes were gleaming.

She was nervous. And she couldn't quite work out why. Logan had changed into a white open-necked shirt and dark fitted trousers. His dark hair still had that rumpled look that she'd always loved. It was like a magnet—all she wanted to do was lift her hand and run her fingers through it.

She shifted her legs nervously in the car, crossing them one way then the other. If he noticed he didn't say anything. She eyed her shoes warily. 'Where is the restaurant?'

Logan was completely cool. He didn't seem at all unsettled at being around her. 'It's a converted farmhouse on the edge of the village. The chef's family have owned the restaurant for years, his wife-to-be is the maître d'—she's from the US.' He gave a little smile. 'It's an explosive combination.'

With Logan this was all about business. She would clearly have to adopt the same attitude.

He pulled up outside the restaurant, switched off the engine, and before she even had a chance to think he had come around the car and was opening her door and holding out his hand towards her.

She stared at his tanned hand and fingers. *Touch him.* She'd done it once. Her palm had burned for around an hour afterwards. Did she really want to touch Logan Cascini again?

How on earth could she say no?

She placed her hand in his. The sparks didn't fly this time. Probably because she was a little more prepared. This time it was a warm buzz, a little hum running up her arm and straight across to her heart.

Twelve years on, and he could still do it to her.

It was unnerving. She could hardly keep her thoughts straight.

The first glimpse of Logan had sent tingles around her body. But that had been quickly followed by a rush of emotions associated with bad memories. Memories that were locked away deep inside her.

There was a reason she wasn't happily married with a family. There was a reason she always backed off when a few dates started to turn into something else.

Professionally, her life was good. She had a gorgeous apartment, a motivating and challenging job, along with a whole host of good friends and colleagues.

That would be enough for most people. That *should* be enough. And right up until she'd glimpsed Logan again it had been.

Now she felt...unbalanced.

She walked into the farmhouse converted into a restaurant. Thankfully there were no cobbles outside and the added height from her stilettos seemed to buffer her confidence a little.

It was cute. There were shutters on the windows and exposed brickwork on the walls. Wooden tables filled the dining room, but they weren't all uniform, like in most restaurants. They were all different shapes and sizes, perfect for all numbers of guests, and it gave an old-world charm to the place.

They were shown to their table and the waiter lit the candle, then handed over the wine list. He nodded at Logan and pointed to the back wall. 'As you can see, we have a wide variety of wines from all the local vineyards. If you need a recommendation just let me know.'

Lucia ran her eyes down the list and sighed. Italians

were passionate about their wine and the wine list was thicker than the actual menu.

'What's your preference?'

Couldn't he remember? Had he forgotten everything about their time together?

Before she had a chance to speak he waved to the waiter. 'Can we have some bread, olives and some oil while we decide?'

The waiter gave a nod and disappeared. It seemed he hadn't quite forgotten everything after all. Lucia had always enjoyed taking her time to peruse a menu, and Logan had always been starving.

She swallowed, her fingers drifting back to the file she'd brought with her. This made it seem more real. This was work. The reason she'd agreed to dinner tonight.

She licked her lips. Nerves were doing strange things to her. 'I think I'd like to keep things simple. I'd like to have some white wine, I think, something light. A *frascati*.'

She knew he'd be surprised. During their time together they'd both favoured red wines, Merlots and Chiantis.

'And I like the look of the set menu. Sometimes it's nice to have someone else pick for you.'

She'd only glanced at the set menu and nothing had jumped out at her. Most restaurants offered a set menu of some of their best dishes. She only hoped Mancini's was the same.

In years gone by she'd been picky about her food, sometimes refusing to go to some restaurants if they didn't serve a particular dish that she liked. But she wanted to start this meeting by letting Logan realise that he didn't really know her any more. Just because he was working on this project it didn't mean that he'd get any special treatment. And she wasn't swayed by a royal wedding either.

She took her job seriously. If the fresco had been by Michelangelo everything would have ground to a complete halt. She was fairly certain it was by a lesser-known artist—one who was still recognised and his work would be protected. But the chapel was fairly well maintained. There was no damp, no immediate threat to the fresco—just the new work that was going on to make it ready for the wedding.

Once the identification part was done, things should be fairly straightforward.

Logan set his menu on the table. 'Both are fine with me.' He had a hint of a smile on his face. As if he knew she was trying to be different but it was all really just a pretence. 'How have you been, Lucia?' he asked huskily. That voice. That accent. Little waves were rolling down her spine. It was the memories. It was anticipation of what had used to come next when Logan had spoken to her like that.

Those days were long gone. Vanished for ever. It didn't matter that the words were bland and perfectly normal. It was the *way* he said them that counted.

'Twelve years is a long time, Logan.' Her voice was sharp.

He waited a few seconds before answering. His voice was low. 'You're right. It's been a very long time. Almost a lifetime ago.'

What did that mean? That for him it was gone, forgotten about? How could anyone forget losing a child? She could feel herself bristle.

'How have you been?' She bounced the question back to him. Her insides were curling up in case he told her—even though he didn't wear a ring—that he was indeed married with a houseful of children.

He nodded slowly. 'I've been busy. Building your own business takes time.' He shrugged. 'Nearly all of my time. I like to be on-site for the restoration projects. I like to make sure that everything is going to plan.'

She felt her shoulders relax a little. 'You don't like to sit in your office and drink coffee?' It was something they used to joke about years ago. Creative people ending up in jobs behind desks, drinking endless cups of coffee.

He gave a smile and shook his head as the waiter approached again, taking their order and returning a few moments later to pour the wine and leave the bread, olives and oil on the table.

Lucia took a sip. The first taste was always sharp. The second much more pleasing as her taste buds adjusted.

'Where are your offices?'

He tasted his wine too and nodded in approval. 'Florence. But I don't spend much time there.'

She tried not to raise her eyebrows. Office space in Florence was expensive. His business had obviously done well. 'Do you still live in Florence?'

He hesitated a second. And she wondered if she'd just stepped over some invisible barrier. They'd lived in Florence together. But she didn't expect him still to be in the small one-bedroomed flat a few minutes from the university.

He nodded and dipped a piece of bread in the oil. 'I have an apartment overlooking Piazza Santa Croce.'

'Wow.' She couldn't help it. It was one of the main areas of Florence. Apartments there weren't cheap and although the existing buildings were old, they'd usually been refurbished to a high standard, hence the expensive price tags.

She gave a little nod of her head. 'I can see you staying there. Did you get to renovate the place yourself?'

He shook his head. 'If only. The apartment was renovated before I got there. But all the original architecture is still there. That's what's important.'

'Do you like staying there?' She was dancing around the subject that was really in her mind. *Did anyone stay there with him?* It shouldn't matter to her. Of course it shouldn't. But she couldn't help but feel a natural curiosity. And there was no way she would come right out and ask the question.

'It's fine. It's Florence.' He looked at her carefully. 'I've always loved living in Florence. I just don't get to stay there as much as I would like.'

'Really? Why not?' *Because your wife and child stay somewhere else?*

He shrugged. 'I've spent the last ten years building up my business. I go wherever the work is. It takes time, energy and commitment. When I'm doing a restoration—like now—I like to be on-site. I've stayed in my apartment probably only three months of the last year.'

'I see,' she said quietly, as the waiter appeared and placed their starters in front of them—wild mushroom ravioli with butter and Parmesan sauce. She was glad of the distraction. Glad to stop being watched by those too-intense green eyes.

It made sense. Logan had always been passionate about everything he'd been involved in. From his work, to his family, to his relationships. But it sounded very much like he didn't have anyone back in Florence to worry about.

'How are your family in Scotland?' she asked.

He smiled. 'They're good. They have three restaurants in Glasgow now. The one in George Square is still the main one and my *nonna* refuses to get out from behind the bar. She still sits there every day and criticises what everyone else does.'

Lucia laughed. She'd met his *nonna* on a few occasions. She was fiery little woman who was both fiercely protective and critical of her family.

'They still ask after you,' he said quietly.

Her laughter died and she swallowed quickly. There was a little tug at her heartstrings. Although both families had roots in Italy, Logan's family were much more welcoming and outgoing than her own. She'd felt more at home in their house in Glasgow than in her own mother and father's house in the small town of Osimo.

She didn't reply. She couldn't reply. Too many memories were starting to flood back. This was the problem with seeing Logan after all this time. All the things she'd literally pushed to the back corners of her mind were starting to poke their way through again.

But it wasn't just unhappy memories that were crowding her thoughts. Logan had other little places in her mind. Just sitting here with him now made a little warm glow spread throughout her body. His eyes, his accent, the way he ran his fingers through his hair when he was searching for the right words. Beautiful, sunny days in Florence, long afternoons drinking endless cups of coffee and dusky evenings with wine leading to long nights together

Passionate. Intense. The two words that sprang to mind to describe their relationship. The third word was tragic. But she didn't even want to go there.

She was still toying with her food, wondering if either one of them would bring up the elephant in the room.

But Logan wasn't ready to go there yet. 'What do you think of Louisa?'

She put down her knife and fork. It was a curious question. The Logan she used to know would size someone up in a matter of minutes. The fact he was asking about Louisa meant he obviously wasn't quite sure.

She frowned. 'I'm not sure. I haven't really had a chance to talk to her yet. She's American, isn't she? How did she manage to own a vineyard in Tuscany?'

'From what I know, she inherited it. She's the last living relative of Signor Bartolini. It seems she might have inherited some time ago but has never visited before. As far as I can make out, Nico—who owns the neighbouring vineyard and who was a friend of Signor Bartolini—has kept it semi-functioning for the last few months. But I'm not entirely sure that Nico and Louisa have hit it off.'

She nodded thoughtfully. She hadn't met Nico yet but had heard him yelling instructions to some of the vineyard workers. He was obviously intent on keeping the vineyard working.

Logan took a sip of his wine. 'How do you find Venice?'

'It took a little getting used to. Florence was always busy, but Venice is off the scale. Cruise liners come in every day and the Piazza San Marco is so busy you can barely move.'

He gave a little nod. 'Where are you staying?'

'I was lucky. I managed to get an older apartment—much like you—on the Grand Canal. My building and street are off the main thoroughfare, but any time of the day or night I can open my doors and look out over the canal. There's never a quiet moment out there.'

'Do you live alone?' She sucked in a breath but couldn't help the amused smile that appeared on her face. It seemed that Logan didn't mind being direct. She'd skirted around the issue but he had no intention of doing that.

A tiny little part of her wanted to lie. Wanted to tell him she had a billionaire husband and three perfect children at home. But she had never been a person to tell lies. Her secret hopes and desires for her own life were just that—secret.

'Yes. It's just me. I lived with someone for a while but things didn't work out. I was consumed with work and didn't really have time for a relationship. It turned out he really didn't want a career woman for a wife anyway.'

She said the words flippantly, not giving away how much it had hurt at the time. But time, in some cases, gave a chance for reflection. That relationship would have always come to an end.

Logan's eyebrows had risen as she'd been speaking. Wasn't she supposed to move on?

But it seemed he'd opened the door now and given her a right to ask whatever she wanted. 'Why haven't you got married and settled down?' she asked.

The waiter appeared, clearing one set of plates and setting down their main course—Tuscan veal chops with Parmesan *tuilles*. The smell drifted up around her

She picked up her fork and sighed. 'This is the kind of thing I wish I had the time and talent to make.'

'Your cooking talents haven't improved with age?' He laughed. Lucia's cooking attempts had been a constant source of amusement for them. She'd once declared she could burn water—and she probably could.

The initial preparation and cooking attempts hadn't been a problem. Distraction had been the problem. Something else had always managed to crop up while she was supposed to be watching a timer or stirring a pot.

'How have you survived without someone to feed you?'

She gave a resigned nod of her head as she tasted some of the succulent veal. 'I eat out. A lot. The kitchen and I will never be friends.'

He laughed. 'I should get Nonna to package up some food for you.'

She waved her fork at him. 'Nonna should package up food for the world. She could make a fortune if she released a recipe book, or sold them to a food manufacturer.'

Logan's eyes connected with hers. 'You really expect Nonna to reveal her secret family recipes to an unsuspecting world?' He was teasing. She could tell. This was the way it used to be with them. Constant joking back and forth.

She shrugged. 'I'm just saying you have an untapped family fortune out there. That could be your nest egg, you know.'

He shook his head. 'I don't think I'd live to tell the tale.'

'Probably not.' She took a sip of her wine. This wasn't

quite as bad as she'd feared. Logan wasn't being difficult, he was his usual charming self. She'd just forgotten how hypnotic those green eyes could be. Every time
his gaze connected with hers she had to blink to remind
herself to breathe.

Logan had always been charming. His family had
joked he could charm the birds from the trees and the
gods out of Olympus. And she'd loved it. She'd loved
the way he could make her feel like the most important woman on the planet. Because even though Logan
had been a charmer, he'd also been a one-woman man.
He'd never shown a glimmer of interest in anyone else
when he'd been with her. She'd felt assured in his love.

It had been a long time since she'd felt so cherished.

A little warm wave rushed over her skin as she
smiled at him and took another sip of her wine. She
was relaxing more as the night went on, remembering
the good times instead of the bad.

Logan didn't deserve the negative associations that
she'd built up in her brain. He deserved much more
than that.

But if that was how she remembered him, how did
he remember her?

This was more like the Lucia he'd once known. It was
the first time he'd seen a genuine smile since she'd got
here. When she'd walked outside to meet him earlier
his heart rate had rocketed. With her perfect hourglass
figure, the white flared skirt, fitted red shirt and silk
scarf knotted around her neck she'd looked like a nine-
teen-fifties movie star. As for those killer red stilettos…

With her tumbling locks and red lips her picture
could have adorned a thousand walls. His fingers

couldn't decide whether they wanted to unknot the scarf around her neck and pull it free, or run down the smooth skin on her tanned legs towards those heels.

Lucia. It was odd. She tried to act so independent, so aloof, but there was an inherent vulnerability about her that made him lose focus on everything else. He felt strangely protective and proud of her. The last time he'd seen her she'd been a shell of her former self. Losing their child had devastated them both.

Although the pregnancy hadn't been planned they'd both been delighted when they'd found out a baby was on the way. They'd spent hours talking about their future together and making preparations for their baby. At one point it had seemed that the whole apartment had been full of brochures for cribs, cabinets, prams and high chairs.

The twenty-week scan had revealed a perfect daughter waiting to be introduced to the world.

No one could explain the unexpected premature labour.

No one could explain why Ariella Rose hadn't managed to take those first few vital breaths.

Of course, the doctor had tried to say that her lungs hadn't been developed enough and there had been no time to give Lucia steroids to help Ariella's lungs mature.

It had been that terrible time when doctors tried to decide if a baby's life was viable or not.

Some babies did breathe at twenty-three weeks.

Ariella Rose hadn't.

The beautiful, vivacious woman he'd known had disintegrated before his eyes, their relationship crumbling around him. He'd spent months desperate to get her to talk to him. But Lucia had put up walls so thick nothing had penetrated.

Every time he'd tried to draw her out of her shell she'd become more and more silent and withdrawn. He'd pulled back too, focusing on his work, because right then that had been all he'd had. But Lucia had slipped through his fingers like grains of sand from the beach.

He'd been grieving too, watching the days tick by on the calendar, waiting for the day they would have welcomed their daughter into the world.

That had been the day Lucia had packed her cases and left.

No amount of pleading had dissuaded her. Florence had had too many bad memories for her—too many painful associations. She'd accepted a job in Venice. She'd wanted to leave, and she hadn't wanted him to follow.

Now his insides twisted. He'd always regretted that he hadn't fought harder. Hadn't found the words to persuade her to stay.

It was almost a relief to see her now. There was a stillness about her—something reserved that hadn't been there before they'd lost their daughter. He could still see a remnant of sadness in her eyes.

But this Lucia was different. She had a different kind of confidence around her. She was a little more self-assured. She'd been through the worst and come out the other side. There was a real resilience there that bubbled underneath the surface.

Her clothes and demeanour were back to the woman he remembered. She'd always worn her stilettos with pride, as if to take someone to task for her diminutive height. And her hair was every bit as tempting as it had always been. It had always felt like silk and smelled of roses. Even now, there was a faint floral aroma drifting across the table towards him, curling its way around him and kicking his senses into gear.

The waiter appeared to clear their plates. 'Dessert?'

'No, thank you.' They both answered in unison and Lucia threw her head back and laughed.

Now his fingers were definitely itching to reach across and tug that scarf from her neck and reveal the paler sensitive skin around her décolletage.

It was her tender spot. The area that when kissed sent her into a spin. It had always been guaranteed to make her go weak at the knees.

He shifted uncomfortably in his chair. Parts of his body were awakening that shouldn't—not in a public restaurant. 'Do you want to have coffee?'

She shook her head. 'I'm tired. I still need to do some work online.'

Work. Of course. The reason they were here. He'd barely even discussed the project with her. He was normally so pedantic about every detail of his build. It seemed that even being around Lucia for a few hours was making him lose focus.

He should be worrying about delays. He should be panicking that his business could be affected by the non-completion clause in his contract.

If things weren't ready on time for the royal wedding he might have to face the wrath of the wedding planner, Lindsay Reeves. She was already phoning him twice a day for updates and photos of the chapel.

He took a deep breath and tried to collect his thoughts. 'Can we continue our work in the chapel?'

This was useless. Now he was looking at those deep brown eyes. Lucia's eyes had always been able to draw him in completely. In twelve years they hadn't lost their magic.

People said that eyes were the window to the soul. Lucia's brown eyes were very dark, very deep and flecked with gold. He could get lost in them completely. Always had.

She blinked. 'In truth, probably not. Give me another day. I have a few ideas. If I needed to go elsewhere to verify who painted it, would you have someone who could ensure the safety of the fresco?'

He straightened in his chair. 'Why would that be needed? It's been safe for the last five hundred years beneath the panels in the chapel?'

She gave an apologetic smile. 'But now it's been discovered. Now it's open to the elements. And now we have a whole host of tradesmen who know that it exists.' She shrugged. 'What if people have thoughts like you first did? What if they think that there is a tiny possibility this could be a Michelangelo work? What if someone tells the press?'

She held out her hands. 'In the space of a few hours this whole village could be swamped by a whole host of people—not all of them with good intentions.' She spoke with complete sincerity. He'd always respected Lucia's ambition, but he was now seeing a true glimpse of her professional expertise.

He nodded slowly. 'Of course. Louisa has already expressed some concerns about publicity. She's worried enough about the royal wedding without having to deal with something else.' It was easy to know who to discuss this with. 'Connor Denoon is the head of security for the royal party. He'll know exactly how to keep things safe and protect the fresco in the meantime.'

She gave him an amused smile. 'Isn't he more at home looking after real-life people than artefacts?'

Logan lifted his hands. 'He has the skill and expertise we need. What's more important is that I trust him. If he says he can keep the fresco safe, then I believe him.'

He signalled to the waiter for the bill. Lucia had told him she still had work to do. It didn't matter that he wasn't in a hurry for this evening to end. He had to respect the job she was here to do.

It only took a few minutes to pay the bill and head back out to the car. The sun was setting behind the deep green Tuscan hills, sending shards of orange and red across the sky.

Lucia took a deep breath as they stepped outside. 'How beautiful.' She spun around in her heels, her skirt swishing around her, a relaxed smile on her face.

He caught her arm as she spun, feeling her smooth skin against his palm. 'You've never experienced a Tuscan sunset. It really is something, isn't it?'

The evening was still warm and pleasant. 'Why don't we go for a walk before we head back to the *palazzo*?' The words were out before he thought about it and he could sense her immediate reluctance.

But what struck him straight away was the way his stomach curled. He hated seeing Lucia like this, prickly and difficult around him. Towards the end of their relationship she'd been so flat. Almost emotionless, as if everything had just been drained from her. It had just been another stage of grieving—he appreciated that now.

But at the beginning she'd been bright, bubbly and vivacious. He didn't know this prickly and difficult version. More importantly, he didn't know how to *act* around her.

He waved his hand. 'Of course, if you want to head straight back, that's fine. I just thought you might want to have a chance to see around Monte Calanetti a little.'

It was official.

She was caught between a rock and a hard place.

Strange as it seemed, getting a sense of the village might actually help her identify who the artist of the fresco might be. Often, if someone had stayed in an area there might be historical stories or some folklore about them. Sometimes getting a sense of a place, seeing other work done in the area could actually help. And, in some respects, Logan's brain worked exactly the same way that hers did.

She sucked in a breath, holding it for a few seconds, her eyes fixing on her red stilettos. They'd seemed like a good idea at the time. But she'd seen the streets of Monte Calanetti. Cobbles. Everywhere. She'd probably land on her back.

She bit her lip. Logan's gaze was fixed on the sunset, his face basking in the orange glow. Her reserve softened. With his dark hair, tanned skin and dark suit jacket he was definite movie-star material. Age suited him. The little lines around his eyes gave him even more charisma, and Logan had oozed it already.

'Okay, then.' *Where had that come from?*

She was almost as amazed at her words as Logan was, judging by the expression on his face. He recovered quickly. 'Great, let's go.'

He drove the car into the town centre and parked outside a bar. He walked swiftly around and opened the door, holding his hand out to her as he had before.

She didn't hesitate. Didn't think about the contact. She was making too much of this. It was probably just all in her head anyway.

Wrong move. She could almost see the spike of electricity.

One of her heels automatically slipped in a gap in the cobbles and he caught her elbow, sliding one arm behind her waist. She pretended it was nothing. Nothing—to feel his body right next to hers.

Her throat was so dry she couldn't even swallow. This wasn't supposed to happen. She was in self-protect mode.

She could smell him. Smell his woodsy aftershave, his masculine scent winding its way around her body. So familiar. So scintillating.

He slammed the car door, keeping one hand around her waist. 'Don't want you to stumble,' he said throatily.

It was an excuse. She knew it was an excuse to keep her close. But she didn't feel in a position to protest. The likelihood of her landing on her backside had just increased tenfold. The cobbles weren't the only thing affecting her balance around here.

He steered her towards the centre of the square, near a fountain and old brick well.

Now Lucia really had a chance to see the beauty of the square, the most quirky thing being that it wasn't exactly a square. The fountain was similar to lots found in small Italian villages. Built with travertine stone, it was circular with a sleeping nymph at its centre. The old well was solid with mismatched stones. Like most of Italy's traditional village wells some modernisation had taken place and water from the well could be accessed via a pipe at the side. Logan pressed the button and reached over for her hand. She didn't have time to pull it back before cool, clear water poured over their fingers.

He lifted his hand, letting the drops fall into his mouth. Her legs quivered. She put her fingers to her lips and tasted the cold water. It was surprisingly fresh. She smiled as a drop trickled down her chin.

Logan moved instantly and caught the drop with his finger. She froze. Before it had just been touching hands, arms. Even holding her close, she was still completely clothed.

But touching her face was different. Touching her face was a complete and utter blast from the past. Logan had always touched her face—just before he kissed her.

It had been their *thing*. She'd used to close her eyes and he'd trace his finger over her skin like butterfly kisses. It had always driven her crazy.

And even though she willed it not to happen, as soon as he touched her chin her body reacted. She closed her eyes.

This was something she wasn't prepared for. This was something she'd *never* be prepared for. She sucked in a sharp breath and forced her eyes back open.

Their gazes meshed. So focused, so intense it made her want to cry.

Logan's deep green eyes were so clear, so solid. He was everything she'd ever wanted. Everything she'd ever needed. The person she'd love for ever. The person she'd never forget.

Something flashed across his vision. Panic. Something she'd never seen before in Logan's eyes. He was the calmest, most controlled man she'd ever known.

He pulled his finger back and stared at it for a second, as if he were being hit with the same overload of memories she was.

She wobbled, adjusting her weight in her stilettos. Logan blinked and lifted his hands onto her shoulders, walking her back a few steps to the edge of the fountain. She sagged down, breathing heavily, trying to ignore the pitter-patter in her chest.

She adjusted her position at the edge of the fountain and her eyes fixed on the nymph in the centre of the cascading water. It was exquisite. Serene and beautiful, holding a large clamshell above her head.

Logan stepped in front of her. She was so conscious of him, of his strong muscular thighs barely hidden inside the dark suit trousers. He didn't speak. He didn't try to touch her again.

Her brain tried to clear a little. This was ridiculous. She wasn't the young woman she'd been the last time she'd been around Logan. She'd lived and aged twelve years. Sometimes inside it felt like she'd aged another forty.

She tried to focus her attention on something else. Something safe. The sculpture of the nymph.

Most nymphs were naked. This nymph wasn't. It was clothed. In a cloak. A cloak with characteristic folds.

She straightened up.

'What is it?' Logan crouched down next to her.

She pointed to the nymph. 'Do you know anything about this?'

He touched the wall of the fountain where she was sitting. 'About the fountain?'

She shook her head. 'No. About the nymph. Do you know who sculpted it? Is there any village history that would tell us?'

His eyes were fixed on hers. 'I know the legend attached to the fountain.'

Her heart started to beat faster. 'What's the legend?' She was watching the fine billowing mist that seemed to glow in the lowering sun. Of course. Every village fountain in Italy would have a legend.

He gave her a wistful kind of smile. 'They say that if you toss a coin and it lands in the clamshell you get your wish.'

Her stomach clenched. It wasn't exactly what she'd wanted to hear. But it reached into her and grabbed a tiny part of her soul. Oh, she had a whole host of things she could wish for. But most of them were in the past. And nothing would change that now.

Wishful thinking. That's all that could happen around this fountain. And a fanciful legend didn't help her identify the sculptor. 'Do you know anything else? Anything more realistic?'

He looked as if he'd been stung. He frowned. 'I have no idea. Is it important?'

She stood up and spun around to face it. 'It could be. See the folds of the cloak?'

He leaned forward. 'Yes ' His voice was hesitant.

She touched his arm. 'Does it look familiar to you?'

His face broke into a smile, there was a mischievous twinkle in his eyes and he held up his hands. 'Is yes the right answer?' It was clear he had no idea.

But something had sparked a fire within her. 'I think it might. Most Renaissance artists didn't just paint they also sculpted. It could be the nymph was sculpted by the same person who painted the fresco. The folds of the cloak are quite characteristic. If I can compare the fresco and the nymph to the works of art that are held in Venice, it could help identify the artist.'

He started to nod his head in recognition. 'You still think its Alberto Burano?'

She smiled. 'It could be.'

This was work. Work she could do. Talking about work made her feel confident again. Made her feel safe.

'So what happens now? How long will it take you to find out?'

She paused. Of course. 'These things can take weeks—sometimes months. The Italian Heritage Board is cautious. We have to be careful before we make any kind of declaration about the potential artist of any fresco. It can always be challenged by others.'

Logan shook his head. 'But what happens in the meantime? Can the wedding still go ahead in the chapel? Louisa is absolutely adamant that things must go to plan. I suspect she's counting on the money from the royal wedding to help her complete the renovations on the *palazzo*. If we can't progress...' His voice tailed off.

There were deep furrows in his brow. He put his hands on his hips and stared out across the village. It was obvious that something else was bothering him.

'If we can't progress—what?'

He let out a deep breath and turned to face her. 'We have a non-completion clause in the contract. It's standard practice in the renovation business.'

'What happens if you don't complete on time?' Now she understood why he looked so worried.

He couldn't meet her gaze. Her brain whirred. She

knew exactly what would happen. Logan's company would have to bear the brunt of any costs.

Something twisted inside her. It had been a long time but Logan had been the father of her child. She knew exactly how much something like this would matter. If he failed to complete this job his reputation would be ruined—he could kiss his company and all his hard work goodbye.

'Is there anything I can do to help prevent the delays?' There was an edge to his voice. Determination.

From the second she'd got here all she'd wanted to do was get away. Being around Logan was claustrophobic, too cluttered—stifling, too many memories.

But she couldn't let his business fall apart because of things he had no control over. This wasn't his fault.

She hesitated. 'There will be a whole lot of paperwork that will need to be completed in Venice. That's always the thing that causes the most delays. If Louisa will allow you to be a signatory for her it could make things much easier. As you know, Italian paperwork can be complicated.'

'You want me to come to Venice?' He sounded a little stunned.

But so was she. Had she really just suggested that?

'Well...it might move things along more quickly. I will be working on the comparisons with other frescoes. If you could find any history of the village that might link Alberto Burano to being here it could also be a huge benefit.'

He nodded slowly. She could almost see him thinking everything over, weighing up the best way forward.

He stepped forward. A little closer than she expected and as she breathed in all she could smell was his woodsy aftershave.

'What day do you want me in Venice?' His voice was determined.

'Friday,' she said quickly, trying not to think about it too much.

Friday was only a few days away. She would have done some of the groundwork before he got there.

He seemed to wait a few seconds before he replied. His voice was low and husky, sending shivers down her spine. 'Friday it is.'

What had she just done?

CHAPTER FOUR

THE HEAT IN Venice was stifling. It seemed the whole world had descended on it to hear one of the world's biggest rock bands play in a concert. Piazza San Marco was positively heaving, the streets crowded beyond measure and tourists juggling to pay the inflated prices in the surrounding cafés and bars.

Venice was always hot in the summer and Lucia was used to it. Living in the middle of permanent tourist attractions meant it was rarely quiet but today was the busiest she'd ever seen it. The queue of people to get inside St Mark's Basilica snaked around the centre of the piazza twice.

Lucia glanced at her clock again. She'd expected Logan to call her over an hour ago. When they'd made the arrangement for him to come and help complete the paperwork she'd had no idea about the rock concert. It hadn't even been on her radar. She didn't want to think about what Venice Marco Polo Airport was like right now. She knew that the wait for the water buses was over an hour and that everything was going much slower than expected.

But the heat in her office was becoming claustrophobic. Even with her windows opened wide over the

Grand Canal there was no breeze. She glanced at the clock again and pulled her fitted blouse away from her back. The air conditioning rarely worked at the Italian Heritage Board. Today was no exception.

She gathered up the papers she might need, closed her windows and headed for the door. Her mobile sounded just as she walked down the stairs. Logan. She answered quickly, but could barely make out his voice for the background noise. 'Logan, where are you?'

She walked out into the bustling crowds, her feet turning automatically in the direction of San Marco, the waterbus drop-off on the Grand Canal. His voice was lost as she struggled to hear, so she continued through the thronging crowds towards the drop-off point. There, in the distance, she could see Logan and a smile flickered to her face.

His bag was clutched in one hand, alongside a pale beige jacket and his mobile phone. His white shirt was wrinkled, his hair rumpled and his face red. It was the first time in her life she'd ever seen Logan looking hot and bothered. It was kind of nice to know that could actually happen to him too.

He ran his fingers through his hair and looked around him, scanning the crowds. The rock concert had obviously caught him equally unawares.

She lifted her hand and waved at him, snaking her way through the people. A flash of relief was all over his face and gave her an unexpected glow. He moved towards her. 'Lucia, thank goodness.' He held up his hands. 'This place is even madder than usual. It wasn't until I hit the airport that I heard about the concert. I guess I should have got an earlier flight. The queue for the water taxis and buses was a mile long.'

She gave a nod and glanced at his bag. 'You look hot. How about we find somewhere to sit down and get something cool to drink?'

Logan let out a long breath, his brow furrowed. 'Do you think you'll be able to find anywhere?'

Lucia gave a little nod of her head. 'You forget, Logan. I've been here more than ten years. I know all Venice's best kept secrets.' She nodded her head for him to follow and weaved through the crowds. She was glad she'd opted out of wearing her normal business attire today. In these conditions she would have sweltered in her fitted suit dress. Instead, the lighter short-sleeved white blouse and knee-length navy skirt helped to keep her cooler. She pulled her sunglasses down from her head and snaked her way through the cobbled side streets of Venice. These were instantly cooler out of the sun's blistering rays and after a few minutes' walk they were away from the madding crowds.

She pointed towards a café with tables and parasols set on the street. Logan gave a sigh of relief and sank down into a chair. 'Perfect,' he said.

The waitress appeared instantly and they both ordered two drinks, one cool and one coffee for later.

She was still amused by how flustered he looked. 'I'm sorry about being so late, Lucia. I hope I haven't ruined your schedule for the day.'

She shook her head. 'No problem. I'd just decided to leave a little earlier because it was so hot. I'm happy to meet you outside rather than in the office.' She pulled out her files. 'I brought the paperwork with me. We can do it now, if you like.'

The waiter appeared and put their drinks on the table. Logan finished his cool drink within a few seconds, then sat back in his chair and sighed. He gave her a quirky smile and held up his hands. 'I don't remember Venice ever being this hot. What on earth is happening?'

She shrugged her shoulders. 'A cross between a heat wave and an extra twenty thousand people descending on the city at once?' She pushed the papers over towards him. 'These are the ones I need you to complete. Then we can file the fresco as a "new find" with the Heritage Board. They are the ones that can authorise any restoration that might need to take place.'

Logan was scouring the papers. He lifted his eyes towards her. 'And who would do that?'

She paused for a second, wondering if it was an answer he really wanted to hear. 'It would probably be me. I've done most of the work on all of the last frescoes that needed to be restored. It used to be my boss, Alessio Orsini, who handled fresco restoration, but once he'd trained me and overseen my work a few times he was happy to hand over the reins. I think he's looking to retire soon.'

Logan nodded slowly. He sat down his pen. 'How would you feel about working in Tuscany? There is a good chance that I'll still be there for the next few months.'

Logan was being cautious, but for some reason she felt as if a little man with icy feet was marching down her spine. It was almost as if he didn't want her there. She felt insulted.

She looked at him steadily. 'I'll go wherever I'm needed. My job is very important to me. The other personalities involved aren't important.' She picked up her cappuccino and took a sip, breaking the little caramelised biscuit at the side into pieces.

'That's not what I meant.' He reached over and grabbed her hand.

It was unexpected. A little part of the biscuit dropped from her hand onto the cobbled street.

Her eyes fixed on it lying amongst the cobbles, rather than looking at his hands or his face. She didn't pull her hand back. 'I get it, Logan. You'd rather not have to work with me. But I won't compromise on my job. We're just going to have to both be professional about it.' She lifted her gaze to meet his.

His eyes widened. 'No, Lucia. You're reading this all wrong.' He squeezed her hand. 'I know we had a difficult past. And seeing you after all these years…it's been…' He seemed to struggle to find the right word. 'It's been hard.'

She felt her heart squeeze.

He moved the position of his hand. This time his thumb was inside her palm, moving in tiny circular motions, while the rest of his hand rested over hers.

He lowered his voice. 'But it's been good to see you, Lucia. Really good. It's left me wondering why we didn't do this earlier.'

She didn't hesitate. 'Because it would have been too hard.' Her gaze was steady on his. 'And you're right, it is still hard.'

'But it doesn't have to be?' There was an edge of optimism in his voice. A little glimmer of hopefulness.

Tears prickled in her eyes. A lump rose instantly in her throat. This was dangerous territory. Business was business, but this was something else entirely. She swallowed. 'I think it always will be. There's too many memories. Too many associations.'

He didn't move. Didn't flinch. Logan had always

been like this. His thumb kept moving in little circles, the way it always had when he was trying to soothe her. And for the most part it worked. Logan had always been cool, almost like the eye of a storm. Few things made him ever raise his voice. Few things made him rattled.

She looked at him again. He was still her Logan. Still so handsome. Still so protective. Grief had made his love feel suffocating. But the truth was Logan had never been suffocating. He'd encouraged her to blossom and grow while they'd been in Florence together. He'd be the very person to tell her never to hide her light under a bushel.

Why on earth hadn't he met someone over the last twelve years? Why wasn't he married with children? It had always been what he wanted. And he'd seemed to cope so much better with the death of Ariella Rose than she had.

He'd been grief-stricken for sure. The plans they'd made for baby furniture and paraphernalia had silently disappeared. He'd spoken to the doctors regarding a proper burial. Things were difficult when a baby was so young. But Logan's calm and assuring manner had persuaded them to go along with his wishes and they'd got to lay Ariella Rose to rest in a cemetery just outside the city walls.

The short ceremony by the priest had been beautiful, the flowers and funeral arrangements all carried out by Logan—she'd been too numb to help with any of it.

It was only now, in hindsight, that she could appreciate just how hard that must have been for him. She hadn't been the only one to cry over the death of their daughter. And after he'd spent days trying to get her talk and she hadn't responded he'd finally stopped and mirrored her behaviour. Closing in on himself and shutting out the world around him.

He finally replied. 'Let's just see how things are. I'm glad we've met again, Lucia. I'm glad that you're settled in an amazing city and doing a job that you love.'

There it was. The unspoken words.

I'm glad you've finally moved on.

But had she?

All he wanted to do was reach across the table and hold her. Lucia was at her most fragile right now. He could see the hidden pain in her eyes and he hated it that he was the person who had done that to her. Hated that her association with him was her most painful memory.

He had painful memories too. But he was still able to remember the good times in Florence—running through one of the fountains during a rainstorm, watching her face when he'd come home with every flower that the street vendor had been selling, sneaking out in the morning to buy her favourite pastry and watching her nose twitch as she'd woken up to the smell. For a long time Lucia had been his joy—and the feeling had been mutual. He only wished he was still hers.

She'd haunted his dreams on and off for years. Dreams about them meeting again in some random place, having dinner together, or catching each other's eye across a crowded room.

He'd always dreaded hearing the news that she was happily married or settled with a family of her own, but somehow seeing her like this was equally hard. More than anything he wanted Lucia to be happy.

Seeing her again was sparking a whole host of emotions that he'd long forgotten. He'd never imagined that the spark between them would still feel so electric. He'd never imagined that once he'd stared into those brown eyes again he'd feel rooted to the spot and never want to break away.

Lucia brushed her chocolate hair from her shoulder. It was a little shorter than he remembered and it suited her. She pulled her hand back steadily, keeping her gaze on his. He could almost see her retreating back into herself and putting a carefully drawn line between them.

She picked up her coffee cup. 'How soon do you think you'll get the paperwork completed?'

Business. That was all she wanted to discuss with him. Even after all this time.

He nodded, picking up the biscuit from the side of his cappuccino and placing it on her saucer. He didn't miss the little hint of a smile from her.

'How soon can you tell me I can finish my renovations?'

She blinked. 'Well…' She paused. 'Actually, I'm not sure. We have to file your paperwork, then I need to do some investigating. I've made a private appointment tomorrow to view another fresco by the artist we think is involved.'

He sat back in his chair. 'Well, that's fine. I'll come with you.'

She looked surprised. 'Why would you want to come with me?'

He shrugged. 'There's not much point in me going back if I can't give Louisa good news. She needs to know that the renovations and wedding plans can continue. At the moment most of the work in the chapel has ground to a halt. There's still work ongoing in the *palazzo* but it doesn't require my supervision every day.

The chapel will be the difference between this wedding going ahead or not.'

Lucia looked thoughtful. Her fingers started twiddling with a strand of her hair and she crossed her legs, giving him a flash of her tanned skin. 'What do you know about the royal couple?'

He shook his head. 'Virtually nothing. I've mostly dealt with Lindsay, the wedding planner.' He laughed. 'Now, there's a woman I don't want to call to say there's an issue with the chapel.'

Lucia smiled. 'Will she chew you up and spit you out?' There was a little spark of amusement in her eyes. It suited her. It made her more like the Lucia he remembered. The Lucia he *wanted* to remember.

'In a heartbeat,' he said quickly. 'There's no point in going back until I know I'm safe.'

Lucia frowned. 'Where have you made arrangements to stay?'

This time he frowned too. Oh, no. 'Well, I haven't. Not yet anyway.' His brain started spinning. 'There's a small boutique hotel I stay in if I ever come to Venice. I can give them a call.' He pulled his mobile from his pocket and started dialling.

Lucia shook her head and held out her hands. 'Have you seen this place? I've never seen Venice this busy. I think everywhere will be packed out.'

So do I. He was cringing inside. He'd known as soon as he'd arrived that he would never make his flight back. It was leaving right around now. And he hadn't even made any attempt to book another. With this number of tourists he imagined that every flight and train journey, in and out of Venice, was booked for the next few days.

He pressed the phone to his ear. 'Hi, there, it's Logan Cascini. I wondered if there was any chance of reserving a room for the night.'

He listened to the reply and tried to stop the sinking feeling settling over him. 'No problem. Can you recommend anywhere else?'

The crease across Lucia's brow was deepening.

He listened to the receptionist telling him what he already knew. Venice was packed. Every hotel was fully booked for the next two days. He cut the call and gave his best attempt at a shrug. 'I'll try somewhere else.'

Lucia sucked in a breath. 'Why do you want to stay, Logan? There isn't anything that you can actually do. Did you book a flight back to Tuscany?'

Her tone was almost accusatory. He pressed a button on his phone and spun it around, showing her his online boarding card for the flight that was due to take off any minute.

Her eyes widened. 'Oh.'

She bit her lip again. 'Why do you even *want* to stay?'

The same question again. This time with a different emphasis on the words. It was obviously preying on her mind, just like it was preying on his. When he'd booked his flight he'd planned to be in Venice for four hours and leave again later today and go straight back to Tuscany. It had all seemed straightforward. Except in his mind, where a little voice kept niggling at him.

This was the contact he'd always imagined making. The renovations were a perfect excuse to be around Lucia. He hadn't planned it. It had surprised him just as much as it had surprised her. But sometimes fate had a mysterious hand in things.

After the first few awkward moments curiosity had been killing him about Lucia. He wanted to know everything about the last twelve years. He wanted to know her plans for the future. If she was happy. If she was settled.

And absolutely none of it was his business. But that didn't stop the little craving that had always been there growing into something a whole lot bigger.

There would always be something between them. Right now, it still felt as if there was a big black cloud hanging over them. But for him, he could see little remnants of sunlight struggling to get through. And he wanted them to get through. So badly.

But still something was holding him back. Holding him back from saying their daughter's name and asking Lucia if she was ready to talk about her.

So he took the easy way out. The safest way out, if he wanted to still have contact with Lucia.

'I want to stay because I want to help move this project along. I would love to see Burano's fresco. I would love to see how it compares to the Madonna and Child and to the nymph sculpture. You know I love this stuff just as much as you do.'

Part of him felt guilty. These were careful words, designed to push the little buttons inside her and help things spark along.

There was a glimmer in her eyes. He was talking her language. A language she related to and understood.

He pulled something from his bag. 'Look at this. You told me to try and find any evidence that Burano had been around the village. I've photocopied something from the local museum. One of the guest houses had an ancient register. People used to stay for months at a time.' He pointed to a blurred entry from 1530. 'I thought that might be Alberto Burano.'

She screwed up her nose and squinted at the blurred entry. It was difficult to judge but he could see the glimmer of excitement behind her eyes.

'I'm sure we'll have a sample of his writing somewhere at the heritage board.' She met his gaze. 'This could be really important, Logan. You did well to find this.'

It was the first note of approval he'd had from her and it made his heart swell in his chest. He wasn't going to tell how he'd had to bribe the local museum curator to let him riffle through all the old paperwork. He wasn't going to let her know he'd spent all of last night checking through mountains of ancient chests in order to find anything that might help.

'Can I take this?' she asked, holding up the photocopy.

He nodded as he zipped up his bag again.

'This can definitely help.' She looked around them. The number of people in the quiet street was starting to pick up. 'But where will you stay?'

The million-dollar question. He shrugged as he desperately tried to think of someone, *anyone* he still knew in Venice.

His fingers flicked through the numbers on his phone. He had a multitude of contacts in Florence, Rome and Pisa. Venice? Not so much.

'You can stay with me.'

The words came out of the blue. It was absolutely the last thing he was expecting to hear.

'What? No, I couldn't possibly put you to any trouble.' His stomach clenched.

He couldn't miss the expression on her face. She was saying the words, but it was reluctantly—this wasn't a warm invitation.

And he hated that. He hated that she felt obliged to offer him somewhere to stay—when it was obvious she didn't really want to.

That hurt.

But the reality was that he really didn't have anywhere else to go. Chances were he could spend the next two hours phoning every hotel and just get the same answer—fully booked. There was a strong likelihood he wouldn't find a bed for the night.

Part of him wanted to refuse graciously and just walk away.

But something else was burning inside…a persistence.

Lucia used to be his. She used to fill his whole world. And he knew that the feelings had been mutual.

They were both adults. They were twelve years away from their shared past. Determination was overcoming him.

He didn't want to walk away from Lucia—no matter how awkward she felt.

In another world she would love him just as much as she always had, and would be delighted to offer him somewhere to stay and he would be delighted to accept.

But in another world they wouldn't have lost Ariella Rose.

His fingers itched to reach over and touch her soft hand.

Her own hands were knotted together, turning over and over in her lap.

The rational part of his brain kicked in. He needed

to get this job back on track. He needed to finish the renovations at the *palazzo* and the chapel.

And the history-loving part of him would love to see the other fresco. This wasn't such an unreasonable offer to accept. Another night in Venice might give him a little time to get to know Lucia again.

And it seemed as though the rest of Venice might be attending a concert somewhere, leaving the beauties of Venice still to be explored...

He lifted his gaze to meet hers. 'Thank you, Lucia. You're right. I probably won't be able to find anywhere else to stay. As long as you're sure it's not too much trouble, I'd be delighted to stay.'

CHAPTER FIVE

WHAT HAD SHE just done?

Was her apartment even reasonably tidy? She didn't have any food. Well, not the kind of food to entertain with and make dinner for a guest. Chilli-flavoured crisps and orange-flavoured chocolate might be her favourite dinner but she couldn't offer it to a guest. What on earth had she been thinking?

She was desperately hoping that she appeared outwardly calm. But her heartbeat was thudding against her chest at a rate of knots. Logan gestured to the waiter and settled their bill, picking up his bag and giving her a casual smile. 'Shall we finish this paperwork back at your place?'

It was a reasonable, rational question. He couldn't possibly imagine the way the blood was racing around her system and the breath was sticking in her lungs.

'Of course,' she said as coolly as possible, with a nod of her head as she stood up.

'How far away do you live?' he asked.

She tried to smile. 'Well, that depends entirely on traffic and the time of day.'

She weaved her way through the cobbled streets towards the water-taxi stop. 'I'm only two stops along. It only takes a few minutes.'

They were lucky. The water taxis on this side of the canal weren't quite so busy. They jumped on and back off within five minutes.

Her skin was prickling. Every little hair on her arms was standing on end even though the sun was splitting the sky. Now that Logan had had a chance to cool down he was back to his normal, unruffled self. She kind of wished he was still as flustered as he had been for a few moments earlier. It made him seem less infallible. A little more vulnerable—just like she felt.

But Logan had never been vulnerable. He'd always been rock solid. Even in grief.

He jumped out of the taxi before her and held out his hand for her as she stepped from the bobbing boat. She lifted her head and tried to walk with confidence. Although her apartment overlooked the Grand Canal the entrance of the traditional building was around the back. It had been hundreds of years since people had entered directly from the canal, and the original entrance had long since been plastered over.

She couldn't hide her smile. The architect in Logan could never be hidden. His eyes were roaming over the traditional building, his smile growing wider by the second. 'You stay in an old Venetian palace?'

The admiration and wonder in his voice was obvious. She'd always known Logan would approve of her choice. The fifteenth-century building facing the Grand Canal was one of the most photographed in the district. It had distinctive Venetian floral Gothic-style architecture. The façade was pink plaster facing with intricate white detailing around all the windows and balconies that overlooked the canal. The arches on the balconies were topped with delicate quatrefoil windows, resembling flowers with four petals.

She gave him a smile as she opened the entranceway. 'Just wait until you see the inside. We have our own high ceilings, beams, alcoves and frescoes. The whole place is full of original features.'

Logan was nodding, his eyes wide as they stepped inside. She'd always loved this about him. The way a glimpse of architectural details of a building could capture his attention instantly. He would become instantly enthralled, desperate to know more about the building and its history. Architecture had always been Logan's dream. But renovating ancient buildings? That was his calling. Always had been.

A bit like hers had been painting.

The memory swept through her like a gust of stormy weather.

Another part of life put into a box. When she'd first got together with Logan, their apartment had been littered with brushes, easels and oils. She had painted all the time, usually wearing nothing more than one of his shirts. She'd loved the feel of having him right next to her as she'd created, and if he hadn't been there, the scent of him—his aroma and aftershave—would usually linger on one of his shirts waiting to be washed. Thoughts of Logan had always fired her creative juices.

A warm feeling crept across her stomach. Logan had always loved finding her like that, his shirt loose around her body and her hair twisted on top of her head with an errant paintbrush holding it in place. He'd usually pulled it free, followed by the shirt, and the following hours had been lost in a rush of love.

But that light had flickered out and died along with the death of their daughter. For a long time she couldn't even bear to look at a paintbrush, let alone hold one.

Working for the heritage board had helped her heal. She didn't paint her own creations any more. But she did paint. Restoration work was painstaking. In every fresco she restored she tried to re-create the passion and drama that the original artist had felt when he'd envisaged the work.

There was still a little part of her that longed to feel like that again too.

There was a lift inside her building but Logan was captivated by the grandiose staircase inside the entranceway. As it curved upwards there were archways hollowed out in the plaster in the walls. A long time ago each had been painted individually and had held sculptures. In between each hollowed archway was a large circular fresco embedded into the plaster on the walls.

Logan moved quickly up the stairs, stopping to admire each individual one. 'These are amazing,' he said, his hand hovering about them. Logan's professional expertise knew far better than to actually touch.

She followed him upwards. A warmth was spreading through her. She was proud of her home—and secretly pleased that the man she'd shared part of her life with loved it just as much as she did.

As they walked upwards she leaned a little closer and whispered, 'I might have restored some of these.'

His head shot around towards her. 'You did?'

She nodded as his eyes fixed on the walls again. His fingers were still hovering just above a fresco of Moses. 'You've made an amazing job of these.'

'Thank you,' she said simply, as they reached her

floor and she pulled out her key and opened the apartment door.

He walked inside and looked around. Her living area was spacious and held a dining table and chairs and two wooden-footed red sofas. As with most Italian traditional apartments the floor was marble. A dark wooden bookcase adorned one wall, jam-packed with books.

But the most spectacular aspect of the apartment was the view. Lucia strode across the room and pulled open the black-and-gilt-edged glass doors. The warm air and noise from the Grand Canal below flooded in. It was like flicking a button and bringing the place to life. Next to the doors was a small wooden table, a chaise longue and an armchair. It was like having a real-live television. You could sit here all day and night and watch the world go by.

She knew his head must be spinning. This apartment was sumptuous. Well out of her price range. She stood shoulder to shoulder with him, watching the *vaporetti* and private boats motor past. On the other side of the canal stood another magnificent long-abandoned palace. Renaissance in style again, with Gothic-styled windows and ornate frescoes on the outside of the building.

He turned towards her and smiled. 'It's almost like your perfect view, isn't it?' There was an edge of curiosity in his voice. But he wasn't going to ask the question out loud. Logan was far too polite for that.

'Coffee?' she asked, as she walked towards the kitchen. It was right next door to the open living area and again had windows looking out on the canal. He nodded and walked in next to her, sitting down on one of the high stools looking over the canal. She switched on her coffee-machine and put in her favourite blend.

She leaned back against the countertop. 'I haven't always stayed here,' she said quietly. 'After I'd been in Venice for two years one of my colleagues retired from the heritage board. They subsidise our living arrangements because—as you know—Venice can be very expensive.' She held out her hands. 'I sort of inherited this place. I pay roughly the same as we did for our apartment in Florence.' She watched his eyebrows rise and couldn't stop the smile. 'It was like all my Saturdays at once.' She laughed as she watched the coffee brew and pointed across the waterway. 'Do you know, they actually asked me how I'd feel about staying here? It was all I could do not to snatch the key and just run.'

The warm feeling was spreading further. She rarely brought friends back to her apartment. This place was her sanctuary. From the moment she'd stepped inside it had always felt like that.

She'd thought having Logan here would be unbearable. She'd been so busy focusing on all the negatives she hadn't even considered the positives.

He was fascinated by the building's history and traditional architecture. He respected the heritage just as much as she did.

She poured the coffee into two mugs and set them on the table, watching the steam rising while she frothed some milk and added it to the mugs.

She gestured with her hand. 'Come and I'll show you where your room is.'

She hadn't even had time to prepare anything and she had to hope that nothing was out of place in her barely used guest suite. She led him down the corridor off the kitchen. It was the only place in her apartment that didn't have natural light.

He grabbed her elbow as they walked down the corridor. 'Are you sure this is okay?'

She turned to face him. He was much closer than she'd expected, his warm breath hitting her cheek. For a second she was frozen. This was as up close and personal as she'd been to Logan in years. The closeness took her breath away.

Even in the dim light of the corridor his green eyes made her struggle to think clearly. He was worried. He was worried about her. And glances like that brought back painful memories.

A tiny little part of her wished that Logan was looking at her in a different way. The way he used to, with passion and laughter in his eyes. She wanted to reach up and touch him. Touch the skin on his cheek, the shadowed outline of his jaw, and run her fingers through his dark hair. She wanted him to step forward just a few inches to see if their bodies still fitted together after all this time.

Her heart was racing and Logan blinked. He was staring at a spot on her neck where she was sure he could see the rapid beating of her pulse.

She took a deep breath and turned away, trying to blink back threatening tears. This was why everything about this was a bad idea.

She swung open a dark wooden door, flooding the corridor with light and stepping into a white and blue room. It was still traditional. A double bedroom with a window overlooking the canal, pale blue walls and fresh white bed linen. It wasn't quite as sumptuous as the other rooms in the house as it was rarely used.

She nodded her head. 'The bathroom is next door. Don't worry, we won't have to share. The box room was converted to an en suite. Would you like some time to settle in?'

He shook his head. 'Your coffee smells too good to let it go to waste. Let's finish the paperwork then we can decide where I'm taking you to dinner.' There was a glimmer in his eye. 'I don't expect you to cook for me—not if I want to live to tell the tale.'

He'd caught her unawares and she threw back her head and laughed. 'I offer you a room for the night and this is the thanks I get?'

He gave her a steady smile. 'Let's just wait until dinner.' She could almost hear his brain ticking over and her stomach gave a little leap.

What on earth did he have planned?

Logan washed up and changed his wrinkled shirt. Thank goodness he always had a spare in his bag.

He looked around the room. It was comfortable but sparse—it was clear this room didn't get much use. Didn't Lucia have friends to stay? She'd had a few girl-friends at university but he had no idea if they'd kept in touch.

He sighed and looked out of the window. It was ridiculous but he was having a hard time with this.

Lucia had a job she loved and a fabulous apartment in one of the most cosmopolitan cities in the world. He should be overjoyed for her. In his head, all he'd ever wanted was for her to be happy. In a twisted kind of way this was his ideal situation.

She was happy. She was settled. But there was no husband and kids on the scene to let the tiny leaves of jealousy unfurl. To let him know that she'd taken the final steps.

He couldn't quite work out why he was feeling so unsettled. All he knew was that there was something in her eyes. A guarded part. A hidden part. A little piece of her that didn't look quite…alive.

That was what bothered him. Lucia had a fabulous life. But was she really living?

He glanced around. While this room was sparsely furnished, the rest of the apartment was sumptuous. The reds and golds complemented the grandeur of the ancient palace. There were lots of similar buildings scattered across Venice. It seemed everyone who'd ever been slightly royal had built a palace in Venice. It was no wonder the heritage board wanted to keep someone in here.

He walked through to the main room. Lucia was sitting in a chair next to the open doors, the sights and sounds of the Grand Canal drifting up towards them. She'd changed into a purple jersey wrap-around dress, her dark chocolate-brown hair falling over her shoulders in waves. Her legs were curled up underneath her and she was reading a book.

Sitting on the table next to her was a glass of red wine. He smiled. 'Merlot or Chianti?'

Her head lifted in surprise. 'What do you think?'

He glanced out at the busy traffic on the Grand Canal. 'A warm summer evening? An aperitif before dinner?' He put his finger on his chin. 'I'm trying to think what you've planned for dinner—will it be meat or pasta?'

She used to be so fussy. He could imagine there were only certain local restaurants that she'd visit.

She held up her glass towards him. 'Maybe it will be both?'

She was teasing. He shook his head and pointed to the glass. 'It must be Merlot. It's too warm an evening for steak. You're planning for pasta.'

Something flickered across her face. She didn't like it that after twelve years he could still read her. She gestured towards the dining table where the bottle of wine and another glass sat. 'Find out for yourself.'

Logan walked over and filled his glass, resisting the temptation to smile. 'Where do you think we're eating tonight?'

She raised her eyebrows. 'What makes you think we'll be eating anywhere? Haven't you heard—it's the busiest night of the year in Venice?'

He sat down on the chaise longue next to her chair. 'But I might know an out-of-the-way place that the tourist hordes don't know about—like Erona's in Florence.'

There was a flash of something behind her eyes and she stood up quickly. He'd upset her.

She didn't want direct reminders of their time in Florence. 'You're not from here. How would you know where to eat?'

'Let's just say that your boss, Alessio, gave me a few hints.'

She slid her feet into a pair of red-soled black patent stilettos with impossibly high heels.

'Wherever we're going, I hope they have flat surfaces,' he muttered. Alessio had told him to get to the restaurant—just not what the streets around it were like.

'Let's go, Logan. Our viewing is early tomorrow morning. I want to get an early night.'

The words sent a flurry of sparks across his brain. An early night. With Lucia Moretti. It was enough to send his whole body into overdrive.

His eyes focused on her behind as she crossed the room ahead of him in her impossibly high heels. Her dress clung to every curve.

He swallowed. This was going to be a long, uncomfortable night.

Venice was virtually silent at this time in the morning. The private motor boat glided through the water towards the Venetian island of Giudecca.

Logan was curious. 'I thought all the artefacts of historical value would have been commandeered by the Italian Heritage Board?'

Lucia gave a sigh. 'In theory, they can. But part of this island is private—has been since before Renaissance times. It's owned by the Brunelli family. They built the church here and commissioned the artist, Burano, to paint the fresco. Technically, we're just their guests. We're allowed access to the fresco on request. You'll understand why when you see it—it's a little unusual.'

The boat came to a halt at the dock and they disembarked onto the wooden structure. A white stone path led them directly to the church, where a dark-suited man was waiting for them. Logan recognised him immediately—Dario Brunelli was frequently nicknamed Italian's most eligible bachelor. *He knew Lucia?*

'Lucia,' he said swiftly, bending to kiss her on both cheeks, 'it's good to see you again. How have you been?'

His familiarity with Lucia grated instantly. Her reaction was even worse—she seemed relaxed in his company. 'I'm good, thank you.' She turned towards Logan. 'Dario, this is Logan Cascini, a specialist restoration architect from Florence. He's working with me on the project in Tuscany.'

It was completely true. But it made it sound as if they'd only just met. As if there was no shared history between them at all.

For a second he held his breath, wondering if Dario was having the same thoughts that he'd had this morning when he'd first seen Lucia. Her cream fitted business suit and pale pink shirt hugged her curves. The knee-length skirt exposed her slim legs. And her dark hair and eyes complemented the package perfectly. Lucia looked good enough to eat.

Dario nodded towards Logan but it was clear his focus was on Lucia. 'So, do you think you've found another of Burano's frescoes?'

Lucia's smile was broad. 'I think there is a distinct possibility. With your permission, I'm going to take some high-resolution digital shots to compare the brush-strokes.'

Dario was nodding enthusiastically. 'In Tuscany? I wonder how in the world Burano ended up working there? Wouldn't it be wonderful if it was another of his works?'

A Renaissance art lover. The passion and enthusiasm in his eyes was for the art, not for Lucia. Not for his woman.

Where had that come from?

Cold air prickled his skin and he shifted on his feet. Lucia hadn't been his woman for twelve years—she hadn't wanted to be.

And he'd had to live with that. He'd had to support the fact she wasn't able to continue their relationship and allow her the space she'd needed to heal. No matter how much it had ripped his heart in two.

No one else had ever come close to the love he'd

felt for Lucia. How could they? She'd been the mother of his child. And even though that was something she wanted to forget, her place in his heart had been well and truly cemented there.

But even he hadn't realised how much.

'Forgive me.' Dario nodded. 'I have to go. I have business to attend to. Please, take all the time you need.'

Lucia gave a gracious nod of her head as Dario walked swiftly down the path towards the waiting motorboat.

She turned and pressed her hand against the heavy wooden door of the church and smiled at Logan. There was a gleam of something in her eye. He only hoped it was for the contents of the church and not for the retreating back of Dario. The spike of jealousy had been unexpected—a feeling he hadn't dealt with in years.

'Ready?' she asked.

He nodded and she pushed the door and it groaned and creaked loudly on its hinges as it swung back. The church wasn't lit.

The only light that streamed in came through six muted stained-glass windows above the altar.

It took a few seconds for his eyes to adjust to the dim light. He caught his breath.

The fresco on the wall was magnificent and stretched from one end of the church to the other. His feet moved automatically towards it.

Over his years in Italy he'd seen many frescoes—but none quite like this. It was completely and utterly unique, almost like a timeline through the first book of the bible.

She rested her hand on his arm. 'I've never seen anything like it before, and I'm quite sure I'll never see anything like it again.' He could hear the amusement in her voice at his reaction. 'It's a little different from the Madonna and Child, isn't it?'

He shook his head as he took in more and more of the fresco. He recognised the characters—at least, he thought he did. Adam and Eve, Noah, Moses, Jacob and his sons. But the thing that made these characters unique was the fact they were all completely naked.

He spun to face her. 'What on earth…?'

She laughed. 'I know. It's why the Italian Heritage Board hasn't bothered to make demands on the family. The Catholic Church would be outraged by these scenes.'

Logan moved forward. He just couldn't stop smiling. He was trying to think rationally. 'Adam and Eve—you might expect them to be naked. But the rest…' He kept looking at the scenes. 'It's amazing. I mean, apart from their nakedness the depictions are accurate. Eve with the apple, Moses leading the Israelites through the Red Sea, Noah on the ark, and Jacob with his twelve sons.' He let out a laugh. 'Joseph is even holding his multi-coloured coat instead of wearing it.'

She shrugged her shoulders. 'Naked bodies were pretty much the fashion during Renaissance times.' Her brow creased slightly. 'But usually they had something—anything—draped around about them. These ones are totally original.'

Logan stepped back a little. 'But there's something else, isn't there? I can't quite put my finger on it.' He paused, staring hard at the scenes, looking between one and another.

She nodded, with an amused expression on her face. 'Give it time, Logan. You'll get it.'

She was teasing him. It was almost like throwing down a challenge. So he took a few minutes, concentrating hard until, finally, the penny dropped.

He turned to her in amazement. 'It's the faces, isn't it?' He stepped right up to the fresco, staring first at the face of Adam then at the face of Moses, then Noah. 'It's the same face.' His eyes scanned one way, then the other. 'It's the same man and woman in every scene.'

Lucia was laughing. 'You're right. The family don't have any official records about who commissioned the fresco. The name of Burano has just been passed down through the family. That's why we'll have to do a comparison. And we're not quite sure why it's the same faces in all the scenes. I've spoken to the family about it at length. We think there's something a little narcissistic in it. We think that when the original Brunellis commissioned the artist they asked for the faces to be made in their image.'

Logan let out a burst of laughter. 'You mean, even all those years ago we had fame-hungry people?' He shook his head. 'Wow, just wow.'

He took another few seconds and stopped in front of the young Joseph holding the coat. 'I still can't believe they wouldn't let Joseph wear his multi-coloured coat.'

She bent down in the front of the fresco. In the dim light he could see her dark eyes were still gleaming. 'Yes, but look at the folds in the cloak. What do you see?'

He looked closer. 'Of course. They look exactly like the folds in the Madonna's dress in the fresco in Tuscany. That's what you noticed.'

There wasn't a sound in the dark church. They were entirely alone, crouching on the floor. The lack of artificial light was almost like a safety blanket around them.

His face was only inches from hers. Their gazes meshed. It was a moment. An instant. For just that second she had the same passion and wonder in her eyes that she'd had twelve years ago. Twelve years ago when they'd thought they could conquer the world.

He'd been trying so hard to hold his tongue, trying to keep a handle on how he felt about everything, but the memories of Lucia were just overtaking him. The spark of jealousy, the protectiveness, the connection between them. Hc was like a pressure cooker just waiting to go off.

Her pupils were dilating in front of him, the blackness overtaking the chocolate brown of her eyes. He was pretty certain his were doing exactly the same.

All of a sudden he couldn't stop himself. He leaned forward, just a few inches, and caught the back of her head in his hand, tangling his fingers through her hair as he pulled her towards him.

And then he stopped thinking entirely...

She was instantly transported back twelve years. The familiarity was astounding.

No one had kissed her like this in twelve years.

No kiss had felt so right.

No kiss had felt so perfect.

Her body moved on automatic pilot, ignoring all the little neurons that were firing in her brain. Ignoring every single rational thought that might be there.

She could only act on instinct. Her hands slid through his thick, dark hair, her fingers tugging and pulling at his head. She could taste him. She could smell him.

Everything about him was familiar. His scent was winding its way around her like a coiling snake. Her hands moved, sliding across his muscled shoulders and arms and down the planes of his chest.

His lips never left hers. Their teeth clashed, his tongue tangling with hers. Crouching on a floor wasn't comfortable for kissing. Logan sensed that and pulled her up against him, his strong legs lifting them both upwards, keeping their bodies in contact the whole time.

She could feel his heart thudding against her chest. Feel her breath catching in her throat.

It was so easy to be swept away. It was so easy to forget about everything else. His fingertips brushed across the front of her breasts as she sucked in a sharp breath, then rounded her hips and stopped firmly on her behind, pulling her even closer to him.

There was no mistaking his reaction to her. There was no mistaking he was every bit as caught up in this as she was.

So when he stopped kissing her she was shocked.

He pulled his lips back from hers and rested his forehead against hers, breathing heavily. His body was still interlocked with hers. It seemed he had no intention of moving.

Her hands, resting against his chest, clenched.

Embarrassment swamped her. She wanted to step back but couldn't.

What on earth was he thinking?

Then, to her surprise, he let out a deep laugh. It wasn't a mocking laugh. It wasn't derogatory. It was more one of astonishment.

In the dark church his voice was husky. 'So that's what I've been missing.' He took a deep breath. 'I sometimes wondered if my mind was playing tricks on me. If I'd imagined how good it was.'

He was echoing her thoughts. She'd felt exactly the same way. Any time she'd allowed memories of Logan to sneak into her brain, she'd always thought it couldn't possibly have been as good as she remembered it. Everything before Ariella Rose, that was.

The portcullis that was always stiffly in place was shaken a little. The thick gate had risen just a tiny bit, leaving the thinnest gap underneath. The black cloud of self-protection that usually cloaked her was thinning in patches.

Their foreheads were still touching. She could feel his warm breath on her cheeks. 'It wasn't all that bad, was it?' she whispered.

His fingers stroked through her soft hair. 'Some parts were really good,' he breathed quietly.

She stayed where she was—for a few more seconds.

This was only a moment of madness. A tiny little step back in time.

It wasn't real. None of this was real.

Real life meant that now she lived and worked in Venice and Logan lived and worked in Florence.

The meeting at Tuscany was merely a blip. The next few weeks of working together would only be a continuation of that blip. She could almost feel the protective coating going around her heart. She had to be careful. She had to be sensible.

She lifted her head back from his, trying to ignore the warm feeling of his beating heart beneath her palm.

It was time to put all the safeguards back in place.

She gave him a rueful smile and stepped back, freeing herself from his grasp.

The movement jolted Logan. He straightened his

back, watching her carefully. It was almost as if he knew what was coming next.

'We don't really have time to reminisce, Logan. I have work to do. You have work to do. The sooner we can verify the artist of the fresco, the sooner we can both move towards our goals.'

What were her goals? She'd always been clear about them in the past, but right now they were looking pretty muddy.

Silence hung in the air between them. It almost shimmered in the slowly brightening daylight.

She could almost hear him processing what she'd said.

He chose his words carefully as he stepped forward and gently touched her cheek. 'You're right, Lucia. It's best we leave things as they are.' He nodded his head. 'We both need to focus on work.'

Something squeezed in her chest. For a few seconds she felt as if she couldn't breathe.

Part of her wished he'd said no. Part of her wished he'd pull her back into his arms and kiss her all over again. Acknowledge this thing that shimmered in the air between them and refuse to walk away from it.

But that was all a fairy tale. This was real life. She could tell from the slight waver in his voice that he was saying what he thought he should. This was just as hard for him as it was for her.

If this was anyone else she might think they were toying with her. But Logan just wasn't capable of that kind of thing. Not after what they'd shared.

This was for the best. It didn't matter that little parts of her brain were screaming at her. Every female hormone she'd ever possessed was currently marching in a charge towards all parts of her body.

She blinked back the tears that were hovering behind her eyes. His fingers felt like butterfly wings on her skin. It was all she could do not to tilt her head towards his hand.

She bent down and picked up her papers, which were strewn on the floor, trying not to acknowledge her trembling hands.

His feet took a step backwards. She could sense him bending over her, probably reaching towards her, then he took a few further steps back. It was almost as if he forcing himself into a position of retreat.

She straightened up and fixed a false smile on her face. 'Let's get to work, Logan. Can you see if we can find some light?' She pulled her camera from her bag. 'The sooner we get these pictures, the sooner we can move forward.'

She tried not to wince at her choice of words.

But Logan's expression was resolute. Guarded. She had no idea what was going on behind those green eyes.

He gave a brief nod. 'Of course.' And walked back towards the door to let in some light.

She turned back to the fresco.

Work. The only thing that was currently keeping her sane.

CHAPTER SIX

WORK WAS THE easy part. It didn't take any time at all for Lucia to take the photos and to take the boat trip back to her office. The rest of Venice had woken up now, with the city becoming loud and colourful as their boat glided back through the water.

The Italian Heritage Board building was every bit as exuberant as Logan had expected it to be. The architecture was a welcome distraction, with some of the really exclusive Renaissance pieces of art housed in the building.

Lucia had uploaded the pictures to her computer and was running a comparison computer program that would take a few hours.

All they could do was wait.

And waiting was something Logan Cascini had never been good at.

After that kiss he was finding it difficult to keep his cool, collected manner in place. One touch of Lucia's lips had been enough to ignite all the sparks in his brain and frustration had been building ever since.

He'd had enough. Not of Lucia. He'd had enough of them being in the same room together and not talking about the big elephant between them. Ariella Rose.

It was twelve years on. It was time. Even if Lucia still felt that it wasn't.

There was no way he was getting on that plane back to Tuscany without tackling the subject. No way at all.

But how?

She had barriers erected so tightly around her she might as well have been wearing a spacesuit. The kiss had been one thing. She'd probably already written it off as a blip.

But Logan couldn't do that. He wanted more. Much more.

No wonder every other relationship he'd had had fizzled out. No wonder he'd never wanted to commit to someone else.

This was nothing to do with losing his daughter. This wasn't about the fear of another pregnancy or another child.

It was much more primal than that. It was about the fear of never finding someone he had the same chemistry with, the same connection with, as he had with Lucia.

Life was hard. Life was tough. But twelve years of drifting had given him new determination.

Seeing Lucia for the first time again had been like a lightning bolt. Kissing her again...well, that had been so much more.

It was time to face things head-on.

He turned from the view of Venice to face her. She was sitting behind her desk, twiddling her long dark hair around one finger.

He reached forward and grabbed her other hand, pulling her to her feet. 'Let's go.'

She looked shocked. 'Let's go where?'

He held out his other hand. 'Out there. Let's see Venice.' He pointed to the screen. 'You already said the computer program would take a few hours. Let's spend them wisely.' He grinned at her. 'Today I am a tourist. Today I want you to show me Venice.'

A hint of a smile appeared on her face. She waved towards the window. 'But it will be crazy out there. There's another concert tonight. We'll have all of last night's gig-goers and all of tonight's too.'

He raised his eyebrows. 'What, we can't handle a few tourists?'

She shook her head and let out a little laugh. 'Now I know you're definitely crazy.' She picked up her handbag and swung it over her shoulder. 'You're right, the program will take another few hours, and as long as we start with ice cream I'm in.'

He held out his hand towards her.

She hesitated. She wavered. He could see it in every inch of her body. She finally let out the breath she'd been holding and put her hand in his.

'Let's go.'

It was hotter than hot. Her jacket was hanging over the top of her shoulder bag to try and deter any pickpockets and her shirt was in danger of sticking to her back.

The queue for ice cream was snaking its way out the door of her favourite gelateria. She tugged Logan towards the end of the queue. His hand was still in hers. It felt odd, but she hadn't quite managed to pull her hand free of his.

The walk through the twisting cobbled streets had been like a step back in time. She'd noticed the women's admiring glances. Logan was every woman's Italian dream—dark-haired, broad shouldered, well dressed and devilishly handsome. His unexpected bright green eyes added a little twist.

And he was free with his natural charm. He nodded and smiled at the numerous pairs of acknowledging eyes. A tiny swell of pride surged in her chest. Memories flickered in her brain. People thought they were a couple. People thought that Logan was hers.

He turned to face her as the queue slowly moved forward. 'What kind of ice cream do you want? I take it you've sampled them all?'

She gave a little smile. 'All in the name of research. Dark chocolate and *limon* are my two favourites from here.'

He nodded at her choices. 'In that case we'll get one of each. Why not try everything you like?' He was smiling as he said the words, and the woman in front turned around with a gleam in her eyes.

Lucia shifted on her feet. She didn't want to allow the tiny seeds in her brain to flower and grow.

Logan reached the front of the queue, ordering their ice creams and only releasing her hand when he reached to pay for them. They walked out into the building heat and he held both hands out towards her. 'What'll it be? The dark, tantalising chocolate or the sweet, zesty lemon?'

He was teasing her. But the surprising thing was, she kind of liked it.

She held her hand out for the chocolate. 'I'll start with dark and delicious.' Her fingers brushed against his. 'But don't count on getting to finish the lemon yourself,' she said smartly as she walked past.

Within seconds he was walking shoulder to shoulder

with her. 'Where do you want to play tourist, then?' she asked. 'I can't imagine that you want to visit Piazza San Marco, St Mark's Basilica or the Clock Tower.'

He shook his head. 'Too busy, and anyway I much prefer Piazza San Marco at night. Much more romantic,' he added.

She ignored the comment.

He pointed over in the distance. 'What I'd really like to do is catch a *vaporetto* to San Giorgio Maggiore and go up the campanile. It's still early. There will hardly be any crowds.'

She gave him a sideways glance as she veered towards the nearest *vaporetto* stop. 'Hmm, so you're still a tourist at heart, then?'

He shrugged. 'It's been a few years since I've been in Venice. But I'm an Italian, I still know where to go to get the best view of the city.' He held out his ice cream towards her. 'Swap?'

She nodded. The dark chocolate was starting to taste a little bitter. She took a nibble of the lemon and sweet, tangy zest nearly made her taste buds explode. But her brain didn't have time to focus on that because Logan had slung his arm around her shoulders and was walking easily next to her as if they did it every day.

And it *did* feel like they did it every day. She fitted under his arm. Always had—always would.

He chatted as they made their way along to the *vaporetto* stop, joining the small number of waiting people and climbing on board as soon as it arrived. Most of the rest of the passengers were heading to Murano—the island famous for its glassware. He glanced at her as the boat stopped. 'Did you want to get off here?'

She shook her head. 'I love Murano glass—I have the

most gorgeous red and gold vase in my apartment—but I don't like the hordes of tourists, or what they make for them. If I see one more orange fish in a clear square cube I'll scream.'

She was standing near the front of the boat and he laughed and pulled her down next to him as the next load of passengers climbed on board. 'You old Venice snob.'

'Oh, come on, you were exactly the same way in Florence. You hated the millions of ornaments of the cathedral and baptistery.'

He lifted his ice cream towards her. 'Guilty as charged.' Then he glanced at the activity on the Grand Canal. 'But sometimes it's nice to play tourist.'

They sat in silence for a few minutes as the boat glided along the canal. It was busy this morning, making the ride a little bumpy, and she inched closer and closer to him. His arm stayed loosely on her shoulders as they reached the stop for San Giorgio. Ice creams finished, they wiped their hands on the napkins provided and climbed out of the boat.

It was getting hotter but most of the tourists hadn't reached the island yet and the queue for the lift to the top of the campanile meant they only had a ten-minute wait.

Logan shook his head as they approached. 'This is one of the architectural glories of Venice. Palladio is one of my favourite architects. Look at it, the gleaming white Istrian marble façade and lithe brick and bell tower—why, it almost seems to float in the middle of the Bacino San Marco, supported on its own tiny island. It's only a few hundred yards off St Mark's Square but most people just take a photo on the way past. They have no idea it's decorated with works by Tintoretto,

Carpaccio and Jacopo Bassano. This is the one place in Venice I just wouldn't want to miss.'

Lucia smiled at him. The passion and enthusiasm in his voice was so good to hear. She could see heads turning at his voice, obviously relieved they'd chosen this venue to visit.

The lift opened to take them up the sixty-metre-high bell tower and a few minutes later they stepped out on to the observation deck. Logan held out his arms and spun around. 'And this is why I love this place. Hardly a queue to get in, only a couple of euros and no crowding up here. The view is perfect.' He pointed across the water towards the campanile San Marco. 'While our brother over there has long lines, a higher price tag, is crowded and doesn't have the same panoramic views.'

Lucia grinned. 'But you can get a full-on postcard shot of the Piazza San Marco just across the water.' She pulled out her phone and held it in front of her, snapping a quick photo.

'Hold it.' Logan pulled out his own phone, but put his hands on her shoulders and turned her, so instead of having a background shot of Piazza San Marco he had a full shot of the Grand Canal. 'Smile,' he said as he held up his phone. 'You know, on a clear day you can see right across the Adriatic Sea and all the way to the Alps.'

The smile was still on her face and she didn't have much time to think about the fact that Logan would now have a picture of her on his phone. As soon as he'd snapped the shot he walked over and leaned his elbows on the balcony, looking out at the panoramic view. 'This is what Venice should be about,' he said quietly.

She spun around and put her elbows next to his. There were a few other people wandering around on the observation deck, but it was nowhere near as busy here as it was on the other side of the water. St Mark's Square was already packed. It seemed most of the people who'd attended the concert hadn't had much sleep.

She could hardly blame them. Anyone who was lucky enough to visit Venice—even for a few hours—usually tried to squeeze in as many of the sights as they possibly could.

Something flickered through her brain. With one concert last night and another tonight there would be a whole host of new people in and out of the city today. 'You won't be able to get a flight home today either, will you?'

A gentle breeze blew across her skin. She wasn't quite sure how she felt about this. Having Logan stay over one night had seemed like an unavoidable hiccup. Having him stay for two nights was something else entirely.

He didn't answer for a few seconds, fixing his eyes instead on the hustle and bustle of the masses of people on the other side of the canal. 'I'm sorry, Lucia.' He ran his fingers through his hair. 'I had no idea about any of this. I didn't mean to put you in a difficult position.'

He looked a little uncomfortable but not entirely unhappy. She'd hardly slept a wink last night. How could she, knowing that the person she used to love with her whole heart had been lying naked next door?

Logan had always slept naked, hating anything on his skin once he was in bed. The only thing he'd ever wanted next to his skin had been her.

She was trying so hard to seem cool, to seem professional. The atmosphere between them today had been lighter, less pressured.

Exactly the opposite from what it should have been after that kiss.

But that kiss had ignited the good memories in her brain. Before that, everything about Logan had been a build-up of frustration and a reminder of grief.

It was almost as if that kiss had brought alive the side of her brain she'd shut off. She just didn't know what to do with it.

'It's fine, Logan,' she said quickly, as she held out her hand towards the busy St Mark's Square. 'The hotels will be every bit as busy again today. Don't worry.'

His head turned towards her and he lifted his hand, running one finger down her arm towards her hand. 'But I do worry, Lucia. I'll always worry about you.' His voice was low, husky and it sent a little tremble up her spine.

She couldn't turn to face him, just kept looking out at the people of Venice as her skin tingled and his hand slid over hers, slowly interlocking their fingers.

Her breath caught in her chest. Just when she'd thought she was safe around Logan. Just when she'd thought she could relax, he did something like this.

Something that made her catch her breath and nibble her bottom lip.

It was the closeness that made her feel vulnerable. Made her feel as if she was on the verge of opening herself up to a whole host of hurt. She'd spent so long protecting herself, hiding herself away.

Logan was a whole part of her life that she'd chosen to close the door on. But having him standing next to her, his breath warming her cheek and his hand interlocked with hers, was like dangling her over a precipice she wasn't ready for.

And it was as if he could sense it. He didn't go any further. Didn't make any other move. Didn't bring up the biggest subject in the world.

Logan was carefully skirting around the edges of her life. But he wouldn't stay there for ever.

'How do you enjoy living and working in Venice?'

She swallowed, trying to push all other thoughts away. 'I love Venice. But it's not the city that captures my soul. I still miss Florence.'

The words took her by surprise. She'd always felt like that. She'd just never said it out loud.

He was facing her again and she could feel his eyes watching her carefully. She wondered if he'd pick her up on what she'd just said. But he didn't. He let it go, keeping things in safe territory. 'How do the restorations work?'

She lifted her other hand and pulled her hair off her neck. It was getting even hotter. 'I've done at least one every year I've worked for the heritage board. Always on frescoes. If they decide the fresco in Tuscany is genuine and is to be restored, then that will be my job.'

She knew why he was asking. He would be in Tuscany for the next few months and he was trying to think ahead. If a few days were difficult, how would they manage to work in the same environment for a few months?

At least, she thought that's what would be on his mind.

It couldn't be the kiss. It *wouldn't* be the kiss. Not when there was so much more to think about.

'How do you feel about coming down to Tuscany?'

It was work. Of course it was work. She didn't know whether to feel disappointment or relief. The touching

and handholding was nothing. It was just Logan back
to his usual charming self, trying to make everyone
around him feel good.

She stared at the packed street across from her and
smiled. 'While I love Venice, and I love my apartment,
the summer months are extremely busy. Tuscany seems
a lot more peaceful than here. It might be nice to have
some clean fresh air and some quiet to be able to concentrate on the restoration work.' She turned her body
towards him, finally relaxed enough to give him a smile.
'I think I'll like it.'

But Logan wasn't staring at her the way she'd
thought. He'd moved his thumb underneath their interlocked fingers and was gently making circles on the
underside of her palm, This was what he'd used to do
when he was deep in thought…when he was contem-
plating something carefully. His eyes were lowered and
his voice quiet. 'How would you feel…?'

She inched a little closer to hear him.

He tried again. 'How would you feel if I asked you to
stay with me when you came back to Tuscany, instead
of in the main *palazzo* with Louise?'

Now he did look up. But he didn't have the quiet as-
suredness that usually always possessed him. Now he
looked wary.

The words were very unexpected. She'd just gone
back into that 'safe' zone, the one where no one could
touch her and no one could threaten her. His words catapulted her straight back out.

The voices in the background blended together into
one constant murmur as the rapid beating of her heart
thudded in her eardrums. His thumb hadn't stopped
moving in those little circles. It was almost as if he'd

been trying to prepare her, to soothe her, before he'd asked the question.

Her brain felt jumbled. She didn't quite know what to say. 'I don't think… I don't think that would work,' was all she could fumble out.

His fingers tensed around hers. 'Why? Why wouldn't it work? You're my oldest friend. Twelve years have passed, Lucia, and you and I are still trapped there. Why aren't you married to someone else with a houseful of kids? Why aren't I?'

Now it was too much. That little question had turned into a whole lot more. She was standing overlooking this beautiful city, people all around her, and yet she felt hideously exposed. If she could transport herself, right now, back into her bed and under her covers, that's exactly what she'd do.

'I don't want to be married,' she blurted out, causing a few heads to turn in their direction. Instantly, she understood what she'd done. People were casting their eyes down in sympathy, as if Logan had just proposed and it had gone horribly wrong.

She shook her head. 'I'm happy with my work. I'm happy with my life.'

He put his hand behind her waist and pulled her towards him. His voice was quiet but there was an edge of frustration that only she could hear. Only she could understand.

'Look at me, Lucia. Look at me and tell me that you've tried to have other relationships. Tell me that you've met some suitably nice, handsome men—just like I've met some beautiful and good women—but something just hasn't been right. It hasn't felt the way it used to feel—the way it *should* feel. You could never

go on and take the next step because you knew, deep
down, that you'd ultimately hurt this good and loving
person. You'd never quite love them the way that they
loved you.'

It was almost as if he'd stepped inside her brain and
was reading her mind and all her past memories. All her
hidden regrets. She could see them all reflected on his
face. He knew this, because he'd been living this life too.

That kiss had catapulted him into another space.
Given him a painful reminder of what he wanted to
capture again. Just like it had her.

She put her hand up to her chest, which was hurting, tight.

She was still shaking her head, aware of the anxious
glances around them. 'I don't know, Logan. I just don't
know.' She looked up and met his gaze. He looked hurt.
He looked confused and something twisted inside her.
It had been a long time since she and Logan had been
like this.

Last time around she'd felt numb. She'd been unable to cope with her own grief so she certainly hadn't
coped with his. But now he looked just as exposed as
she felt.

His hair was mussed from where he'd run his fingers
through it. The wind was rippling his shirt around his
shoulders and chest. She almost hated the fact he could
relate to how her life had turned out. To how every relationship she'd had since him had turned out.

But she hated even more that he'd mirrored her life
with his own. She'd told herself that she'd always hoped
Logan would move on, meet a girl, fall in love and have
a family of his own.

Seeing him in Tuscany a few days ago and feeling

that flicker of excitement when he'd told her he was unattached had revealed a side to her she didn't like.

He was fixed on her with those green eyes. They were burning a hole into her. To the rest of the world they would be the picture-perfect couple with the backdrop of Venice behind them. No one else would know the way their insides had been ripped out and left for the vultures.

Her heart squeezed. She was bad. She was selfish. Part of her did wish Logan had a happy life but then again part of her always wanted him to belong to her. But at what price?

He hadn't moved. One hand was still wrapped around her waist, pressing her body against his, the other interlocking their fingers. She could break free if she wanted to. But after all these years she just didn't know how.

He blinked. 'I won't pressure you any more. I won't bring it up again. Just promise me you'll give it some thought. You can tell me before I return to Tuscany tomorrow.'

She gave the briefest nod and it coincided with a swell of relief from her chest as he stepped back, breaking their contact. In their exposed position on the observation deck a gust of wind swept between them. It startled her, sweeping away the feeling of warmth from Logan's body next to hers.

The expression in Logan's eyes changed. Gone was the tiny smudge of vulnerability that she'd seen before. It had been replaced by the determined, focused look she knew so well.

'Are we done with photos?' he asked, just a little brusquely.

She nodded as she pushed her phone back in her bag. He took her hand again, firmly this time, no gentle touch, as if he was determined not to let her escape. They walked back to the lift. 'Tonight I'm going to pick the venue for dinner.'

It was clear there was no point arguing. She gave a brief nod as the doors slid closed in front of them.

The stiff atmosphere remained for the next thirty minutes. His hand grasped hers rigidly as they boarded the *vaporetto* and made the short journey back to Piazza San Marco.

It was even more crowded but Logan seemed to have got his bearings in the city and led her through some of the backstreets. Her phone rang just as they were about to cross one of Venice's bridges.

She pulled it from her bag. 'It's work,' she said. 'I need to take it.'

'No problem. I'll have a look in some of the shops around here.'

As her boss spoke rapidly in her ear she lost sight of Logan's broad shoulders in the crowds. It was twenty minutes before the conversation was over and Logan appeared at her side holding a large loop-handled bag with a designer logo on the side. He held it out towards her.

'What is it?'

'Yours. For tonight.'

She was more than a little surprised. She opened the bag and saw a flash of red but he shook his head.

'Leave it. You can try it on when we get back to the apartment.'

In some ways she should feel flattered. Logan had always had exquisite taste. He'd bought her clothes in the past and she'd loved every single item. But they weren't a couple any more—they weren't lovers and she wasn't sure this felt entirely appropriate.

'Why on earth would you buy me something?'

He shrugged his shoulders. 'It's a thank-you gift,' he said casually. 'A thank you for letting me stay at your apartment when I obviously should have planned better.' He made it sound so matter-of-fact, so easy and rational. But the contents of the bag didn't seem impartial.

Red was her favourite colour. And although she hadn't had a chance to examine the dress she was sure it would fit perfectly and be a flattering style. It was all part of Logan's gift.

'What was your call?' He wasn't giving her time to think about this too much. Probably in case she started to object.

She gave a little smile. 'The electronic comparison of brushstrokes indicates the fresco is indeed by Burano. The paint sampling won't be completed until early next week.'

'When?'

'Probably Monday. Technology is a wonderful thing these days. They will be able to give me an exact match of the product and colours that Burano used in his fresco for the restoration work.'

They started to walk across the bridge now, stopping in the middle just as a gondola with some tourists on board passed underneath. 'And how long do you think the restoration work will take?'

She put her elbows on the bridge next to him. The sun was beating down now, rising high in the sky above them. She gave a nervous laugh. 'That's the one thing that doesn't happen quickly. Probably around a few months.'

'And it will be definitely you who does the work?'

Was it possible he didn't want her to be working next to him, no matter what he'd been saying? Maybe Logan was only looking for a quiet life. Maybe he was only trying to keep her onside to make sure his project didn't miss his deadline?

But he didn't look unhappy. He still had that determined gleam in his eye. He pointed to a baker's shop on the other side of the bridge. 'Why don't we grab some food and head back to the apartment? It's going to be too hot for sightseeing this afternoon and we both have work we can probably do before dinner tonight.'

She gave a nod of her head. It made sense—even if the thought of sharing her apartment space with Logan all afternoon made it feel as if the walls would close in around her.

'Where are we going later?' she asked, as they walked over the other side of the bridge.

He tapped the side of his nose. 'Leave that to me.'

CHAPTER SEVEN

IT WAS RIDICULOUS and he knew it. Why did he feel as if so much rested on one night?

He'd planned everything to perfection, pulling strings wherever he could. What he wanted most was for Lucia to be relaxed around him, maybe just enough to let her guard down and let him in.

It sounded cold, it sounded calculating. It was anything but.

He needed her to open up to him, to talk to him. It's what they both needed in order to move on with their lives.

It didn't matter that he had hopes for the direction in which they moved. He had to push those aside right now. He wanted her to talk. He couldn't see any further forward than that.

'Are you ready?'

He'd been pacing in the main room for the last half hour, watching the sun beginning to lower in the sky, bathing Venice in a beautiful orange glow.

'I'm ready.' Her voice sounded a little shaky and he spun around.

She looked a picture. The red dress was exactly as he'd envisaged it, hugging her curves in all the right places. He'd known as soon as he'd seen it that it was perfect for her. A red jersey underlay with red crochet lace on top, it reached her knees and only gave the tiniest hint of skin underneath. Lucia had never liked anything too revealing.

She was wearing her black patent impossibly high heels with red soles and clutching a sequin bag in her hand. But something wasn't quite right.

She flicked her long hair on her shoulders and meshed her fingers together. Lucia was wound tighter than a spring.

He walked over and handed her a glass of red wine. 'Let's sit down for five minutes. We have time.'

He gestured towards the chaise longue.

She waited a few seconds. Her nerves seemed to emanate from her, and even the hand holding the glass had an almost imperceptible shake. After a few moments she sucked in a deep breath and walked across the room.

'Thank you for the dress. It's perfect,' she said simply, as she sat down and crossed her legs.

'I knew it would suit you,' he said calmly. 'You look stunning.' It was true and he was quite sure that every man in Venice who saw her would agree during the course of the evening.

She took a sip of her wine. 'Are you going to tell me where we are going for dinner?'

He smiled. 'We're in Venice. We're going to Rubins overlooking Piazza San Marco. Where else would we go?'

A hint of a smile appeared on her face as she relaxed back and took another sip of wine. 'How on earth did you manage that? You couldn't find a hotel room, but you managed to get into the most exclusive restaurant in Venice?'

He wrinkled his nose. 'Let's just say I might have helped them at some point with an architectural matter. Unfortunately, they don't have beds for the night—so dinner it is.'

He actually couldn't believe his luck. The restaurant overlooking Piazza San Marco and based in the Procuratie Nuove had had issues a few years ago when some of the stonework around the elaborate archways had started to crumble. Logan had been able to help them find the same stone, from the original source, to allow complete restoration. It hadn't been an easy task. And right now he would take any advantage he could get.

They sat for a few minutes longer, watching the world go by on the Grand Canal, as she finished her wine.

He stood up and held out his hand towards her. 'Are we ready?'

She nodded and slid her hand into his. The momentum of pulling her up made them almost bump noses and she laughed and put her hands on his chest. 'Where did this dark suit come from? You surely didn't have this in your bag?'

He shook his head. 'I picked it up an hour ago when you were getting ready. I think you've seen enough of the cream jacket and trousers.'

Her eyes ran up and down his body. It was amazing how that tiny act could make his hairs stand on end and make him feel distinctly hot under the collar.

She gave an approving nod. 'I like it,' she said as she stepped away. 'I like it even more that you didn't bother with a tie.' She spun towards him in her heels. 'I never did like a man in a tie.'

His heart leapt in his chest. Her mood was lifting. She was definitely beginning to relax. He caught her elbow and spun her back towards him, resting his other hand on her hip.

He wanted this to be the start of something new. He wanted a chance to make things work with the only woman he'd ever really loved.

He knew they both had to move on. He knew they might not be able to move on together. And he knew at some point they had to talk about Ariella Rose.

But his heart was squeezing in his chest.

Tonight could be perfect. Tonight could just be about them. And somehow he knew that if he gave her the guarantee of no pressure, it could change everything.

'What do you say that for tonight I promise you that I won't mention Ariella Rose. We won't talk about what happened. And we'll only concentrate on the here and now. We'll only concentrate on the good things.'

He slid his hand through her silky soft hair.

She'd outlined her eyes in black and put on some lipstick that matched her dress. Right now Lucia was every bit the Italian siren.

Tonight wasn't about upsetting her. Tonight wasn't about grieving.

Tonight was about reminding her how good things had been between them. Reminding her what it felt like to truly connect with a person—and hoping she might realise that some things were worth fighting for.

She blinked quickly, trying to lose the obvious sheen on her eyes. Her voice was shaky. 'You promise?'

'I promise.' He didn't hesitate. This was the only way. The only way to try and take the steps to move forward. He wouldn't leave Venice without having that

conversation with her but for tonight—just for tonight—
he wanted to capture just a little of the old Lucia and
Logan again.

She locked up the apartment and they headed downstairs. He gestured her towards the other entrance of the
building, the one that looked out over the Grand Canal
and had a private mooring dock.

She shook her head. 'We never use that any more.'

He smiled as he pulled at the older doors. 'Well, tonight we're going to.'

Her stomach had been doing little flip-flops since early
afternoon and didn't seem to want to stop any time
soon.

The dress he'd bought her was beautiful, elegant
without being revealing and still managing to fit like
a second skin. It might as well have been made especially for her.

When she'd put it on she'd felt a surge of confidence
she hadn't felt in years. And seeing Logan in his dark
suit had almost toppled her off the edge where she was
dangling. It was like recapturing a moment from twelve
years ago, when they'd used to dress up regularly and
go out eating and dancing together. Back when neither
had had a care in the world and she'd had no idea what
could lie ahead.

Logan's green eyes were twinkling as he opened the
door to the Grand Canal. Bobbing on the water was a
sleek black gondola edged in red and gilt with its own
private canopy.

Lucia sucked in a breath. 'What on earth have you
done?' She knew exactly how much these cost to hire.
Every night the Grand Canal was full of wide-eyed

tourists bobbing around in these private hired gondolas. Most of the local Venetians laughed at them being taken advantage of. She'd never guessed Logan would fall into the trap.

'I've decided to start this evening the way it should continue.' He was smiling and his voice was steady. She could swear the orange-bathed canal was almost shimmering behind him. It made the whole evening just seem a little magical.

She glanced down at her towering stilettos as the gondolier held out his hand towards her. Her footsteps were slightly tottery as she stepped over the dark water of the Grand Canal. While it could seem terribly romantic, she didn't want to land in it and re-emerge like a creature of the black lagoon.

Logan jumped over easily, catching hold of her waist and steering her towards the red velvet love seat on the gondola. She laughed as they plonked down onto the seat under a black canopy and the gondola started gliding along the canal.

It was the first time in her life she'd felt like a tourist in Venice. Logan's arm slid easily behind her back. The love seat was unsurprisingly small, making sure they sat snugly together, his leg touching the length of hers.

It had been years and years since she'd done anything like this.

There was something magical about Venice in the early evening. Voices were hushed, music floated through the air, and quiet had fallen over the city.

'This is lovely,' Lucia murmured. Logan gave her shoulder a little squeeze.

As she watched the world go by she started to relax into his hold. He'd promised her there would be no pressure, no tension tonight. A tiny part of her coiled-up stomach didn't exactly believe him. It was hard to be around Logan and not think about Ariella Rose at all—and she was sure he must feel the same way.

But for tonight it might be nice not to focus on the hurts of the past. It hadn't been Logan who had hurt her. She'd never felt let down by him, or felt animosity towards him.

He was just the biggest reminder of Ariella Rose, and until her head could get around that...

The gondolier moved smoothly through the traffic. She had no idea where they were going but it was obvious he was going the picturesque route, winding their way through lesser canals and under bridges. She could see tourists pointing and taking pictures. Thank goodness for the canopy as it gave some ounce of privacy without spoiling their view.

There was something nice about the sound of the water lapping gently at the side of the gondola. Logan took his arm from her shoulder and bent forward, bringing out a bottle of chilled Prosecco and two glasses. He popped the cork and filled them up, handing hers over and holding his towards her. 'Here's to a fabulous night in Venice.'

She clinked her glass against his and sipped, letting the bubbles explode across her tongue and tickle her nose. 'Here's to an unusual night in Venice,' she said.

He raised his eyebrows. 'You mean you don't travel by gondola every night?'

She shook her head. 'I mean I haven't travelled in a gondola *ever* since I got here.'

'Really?' He seemed surprised.

She shrugged her shoulders. 'Think of it this way.

If you lived in Pisa, how many times would you actually climb the tower?'

He wrinkled his brow. 'I get where you're coming from but this is me—remember?' He turned a little more to face her. She could see the faint shadow on his jawline. He'd probably only shaved a few hours ago but that didn't quell the rapid growth of his potential beard. Her fingers itched to reach out and touch.

Logan wasn't finished. 'Remember when we stayed in Florence? How many times did we keep visiting the baptistery at the Duomo or stand underneath the Renaissance dome?'

She shook her head. 'That's because you're an architect junkie and those things were right on our doorstep.' She raised her eyebrows at him. 'I do remember you found a way to charm guards at every attraction and skip the queues.'

He gave a wave of his hand and glanced at her mischievously. 'There's a reason Italian men were born with charm. Anyway, we were natives. The guards knew that.'

'Only because you slipped some money in their hands.'

He gave a deep laugh. 'I don't know what you're taking about.' There were crinkles around his green eyes and her heart gave a little lurch.

Logan Cascini was really every woman's dream guy. She'd forgotten just how much fun they used to have together. It was unusual to meet a guy who shared her passion for the arts as much as he did.

From what most of her girlfriends told her, it was unusual to feel so connected, so in tune with a guy as she had with Logan. Most of her friends went for tempestuous and volatile relationships with plates smashing and clothes being tossed out of windows.

Life with Logan had been passionate but fulfilling. Something she'd never found again.

The gondola slid up next to the service point for disembarkation. It rocked precariously as she tried to stand up and she wobbled as the gondolier leapt ashore and held his hand out towards her.

As her feet landed on steady ground she turned towards Logan again. They were right at the edge of Piazza San Marco—the busiest place in Venice. The crowds might be a little quieter because of the planned concert but it was buzzing with excitement.

'Ready?'

He nodded towards the gondolier, tipped him and slid an arm around her waist, steering her towards the Procuraties. The sun was even lower in the sky now. The Procuraties were lit at night with tiny white lights. It was like a thousand glittering candles flickering in the night. There was no denying the beauty of the setting.

Music drifted down towards them. Some of these restaurants were known as the finest in the world, with Michelin-starred chefs and award-winning menus.

He pointed to a set of stairs heading up towards Rubins. 'After you.'

She felt her stomach flip over. He was being so formal around her. So controlled. The tiny bit of laughter on the boat had been the one true time she'd glimpsed the real Logan. That was who she wanted to spend the evening with.

The restaurant was beautiful. White linen table-cloths, more flickering candles and a harpist playing in the corner. It was full of couples dining in the dimmed lights, capturing a moment in one of the most beautiful cities in the world.

Logan held out her chair as she sat at the table then ordered them some wine. The waiter gave them thick, leather-covered menus. Lucia gave a smile as the wine appeared and was poured. 'It looks like we could have finished the wine by the time we get through this menu.'

Logan smiled at the waiter and closed his menu. 'What do you recommend?'

In the end they ordered a mixture of duck stuffed ravioli, white truffle pasta, fish carpaccio and some veal escalopes with Dobbiaco cheese.

The food was delicious and the wine kept flowing, almost as much as the easy chatter.

'What do you have to work on after the Tuscany project?'

Logan smiled at her. 'I could tell you, but I might have to kill you.' He tapped the side of his nose.

She leaned forward. 'Oh, don't go all James Bond on me. Is it something good?'

He leaned forward too, his voice low. 'It's something great. I'm just waiting for the final word. Let's just say I'll be working on something in Rome. Something I would absolutely love to work on and which could really put my restoration business under the spotlight.'

'Doesn't the chapel and *palazzo* restoration in Tuscany already do that? I'd have thought the royal wedding would mean everyone involved would benefit from the publicity.'

He gave a sigh. 'It does. But this is different, this is real Renaissance architecture. Something special that's needed to be restored for a number of years.'

She shook her head as she kept eating the delicious food. 'You make it sound like my dream job of being asked to restore the Michelangelo frescoes.'

'It's close.'

She almost dropped her fork. 'Really?'

He nodded. 'They are considering a number of different companies. The work definitely needs to be done, it just depends who wins the contract.'

She frowned. She knew just how passionate Logan was about his work, just how particular. 'There can't be many firms that have as good a reputation as you have.'

He met her gaze. 'Thanks for the compliment. Any chance you could be on the selection committee?'

She threw back her head and laughed. The wine was starting to kick in. The venue was exquisite and the food delicious. As for the company...

Logan put down his knife and fork. 'Honestly, what would you do if you got asked to do some restoration work on one of Michelangelo's frescoes?'

His face was completely serious. What on earth had he been asked to do?

'Honestly? I would probably die of shock. And I would be too scared to even contemplate doing something like that.'

He tilted his head. 'But you work for the Italian Heritage Board. Isn't that exactly the place that should be asked to do these things?'

She shook her head. 'We're just one organisation. I would be terrified. The pressure would be overwhelming and the criticism—before I even started—would be even more so.' She sat back in her chair. 'When it comes to things like that, I prefer just to admire along with the rest of the general public.'

'And Burano?'

She shook her head. 'His work isn't as well known. Isn't as criticised. The Madonna and Child hasn't been seen in generations. It isn't even on official records. Restoring it to its former beauty will be an act of joy.'

She could see him suck in a breath at her words. He paused, then looked up between heavy lids, 'And do you think everything can be restored—even people?'

Her skin chilled and her throat closed over. It was almost as if someone had stood behind her and poured icy water over her head.

He'd promised. He'd promised he wouldn't mention this tonight. She stood up swiftly, her chair toppling over behind her.

Logan was on his feet in an instant. It was almost as if he'd realised what had slipped out of his mouth. He walked swiftly over to the waiter, thrusting a bundle of notes at him.

Lucia didn't wait, she turned on her impossibly high heels and took off down the stairs.

But Piazza San Marco wasn't ready to give up on her yet.

As they'd had dinner, a small string quintet had been setting up downstairs outside one of the neighbouring restaurants. With the whole square bathed in flickering lights, the silhouette of the Basilica and Clock Tower at one end and the outlined string players in the middle her feet came to an abrupt halt.

Even she knew that running through the middle of a quintet in the piazza wasn't her best idea.

As she sucked in some air to try and still her thudding heart, she felt a presence behind her. Logan's hand slid across the thin red fabric of the dress covering her belly. She felt his warm breath on her shoulder and he moved in gently, letting her feel the rise and fall of his chest against her shoulder blades.

She was upset. But she wasn't angry at his touch. Instead, it felt like a comfort blanket.

Two of the violinists lifted their instruments and the quintet started to play. It wasn't what she expected. Classical music—usually opera—was often heard in the piazza. But this was different. It was a modern song by a UK male singer, transformed and made beautiful by the strings. She could almost hear his words echoing about love and loss in her ears.

It was almost as if they knew exactly what to play.

She spun around, placing her hands flat on Logan's chest. He didn't say a word, just lifted one hand and let his finger trail down her cheek until it reached her shoulder, where he flicked her curls back.

He was watching her with those steady green eyes and she could see the hurt shimmering from him. He was trying so hard, but was finding this every bit as difficult as she was.

His other hand slid around her hips, halting at her lower spine.

They were locked together. Just the way they should be.

Her palms slid up the planes of his chest and rested on his shoulders. This was her Logan. No one else's. No one else could ever come close to the connection she felt with him.

His body started to sway, tiny movements from side to side. One hand stayed at the base of her spine and the other tangled through her hair.

Dancing. She hadn't danced since...

Since before she'd had Ariella Rose.

She and Logan had once danced all the time. Sometimes in the clubs of Florence, often at family events and sometimes in the privacy of their own home.

Most of all she'd just loved the feeling of being in his arms and the warm touch of his body next to hers.

As the melody moved past the introduction he reached up and captured her hand in his, leading her away from the stairs and onto the patterned floor of Piazza San Marco. Little lights glowed under their feet.

People were still walking past, stopping to listen to the music, with one other couple dancing nearby.

He turned her to face her, putting his hands on her hips. 'Ready to recapture the past, Lucia?' he whispered.

She reached up and put her hand on his chest again. She could feel his warm skin and beating heart underneath the fine Italian shirt.

All she could focus on was the way he was looking at her. It made her feel like the only girl on the planet.

She slid her hands around his neck and rested her head against his chest. 'Always,' she replied.

Their footsteps moved in perfect unison. The warmth of his body next to hers felt overwhelming.

They fitted so well together it almost felt like they'd never been apart. And Logan didn't just know how to sway to the music. He knew how to dance—how to really dance.

It was as if they could read each other's minds and knew exactly what the next steps should be. She moved her hand from his chest, sliding it along the length of his arm and letting their hands clasp.

She felt him stiffen against her and she lifted her head.

There was no doubt on his face. He released her from his grasp against him and spun her outwards. When she danced with Logan she always felt like she could fly.

He could lift and spin her as if she were as light as air. Her dress spun out, the ripples of red fabric twisting high from her thighs, the stiletto heels forgotten as she continued to follow his lead.

She could hear the murmurs around them as people stopped to stare. But all she could focus on was the beat of the music and the feel of Logan's hard muscles as they connected briefly through the parts of the music.

Logan knew how to lead. He knew how to steer her and how to whip her around, like a matador with a cape.

And she kept spinning. The lit arches of the Procuraties flashing past her line of vision. The evening was still warm and her body temperature was rising quickly.

She couldn't even begin to think straight. The only thing that counted was how right everything felt—how *connected* everything felt.

She dipped her head and spun under his arm three times as the crowd gasped. The momentum of the music was building. He caught her around the waist and dipped her backwards. It was one of their all-time favourite moves. The sensuality of the deep arch of her back, followed by her ever-so-slow stretch back up, ending up nose to nose with Logan.

He was breathing just as quickly as she was. A laugh escaped from her lips. Her hair fell over her face, some of her curls connecting with his skin. But he didn't brush them back, he just dipped his head further forward, allowing them both to be hidden beneath the veil of her hair.

'How are we doing?' he murmured. He ran one finger up her spine, sending shock waves everywhere, a thousand beautiful butterflies beating their wings against her skin.

It couldn't be more perfect than this.

Then he moved. The music was slowing, reaching a building crescendo. He spun her once more, letting her skirt billow around her and her hair stream outwards.

He caught her hips suddenly, stopping her in mid-pivot and pressing his head against hers. She didn't even have time to catch her breath before his lips were on hers.

There was no time to think about where they were or what they had been doing. There was no time to think about the audience or the scenery.

His hands skirted around her behind, her hips and up the sides of her waist, stopping as they tangled in her hair, and he anchored her head firmly in one hand.

She couldn't ever remember being kissed like this—even by Logan.

She couldn't get enough of him. His taste, his smell, the feel of his body beneath the palms of her hand. He was hers. He was all hers. And she didn't want this to stop.

He pulled his lips back from hers, staying close enough to let her feel his breath on her skin. 'It's you, Lucia. It's always been you.'

The music died around them, but she hardly noticed. Her heartbeat was roaring in her ears. The world around them was still spinning—just like her brain. It hadn't stopped. Not for a second.

Logan held her tightly to him. She could feel his knotted muscles, the tension as he held her. She had no doubt about the effects she had on his body.

Of the effects he had on hers.

It had been so long. She'd forgotten what passion like this felt like. Something had been ignited inside her. A tiny flame that had been dimmed for so long. Now the fire was burning so brightly she couldn't imagine putting it out again.

Logan's eyes fixed on hers. They were steady but had never seemed so determined—so heated.

He clasped one hand in his. 'Let's go.' He didn't wait for a response. He walked away briskly, pulling her behind him as he parted the crowd around them.

His long strides covered the expanse of Piazza San Marco easily, and she was running in her stilettos to keep up.

She was surprised to see the sleek, black gondola still waiting. He didn't wait for the chatting gondolier to pay attention, just turned and lifted her straight onto the swaying gondola, shouting an instruction to the gondolier.

With one tug the canopy was closed, leaving them in a pool of darkness, with only a few of Venice's lights flickering behind them.

A seed of doubt flashed through her brain. All the rational thoughts that she'd completely ignored for the last few hours started to take seed and let their roots unfurl. She couldn't stop the rapid thud-thud of her heart. Every inch of her skin was on fire, the tiny hairs on her arms standing on end.

Her eyes started to adjust to the dim light. Logan hadn't moved. It could only have been a few seconds, but it felt like so much longer. It felt as if his brain must be crowding with the same doubts that she was feeling. Her stomach clenched. Everything suddenly felt like a huge mistake.

Logan shifted his body towards hers, reaching up his hand towards her face. He ran one finger across her forehead. Her eyes automatically closed and the finger traced down over her eyelids, cheeks, across her lips then under her chin and to the tender skin of her décolletage.

He leaned closer, the heat from his body spreading towards hers.

And then he murmured those words again.

'It's you Lucia, it's always been you.'

Before, she'd been shocked. They'd been in the middle of Piazza San Marco with a crowd of onlookers. Here, it was entirely private. All she could hear was the movement of the gondola slipping through the waters of Venice.

She squeezed her eyes closed again for a few seconds. Her hand reached up towards him. She couldn't help it. She couldn't be this close to Logan and not touch him. It was all she could think about.

She felt him suck in a breath as she ran the palm of her hand along his now-stubbled jaw.

If she could suspend the past—suspend the memories—then everything about Logan was perfect.

Now, as he said the words it was just the two of them. Her heart wanted to melt. Her lips wanted to respond. She wanted to say it had only ever been him. She wanted to tell him that she'd never felt the same about anyone else—she *couldn't* feel the same about anyone else.

Without Logan she wasn't living. She was only existing.

She didn't want to just exist any more.

This time when he bent to kiss her she matched him move for move. She ran her hands through his dark hair and pulled him closer to her, pressing her breasts against his chest.

Logan knew how to kiss. He really knew how to kiss. There was a zing as their lips met. Teeth grazed her lips. Then his lips were firmly on hers. Tasting her, caressing her. Full sweet lips on hers, filling her with so much promise, so much expectation.

The zings didn't stop at her lips but carried on right around her body, like an army on rapid attack. She couldn't help her responses. She couldn't help but push harder against his body, her hands exploring his back and shoulders.

The kiss intensified with every passing second, sparking a whole host of memories throughout her body. It didn't matter that their eyes were closed. With this kiss Logan could see every part of her, burrow his way to the centre of her closed-over soul.

She'd always felt threatened by their closeness after the death of their daughter. Fear had pushed her into a position of retreat, because even though she'd told Logan she couldn't talk about things, once he'd kissed her she always felt at her most vulnerable. Her most open.

His earthy scent swam around her. His fingers stroked the back of her neck, giving her a promise of what was to come.

His kisses moved lower, along her cheek and down the delicate skin of her neck. For a moment she almost objected. She didn't want his lips to leave hers.

But Logan knew all her secret places. Knew the tiny spot at the back of her ear that made her gasp with pleasure and lose all rational thought. Before she'd even thought about it her head was arching backwards, opening up the more sensitive skin at the bottom of her throat.

And Logan didn't hesitate. He was on it in a flash. She wanted to move. Her dress was inching upwards, his hand brushing against her thighs. But space was cramped under the canopy, with nowhere really to go, and they both jumped apart as the gondola jerked suddenly as it scraped against wood.

She sat back in the love seat, trying to still her ragged breaths. There was another couple of bumps.

It had been deliberate. Of course it had. They'd reached their destination and their gondolier had enough experience to allow his guests a moment of warning.

Was this it? Was this where this evening ended?

Logan pulled back the canopy and stood up, straightening his rumpled jacket and shirt and then turning towards her. He didn't speak, just held out his hand towards her.

What happened next was up to her.

It was her apartment. Her space. She'd offered him somewhere to stay for the weekend, without even considering this as a possibility.

The sun had set now. The warm orange glow from earlier had disappeared.

But now Venice was alive with a million different lights brightening up the almost black sky. Logan was outlined like a film star on his final movie shot.

The backdrop was stunning with the beautiful architecture along the Grand Canal and silhouetted gondolas around them.

But all she could focus on was Logan.

Because she knew exactly how this night would end.

It was already written in the stars twinkling in the sky above their head.

She slid her hand into his and he pulled her towards him as the boat rocked on the water.

This was fate. It had to be.

And who was she to fight fate?

CHAPTER EIGHT

THE ROOM WAS bathed in the pale light of morning.

It wasn't what he expected—not at all. Last night he hadn't paid attention to anything around them. They'd barely managed to close the apartment door behind them before they'd stumbled through to her bedroom.

Lucia's room wasn't the stark white of the guest bedroom along the corridor. It was sumptuous and opulent, furnished in the colours she'd used to favour when painting. Purples and golds with a tiny flash of red. It suited the general feel of the apartment—the whole place still had the hint of a palace about it. And the beautiful décor and furnishings in the room were more personal—more Lucia—than the room he'd stayed in.

Lucia was still tangled in his arms, her head resting on his chest and her dark locks fanned out on the purple bedding. Her breathing was slow and steady. The early morning light and noise from the Grand Canal hadn't woken her yet.

He didn't want to move. Didn't want to breathe in case it disturbed her.

This was perfection. This was exactly the way things should be between them but he knew he would have to destroy it all.

It would be so easy. So easy to say nothing at all and ignore the huge elephant that sat in the corner of the room every time they were together. But Logan didn't want only part of Lucia. He wanted all of her. He'd waited this long. And if he couldn't have all of her...

His hand reached up and stroked her head. They would have to spend the next few months working together in Tuscany. They could flirt, laugh, love and sleep together and make a poor attempt at having a relationship.

But the truth was that any attempt would be futile until they'd spoken about Ariella Rose. They had to start from scratch. They could only build this relationship once they'd grieved together for their daughter. And he still didn't know if Lucia was capable of that.

His phone beeped on the table next to the bed. The noise stirred Lucia from her peaceful sleep and she woke gradually.

Her arm drifted across his chest. She was smiling as she woke, as if she were in the middle of some alluring dream.

Her eyelids flickered open, revealing her dark brown eyes surrounded by thick black lashes. All traces of last night's make-up had vanished. Lucia didn't need any. Her flawless skin and naturally red lips were enticing enough.

His stomach clenched as he waited for anything—any trace of regret about last night. 'Good morning, beautiful,' he said softly.

She smiled and closed her eyes again, pushing her naked body closer to his. Her fingers started tracing circles on his chest. 'Good morning, handsome,' she said sleepily.

Some of his tension dissipated. He could leave this. Say nothing. Stroke his fingers across her skin and pull her beneath the covers. It was the biggest temptation in the world right now.

And while it might offer some temporary sanctuary and pleasure it wouldn't take him to the place he ultimately wanted to be.

Somehow he knew it didn't matter how he phrased the question—he already knew how she would react.

It was horrible—knowing that the path they would have to tread would be a painful one. But he was ready for it. He'd been ready for it for the past twelve years.

'How are you feeling?'

She pushed her head up onto one hand as she lay facing him. Her face still had that relaxed, sleepy, dreamy quality about it. It was the most chilled he'd ever seen her.

'I'm fine.' She smiled. 'How are you?' There was a teasing tone to her voice—as if she wanted to take this to a whole other place.

His fingers wanted to reach out and touch her soft skin. It took all his will power not to move and instead to clench the purple sheet in his fist.

'We need to talk, Lucia. You know we need to talk.'

The muscles around her neck tensed. She turned her head away from him. 'No, we don't.'

It was an immediate, instinctual reaction. He knew that. He pushed himself further up the bed. The sheet moved with him, pulling from Lucia's skin. She made a grab for it. It was amazing how a few words could make you feel naked all over again.

He sighed. 'We have to work together, Lucia. We're going to be in Tuscany together. I don't want things to be awkward between us.'

Her head shot around. 'And this is how you stop it?' It was an accusatory tone. And he got that. He did. Lucia would much rather they never spoke about this at all.

He moved to the edge of the bed and picked up his discarded shirt from the floor, pulling it over his head. He shook his head. 'No, Lucia. This is how I start things. This is how we should start things. By talking.' He stood up. 'Now get dressed. We're going to go for breakfast together.'

He moved across the floor, finding his underwear, crumpled trousers and shoes. If he were a young man, concerned about his appearance, he might be cringing right now at the thought of going out in Venice in last night's clothes.

But he was a grown-up. An adult. And he had so much more to worry about.

Lucia was scowling at him. The beautiful red dress he'd bought her was bunched up in a little ball. He doubted it would ever look the same. 'I'm not coming.'

'Yes, you are.' He opened the door of her wardrobe, his eyes running rapidly over the colours, and pulled out a flowered dress, throwing it on the bed. 'Would you like me to select your underwear too?' He didn't mean to be cruel. But he wasn't prepared to take no for an answer. Not after all this time.

She pulled the sheet up under her chin. 'Stop it, Logan. You can't bully me into doing what you want. I'm not a child.'

He bent down next to her. 'I have never bullied you, Lucia. I never will. And you're right, you're not a child. You're a mother—just like I'm a father. Just because our child isn't here any more it doesn't change that.'

Her eyes widened. She was shocked. It was the last

thing she'd obviously expected to hear. And he wasn't quite sure where it had come from.

After a few seconds her fingers released on the sheet a little. He sensed the moment and opened the drawer next to her bed, pulling out matching white underwear. 'I'll give you a few minutes to get dressed,' he said, walking to the door and standing in the corridor.

Every part of him was on edge. He had no idea right now if he'd handled this right. He'd spent so long tiptoeing around Lucia that now it felt as if he'd just leapt in wearing a pair of clown-size shoes.

He held his breath, listening for any sign of movement. Any tiny noise.

After a few seconds he heard something. The gentle movement of a sheet. He leaned back against the wall. It didn't matter that she hated him right now. All that mattered was that they talk. That they *really* talked.

He walked through to the guest bedroom and quickly washed his face and hands, running his fingers through his hair and brushing his teeth. He had another shirt in his bag but it would probably be equally as rumpled. He hadn't planned on staying in Venice so clothes were definitely scarce.

It was too warm for a jacket so he walked through to the main room and waited for Lucia to appear.

It only took a few moments. She hadn't bothered with make-up and her hair was pulled back in a clasp. The yellow and pink flowered dress made her look much younger.

His heartbeat turned up a little notch. It was almost like turning back time. She had a white canvas bag in her hand and some flat sandals on her feet. But she'd never looked so beautiful.

He walked over to the main door and held it open. 'Let's go.'

There was a sinking feeling in his stomach. Almost as if he knew how this could turn out.

Lucia didn't even glance at him as she walked past. She had that determined edge to her chin.

But he could be equally determined. It was time to show her how much.

Talk about an awkward morning after. She couldn't believe she'd allowed herself to get into this position.

She knew so much better than this.

She was an adult and knew exactly what going for dinner and wine with Logan could lead to. The sexual chemistry between them had always been off the chart, but add into that the dress-buying and dancing and, well…what chance had she really had?

She held her head up proudly as she walked down the street towards her favourite café. This wasn't like doing a walk of shame the next day after a night-time encounter.

Logan had been the man she'd lived with. He'd been the man who'd cherished and treasured her. He'd been the man she'd loved with her whole heart.

She still did.

Her feet stumbled on the uneven street. Logan caught her elbow and she tugged it away. Where had that thought come from?

She squeezed her eyes closed for a second. This was because of last night. Memories of what had been and how good they had been together. She was being sentimental, nothing more. So why was her stomach permanently in knots?

She stopped at the tables on the street at her favourite café. Logan pulled out a chair for her. The waiter gave her a wave. 'Usual?'

She nodded. Logan caught his eye 'Make it two.'

Little parts of her were starting to unravel, even at those innocuous words. Logan knew that her usual would be coffee with steamed milk and a heated croissant with raspberry jam. He knew her that well and was happy to eat the same as her.

It was almost as if he were chipping away at the barriers she'd erected around herself all those years ago. The ones that had protected her. Stopped her from getting too close to anyone else and kept her safe from being hurt.

Logan folded his arms across his chest. He was sitting directly opposite her, his eyes watching her carefully.

He waited until the coffee appeared on the table and the waft of buttery croissants filled the air around them.

'It's been too long, Lucia,' he said quietly. 'I never wanted you to leave, but I understood you needed time and space.' He picked up his spoon and stirred his coffee. 'But it was never my intention to leave things this long.'

He had no idea what those few words could do to her.

The rest of Venice seemed completely at ease. People were laughing and strolling in the early Sunday morning light. Shopkeepers were just starting to roll up their shutters and open their doors. A street vendor wandered past, clutching buckets filled with beautiful flowers. The assorted scents started to mix with that of the breakfast croissants. It could be a beautiful day. So why did it feel like the worst?

Logan hadn't finished talking. 'I always hoped things would be different. I thought you would be married. I thought you would be a mother.'

He paused. 'I always hoped you would be.'

She felt tears spring to her eyes. It was almost as if he were twisting the knife that was currently piercing her heart. She knew that wasn't his intention. She knew he was trying his best to move things forward.

But Lucia had never moved forward. She could remember everything about Ariella Rose as if it had just happened yesterday. She could remember the sudden unexpected pain, the cramps, the awkward delivery. She could remember the tiny fragile bundle. Ariella had been so small she could fit in one hand, wrapped in a pink blanket made by Nonna.

The almost transparent skin. The tiny little blue veins underneath. She could remember how she'd had to gently ease up a tiny eyelid in order to see her baby's eyes. Eyes that would never see the world.

Lungs that would never fill with air.

She could remember all her hopes and dreams for the future evaporate with the silence in the air. The heavy, ominous silence of nothing.

Her horror had been so complete she'd only been able to shed a few tears. Tears of shock. It had been as if every emotion in her body had switched off. Gone into complete self-protection mode.

Now Logan was trying to open her all up to this again.

'Maybe I decided that wasn't what I wanted.' The words came out tight, almost angry, and Logan eyebrows arched slowly.

'You were made to be a mother, Lucia.' He held her

gaze as she tried to swallow. 'You would be the finest mother in the world.'

She was frozen. Couldn't breathe. Her mouth had never felt so dry, but the aroma of coffee was acrid to her now. The croissant mocked her.

Some modern career women would find his words insulting. But she didn't. Logan knew her better than anyone. He knew how much she'd relished being pregnant. He knew how much she'd planned for their daughter—they both had.

Although she was passionate about her career, she'd longed to raise their daughter.

She lifted her coffee cup with trembling hands. 'Things change.'

He shook his head and reached across the table towards her.

But she didn't want him to touch her. She couldn't take the feel of his skin on hers right now.

He leaned his elbows on the table and just kept talking. 'I've dreamt of being a father too. But it's never happened. It wasn't meant to happen—not with anyone but you.'

He said the words so easily. As if he'd contemplated them for a long time and had come to accept that this was his lot in life.

'I've met some wonderful women, but none that I wanted to marry, none that I wanted to raise children with. I only ever wanted to do that with you.'

She could feel the anger build in her chest. 'But we never planned Ariella Rose. You make it sound as if we had our future all written out.' She spat the words at him.

She couldn't understand how he could talk about any

of this so calmly. It felt as if he'd reached a fist into her chest and was squeezing all the blood from her pumping heart.

'My future was written the second I saw you, Lucia.' He hadn't raised his voice once. His words were calm and steady. He was so resolute.

She leaned across the table towards him. 'I can't talk about this,' she hissed.

It was the first time she saw a little spark in him. He gritted his teeth. 'Well, you have to. It's about time. You owe it to our daughter.'

She pulled back as if he'd wounded her. But Logan wasn't finished. 'You owe it to our daughter to talk about her and give her the love and respect she deserves.'

Her head was swimming. 'How dare you! You know I loved Ariella.'

'But you don't honour her memory.'

'What does that mean?'

Logan rubbed the palms of his hand on his trousers. It was obvious this was upsetting him just as much as it was upsetting her.

He took a deep breath. 'It means you walked away, Lucia. You walked away from the memory of our daughter and the memory of what we used to have. I think about her every single day. It doesn't matter that you're in Venice and she's in Tuscany. I visit her grave every month. You could too. But as far as I know you haven't been there since the day we buried her.'

Fury erupted inside her. Tears were brimming in her eyes but they just couldn't come any further— she hadn't been able to cry since the day they'd buried their daughter. From that point on everything had been locked inside.

'I can't go there. I can't visit.'

'Why?' He wouldn't stop. He wasn't going to let this go. It would have been better if they'd never seen each other again. The last thing she needed was stirring up the memories of Ariella Rose and any association with Logan did just that.

She wasn't able to separate the parts of him from their daughter. She couldn't just remember his kiss, his touch without remembering where it had led them. Couldn't block out all the pain it had caused.

'I just can't.'

'Then maybe that's what we should do.'

She felt herself bristle. 'Don't tell me what to do, Logan. We haven't known each other in a long time— you have no right.'

He stood up sharply, his chair screeching backwards, and she held her breath, wondering what would come next. The waiter stuck his head out of the door of the restaurant, watching carefully.

But Logan just shook his head, stretched out his back, then took a few steps towards her and knelt beside her chair.

She was still holding her breath as he slid his hand up and took hers. She hadn't realised it but her hands were cold and the warmth from him completely enveloped her.

His voice was quiet again, this time almost pleading. 'I have every right. We lost our daughter together. Who do you think I get to talk about Ariella Rose with? Who do I get to share the memories of our daughter with? I want to remember what we lost, Lucia. I loved her with every part of my heart—just as you did.' He sighed and looked up, meeting her gaze.

'This isn't just about you any more, Lucia. It was twelve years ago. I would have done anything to help you grieve, to comfort you after the loss of our daughter. But I've realised this is about me too. It wasn't enough just to make the arrangements. It wasn't enough to say a prayer. It wasn't about giving you the space you needed. I watched you fall apart right under my nose, I watched you shut yourself off from the world and bury yourself away. I thought I had no right to force you to talk. I thought I had to let you do this your own way. But twelve years on? I was wrong, Lucia. I was very wrong. For you, and for me.'

She squeezed her eyes closed again. She couldn't take his intense and sincere glance. This was exactly what she'd always tried to avoid.

It had been too much. Too much to think about. She couldn't bear it.

And now here was Logan—her strong, able Logan—telling her how much he'd been hurt too. He'd never worn his heart so much on his sleeve as he was doing now and it was tearing her apart.

She'd never even contemplated his hurt. His grief. She'd been too selfishly trying to cope with her own. Logan had appeared so composed, so strong. Now his face looked as if it had worn a river of grief across it. She could see her own pain reflected in his eyes, the tight grip of her hand telling her more than she wanted to know.

'You have to face this, Lucia. You're never going to get past this, *I'm* never going to get past this, if we can't talk together.'

Logan. Her handsome, strong Logan. She'd always hoped he would have married and had kids. He deserved to be a father. He deserved to spend his summer evenings playing in a garden, with his arms wrapped around the woman that he loved.

Twelve years ago she'd hoped that might be her.

He still wanted to save her. Even after all these years he wanted to patch her up and put her together again. But he couldn't do it then. And he couldn't do it now.

But things were different now. He'd realised how much *he* still hurt.

It didn't matter if Lucia wrapped her arms around his neck right now and told him she wanted to try and make things work again. It didn't matter that she might want a future with them together.

Now he'd realised exactly what he needed. For him. And for her.

He lifted his hand then ran his fingers through her hair at the side of her head. 'I loved Ariella Rose. I loved it that her eyes were so dark blue, though they probably would have turned brown—just like yours. I loved the fine downy hair we could see on her head. I loved that her fingers and toes were perfect. I dream about the person she could have become. And I wonder about the type of personality she would have had.'

He moved his fingers down her cheek. 'I wonder if she would have been like me, or if she would have been like you.'

He brought his hand down next to his other, clasping both of her hands in his. 'I love it that we made a little person. But I watch the calendar every year. Every year when it's her birthday I think about another year that we've lost. I think about the little girl who would have grown up and laughed and played and gone to school. I think she would be at an age right now where she would hate her overprotective dad. She would hate the fact I didn't want her to speak to boys or to wear clothes that made her look like a teenager. I would want to keep her all buttoned up in pink dresses and sandals.'

Lucia was shaking. And not just her hands. Every part of her body was shaking. It was as if his words were starting to penetrate her fortress-like exterior.

He could see the waiter casting anxious glances in their direction. But he didn't want to do anything that might distract her.

'Tell me how much you miss her, Lucia. Tell me what your hopes and dreams were for our daughter.'

He couldn't do anything to stop the shaking. He knew it was just her body's natural response. He just kept her ice-cold hands in his, hoping and praying she would finally start to open up.

Her voice was tight. Her fingers started to grip his hand more tightly. Almost as if she were clinging on for her life.

'I miss her every day.' The words came out in a rush. Then there was silence. Silence he was determined not to fill. It was the first time she'd ever said anything about their daughter.

Lucia finally started to talk again. 'I get so angry because I don't know whether she would have had dark hair, or blond hair like your sisters. I don't know whether she would have had curls or straight hair. I don't know whether she would have been a tomboy or a ballet dancer. Whether she would have wanted red shoes or pink or white.' She shook her head. 'There's so many things about my daughter that I don't know.

Will never know. And I feel cheated, completely and utterly cheated.'

His chest was tight. But tiny little parts of the tightness were giving away to relief. She was finally, finally starting to talk. Starting to talk about the life they had lost.

'Then I think about things that would never, ever have mattered. Not in the scale of things.' She looked upwards to the sky.

'What do you mean?' he prompted gently.

'I mean, would she have liked cats or dogs? Would she have been artistic? Would she have liked staying in Florence? How would she have got on at school? All the things that—if our daughter was actually here— we probably would have argued about and fussed over. But in the end, it doesn't mean anything.' Her eyes lowered and fixed on the canal next to the café. A few boats were puttering past. People going about their daily business.

No one else could know or imagine what was at stake at this table.

Logan took a deep breath. He had so much more to say. Even though he'd been much more able to talk about his grief than Lucia, there was something about it just being the two of them here that made it different.

No one else could really understand how they both felt— not unless they'd lost a child too.

He straightened up and sat back down in the chair opposite her again. But this time he pulled it closer, away from the table and round to the side so their legs were touching.

'I miss things,' he said softly. 'I miss us. I miss what

we used to have together. I didn't just lose a daughter, Lucia. I lost the love of my life too.'

He could see her swallow painfully. It wasn't just him that felt this way. But somehow Lucia didn't want to go there. It was as if, now she'd finally managed to say something about Ariella, she didn't know how to stop.

'Sometimes I think we were lucky. Sometimes I think that I'm selfish.'

His head shot up in surprise. 'What?'

She scrunched up her face. Her voice was sad. 'I look at other people who've lost children. You see them on the news all the time. They had a little person, a real little person with life and spark and personality, and it's just...' she shook her head '...ripped from their grasp. One day they have a little boy or girl in their room at home, talking, laughing, playing, then the next day because of disease or accidents or war their precious little person is stolen from them. Gone, in the blink of an eye.'

Her eyes fixed on the uneven ground beneath their feet. 'That's when I think that most of the time I don't know what I missed. I can pretend. I can build up all these thoughts of what Ariella Rose could have been like in my head.' She met his gaze. 'But the truth is, you and I will never know. Is it easier to lose a baby that you loved and hoped for than it is to lose an actual child you've spent years bringing up?' She shook her head again.

'I try to rationalise why I feel so empty. I try to make excuses about why I don't want to be around pregnant colleagues or friends.' She gave him a sad kind of smile. 'I have twelve years' worth of excuses, Logan, with reasons for not visiting new babies or friends playing happy families. It would surprise you how often I'm away with work.'

He could feel the tiny hairs standing up at the back of his neck. It just didn't feel quite right. He could feel her stepping back, detaching herself from the thoughts and feelings she'd been having a few moments ago. It was the slight change in the tone of her voice. The cool way she could look at him now.

For a few seconds her heart had been virtually on display. Her fears and hidden emotions had been coming to the surface. But even though she hadn't moved, was still sitting on the chair next to him, still letting their legs touch, she was pulling back again.

The only reason he could pick up on the tiny clues was because he knew her so well.

She straightened her spine in the chair. He could sense her sorting out her thoughts, finding a way to steal herself back from what she'd almost revealed.

He reached out to take her hand again. 'How would you feel about taking a visit to Florence again? How would you feel about us going together to Ariella Rose's grave?'

She pulled her hand back sharply from his, almost as if she'd been stung. It was too much. It was a step too far.

She wasn't ready to take it. She might never be ready to take it.

And with that realisation he felt the woman he'd always loved slip away from him once again.

Her face had turned into a mask. 'I don't want to do that, Logan. I don't think it's necessary.'

Her phone beeped in her bag and she bent forward, obviously glad of the distraction.

Their coffees and breakfast were virtually untouched, discarded.

A bit like how he felt right now.

She gave a false smile. 'It's work. With the computer program verifying Burano as the artist of the fresco, we can start to plan for the restoration now.'

She stood up quickly. It was almost as if their conversation had been forgotten.

For a few seconds he didn't move. He'd almost got there. *They'd* almost got there.

For him it was all or nothing. He knew that Lucia was the woman that he wanted, but he wasn't just prepared to accept a small part of her. And just when she'd started, just when she'd finally managed to talk about their daughter, it was almost as if he'd been able to see the shutters come down over her eyes, closing off the part of her that was most exposed, most vulnerable and cocooning it back in herself.

He had so many hidden hopes and plans for them. Last night had been wrong. Last night had made him think that there might just be hope for them. That this relationship could actually bloom and grow after all these years.

She didn't get it. She didn't get it that in his head they would grow old together. When they'd both lost their beauty, their youth and their health, they would still have each other. And that would be enough. That would always be enough.

Only it wasn't now. Not when he knew that the woman he loved with all his heart would never love him the same way. She couldn't. Part of her heart was permanently locked away. Had been for the last twelve years and it looked like it would stay that way for ever.

He stood up and put some notes on the table to cover breakfast. Lucia's whole face had changed. It was as if it had been replaced by a mask.

His stomach turned over. He could have played things so differently this morning. He could have ignored the past and just continued with the present, no matter how little of her he actually got.

But it would never have been enough. And even though his heart felt as though she'd ripped it in two, he knew this was right. For him at least.

He kept his voice as detached as he could. He would never make a scene. Never do anything to deliberately cause her embarrassment or upset.

'Shall we make travel plans back to Tuscany?'

Her shoulders dropped a little as he spoke. Was that relief that he saw? Relief that he'd finally let things go?

Her words came out rapidly and her footsteps matched his on the cobbles next to the narrow canal. 'I can arrange the return flights. We should be able to go back first thing tomorrow morning. The samples that I took earlier will be sent for automatic colour and pigment matching. I can only restore the fresco using products as close to the originals as possible. Thank goodness for modern technology.' She gave a wave of her hand and kept chattering as they crossed the bridge.

Logan felt numb. This was it. This was it for him and her.

He'd have to spend the next few months in Tuscany, working next to Lucia but keeping her at arm's length. Every glimpse whipped up a whole host of memories of the night before. He couldn't possibly be in her company and not think about what the two of them had lost and never recovered from.

There couldn't be a Logan and Lucia. Not if she still couldn't mourn their daughter.

It would be best for them both.

CHAPTER NINE

SHE FELT NUMB. It was the only way she could survive.

Last night had been a blur. They'd got up this morning just as the sun had been rising and made their way in a water taxi to the airport. Logan had spoken barely a word to her.

And that was what hurt most.

He'd been polite, of course, courteous even. But it had all been strained. Any time she'd caught a glimpse of his once gleaming green eyes all she'd been able to see was the blankness that had been pulled over them.

They stood patiently in the queue, checking in and filing through to Departures. As soon as they made their way through she made a feeble excuse that she needed to pick up some things.

Logan gave a nod of his head and said he was going for coffee and would meet her at the departure gate. He seemed almost as relieved as she was to get some space.

Lucia ducked into the nearest shop. She didn't even care which one it was—and started walking blankly through the aisles.

Lingerie. Just what she needed. She cringed as she passed a couple winking and nudging each other near the sexiest black and pink lingerie in the shop. She couldn't even remember the last time she'd spent money on matching lingerie. And she certainly wasn't going to need some any time soon. Not at these prices anyway. Who actually spent this kind of money on underwear?

Something inside her sparked a wave of fury. Her steps became quicker, more determined. She marched along the aisles until she saw something that caught her eye, something she might actually wear.

It was a pale pink satin nightdress trimmed with exquisite lace. It was not as short as she might usually wear, reaching down to at least her knees. She reached out and touched it. The heavy satin was silky to touch, pure of quality and luxury. She picked out her size and walked to the cashier's desk without a second thought.

The cashier folded and wrapped the nightdress in tissue paper and Lucia didn't even blink when she handed over her credit card.

Why shouldn't she buy herself something beautiful? As she pushed the package into her bag her mind flashed back to her bedroom and the beautiful red dress that Logan had bought her lying crumpled on the floor.

She hadn't even picked it up. She didn't need any reminder of the night they'd spent together. It was already ingrained in her brain.

She didn't need anything to remember the feel of his fingers on her skin, the feel of his lips on her neck and throat. The smell of his scent winding its way around her. The squeeze in her heart the next day when he'd told her they needed to talk.

And the look in his eyes when she'd finally stood up and walked away, pushing everything else back into a space she didn't have to deal with.

She'd been walking on eggshells ever since.

And not just around Logan. Around herself too.

For a few tiny seconds she allowed herself to think about Ariella Rose. She'd allowed herself to say a few words, to contemplate what might have been and what she'd lost.

But it had been too much. The wave of emotions that had swept over her had had to be quickly quelled. On that warm summer's day she'd never felt so cold. The tremors that had come over her body had been overwhelming.

It would have been so easy to bury her head in Logan's shoulder and just hold on for grim life. But she was too scared. Scared that if she went there she might never come back.

The truth was that no adult should outlive their child. And only someone who'd been there could understand that. Her friends and family had no idea of the type of thoughts that had crept through her brain in the few days after her daughter's death. She'd never acknowledged them to anyone.

Instead, she'd kept things locked away—even from Logan. How did you tell the man you loved with your whole heart that you would rather be with your daughter than him?

It had been too cruel. Even for her.

Her eyes scanned the coffee shop. Logan was sitting staring out of one of the windows, his hand stirring his cappuccino endlessly.

She dumped her bags in the chair next to him. It wouldn't be long until their flight was called. She walked over to the counter. 'Full-fat caramel latte with whipped cream and a strawberry frosted doughnut.'

A whole day's worth of calories about to be consumed in ten minutes. But she just felt like it. Some-times days were just like that.

And from the look on Logan's face his day was en-tirely like that too.

It seemed the longest flight in history.

It was amazing the things you could think up to do rather than talk to the person sitting directly at your elbow.

Lucia was wearing a bright orange dress, and match-ing stilettos. She had a large brown leather bag—which looked as if it could carry the entire contents of her kitchen—slung over her shoulder.

Her wheeled suitcase looked bigger than his car. It was clear she was here to stay.

For a second he'd wondered if she was having sec-ond thoughts. She'd disappeared at the airport for a bit, then reappeared, eating a whole host of things that would never normally cross her lips.

Logan was far too wise to comment. Lucia hadn't been known for hormonal binges. But it had been twelve long years. Lots of things could have changed that he knew nothing about.

And, frankly, it wasn't his business any more.

As they landed at the private Tuscan airport and waited for their car, one of the signs at the newsstand caught his eye.

He gave her a nudge. *'When was the last time Prince Antonio saw his Cinderella bride?'*

For the first time since they'd left Venice the glazed expression left Lucia's face and her eyes widened. 'What on earth have we missed? We've only been gone a few days.'

He shook his head as the car pulled up in front of them. 'I have no idea. We'll need to talk to Louisa as soon as we reach the *palazzo*. I wonder if this will have implications for the wedding?'

He opened the door for Lucia and they climbed inside. After a few seconds she pulled out her laptop and started working. Logan sighed and leaned back, watching the green Tuscan hills roll by.

The journey from the airport took them back through the village and he took a few moments to study the surrounding architecture again. It was important that he keep the *palazzo* as in keeping with its surroundings as possible. Any kind of modern renovation would be disastrous. So, while modern fixtures and fittings could be included, they had to be sympathetic to the history of the house.

They pulled up outside the *palazzo*. It was a hive of activity. Monday mornings in the Italian building trade could notoriously start slowly. Not today.

Connor was in talks with someone outside the chapel building. It was obvious he was keeping on top of the security of the fresco.

A delivery of the special pink-coloured stone used in the *palazzo* was being unloaded. Some of the outer restoration work still needed to be completed. He could see his special stonemason signing for the delivery.

Louisa came walking out of the main entrance as Lucia grabbed her case. Louisa looked distracted, as if her mind were on a hundred other things. She hadn't even noticed their return.

'Louisa?' he said, trying to be heard above the building work around them. She was frowning and it marred her pretty face. Her hair was pulled back in a rumpled knot and her long tunic looked like yesterday's.

Her head flicked up. 'Logan.' Her eyes darted over to Lucia. 'Lucia. You're both back.' She walked over quickly. 'Do you have news?'

Lucia gave her a cautious smile. 'We do. The fresco *is* by Burano, he lived and worked in the Renaissance period and we have other examples of his work. He was both a painter and a sculptor. We're making arrangements to look at the sculpture on the fountain in the village. It could be another piece of his work.'

Louisa gave a smile and a quick nod. 'That's great. Really great. What happens next?'

Lucia glanced towards Logan. It was obvious that she was picking up the same vibes that he was. Louisa's body language was all over the place. She was saying the right words but her hands were continually knotting in front of her abdomen.

'Things will be fine. I'll begin the restoration work on the fresco. It could take a few months. All the costs will be covered by the Italian Heritage Board.'

'A few months?' Louisa looked shocked. 'But what about—?'

Logan stepped forward and took her arm, cutting her off. 'Are you okay? Don't worry about Lucia's work. It won't interfere with any of the plans here.' He nodded towards Lucia. 'We'll make sure of that.' He lowered his voice. 'Is this about the headlines? We saw them when we landed at the airport. Is the wedding still going ahead? Is there anything you need to tell us?'

Louisa's face tightened and she pressed her lips together. 'Of course the wedding is still going ahead. There's nothing to tell. Nothing to tell at all.'

It was clear by the tone of her voice that she wasn't willing to discuss anything.

She waved her hand towards the *palazzo*. 'Lucia, you're welcome to stay here, but...' she glanced at Lucia's stuffed suitcase '...you might need to make other arrangements while the wedding is taking place.'

Logan turned and stared at Lucia just as she turned and stared at him. Both of them had wide eyes. It was like a cartoon scene. It was something that hadn't occurred to either of them.

Of course Lucia would need somewhere to stay for the next few months. He'd invited her to stay with him in the farmhouse, but that had been when they'd been at the top of the campanile. It seemed like a million years ago. She'd promised to consider it and they hadn't discussed it again since.

He knew that he should say something here.

Logan's arrangement was different from everyone else's. He was staying in one of the old converted farmhouses on the estate. It was comfortable. It was private. And it was big enough for two people.

There were two reasonable-sized bedrooms. He had hardly set foot in the other one—even though he could have used it as his office. His computer and paperwork were currently spread over the dining-room table. Dining for one didn't really require the full use of the table.

He caught a glimpse of the expression on Louisa's face. She was caught in the middle, probably unable to fathom out what their relationship was. She waved her hand. 'I'll leave that to you two.' She walked away into the vineyards.

Lucia was watching her retreating back. 'Do you think she's okay?'

He shrugged. 'She certainly didn't want to be drawn into any gossip. She could be worried about how this could affect the prospects for the vineyard and the *palazzo*. I can only assume that the wedding costs are covering all the renovations around here. If they back out now...' He let his voice drift off. They both knew exactly what that could mean for Louisa.

Lucia gave a little nod and tugged at her case. 'In that case, I have things I need to do. I'm going back to chart some of the fresco and make an approximate estimate of how long the restoration work will take. I'll share the timetable with you when it's finished.'

Logan looked around. There was a mountain of work here for him too. A little gust of wind swept past and carried Lucia's rose-scented perfume towards him.

He cringed as it automatically evoked memories in his brain. Nights. Days. Passion. Love. And loss.

Avoiding Lucia in Palazzo di Comparino could be harder than he'd thought.

It could be nigh on impossible.

'See you later,' he said briskly as her eyes met his.

For the tiniest second he held his breath. There it was again, that connection. It sparked every time he looked into those deep brown eyes and reflected the pain and passion that had affected them both.

He dug his hands in his pockets and turned away.

It was best to break the connection.

Best for them both.

Lucia couldn't sleep. The windows in her bedroom were open wide and she could practically hear the music of the Tuscan hills calling to her. Every rustle of the vineyard leaves, every noise from the watering system, the tiny cranking noises of some of the mechanical systems were all being carried in the warm night air.

The bed was comfortable, but even wearing just her new satin nightdress and only having one sheet was proving too much. She couldn't settle. Every time she closed her eyes for a few seconds her brain started to replay the last few days with Logan.

And it was infuriating. Because it wasn't one tiny part—it was everything…almost told in parts like a TV series. Her nerves at speaking to him for the first time. That *whoosh* that had swept over her body when she'd set eyes on him again. The way her skin had prickled just from being near him. Feeling the heat from his body when he was in close proximity to her. The touch of his lips on hers, awakening all the old sensations. Being held in his arms as they'd danced at Piazza San Marco. And the feel of his skin against hers when they'd finally gone to bed together.

Being around Logan seemed to have set all of her five senses on fire. And now they'd been reawakened it seemed they didn't want to go back to sleep.

She sat up in bed for the twentieth time and slid her feet onto the floor. The tiles of the floor were cool and it took a few seconds to find her flat sandals.

She stood at the window for a moment, wondering if she should go outside. There was not a single person in sight. That wasn't unusual—it was the middle of the night. She glanced around her room.

There was somewhere she wanted to be. Was it worth getting changed? The chapel was only across the courtyard from the *palazzo*. Could she just sneak across the way she was?

She grimaced at the stuffed-full suitcase. Packing

when your mind was on other things wasn't exactly ideal. She hadn't brought a dressing gown. Or her running gear. Or a hairdryer.

She opened her door. It creaked loudly and she held her breath for a few seconds to see if anyone had noticed the noise.

The air in the corridor was still. Her sandals made barely a sound as she crept along and down the stairs. The front door of the *palazzo* wasn't even locked.

She slipped outside and her footsteps quickened as she crossed the courtyard, the warm air making her nightdress flutter around her. It didn't matter, there was nobody to see her. She couldn't explain it. Couldn't even think about it too much. But she was being drawn to the chapel like a magnet.

Except it wasn't really the chapel she wanted to see— it was the fresco.

The thick wooden door was heavy and she had to put her shoulder to it to finally push it open.

The slightly colder, stiller air of the chapel swept around her as soon as she stepped inside. Her footsteps stopped as the tiny hairs on her arms stood upright.

It was like walking into a scene from a scary movie. She was being ridiculous. Of course the chapel was slightly colder. The walls were thicker than the *palazzo*'s and the cooler air had probably helped with the preservation of the fresco.

It was pitch-black. Only a few strands of moonlight were sneaking through the stained-glass windows. Nothing was really visible. She hadn't thought to bring a candle with her.

She took a few small steps forward, hoping her eyes would adjust to the darkness around her. Her hand reached out to touch the cold wall. It was odd. This chapel must have hundreds of years' worth of history, hundreds of years' worth of stories to tell. Weddings, birth, funerals all held in here.

In a way it was nice the royal wedding was being held here. A piece of history was being brought back to life, back to its former glory. If they hadn't proposed to use this site, Burano's fresco might never have been discovered.

'Yaow!' She stubbed her foot on something—some kind of carpenter's toolbox—and bent to rub her bare toe. Her hand touched something on the floor. She fumbled for a second. A flashlight. Perfect. She flicked the switch and a thin beam of light cut through the darkness.

Now she could move more easily. She spun the torch around towards the fresco wall, the light hitting squarely on the Madonna's face. Lucia sucked in a breath. Her feet moved forward automatically. An invisible hand had reached into her chest and was squeezing at her heart.

This was it. This was what she'd needed to see. She moved the light a little downwards onto the face of baby Jesus, then back towards Mary. She drew up directly to the fresco, her hand shaking a little as Mary's face was illuminated in all its glory.

Every hint of colour, every hair on her head, every tiny line of her face—it was the expression that had been captured so beautifully. The expression that made her knees tremble.

She'd never seen it captured quite so perfectly. Even though it was paint that was centuries old she felt as if she could reach out and touch Mary. Stroke her cheek, feel the warmth of her skin, see the wonder in her eyes.

This was what she'd remembered. It was the thing that she'd pushed to the back of her head when she'd first seen the fresco. Now it was drawing her back.

Now she couldn't deny it. She couldn't ignore it.

This had all been in Burano's imagination. It felt as if he'd stepped back in time and caught that moment when a mother first looked at her child and was overcome by that huge wave of emotions and undeniable love. Baby Jesus was looking back at his mother with childlike wonder and awe. The look of love that only a child could give his mother—making the bond complete. The light behind the depiction of the Madonna and Child was almost ethereal. The glow around them was all-encompassing. All-consuming.

Her legs trembled. Her whole body was shaking.

And something, something from deep inside, was pushing its way out.

This was what she had missed. This was what she'd missed out on. This was what would never be hers. Never be shared between her and her daughter.

Her legs gave way, collapsing beneath her onto the dusty chapel floor as the sobs started to come out.

And twelve years' worth of suppressed grief started to flow.

Logan was pacing. He hadn't even made an attempt to go to bed. He'd heard rustling in the vineyard and had taken a restless walk to investigate. It had been fruitless. He'd found nothing. It had probably only been a fox.

But as he had been crossing back towards his farmhouse, something had caught his eye. At first he'd thought he had finally gone crazy and was imagining it. Then he'd looked again.

Lucia. Dressed in very little with bare legs, bare arms and a pale pink lace-trimmed nightdress fluttering around her in the warm breeze and clinging to every curve of her skin. Was she sleepwalking?

She seemed so focused, so light on her feet, that she almost floated across the courtyard, straight to the chapel entrance. He'd started to move in her direction but his footsteps had faltered as she'd paused at the chapel door, pushing it with her shoulder to lever it open.

Then she disappeared into the darkness.

Logan stopped. His heart was thudding in his chest. Should he follow, or should he leave?

Every part of his rational brain told him to step away. No matter how much he wanted to, he couldn't pursue a relationship with Lucia. Not like this. Not when they were both in different places.

But the protective element in him couldn't walk away. Couldn't leave her like this.

He walked quietly towards the chapel. A little beam of light appeared inside the chapel, cutting across the stained-glass windows. What was she doing?

He held his breath as he reached the doorway. Stepping inside the dark chapel was intimidating—and he was fully dressed. The thin beam of torchlight was focused on the fresco on the faraway wall.

He'd never seen it lit up like this before. He'd only ever really studied it in daylight. It looked entirely different under the concentrated light of a torch beam. The architect-minded part of him wondered how it must have looked hundreds of years ago in flickering candlelight.

Lucia had the beam directly on the Madonna's face. Under the artificial light her face was brightly illuminated. In a reach-out-and-touch kind of way

The beam wobbled and he stepped forward. Part of his stomach was curled up in a ball. Lucia had come out to the chapel in the middle of the night. In the light reflected back off the fresco he could see her trembling, shuddering skin. Every muscle, every bone was shaking.

His response was automatic. He stepped forward just as she crumpled to the floor, her sobs cutting through the night air. The torch fell to the floor with a crash, the light sputtering out.

He was stunned. In twelve years he hadn't heard her cry. There had been a few tears just after the birth of their daughter—but none after that.

He wrapped his arms around her. Her skin was cold, chilled in the coolness of the chapel, so he pulled her against his chest and stroked her hair. He didn't care about the dust. He didn't care about the broken torch on the ground.

He just held her.

And she sobbed. Like no one he'd ever heard before. These weren't quiet, tiny sobs. These were loud and spluttering, echoing around the thick chapel walls. Her body was racked with them and he could feel her pain, feel her anguish. It was as if twelve years' worth of grief and sorrow had just erupted from her soul.

It was horrible to see the woman he loved like this. But he knew exactly how she felt. Only he could understand. So he waited and he held her, gently stroking her hair and whispering in her ear.

He had no idea how long they stayed that way. Eventually her sobs quietened, turning into little shudders instead of big outbursts. He changed position, pulling her up onto his knees, taking her bare legs away from the cold floor of the chapel.

His hands sneaked around her satin-covered waist and he pulled her against his chest. Her hands snaked up around his neck and her head tucked under his chin. He could feel her ragged breaths against his skin.

'I know, Lucia,' he said softly. 'I know how you feel. I loved her just as much as you did.'

She gave a little whimper and her fingers tightened around his neck. He waited a few seconds then gently lifted her head up. There was only a tiny bit of moonlight streaming through the stained-glass windows but he could see her tear-streaked face and he lifted both hands to caress it.

'Talk to me,' he whispered.

She shuddered, then nodded slowly.

It was odd. The strangest feeling in the world, but it was almost as if his body gave a little cry of relief.

'I miss her,' she said in shaky breaths. 'I miss her every day.'

His heart squeezed in his chest. He wanted to wrap his arms around her again and kiss her. But he needed to let her speak.

'I don't want to talk about her,' she said, her voice tinged with regret. 'If I don't talk about her, then none of it was real. None of it really happened.'

She shook her head as her voice rose in pain. 'Why, Logan? Why our baby? Why did we have to lose her? Do you know where we could be right now? Do you know what kind of life we could be leading?'

He nodded his head. 'Of course I do,' he whispered.

'But you were so calm, so controlled,' she said angrily. 'I couldn't be like that, I just couldn't. You did everything. You organised the flowers, the funeral, the casket. You spoke to the family.' She shook her head, her voice rising. 'How could you even do that? How could you even function? Our daughter was dead!'

'You think I didn't know that? You think I didn't hurt every bit as much as you? I hated that, Lucia. I hated every second of that. I hated the fact you wouldn't eat, you wouldn't sleep and you wouldn't talk to me. Organising was the only thing I *could* do. I wanted the world to know that Ariella Rose had existed. I wanted her to matter. I wanted to bury our daughter with the respect she deserved.' He hadn't realised this had been buried inside him. He hadn't realised he'd wanted to say all this to her.

'And I didn't?' She was crying again. 'You were so... capable. And I felt useless. I couldn't be the person I'd been. I couldn't be your other half. I couldn't look at you without thinking about her and what had been stolen from me!'

He clasped her head between his hands and leaned his forehead against hers. 'Stolen from *us*, Lucia,' he said quietly.

'I needed you. I needed you every second of the day. But I couldn't get to you. You locked yourself away from me and after a few weeks I realised that you needed to grieve differently from me. I didn't want to let you go. I never wanted to let you go. No matter how sorry I was, no matter how much I hurt, I still wanted you, Lucia. Every second of every day. You're the only person in this world for me. The only person I want to grow old with.' He traced a finger down her damp cheek. 'I just needed to see you cry. I just needed to know that you could acknowledge our daughter.'

She was still shuddering. He ran one hand down her

arm and could feel the tiny hairs on her arms standing on end.

'Why now? What's changed?'

She met his gaze with tear-filled eyes. 'You. I've avoided you for so long. Seeing you again, being together, remembering everything we've shared together, I couldn't hide away from it any more. It's just been bubbling underneath the surface the whole time. I couldn't keep it locked away any more. Not if I want to live.'

He gave his head a shake. 'But you wouldn't talk to me in Venice. You said you couldn't do it.'

She squeezed her eyes closed for a moment. 'I know.' Now she reached up and touched his face, his jaw. 'I think something just lined up for us, Logan.' She pointed towards the fresco. 'If you hadn't got this job, if this fresco hadn't been found, we probably wouldn't have met again.' She placed her hand over her heart. 'I *needed* this. I needed all this to happen.' She looked up towards the fresco. 'Hundreds of years ago Burano must have met someone, must have known a new mother, to capture the love and adoration in his painting. Because he's captured it so beautifully. When I first saw his fresco I wouldn't let the painting touch me. I wouldn't let it inside. I was jealous. I couldn't acknowledge the painting because *I* wanted to be that person. *I* wanted to be that mother who looks at her baby with such joy and pleasure, wondering what the world will hold for them.' The tears were falling freely down her face again.

All he wanted to do was comfort her. All he wanted to do was love her.

He sucked in a deep breath. 'Lucia, you can be that person. I want you to know that I love you. I want you—just the way you are. But if you want to try and have a family again then I'll be with you, every step of the way.' He stroked his thumb across her cheek. 'Likewise, if you just want to grow old and grey together and wander through the streets of Venice, or Florence, or even the Tuscan hills, I'll do that with you too. As long as I'm with you, I know I'll be happy.'

Her hands kept trembling as she wound them around his neck again, pressing her body against his and whispering in his ear. 'Can I be enough for you, Logan? Enough for you on my own? What if we weren't meant to have babies? What if that's never going to happen for us?'

He stood up, pulling her to her feet alongside him but keeping their bodies locked close together. He slid his hands along the satin slip covering her back and anchored her to him. He kissed one cheek and then the other. 'Then that's the way things are supposed to be. As long as I'm with you I can take whatever hand life deals us.'

He bent to meet her lips.

It was like the first kiss all over again.

This was the woman he'd fallen in love with all those years ago.

This was the woman he'd had to allow to walk away even though it had broken his heart.

This was the mother of his child.

This was his Lucia.

Her body was pressed against his and she responded to every touch, her fingers threading through his hair. Her rose scent wound around him, pulling him in in every way.

Her cold skin heated quickly, her lips matching every kiss.

For Logan, it was like coming home.

When Lucia finally pulled back he was shocked. She lifted a finger and placed it against his lips, keeping her body tight against his.

She took a deep breath. 'Logan, if this is going to work, there's something I need to do.'

His breath was caught somewhere in his throat. After twelve years there was finally a chance of a relationship again with Lucia. There wasn't anything he wouldn't agree to.

'What is it? What do you need to do? Because I don't want to lose you again. I don't want this chance to slip away from us.'

Her voice was trembling and her hand slid down his arm, interlocking their fingers. 'I was kind of hoping you would agree to do it with me.'

Her dark eyes met his gaze and he squeezed her hand tightly. 'Anything, Lucia,' he whispered. 'Anything for you.'

CHAPTER TEN

IT WAS A gorgeous summer's day with the sun high in the sky above them.

Logan was standing in front of her in his trademark cream suit and pale blue shirt. 'Ready?' he asked.

Her stomach was churning. Over and over. She would have tossed and turned last night if he hadn't held her safely in his arms. She'd even bought herself a new dress. Pale pink with tiny flowers. It was ridiculous. She didn't need it. But she'd wanted to wake up this morning and feel like everything was new.

More than anything, she wanted to be prepared.

Florence was alive. She'd forgotten how much she loved this city. Chattering voices were all around them, tourist parties bustling past and Italian voices mixing with a multitude of other languages.

She slid her hand into his, clutching her pink and lilac flowers in her hand. 'I'm ready,' she said with a certainty she hadn't known she possessed.

The walk through the streets took around fifteen minutes, the crowds lessening the further out they went. No one else was going where they were.

It was a pleasant walk with a few shopkeepers nodding at Logan as they passed by and him pointing out a few changes to the city since she'd left.

As the green archway of the cemetery came into view her footsteps faltered. Logan slipped his hand around her waist. As their bodies pressed against each other she fell into step with him. It felt natural and gave her the added reassurance to continue.

The cemetery was quiet, bathed in warm sunlight, with only a few people dotted around in quiet condolence.

Her throat was closing up as they walked along the white paved path. Like most cemeteries this one had a special section for children and babies. It was tucked away at the back, next to the white wall that separated the cemetery from the rest of the city.

There was a white bench in the middle, with lots of green grass and flower beds erupting with colour. Something inside her clenched. She hadn't allowed herself to think about this. She hadn't allowed herself to realise the beauty of the surroundings.

Within the cemetery walls she couldn't even hear the noise of the city outside. It was like their own private sanctuary.

She squeezed her eyes closed as they passed rows of little white headstones. So many little lives lost. So many other people who'd experienced the same pain that she had.

Had she maybe even met some of them? She'd been so immersed in her own grief that she hadn't stopped to think about anyone else's.

Their footsteps slowed. She'd only been here once and Logan had been numerous times but she still knew exactly where Ariella Rose was buried—it was imprinted in her brain.

They stopped and stood for a second, looking down at the little white headstone.

Beloved daughter.
Ariella Rose Cascini.
Born asleep.

Apart from the date, there was nothing else on the stone.

Lucia laid her head on his shoulder as silent tears fell down her cheeks. She needed this. She'd needed to do this for so long.

A dove swooped in the air above them, landing on the grass at their feet. Lucia gave a little nod of her head as it eyed her suspiciously then walked away. She put her pale pink and lilac flowers into the little white vase at the graveside then leaned over to touch the stone.

It was odd. Any marble headstone she'd ever touched before had been cold. But Ariella's wasn't. It was bathed in the bright light and warmed by the sun.

The horrible closed-in feeling that had been around her heart for so long was gone. The terrible weight and the dark cloud that had pressed on her shoulders for the last twelve years was finally gone.

Today she didn't feel despair all around her. Today she saw a beautiful memorial and resting place for her darling daughter. A place where she could come and sit sometimes if she needed to.

She'd been so afraid for so long. But with Logan by her side she didn't need to be.

'I love you, Ariella Rose,' she whispered. 'I'm sorry

I haven't been here and I promise to visit in the future.'
She stroked her hand along the stone and stood up,
taking the few steps to Logan and wrapping her arms
around his waist.

'Thank you,' she said quietly. 'Thank you for bringing me here.'

'Any time. Any time at all.'

He threaded his fingers back through hers. 'Do you
want to take some time? How do you feel?' His voice
was cautious.

She tilted her head up towards the sun and the face
of the man that she loved and adored. The man she
wanted to grow old with.

'I feel as if I've taken that step. The one that I've
needed to for so long. I'm ready now.'

He clasped both her hands in his. 'Ready for what?'

She met the gaze of his steady green eyes. 'Ready to
move forward. Now I can love the man I want to without feeling overcome with grief.' She smiled up at the
sun. 'Now I can look towards the future.'

There was a swell in her chest. A confidence she
hadn't felt in so long.

He reached up and slid his hand through her hair as
he pulled her to him.

'Then let's start now.'

And he kissed her.

And she kissed him right back.

She was laughing. She was running through the cobbled
streets of Monte Calanetti in her impossibly high heels.

He loved it. He loved every second of it. 'Watch out!'
he shouted. 'You'll break something!'

'Keep up, slowcoach!' she shouted over her shoulder as she made the final dash towards the fountain. He walked up behind her and slid his hands around her waist. He could feel her rapid breaths against his chest wall.

'Do you have them?' she asked.

He unfurled his fingers, revealing the shiny euro coins in his hand. He eyed the clamshell the nymph held above her head in the centre of the fountain. 'First time?' He was smiling. She'd tried this a hundred times before and had never managed to hit the mark—the clamshell that would make your wish come true.

Her deep brown eyes met his. 'First time,' she repeated. Her index finger moved the coins in the palm of his hand as if she was looking for just the right one. After a few seconds she smiled. 'This one,' she said, weighing the coin in her hand.

'That one? You're sure?'

'Oh, I'm sure.' She spun around to face the nymph. His hand was on her abdomen and she pressed her right hand over his, as she took a deep breath, pulled back her left hand and let the coin fly.

His eyes stayed on the coin as it caught the sunlight as it arced through the air, but his left hand was flicking something else into the fountain at their feet.

The coin was on a direct path and landed squarely in the middle of the clamshell. Lucia let out a shriek. 'I've done it! I've finally done it!' She spun around and flung her arms around his neck. 'I've finally done it.'

He picked her up and spun her around, her hair streaming out behind her. 'You've done it,' he cheered as he set her back down. 'Now, what did you wish for?'

For the first time his stomach wasn't in knots around Lucia. Slowly but surely she was turning back into the woman he loved. The dark shadows were going from her eyes. Her steps were lighter. She laughed more. She cried more. And she still loved to dance.

'Isn't the wish supposed to be a secret?' she said coyly.

He swallowed. He'd never felt more nervous, or surer about anything in his life. 'Look down,' he said quietly.

She blinked. It obviously wasn't what she had expected to hear. A frown creased her brow as she stared down, taking a few seconds to see the glint of gold under the clear water.

Her eyes widened and she bent down, putting her hand into the water and pulling out the ring.

'Logan?' she asked as a smile spread across her face.

It wasn't a traditional flashy engagement ring. He didn't want to waste any time. It was a gold wedding band studded with diamonds and rubies. It was a ring of promise. A ring of hope.

He didn't hesitate, just got down on one knee in front of the woman he loved. 'Lucia Moretti. You're the woman of my dreams. The woman I love with my whole heart. You are my perfect match. The person I want to laugh with, cry with, play with and grow old with. I believe this was meant to happen. I honestly believe we were meant to meet again and mourn our daughter together. I don't care where you want to make a life. I don't care if it's Venice, Florence, Rome or anywhere else. All that matters to me is that home is with you.' He pressed his hand against his heart 'As long as I'm with you, I don't care where we are. You're the person I call home. You're all that I need. Will you make me the happiest man alive and marry me?'

She was still staring at the ring, watching the sun

glint off the little diamonds and rubies. The smile was permanently etched on her face.

She wrapped one arm around his neck and sat down on his knee. She didn't hesitate to slip the ring on her finger. 'How on earth could any woman refuse such a romantic proposal at Burano's fountain?' Her eyes were twinkling. She put her hand over his. 'There's no one else I ever want to be with. You're the only man for me.'

He pulled something out from behind his waist. 'I've brought you something else.'

She stared at the wrapped package. It wasn't big, small enough to tuck into his waistband. Plain canvas tied with string. She pulled the string and let the package unfurl. It was new paintbrushes and some oils. Her mouth fell open.

'How…how did you know?'

'That you'd want to take up painting again?'

She nodded as her eyes glistened with tears. 'Because we've come such a long way, Lucia. We've both moved on. You used to love painting and I know that you've found that little piece in your heart again that makes you ready to start again.'

She nodded her head slowly. 'You're right. I have. But I'd only just started to think about it.' She looked around. 'We're in such beautiful surroundings I can't help but feel inspired.'

He leaned forward to kiss her. 'Which leads me to my next question. Where do you want to live?'

She smiled and looked around. 'This might surprise you, but I've kind of grown fond of these Tuscan hills. I like the peace. I like the quiet. Maybe I'm not the city girl I thought.' She bit her bottom lip. 'How would you feel about finding somewhere to live around here?'

He stood and pulled her to her feet, holding her close.
He ran his fingers through her hair. 'I think that this
is a good place, a healing place. And I'm sure there's a
Tuscan villa somewhere in these hills just waiting for
us to renovate it. A villa where we can build you your
own studio.'

She smiled again, 'All work and no play makes
Logan a dull boy.'

She was teasing and he knew it. 'Who says anything
about working?' he murmured.

She pressed a little kiss against his lips. 'Do you want
to know what I wished for?'

'Are you going to tell me?'

She nodded. 'Someone must have been listening.
When I threw that coin I wished for new beginnings.'

His eyebrows rose. 'You did?' It was perfect. It was
as if everything was just meant to be.

'I did,' she said with confidence, and with that she
rose up on her toes to kiss him. 'To new beginnings,'
she whispered.

'New beginnings,' he murmured, and he kissed her
right back.

* * * * *

The Cowboy.

Her heart thudded in her chest. Another one of those giddy waves of joy passed through her, even as the lump in her throat returned. The Cowboy! She'd wished for him and he was here, so soon after she'd made her personal vow that she could hardly believe he was real.

Yet there he was, a man she'd never seen before, holding the bridle and calming the lead horse. The Cowboy— *her* cowboy—was the most physically appealing man she'd ever seen. Tall, dark and handsome barely began to describe him, inadequate to cover the physical confidence he possessed, that aura of calm and control about him as he talked with the other men and kept the horse calm at the same time.

Who are you?

He looked right at her, as if he'd heard her ask the question. Right at her. Over the nose of the white horse, across the dozen people who milled between them, their gazes met and held.

Across the crowd, they shared a slow smile. If it was true that like attracted like, then she and this man sure were alike. When people said "two peas in a pod" to Kristen, they were invariably referring to her twin, but on this special summer day, Kristen knew that she and this man were a match, too. That smile said it all.

* * *

Montana Mavericks:
What Happened At The Wedding?
A weekend Rust Creek Falls will never forget!

THE MAVERICK'S
HOLIDAY
MASQUERADE

BY
CARO CARSON

Published in Great Britain 2015
by Mills & Boon, an imprint of Harlequin (UK) Limited,
Eton House, 18-24 Paradise Road, Richmond, Surrey, TW9 1SR

© 2015 Harlequin Books S.A.

Special thanks and acknowledgment to Caro Carson for her contribution to the Montana Mavericks: What Happened at the Wedding? continuity.

ISBN: 978-0-263-25181-4

23-1115

Harlequin (UK) Limited's policy is to use papers that are natural, renewable and recyclable products and made from wood grown in sustainable forests. The logging and manufacturing processes conform to the legal environmental regulations of the country of origin.

Printed and bound in Spain
by CPI, Barcelona

Despite a no-nonsense background as a West Point graduate and US Army officer, **Caro Carson** has always treasured the happily-ever-after of a good romance novel. Now a double RITA® Award-nominated author, Caro is delighted to be living her own happily-ever-after with her husband and two children in the great state of Florida, a location that has saved the coaster-loving theme-park fanatic a fortune on plane tickets.

For my parents, Larry and Sue,
with gratitude for all the plays and ballets,
the Broadway musicals and the rock concerts,
and for setting the example by
pursuing their passion for the theater.
This theater-loving heroine had to be for you!

Chapter One

Fourth of July

"Do you see them?"

Kristen Dalton shaded her eyes with one hand as she looked up the road, but she couldn't see any hint of a horse-drawn carriage. "Sorry, sis. No sign of the bride and groom yet."

"I can't wait to see her wedding dress. The rumors have been all over the place. I've heard everything from country casual to Kardashian craziness."

Anything could be true. Although Kristen and her sister lived in a small town surrounded by ranches, technology made the world itself a small place. Even to the far northern edge of Montana, a gown from glittering Hollywood could be shipped overnight. Since the wedding dress possibilities were endless, the speculation around town had been, as well. For weeks, Kristen had

~~been patiently~~ listening to her twin, Kayla, list the pros and cons of every type of gown. Although today was the Fourth of July, her twin's excitement was closer to that of a kid on Christmas morning.

Kristen handed her sister her paper cup, then hopped up to perch on the top log of the split-rail fence that bordered the town park. She held out her hands for her cup and Kayla's. "Come sit with me. It could be a while. That photographer has to take pictures of a million Traub family members at the church."

Kayla climbed up to sit beside her on the railing, settling in for the wait. "What a beautiful day for their wedding."

Kristen thought it was a little too warm, nearly eighty degrees, which was as hot as things got this close to Glacier National Park. As she handed back Kayla's cup, Kristen took a healthy drink of her ice-cold wedding punch.

Thank goodness they'd decided to wear sundresses. They didn't match, of course. She and Kayla looked as identical as two peas in a pod, a phrase Kristen had been hearing for as long as she could remember, but they hadn't dressed like twins for as long as they'd been choosing their own clothes. From a distance, she supposed they looked like twins in blue dresses, but up close, they weren't alike at all.

Kayla's dress had an all-over print of tiny flowers. Her spaghetti straps were delicate, and she wore their grandmother's earrings. The shiny filigree drops were shown to their advantage on Kayla because she swept her hair up most of the time.

No one would ever see those earrings if Kristen wore them, because her hair was nearly always down.

And long. And wavy. And—*okay, I'll admit it, Mom*—always blowing in the Montana breeze and getting tangled. Their mother had despaired of keeping it neat and had given up trying somewhere around kindergarten, when Kristen had become quite adept at removing barrettes and bows.

Kristen could also admit that she'd deliberately worn blue because it made her eyes appear their bluest. Her denim halter dress always made her feel like she struck the right balance between sweet and sexy. She got smiles from the town's mavens and mavericks both. Rather than sandals, she wore her western boots. Not the solid, broken-in ones that she wore to do chores around the family ranch, but the ones with the hand-scrolled swirls in the leather. These were the boots she wore for two-stepping, waltzing and square dancing, all of which she hoped to do before, during and after tonight's fireworks.

All she needed was the right cowboy to dance with.

If only...

If only there was a cowboy here in Rust Creek Falls that she didn't already know—and already know wasn't her type.

"I really admire Braden and Jennifer for thinking up this carriage ride," her sister said. "Their first experience as Mr. and Mrs. Traub will be private, just the two of them, as they start their journey together, figuratively, literally—"

"Briefly." Kristen nudged her in the shoulder. "The church is only two blocks away. Then we'll be right here, ready to say hi while we're really checking out the newest Mrs. Traub's gown."

Kayla shot her a look. "We're supposed to admire the bride's gown. It's expected."

"I know, I know. It'll be worth the wait, I'm sure."

"They say the best things in life are." Kayla sounded like she really meant that.

Kristen kicked the heels of her boots against the lower log railing. *Thunk, thunk.* She polished off the rest of her punch, then lifted her heavy hair from the back of her warm neck again. *Thunk, thunk.* "I hope this carriage looks amazing, because it certainly isn't a very fast way to travel."

Kayla nudged her shoulder. "I heard Sutter Traub located true white horses, and they went to someone's place south of Kalispell to borrow a two-seater surrey. Paige and Lindsay bought miles of white ribbon for it and were making bows all week."

"Wow," Kristen said, impressed at the wealth of details her sister knew. Kristen had only heard that the bride and groom were going to arrive at the park by carriage. "You've got wedding fever worse than anyone else in town, and that's saying something, considering the entire town is here for the reception."

Kristen stopped thudding her heels against the cross rail; even a twin might get annoyed at the rhythmic thumping, even an identical twin who understood Kristen's restless nature better than anyone else in the world. Squinting against the bright July sun, she joined Kayla in staring silently down Buckskin Road, past their old high school. Every kid in Rust Creek Falls had been educated there. Every kid still was. Some things in this small town never changed, and that was fine with Kristen.

She'd gone to the University of Montana, majored in theater and spent a summer as an unpaid intern in New

York City. Like Dorothy in a pair of ruby red slippers—a role she'd played onstage at the university—she'd realized there was no place like home. Cities were great fun to visit, but the tiny town of Rust Creek Falls under the big sky of Montana was home. It always had been. It always would be.

Small didn't mean boring. Things were always changing. Their local politics could make the national scene appear tame, but everyone had pulled together to rebuild after a flood had wiped out a substantial portion of the town just a couple of years ago. Old Bledsoe's Folly, an abandoned mountain retreat, was now an upscale resort that had the town buzzing with talk about developing the area's first ski slope.

But it was the people of Rust Creek Falls that were the most interesting. There must be something about Montana's famous Big Sky, because lots of folks who'd come to help with the flood recovery or to turn Bledsoe's Folly into Maverick Manor had ended up staying, partnered up after falling in love in Kristen's hometown.

She glanced up at that blue sky now, automatically scanning the horizon for planes—for a certain plane. It was a habit she'd formed earlier this year, when she'd thought the blue sky was bringing her true love to her. The handsome pilot of a commuter airline had turned out to be a heartbreaker of the lowest kind. Like a sailor with a girl in every port, he'd had a woman at every airport. Kristen still felt like an idiot for falling for him.

She got another shoulder nudge from her sister. "Does he fly into Kalispell on weekends now?"

Leave it up to quiet Kayla to never miss a detail, not even a glance at the sky.

Kristen wrinkled her nose. "I don't care what Captain Two-Timer does or where he flies or who he tells lies to after he lands."

"Or *to whom* he tells lies after he lands."

"You should be a writer, you know." Kristen resumed her rail-thumping. "I don't care 'to whom' he lies. It isn't to me, not anymore. 'Gee, I wish I didn't have to go. I won't be able to call you for a few days. You know I'd rather be with you, but this job is so demanding.' I was an idiot. I can't believe I couldn't see through him."

"You were in love."

"I'm not anymore." She tossed her hair back. "I'm in the mood to dance. I'm hoping for a handsome stranger or two to flirt with, but I'm not going to fall in love again."

"Not ever?"

"Not for a long while. Definitely not today."

Kayla didn't say anything for long seconds.

Kristen stopped looking for the carriage when she realized her sister was staring at her, not at the road. "What?"

"You shouldn't dare the universe to prove you wrong like that."

"Stop that. You're giving me goose bumps." Kristen jumped down from the fence, an easy drop of two feet at most, but somehow she stumbled and nearly fell. She was normally as nimble as a cat, and this sudden imbalance struck her as—funny? Yes, it was funny. It was good to giggle after that serious moment. "You stay here on carriage watch. I'll go get us some more punch. Give me your cup."

When Kayla reached down to hand her the cup, she slipped, too, and fell right into Kristen. They dissolved into giggles together, for no reason at all.

"What do you suppose is in that punch?" Kristen asked. "We only had one cup."

"I don't know, but stay here with me. Just look down that road and wait for true love to come our way."

Ryan Roarke parked his red Porsche in between two sturdy pickup trucks. The high-performance sports car belonged in Los Angeles, but this wasn't LA. In fact, Ryan had come to Montana to get away from Los Angeles. When he'd directed his assistant to reserve a luxury rental vehicle at the Glacier Park airport, he'd expected to be handed the keys to his usual Land Rover or an Audi fitted with a ski rack, the kind of rental he drove when he visited his brother in a different part of Montana, the upscale ski resort of Thunder Canyon.

This was July, however, and the roads were clear of snow, so the clerk had been enthusiastic when she'd handed him the keys to the Porsche. Ryan had attempted to return her smile when he wanted to grimace.

He grimaced now. Pulling into the packed dirt of the parking spaces at the edge of Rust Creek Falls' park in a Porsche was not what he'd had in mind for the weekend. The flashy car was so inappropriate for this rugged town, it made him look like he was having a midlife crisis. Ryan killed the powerful engine and got out, feeling like a giant at six-foot-one next to the low car. He returned the stares from a few cowboys with a hard look of his own.

Ryan knew what a midlife crisis looked like—too many of his fellow attorneys blew their children's inheritances on sports cars in an effort to replace their children's mothers with starlets—but he didn't know what one felt like. He was *not* having a midlife crisis.

He was only thirty-three, for starters, and a confirmed bachelor. He wasn't trying to appear more wealthy or powerful or attractive to women than he already was.

As the second generation of well-known attorneys in Los Angeles, Ryan already owned the sports cars, the Rolex, the hand-tailored suits. Physical intimidation had a subliminal effect even in a courtroom, and Ryan kept himself in fighting shape by boxing with exclusive trainers and surfing on exclusive beaches. When it came to young, blonde starlets finding him attractive, he didn't even have to try.

This was definitely not a midlife crisis.

So why am I standing in the smallest of towns in a landlocked state more than one thousand miles away from home?

He was supposed to be on a yacht, slowly getting sloshed with his fellow millionaires, drinking top-shelf mojitos while waiting for the sun to set over the Pacific and for the city of Los Angeles to blow an obscene amount of money on a fireworks display worthy of a Hollywood movie. One Laker Girl, in particular, was quite upset he'd canceled those plans. But the government had closed the courts of law on Friday for the holiday weekend, and for the past two years, whenever Ryan found himself with a chance to take a few days off, he'd found himself taking those days off in Montana.

The reason he'd first set foot in Big Sky Country was his brother. Shane Roarke had gained fame as a celebrity chef, a man whose dynamic personality and culinary skill had combined to give him the keys to the world. Shane had opened restaurants all over that world, but when it came to choosing one place to live, he'd chosen Montana.

Shane, like Ryan, was adopted. Shane had found his birth family in Thunder Canyon. He'd found a pair of half brothers, a baker's dozen of cousins—and the love of his life. She'd been working right under his nose at his own restaurant in the Thunder Canyon resort.

None of that would be happening for Ryan. Not in Montana, and not anywhere else on the planet. Unlike Shane, Ryan hadn't been adopted at birth. He'd been almost four years old, too young to have many memories of his birth mother, but old enough to have retained an image or two, impressions.

Feelings.

And that one clear moment in time: watching his mother voluntarily walk away from him, forever.

No, there would never be an embrace from a happy second family for him. He was loyal only to one family: the Roarkes. His parents, Christa and Gavin Roarke, his older brother Shane, his younger sister Maggie.

It was Maggie who lived here in Rust Creek Falls, some three hundred miles even farther north than Thunder Canyon. Maggie was married now, and she'd given birth to her first baby less than three months ago.

The Fourth of July wasn't a big family holiday, not like Thanksgiving or Christmas. Between the LA traffic to the airport, the security checks, and the need to change planes in order to cross one thousand miles, Montana was no weekend jaunt. No one was expected to travel for nine or ten hours to see family for a day in July. And yet, Maggie had mentioned over the phone that the whole town would be celebrating the wedding for a couple Ryan vaguely knew from a previous trip, and he'd booked a flight.

Another moment in time, another feeling: *A wedding in Rust Creek Falls? I should be there.*

He was acting irrationally, following a hunch. Was that any worse behavior than the attorneys who really were having midlife crises?

Maggie had told him the wedding would be in the church, a formal affair with five bridesmaids and men in tuxedos. Accordingly, Ryan was wearing a suit and tie. He owned a few tuxedos, of course, but since the wedding was in the afternoon and he was one of an entire town of guests, he'd assumed wearing black tie would be too much.

As Ryan made his way from the parking lot to the main part of the park, he returned a few curious but courteous nods from the locals. His assumption about the tux being overkill had clearly been correct, but even his suit was too much. The reception was also the town's Fourth of July community barbecue. Ryan felt exactly like what he was, an overdressed city slicker, standing in a grassy field that was dotted with picnic blankets and populated by cowboys in their jeans and cowgirls in their sundresses.

He stopped near the temporary stage and wooden dance floor. The bride and groom hadn't arrived yet, but the band was warming up and the drinks were being served. An old man came toward him, going out of his way just to offer Ryan a cup of wedding punch in a paper cup. Amused, Ryan thanked him, realizing the old-timer must have thought he looked like he needed a drink, standing alone as he was.

He was alone, but only because Maggie and her husband were back at their house, hoping their baby would take a nap so they could return for the fireworks later. Being alone didn't mean Ryan was lonely.

Ryan took a swig of the wedding punch, then immediately wished he hadn't. It was a god-awful sweet concoction with sparkling wine thrown in, something he'd never drink under almost any other circumstance. Worse, he couldn't just pour the stuff out on the grass. In a small town like this one, he was as likely to be standing near the person who made the punch as not. Some doting grandma or an earnest young lady had probably mixed the juice and wine, and the odds were good that if Ryan dumped it out, she'd see him do it. He'd break some proud punch maker's heart.

If there was one thing Ryan was not, it was a heart-breaker. His Laker Girl, for example, was irritated at losing a yacht outing, but she wasn't heartbroken. He kept his relationships painless, his connections surface-deep. In LA, it seemed right. Today, here in this park, it seemed...too little.

He polished off the punch, but on his way to the industrial-size trash can, he passed the punch table and found himself accosted by a trio of sweet little grannies.

"Well, don't you look nice?"

"Are you waiting on somebody? A handsome, young man like you must have a date for this wedding."

"It's nearly eighty degrees. You must be ready to melt in that jacket, not that you don't look very fine."

He wasn't overheated. In Los Angeles, the temperature would easily reach one hundred, and he'd still wear a suit between his office and the courthouse. It took more than a reading on a thermometer to make him lose his cool.

Still, he appreciated their maternal concern. Their

faces were creased with laugh lines, and all three of them had sparkling blue eyes that had probably been passed down from the Norwegians and Germans who'd settled here centuries ago. It was like being fussed over by three kindly characters from one of Grimm's fairy tales.

"Here, son, let me refill your cup."

"No, thank you." Ryan waved off the punch bowl ladle.

All three women jerked to attention, then looked at him through narrowed eyes, their fairy-tale personas taking on the aura of determined villainesses.

"Don't be foolish, dear. The day is hot and this punch is cold."

This was Montana, land of grizzly bears as well as grannies. At the moment, it seemed like there might not be much difference between the two groups. When confronted by a bear, one should let it have its way. Ryan forced another smile as the punch pushers refilled his cup.

"Thank you very much." He raised his paper cup in a toasting gesture, took a healthy swig to make them happy and continued on his way.

To where? Just where did he have to go?

To a trash can. He had nowhere else to be, nothing else to do, no one else to see.

His vision burst into stars, like he'd been hit in the boxing ring, a TKO. He put his hand out to steady himself, the wooden fence rough under his palm. He wasn't drunk. It wasn't possible on a cup of juice-diluted sparkling wine. And yet he felt...he felt...

Good God, he felt like garbage.

Useless.

Maggie was with her husband. Shane was with his wife. Even his parents were together back in California, planning their retirement, ready to travel and spend time together as Christa and Gavin after decades tirelessly fulfilling the roles of Mom and Dad.

Lonely.

One thousand miles he'd traveled, and for what? To be a stranger in a strange land? He looked around, keeping his grip on the split-rail fence. Everywhere, everyone had someone. Children had grandparents. Husbands had wives. Awkward teenagers had each other. The teen girls were toying with their hair, whispering and talking and looking at the boys. The boys stood with their arms crossed over their chests, testing their fledgling cowboy swagger, but they stood in a cluster with other boys with crossed arms, all being independent together.

All being independent, together. That was what this town was about. Ryan had first come here after a flood had decimated the southern half of the town. His sister had been helping process insurance claims in the town hall. Maggie was so efficient Ryan hadn't been needed the weekend he'd arrived to help. Instead, he'd picked up a spare pair of work gloves and started using his muscles instead of his brains, picking up the pieces, literally, of someone's broken dream.

Without a lot of conversation, he'd joined a cluster of men and women as they'd each picked up one brick, one board, one metal window frame to toss in a Dumpster before reaching for the next. One by one, each piece of debris had been cleared away. Independently but together, he and the others removed the remains of an entire house in a day, leaving the lot ready for a fresh building and a new dream.

With a few nods and handshakes, all the men and women had gone their separate ways after sunset, to eat and rest and do it all over again the next day. Ryan had never been part of something so profound.

He stared at the split-rail fence under his hand. That was why he kept coming back. For one day, he'd belonged. No one had cared which law firm he was with, which part of LA he could afford to live in, which clients had invited him onto their yachts. He'd been part of this community, no questions asked, and he'd liked it.

But now, they don't need me.

He rejected that thought, hearing in it the echo of a pitiful little boy whose mother had decided he was no longer needed in her life. Rejected that emotion as he had rejected it so many times before. He refused to be an unwanted child. He was a Roarke, a powerful attorney from a powerful family, and when he wanted something, no one could stop him from achieving it.

He just needed to know what he wanted.

The drunken, emotional craziness cleared from his mind as he kept staring at his hand, still gripping the solid wood railing. Slowly, he lifted his gaze, following the line of the fence as it stretched along the perimeter of the park. He could hardly believe the direction his own mind was taking, but his thoughts were heading straight toward one idea. What if he chose a new path in life? What if he came to Montana for more than a long weekend? Could he live here? Would he feel like he belonged, or would he always be skirting along the outside of the close-knit community?

His visual run along the length of the fence was interrupted a hundred yards away by two women in blue dresses who were sitting on the railing, their backs to the people of the town. The one with the loose, long hair threw her head back and laughed at something the other woman said, happy although she was on the outskirts of the party.

Happy, because she's not alone.

Shane and Maggie were happy in Montana, too, because they were not alone. Marriage and parenthood were sobering concepts for him. He didn't think he'd be very good at either one, and he didn't particularly have a burning desire to try, either. He let go of the fence and headed back toward the Porsche, loosening his tie as he went. Maybe he had come to Montana looking for something, but it hadn't been for love.

If he made such a drastic change, if he gave up LA for a life in a small town, he'd do so on his own terms. This was about a different standard of living, a different pace of life. There was only one way to find out if this town could meet his terms, and that was to try it on for size. Just for today, he was going to act like he belonged here. He'd eat some barbecue, dance with some local girls and decide if this community of extended families and battered pickup trucks was really richer than his moneyed life in LA.

If he decided it was, then he'd develop and execute a plan for responsibly resigning from Roarke and Associates in Los Angeles and moving permanently to Montana.

What if they don't like me here, now that they don't need me?

He shoved the boyishly insecure emotion aside as he opened the Porsche's trunk to get to his suitcase. The Porsche had its trunk in the front of the car and the engine in the back, making it just as unusual as

Ryan himself in this humble parking lot. The Porsche was doomed to always be different. But he, with a simple change of clothes, could make himself fit in. He'd brought the jeans he usually wore to ride ATVs in Thunder Canyon and the boots he'd worn when he'd helped out after the flood.

If the town rejected him this time, if he was treated like he was no longer wanted now that the flood was a receding memory, then no harm done. He'd lived through rejection before. He could take any heartache this town could dish out.

He took off his Rolex and tossed it into the trunk before slamming the red metal shut.

Chapter Two

"Well, it won't be long now. The band's tuning up."

Thank goodness. That giggly buzz from the powerful punch had started wearing off, giving way to a different sensation. After a few tipsy laughs with her sister, Kristen now felt more than sober. She felt almost somber, as she shifted her seat on the increasingly uncomfortable wood rail.

Her life needed to get on the right track. Things weren't right. Pieces were missing. She was twenty-five, a college graduate with a passion for the theater, yet she spent her days running to the feed store and performing the same ranch chores she'd been assigned in junior high. Not that she wanted to lose her roots—her family, the ranch, this town—but she wanted more. An outlet for her theatrical passion—something that was hard to find in her hometown. An outlet for real passion, too, someone to lose her head and her heart over—someone who wouldn't trample them this time.

This bad mood was probably just because a plane had flown overhead, reminding her that a good man was hard to find. Maybe she envied her pilot for having a home base but the freedom to fly and explore. If only he hadn't been exploring with other women in other towns...

Jeez, she was spiraling down into a full-blown pity party.

The band began playing its first song of the afternoon. Kristen looked over her shoulder toward the empty wooden dance floor in the distance. If no one else started dancing, she'd get the party started and be grateful for the chance. If there was one thing that could shake Kristen out of the blues, it was a party. And man, was she feeling blue.

Stupid airplane.

The wedding carriage appeared at the end of the block with a flutter of white ribbons and the tossing of a horse's snowy white mane. If Cinderella had been a cowgirl, this would have been her glass carriage.

"Oh, wow."

"Wow."

There were no other words between the sisters. As the surrey rolled steadily toward them, Kristen swallowed around a sudden but definite lump in her throat.

The closer the carriage came, the more clearly she saw the faces of the couple on the high bench. The groom, a man born and bred in Rust Creek Falls like Kristen herself, was transformed. Kristen felt she'd never seen Braden Traub before. Wearing a tuxedo and black cowboy hat, he held the reins loosely in his hands and kept his face turned toward his bride. Whatever she was saying, he found fascinating. He had eyes only for her and never looked at the horses, and yet, had those horses bolted, Kristen knew he would have had them back under his control within seconds, never allowing his bride to be in danger.

"I want what they have," her sister said, reverence in her quiet tone.

"Me, too."

With a love like that, she could branch out, she could fly, she could be fearless. A love like that would be her home base, the heartbeat at the center that made everything else come alive.

Kristen laid her head on Kayla's shoulder. Her sister was supposed to be the serious twin, but Kristen suddenly felt like crying, completely undone by the romance of the moment, by what was possible between a man and woman, by what she'd never experienced herself.

I want a cowboy, capable and strong, who has eyes only for me, who loves only me, 'til death do us part.

She loved her family. She loved her hometown. And someday, she silently vowed, she would love a cowboy who was honest and true. *If only...*

If only she could find the right cowboy.

"No more city slickers for me," Kristen whispered. "I'll have the real deal, or I'll stay single forever."

"To true love." Kayla raised her cup in a toast.

Kristen knew Kayla was trying to cheer her up, so she straightened and lifted her cup. "To true love. Too bad we're out of actual punch for this toast."

"It still counts."

The carriage had been noticed by other people as

it drew closer to the park entrance. Kristen and Kayla jumped down from the fence to join the growing crowd as they followed the carriage into the heart of the park. The bride and groom's tête-à-tête was over as Braden pulled the team to a stop amid applause, good-natured catcalls about what had taken so long and a flurry of activity as the bride gathered up her skirts and bouquet, preparing to get down from the high surrey bench.

"Looks like she went traditional with a sweetheart neckline. I'm going to the other side to get a better look at her dress, okay?"

"Have fun," Kristen said as Kayla slipped through the small crowd.

Braden tied off the reins and set the brake, but for added safety amid the noisy well-wishers, two cowboys held the bridles of the white horses as Braden jumped down from the surrey. One cowboy was Sutter Traub, the town's own horse whisperer, and the other was...

The Cowboy.

Kristen's heart thudded in her chest. Another one of those giddy waves of joy passed through her, even as the lump in her throat returned. The Cowboy! She'd wished for him and he was here, so soon after she'd made her personal vow, she could hardly believe he was real.

Yet there he was, a man she'd never seen before, holding the bridle and calming the lead horse as Braden handed his bride down from the surrey. The Cowboy—*her* cowboy—was the most physically appealing man she'd ever seen. Tall, dark and handsome barely began to describe him, inadequate to cover the physical confidence he possessed as he talked with the other men and kept the horse calm at the same time. The Cowboy had an air of authority that had surely come from a lifetime of handling anything that land or livestock could throw at a man.

Kristen stepped a little to one side, and the crowd parted just enough that she could check him out from his boots and jeans—check and check—to his white button-down shirt. It looked a little dressy for the picnic; he'd probably been at the church for the ceremony. He'd cuffed up the long sleeves, revealing strong forearms.

He was tan, but so were most of the ranchers who worked outdoors. Even the summer sun couldn't lighten his nearly black hair, which he wore short, but not shorn. It was long enough that she could see a bit of a wave in it, and she knew it would feel glorious when she could run her fingers through it. When he was hers, she'd have the right to touch him and casually brush his hair back from his forehead.

Her gaze traveled past his broad shoulders to the strong hands that held the bridle. When he was hers, she'd have the right to touch him anywhere. Everywhere.

Her fingers practically tingled in anticipation.

He wore no cowboy hat, but that wasn't unusual. Half the cowboys didn't wear one when they weren't working. A lot of the local guys wore ball caps with dumb fishing mottos on them, but not her cowboy. He looked too classy for that. He looked...

She couldn't put her tingling finger on it, but he didn't quite look like any of the cowboys from around Rust Creek Falls.

He's not from around here, that's why.

Kristen would have noticed him long ago if he were a local.

Who are you?

He looked right at her, as if he'd heard her ask the question. Over the nose of the white horse, across the dozen people who milled between them, their gazes met and held.

The people and the picnic and the party disappeared. Kristen felt only the heat in his dark brown eyes. He checked her out as thoroughly as she'd been checking him out, his gaze moving across her bare shoulders, down the V of her halter dress, taking in her boots with a brief quirk of his lips. She didn't miss it, because she hadn't looked away for a second. She was no shrinking violet. When he realized she was still watching him, he lifted a brow. She tossed her hair back and shrugged one bare shoulder.

Across the crowd, they shared a slow smile. If it was true that like attracted like, then she and this man sure were alike. When people said "two peas in a pod" to Kristen, they were invariably referring to her twin, but on this special summer day, Kristen knew that she and this man were a match, too. That smile said it all.

Without warning, the horse he was holding threw its head up. The Cowboy lost his grip on the bridle and took a head-butt to the jaw. Of course, he had the bridle back in hand and the horse steady in a second, but as his dark brown eyes met Kristen's once more, his mouth quirked again in a bit of a sheepish smile.

Kristen wanted to toss her head like the snowy white horse. *What do you know? I just made a cowboy lose control of a horse.*

With a self-satisfied smile, Kristen turned toward the pavilion and the punch table. It was time to get two fresh cups and introduce herself to the man of her dreams.

* * *

Ryan rubbed his jaw as he moved with the rest of the wedding party toward the stage.

That horse had hit him as hard as the best boxer he'd ever faced down in the ring. Ryan was grateful that he knew how to take a punch. He'd managed to stay on his feet, so he hadn't looked like a complete fool in front of the exquisite woman he'd been so thoroughly distracted by. He *hoped* he hadn't looked like a fool. She'd disappeared into the crowd.

He'd find her again. The crowd here wasn't big enough for someone to get lost permanently, a point definitely in favor of small towns at the moment. He scanned the people edging the dance floor, looking for her unusual blend of delicate features and a bold gaze.

The lead singer of the band spoke into the microphone. "Ladies and gentlemen, may I have your attention please? I'd like to turn the stage over to the mayor of Rust Creek Falls, Collin Traub."

Another Traub. Was everyone in the town related to the bride and groom? And, by birth and by blood, to Ryan's own brother?

As a man about Ryan's age took the mike amid a round of applause, everyone turned to face the stage. Ryan kept looking through the crowd, scanning the backs of the heads of the people in front of him, looking for one particular woman's long hair.

The attorney side of himself, which was practically the only side he had, yanked his attention back to the stage. If he was seriously considering a move to this town, he ought to be evaluating the mayor. Local government would have a huge impact on the growth of the town and the requirements for operating a business. He couldn't prosper in a town that elected inflexible or un-qualified people to office. Ryan focused on the mayor, who still wore his tuxedo as part of the wedding party, a tuxedo with a bolo tie instead of a bow tie, of course. The men around here were never far from their cowboy roots, even in their formal attire. The mayor's welcome speech was sensible, friendly and, that most appreci-ated trait of all speeches, short.

Like Ryan's attention span. He couldn't focus on any-thing but seeing that woman again. The sun had high-lighted her hair when he'd seen her, framing her in a halo of light. He was looking for a shade of brown that shone with gold, like caramel or honey or something appealing he'd find in one of his brother's kitchens.

Unbelievable. He was turning into a poet. Beauti-ful, long hair was hardly a rarity where he came from, but Ryan would bet a million dollars that he could bury his hands in his mystery woman's hair and not have to politely avoid the anchors of fake hair extensions. So many women in Hollywood paid a fortune to look like they had the kind of hair that his boot-wearing beauty probably had gained through healthy living on a ranch.

In a flash, he saw himself burying his hands in her hair, holding her reverently as she gazed up at him from the pillow, her happiness a part of his pleasure as—

Get a grip, Ryan.

He needed to snap out of this. This day was turn-ing strange, whether it was from the strain of work and travel, the strangeness of ruminating over his siblings' marriages or the sight of a bride and groom, he couldn't say. Maybe it was the higher elevation or the cleaner air or that damned syrupy wedding punch, but he felt off.

The mayor called the bride and groom to the stage for

the best man's toast. Ryan saw the three fairy-tale grannies circulating in the crowd, coming toward him with
trays of paper cups, making sure everyone who didn't
already have a drink in hand accepted one of theirs.

Absolutely not. Ryan Roarke, attorney at law, was
not going to drink punch and spin ridiculous fantasies
about a cowgirl he hadn't even met. He turned on his
heel and headed away from the stage.

"Were you looking for this? I think you're going to
need it."

Ryan stopped abruptly, face to face with the cowgirl
herself. Had he been heading straight for her, or had she
stepped into his path? Either way, she was right here,
stunningly beautiful in denim and sunshine.

She held out a cup and nodded toward the stage behind him. "It's time for the toast."

From her, he'd take the punch. He'd probably stand
here and drink water from the river Styx, as long as he
could keep looking at her. She looked right back, her
blue eyes and heart-shaped face framed by that hair he
so keenly wanted to touch.

"I'm Kristen," she said with a smile.

He nodded gravely, aware that this was an introduction he'd remember.

"Ryan," he said, and he suddenly didn't care about
Montana or Hollywood, about mayors and law firms.
The only thing he cared about was getting to know the
woman who smiled at him in a green park on the Fourth
of July. She was worth traveling a thousand miles.

"You're not from around here, are you?" she asked.

"No, I'm not." Now that he'd decided what he wanted,
he could relax. He found himself smiling at her— with
her—without any effort at all. "But I could be."

The best man finished his toast. "To the new Mr. and Mrs. Braden Traub."

The crowd around them cheered and raised their drinks to toast the happy couple. Ryan tapped his cup to Kristen's, then watched her over the rim of his cup as they drank to the newlyweds' happiness.

The band struck up a song, a country-western ballad for the bride and groom's first dance, and the lovely Kristen turned to face the dance floor.

With the taste of that sweet punch lingering on his tongue, Ryan looked at the faces of the townspeople who were looking at the newlyweds, faces that were young and old and in between. He could practically feel the goodwill and best wishes being directed toward the center of the dance floor as the bride and groom danced alone. Where were the murmured whispers about the prenuptial agreement? The bets that this marriage wouldn't last longer than the bride's previous two or the groom's last three?

Ryan glanced down at the beautiful woman beside him. Her profile was not only pure physical perfection, but the expression on her face looked to him to be genuinely pure, as well, as open and honest as her friends' and neighbors' faces. He rubbed his still-aching jaw in disbelief. He'd had to see this to believe it, the possibility that an entire town could be truly wishing this couple a lifetime of happiness. If he wanted to fit in here, he'd have to leave some of his skepticism in LA.

The song came to an end, and Kristen bit the edge of her cup in her perfect white teeth so her hands were free to applaud with the rest of the crowd.

"Allow me." Ryan tugged the cup from her, charmed by her unselfconscious smile. He slid her empty cup inside his own, then turned to put them down on the nearest picnic table.

The lead singer of the band was doubling as the master of ceremonies. "Everyone is invited to join in for this next dance. For every couple who gets on the dance floor, the bride and groom will get another year of happiness, so don't be shy. Find your partners."

The fiddle player began the first notes of a country-western song in the clear one-two-three rhythm of a waltz.

Ryan didn't know how to two-step or boot-scoot or do any kind of country dancing, but a waltz was a waltz, whether it was danced under the chandeliers of a ballroom or on temporary wood planking in a park. He could fit in here, on the dance floor with the citizens of Rust Creek Falls, and he could waltz with the prettiest cowgirl of them all.

"May I have this dance?" he asked.

"You may." Kristen took her place in his arms with a graceful swirl of her denim dress. They began to move as one.

There was nothing that satisfied Ryan's sense of irony more than holding a beautiful woman in a ballroom dance. It seemed so civilized on the surface, when it was really a way to bring a man and a woman's bodies in sync. While they performed the prescribed moves of the centuries-old waltz, he could touch the smooth skin of her upper back, left bare by the halter dress. He could feel the incredible softness of her hair brushing his wrist as they turned in smooth circles. He could hold her so close that they stepped between each other's legs, graceful movements of her booted feet between his own.

"I love the waltz even more than the two-step," she

said, civilized small talk made while her thighs brushed against his.

"I do, too." Of course, he only knew the waltz, not the two-step, but he'd watch and learn the two-step in record time today. He intended to dance as much as possible with Kristen. This was where he wanted to be, but more importantly, this was the woman with whom he wanted to be. She moved with him effortlessly, lightly, wonderfully. The moment in time seemed perfect.

As if this dance were destined to be.

No. He didn't believe in things like destiny. Men and women had to carve their own lives out of the circumstances they were dealt. As beautiful as the woman in his arms was, as expressive as her eyes were and as easily as her smile came, it was still absurd to think she'd come into his life today because of destiny.

It was even more absurd that he was debating the possibility.

It had to be the wedding. The music. The damned effect of that punch. This was just an average town, a simple song, an average band. There was nothing special about this waltz, and the woman he shared it with was merely a pretty country girl. Those were facts, not fate.

He was an attorney, a man of letters. Like his parents, he believed in laws and rules, not in mystical interpretations of life.

But Mom, I'm not really a Roarke.

Oh, but you are. I think you were always meant to be my son, and I was always meant to be your mother.

The memory caught him by surprise. Did his analytical adoptive mother truly believe in fate, or had she said those words to comfort a boy who'd never forgotten being left behind?

"Are you okay?"

Kristen's soft question brought him back to reality. He gave her a polite, reassuring smile that was little more than a reflex.

"Yes, I'm fine."

How odd that she'd asked. He hadn't changed the rhythm of their dancing or the way he was holding her as he'd remembered his mother's words about destiny. On the surface, everything was the same, all smooth skin, smooth steps, synchronicity. And yet, Kristen had noticed his subtle change in mood.

She was more than a pretty country girl, and he couldn't fool himself otherwise. There was something special about her. This day had become so much more than a weekend away from the rat race. This town, this celebration, this woman all combined to make Ryan feel like he was standing at the brink of something new. Did she feel it, too?

He'd known her for minutes. He couldn't ask her if she believed in destiny, but he could hold her as the band played, so he lost himself in her blue eyes as they waltzed together under the big Montana sky.

The Cowboy didn't seem inclined to make small talk, and she loved dancing too much to want to chatter about nothing when she could be enjoying the music and the motion, so they danced in silence as one song led to the next.

Occasionally, though, she noticed someone on the dance floor would seem to recognize Ryan, and they'd exchanged a friendly nod.

Who are you? Where did you come from?

She was half-afraid to ask. He was too perfect for

her—he even wanted to dance every song, just like she did—so she could almost imagine she'd conjured him up. Like a figment of her imagination, he could disappear as easily as he'd arrived.

Sooner than she would have liked, the band stopped playing and the wedding cake was cut with the usual ceremony. It went without saying that after being so in tune with Ryan on the dance floor, they'd take their cake slices and walk in step toward one of the many card tables that had been set up under the park's shade trees.

Dancing had been all about communicating with movement, but Kristen had no desire to sit across from the man and eat wedding cake in silence.

"Will you be in town long?" she asked, jumping in with both feet and asking the most important question first. Her brothers would probably shake their heads and say she was being too bold again, but her sister would probably tell her she'd make a good journalist, getting right to the point.

"Just until tomorrow." Ryan set his plate aside and gave her his full attention, arms crossed on the table, gaze on her face.

Shivers ran down her spine. Hadn't she vowed to find a man who paid attention to her and only her?

Her sister had been so serious as they'd sat on the fence, telling Kristen she shouldn't dare the universe with her declaration about not falling in love today. If the universe had decided to prove Kristen wrong by setting the perfect man in front of her as a temptation— well, heck, that wasn't much of a punishment. She'd said she wouldn't fall in love, but a girl would be crazy not to reconsider after meeting a man like Ryan.

She flipped her hair back over her shoulder to keep

it out of the white icing. "What did you mean when I asked you if you were from around here, and you said you could be?"

"It's a thought I've been entertaining. It might be time to get out of the fast lane and settle down, somewhere away from the madding crowds. I like Montana."

She licked a little frosting off her finger as she listened. Not a lot of cowboys would describe their lives as being in the fast lane.

"I've visited a few places in Montana over the past couple of years," he said, "but right now, Rust Creek Falls looks just about perfect."

He was looking right at her. Another shiver went down her spine, and she decided the sensation was as delicious as the cake. She was already half in love with Ryan. He was handsome and humorous, with a cowboy's good manners and rock-hard body, and most of all, he seemed to be interested in everything she had to say. If he was considering a permanent move to Rust Creek Falls, the universe had won the dare. She'd fall in love today and be happy that the universe had known better than she had.

"Are you a Traub?" he asked.

"No, I'm a Dalton."

"Good. I was starting to think everyone was a Traub except me."

It could have been her overactive actress's imagination, but he'd said that line with a touch of wistfulness.

"Don't feel too left out. There are oodles of Daltons and Crawfords and Stricklands here, too. You don't have to be a Traub to live in Rust Creek Falls."

One of the Traubs in question passed near their table,

Collin Traub, the mayor, to be exact. He nodded at Ryan, who hesitated just a moment before nodding back.

"You know Collin?" Kristen asked. That was excellent. The more ties Ryan had to this town, the more reasons he had to stay.

"Collin who?"

"The man you just nodded at."

"No, not really." He looked away from her toward Collin, then glanced around the other tables, but his gaze didn't stop on anyone in particular.

He knew no one, then. That could be a lonely feeling. Kristen remembered feeling lost on campus when she'd first arrived at the University of Montana. The modest city of Missoula had seemed like a giant metropolis of heartless strangers.

She didn't want Ryan to feel that way, not in her town. She slid his discarded plate back in front of him, took his fork and scooped up a chunk from the best part of the slice, the corner between the top and side that had the most frosting. Maybe a little sugar would bring the smile back to his face.

She held the fork up. "Here, eat this. You can't let homemade cake go to waste."

He didn't smile. One brow lifted slightly at her impulsive gesture. She hadn't thought it through, but if she'd expected him to take the fork from her, she'd been wrong. Instead, with his intense gaze never leaving her face, he leaned forward and ate the bite off the fork as she held it.

It was a move for lovers. There was an intimacy to feeding someone. She could imagine that mouth on her skin, tasting her, taking his time, savoring the moment...

Kristen sat back in the metal chair and lifted the hair off the back of her neck. The heat of the day hadn't dissipated, although it was getting close to suppertime, but she knew the real reason she was warm, and it had to do with a man who was just a bit older, just a bit more self-possessed, just a bit more devilish, than the men she usually dated. The universe had outdone itself.

She leaned forward once more, determined to match Ryan's confidence. "Collin seemed to recognize you, even if you don't know him."

Ryan nodded once, a crisp acknowledgment of her observation. "I'm surprised. I didn't think anyone around here would recognize me."

The proverbial lightbulb went off over Kristen's head. What kind of cowboy talked about crowds and fast lanes? What kind of cowboy got recognized by people who were strangers to him?

A cowboy who starred in the rodeo, that was who. Collin Traub had once been a rodeo rider, and he recognized Ryan.

In ninth grade, Kristen had gone through her rodeo phase. She'd been able to name all the best cutting horses and recite the bloodlines of all the barrel-racing champions, but even then, she'd been more interested in boys than livestock. She'd been able to name the most handsome bull riders as well as the most noble horses. She'd begged her parents to drive her all the way to the Missoula Stampede. Afterward, she'd cut photos of her favorite cowboys out of the color program and taped them to the inside of her locker.

She'd outgrown that infatuation. Cowboy crushes had given way to movie star mania, and she'd left the ranch to taste life on the stage. Now everything seemed to be coming full circle. Here she was, eating wedding cake on the Fourth of July with a rodeo rider. The Cowboy. *Her* Cowboy.

Bravo, Universe. Bravo.

Since the professional rodeo circuit ran nearly all its events in July and August, she wasn't surprised Ryan had to leave town tomorrow. It was only surprising he'd been able to stop here today. He'd hoped Rust Creek Falls would give him a break from his everyday life in the fast lane. When people recognized Ryan, he returned all their nods politely, but he hadn't been striking up conversations or handing out autographs. He didn't want to play up his life on the professional circuit obviously.

She wasn't about to ask him about his life on the rodeo circuit, either. Her days as a fourteen-year-old fan were long behind her. Now she was the woman who'd fed a man cake while he'd devoured her with his eyes. That man was the person she wanted to get to know.

She only had today to do it. One day for him to decide if he'd ever come back to Rust Creek Falls—or rather, one day for her to decide if she ought to convince him.

One day that could decide the rest of their lives.

Chapter Three

Kristen missed the feel of having Ryan's arms around her, but even the most die-hard dancers had to take a break when the band stopped playing.

As the next band set up its equipment, Kristen got to know more about Ryan than the clean smell of his dress shirt and the way their bodies fit together in a slow dance. Sitting together on a corner of the stage, they discussed everything from favorite sports teams to favorite seasons. She loved the Green Bay Packers and Christmas. He preferred the New York Yankees and summer. He was the middle child of three; she was the baby of five— even if she was only separated from number four by a few minutes. His siblings didn't live in the same state as he did; her entire family lived in the same town.

"In other words," Kristen said, "we have everything in common."

"A perfectly logical conclusion." Ryan kept his expression perfectly serious, too, although she knew he was teasing her.

"It is." She polished off her punch and set her cup down, prepared to check off her conclusions one by one on her fingers. "We both enjoy watching professional sports. We each have one sister. We each have at least one older brother. We talk to our families all the time."

That made four. She wiggled her pinky finger, the last one she hadn't checked off. "And we both love to dance. Like I said, we've got everything in common."

His slow smile was just about the sexiest thing about him, and considering everything about him was sexy, that was saying something. "I have no objection to any of that. But for the sake of accuracy, and to give myself an excuse to keep watching a beautiful woman as she makes an animated argument, I have to point out that our preferred seasons are opposites."

"That is a fact." Kristen was never one to back down from a challenge. She lowered her voice. "Having one thing we don't agree on keeps it…interesting."

His gaze dropped to her mouth. He was interested, all right.

"Differences can be good. For example, you're a boy. I'm a girl." She pointed at his chest, then at hers, his gaze dropping farther, down to where she pressed her finger to her heart. "You're summer, I'm Christmas."

Just as their eyes had met over the head of that white horse, his gaze suddenly left her finger and focused right on her. He looked serious for real this time, no joke to it. "I believe if anyone could make Christmas better, it would be you."

Kristen leaned in a little closer. "If every Fourth of

July could be spent with you, I'd start to look forward to summer as soon as the first snow fell."

He was going to kiss her. Right here, sitting on the edge of the stage in the middle of the town's celebration, he was going to kiss her, and she felt her heart beating under her own fingertip in anticipation.

But he didn't. In silence, he looked at her for one second longer, then lifted his cup to her in a salute, and downed his punch.

"Hi, Kristen."

She looked up to see one of the guys from her high school drama club days standing over her with his guitar.

"My band's on for the next hour. Make sure you clap even if we suck, okay?"

"You'll be great." Kristen stood along with Ryan, and yielded the stage with a wave of her hand. "It's all yours. Break a leg."

The dance floor began filling up again. She spotted Kayla dancing with someone else Kristen hadn't seen in a while, one of their brothers' friends who'd been a few years ahead of them in high school.

High school. Again. She was twenty-five. She didn't want her life to revolve around high school. Hadn't she evolved since then?

Yes, of course she had. She was just overthinking everything.

There was something in the air today. The town seemed different somehow. Maybe because a police officer she didn't recognize had walked past her, heading toward the fountain and the sounds of a fight, although public brawls were rare in Rust Creek Falls. Maybe because a high-stakes poker game had kicked off at the Ace in the Hole bar, and lots of rowdier folk were drifting that way. Members of the wedding party were sneaking off, too, headed for the park exit, where the groom's truck was now parked in preparation for the getaway.

A getaway. It sounded appealing on one level, but she'd already been there, done that. She'd gotten a college degree, even lived in New York City one summer, and then returned to Rust Creek Falls by choice. She wasn't stuck here; she was happy here. People visited and ended up staying permanently, which was proof enough that the town was great. If the Cowboy settled down here, maybe she'd feel more settled herself.

"Where do you want to go?" Ryan asked.

Kristen almost laughed at the timing. "Is that a trick question? Do you mean where do I want to go in life or just in the next five minutes?"

"They say the journey of a lifetime starts with a single step." A smile teased the corners of his mouth. "I've always thought that put a lot of pressure on choosing where to step."

"Let's be daring and step this way, then." She stood shoulder to shoulder with him and deliberately raised her knee high, then took a giant step in the direction of the fence where she'd sat with her sister, waiting for true love to arrive.

Those moments with her sister seemed prophetic now. Her emotions seemed wild and free today, swinging from a kind of drunken silliness to intensely important. Through it all, she'd had Ryan's arm around her on the dance floor, Ryan sitting across from her at the table, Ryan walking beside her now, matching her stride for stride after that first silly step.

"I think the bride and groom are going to make a break for it," Kristen said. "We can wave goodbye from the fence." The fireworks wouldn't begin until after ten since the sun set so late in July, but Kristen had noticed the newest Traub couple saying goodbye to their bridesmaids and groomsmen.

"I guess they're not too worried about seeing fireworks tonight," she said. "Maybe they'll watch them from the balcony of Maverick Manor. That's where they're staying. They'll fly out tomorrow on their honeymoon."

"I'm sure they'll see fireworks tonight." Ryan kept his serious poker face in place as they reached the fence.

She did a little Groucho Marx imitation, wagging her eyebrows and pretending she held a cigar. "Fireworks? Is that what the kids are calling it these days?"

Ryan gave her a boost to sit on the top rail. His laughter was as warm and masculine as the brief touch of his hands on her waist. He stayed on the ground, leaning against the fence, and crossed his ankles as he settled in for the wait.

Kristen enjoyed the novel position of being able to look down on him. All that rich, dark hair, just waiting for her to mess up —and if she sat at just the right angle, she could see a bit of his chest below the unbuttoned V at his throat. He had no farmer's tan, just more yummy bronzed skin...

He looked up at her, catching her staring.

She was so busted, but she didn't bite her lip or blush or look away. She'd learned a long time ago to brazen out embarrassing situations.

"You were sitting right here when I first saw you," he said.

If he'd seen her sitting on the fence, then he'd been

her before the carriage had arrived. She hadn't spotted him first, after all.

Why didn't you approach me right away? That was too bold even for her. She tried a different question. "What did you think about the girl on the fence?"

"That you were happy. You were laughing with your sister. I envied you."

"For having a sister?" She shook her head and answered her own question. "No, you have a sister of your own. You envied us for laughing. Are you not happy?"

"Is that a trick question? Do you mean for the next five minutes, or do you mean my life in general?"

She smiled at his light words, but her curiosity grew. "Let's start with at the moment."

He didn't answer her immediately, looking away to gaze calmly at the horizon and the first streaks of the sunset appearing over the mountain peaks.

She thunked her heels on the railing, stopped herself and smoothed her skirt over her knees. She'd rather be smoothing his dark hair.

"I met a wonderful woman today," he said, "and she's tolerating my company without complaint. I'm happy."

"Good answer, but that was a mighty long pause." She wanted to see his face, so she climbed down and leaned against the fence beside him, watching his profile as he watched the horizon. "I thought 'Are you happy?' would be an easy yes or no."

"I don't usually think in terms of being happy. It sounds frivolous."

She slipped her hand in his. It felt familiar, for they'd been holding hands in the traditional ballroom holds that went with the waltz and the two-step, but it also felt significant. There was no excuse of a dance this time.

He rubbed his thumb along the back of her hand, as if they often held hands while they talked.

"It's not frivolous, though," he said. "Happiness is serious. It's the driving force behind our lives. 'The pursuit of happiness' is a legal right. We all have the right to try to find it."

"To try." She echoed the words he'd emphasized. "Have you been successful in your attempt?"

He raised their joined hands and placed a light kiss on her knuckle.

"Today, yes."

She made him happy.

She sucked in a little breath at the compliment. But he'd said *today*, as if happiness were a rare occurrence.

"Isn't your life usually happy?"

"I'm working on it," he said with all the confidence of a man who was certain he'd solve a problem soon.

That kind of confidence must be nice to have. "How do you work on happiness?"

"My job isn't as fulfilling as it once was. I need to reevaluate. Refocus."

Kristen could imagine that even if he was born for the rodeo, it could easily be more stressful than happy. Rodeo careers were physically punishing and therefore short. He looked to be about thirty. He'd said he was considering a change of pace, getting out of the fast lane, but maybe he was being forced to by circumstances.

"It's more than my career, though. I find myself envying my brother and sister." He paused, and Kristen suspected that he was giving these thoughts voice for the first time. "Within a year of each other, they got married. My sister had a baby just a few months ago, and my brother is expecting his first."

"So now they're happy?"

"I wouldn't have said they were unhappy people before. They had great careers and a family they could rely on, but I can see that they have more now. Even though they weren't missing anything, they found something else, anyway, and now they are really living. Or more accurately, I should say they found some*one* else. Not a thing, a person."

A little distance away, the bride laughingly yelped as she and Braden were pelted with birdseed as they ran toward the opening in the fence. The groom's black truck was parked on the street beyond.

Ryan didn't move as the whole wedding party came closer. "I'm starting to believe it's not how much fame and fortune you have, but whether or not you have someone by your side."

As Braden and his bride ran past them, Kristen waved and shouted "good luck," but they already seemed incredibly lucky to her. She and her sister had started the afternoon by wishing they had what the newlyweds had. It hadn't occurred to Kristen that she ought to do something about it besides hope and wait. Ryan was right about pursuing happiness. It was sobering to realize that she'd been so passive about her life.

"I'm sorry," Ryan said quietly, and she realized he was studying her closely. "Here we are at a happy occasion, and I'm being too maudlin and reflective. Montana has that effect on me."

"Montana makes you sad?"

"Montana makes me think. I wish I didn't have to

leave tomorrow. I feel more at peace here than any-where else."

Then he'd be coming back.

She felt her buoyant mood returning. The truth was, no matter how much she admired Ryan's determination, hoping and wishing had worked for Kristen. Who was she to double-guess how the universe worked?

The groom opened the passenger door of his truck and began helping his bride gather up her full skirts so she could climb in. He knew which door to open for her because his friends had very helpfully used white shoe polish on the window to write the words *Bride Goes Here* with an arrow.

Kristen gave Ryan a gentle nudge with her shoulder. "The truck isn't as romantic as the carriage, but infinitely more practical. It wouldn't be too romantic to ride off into the sunset and then spend the first hours of your wedding night unhitching a team and stabling the horses, would it?"

"I would never argue with a cowgirl. If you say un-hitching horses would delay the fireworks, then I trust you."

"You're just humoring me now." He was doing that serious-joking thing again, implying she knew more about horses than he did.

"I'd bet the ranch that you live on a ranch. You must know horses."

The black truck drove off, the cluster of empty cans that were tied to its tailpipe cluttering loudly behind it. Ryan gave their joined hands a tug and started leading her along the fence, away from the send-off crowd who were now milling about.

"I do live on a ranch, but what made you guess that?

Do I smell like I mucked the stables this morning? I'm not saying I did, but is there hay in my hair? Or do I just snicker like a horse when I laugh?"

He stopped walking once they reached a cluster of spruce trees. She moved a little closer into his personal space.

He didn't back up an inch. This close, in order for him to look down at her, his eyes got that heavy-lidded look. Bedroom eyes.

"Those aren't the clues that you live on a ranch."

"The boots, then?" She felt a little nervous, a little excited. Ryan had been willing to follow her playful lead all day, but the way he looked at her now left no doubt that he was a man who knew where the game was leading—and who'd know exactly what to do when they got there.

"You must be a cowgirl because you have incredible stamina," he murmured, "on the dance floor."

A shiver threatened to run down her spine.

"You practically glow with health. Your hair, your skin. You. Every single inch of you." They were so very close, bodies nearly touching in the quiet twilight, the sounds of the band and the crowd far in the background.

She wanted to kiss him. She could go up on tiptoe and taste his lips as she'd been dying to do forever, but she wanted him to initiate it. Good girls didn't steal the first kiss. How such an old-fashioned notion had been ingrained in her brain was beyond her, but there it was. She kept holding his hand, wanting so much more.

An evening breeze carried the crisp air from the distant mountains into the park, stirring the evergreen sent of the spruce trees, blowing a few strands of her loose hair over her cheeks. Ryan brushed them back, those bedroom eyes making the touch of his hand on her hair as sensual a feeling as she'd ever experienced.

As Ryan tamed her hair, she stayed still, wishing, wishing. His body was so much larger than hers, his muscles moving under the polished cotton of his shirt with the gentle motion of his hand.

Kiss me.

He let the last lock of her hair go, and his fingers brushed the bare skin of her shoulders, then higher, a smooth, light run up the length of her neck, a barely there brush of fingertips on her jaw.

Kiss me, kiss me.

The gentle touch of his fingertips was replaced by the sure warmth of his palm as he cupped her face in his hand. Her eyes closed.

Kiss me.

"Kristen Dalton." When he spoke her name, she felt the whisper of his breath on her lips. "Where have you been all my life?"

"Right here, waiting for you to find some happiness."

He kissed her, and, oh, it was a glorious feeling of soft lips and restraint, a tender you-may-kiss the bride moment. He ended it too soon, and she opened her eyes. Behind him, the sunset had come into its full colors over the snow-capped mountains that had defined the horizon her entire life.

Had she expected the kiss to make him happy? He wasn't smiling. His gaze was direct, his face so serious it was almost a frown.

Before she could say something, anything at all, he let go of her hand to hold her face between both of his palms. Words fled. He pulled her to him for a kiss that rocked her world. Rougher, more greedy. Possessive, more passionate.

Her fingers slid into the hair at the nape of his neck as he pulled her into him more tightly than any dance had allowed. She felt the hard planes of his body, and everything soft in her wanted to give in and melt in the safety of his arms.

She kissed him until his arms felt more sexy than safe. She kissed him until the only reason she was standing was that he held her up.

If he could have laid her down, if they hadn't been hiding in plain sight in a corner of the town park, she would have gone willingly. It would be madness, but finally, she understood the crazy things couples did. Love at first sight, undeniable desire, life-changing decisions made in a split second—it all made perfect sense.

He ended the kiss when she would not have, could not have. As they held tightly to each other, she could feel every breath that filled his chest. She panted softly herself, as if she'd run a mile. Run a mile, and won the race. The endorphin rush, the thrill of knowing that *this* had happened, that she'd found the one man with whom she connected more strongly than she'd known was possible, was almost frightening.

He placed gentle kisses on her temple and at the corner of her eye, little echoes of the passion that had just obliterated all her thoughts. "You smell fantastic, by the way."

It took her a second to remember what they'd been talking about before the kiss. "Not like a stable?"

"Like summer."

"Your favorite."

And then they were kissing again, hungry and intense. She wanted him with a desperation that threatened once more to make her shameless. He broke off the kiss but clutched her closer. His breath was harsh in her ear. "That was damned..."

"Scary?" she whispered.

"Powerful."

She pulled back a little bit. All the emotions overwhelming her were reflected in his expression, too. It made her feel even closer to him, to the one person who was weathering this unpredictable storm with her.

"I think..." She didn't have any clear thoughts, only feelings. Crazy, uninhibited feelings today, here in the town park. She looked up at him through her lashes, hoping to lighten the intensity. "I think we just found a great way to pursue happiness."

His smile was brief. "I still have to leave tomorrow. The fact that I'm falling for the most beautiful girl in the world doesn't change the fact that I have people depending on me."

Falling for her. He was falling for her, and everything was right in the world—except that he had to leave tomorrow. She didn't like it, but she understood it. The rodeo wasn't so different from the theater in many ways.

"The show must go on," she said.

"And on, and on. I get to enjoy the victories for about five seconds before the next challenge begins. But we still have tonight. How would you like to spend it?"

He had to ask?

She kissed him this time. He responded instantly, perfectly, opening his mouth to her demands, anchoring her to him with his hands. He kept the kiss from exploding into desperation this time, setting a slower pace, a more luxurious exploration. It was divine to kiss him, the sensation so perfect that it was like see-ing a new color she'd never known existed or hearing a beautiful piece of music for the first time.

He broke off the kiss with a softly spoken *damn*.

"Ryan," she begged.

"I know." He tucked her securely against his chest. She breathed in the warm skin exposed at his throat. "I know."

Where are you staying? Let's leave the park now. The words wouldn't come, too many years of that good-girl upbringing preventing her from saying what she wanted.

"I have to leave tomorrow," he said, so quietly that she wondered if he was speaking to himself. "It would be…we should just…we shouldn't."

There was nothing else to say. A part of her wanted to plead childishly, *Don't you want to?* Or more impor-tantly, *Don't you want me?*

She stayed silent, her cheek to his chest. He was older than she was and almost certainly more experienced, but she trusted herself to answer those questions. Yes, he wanted to. Yes, he wanted *her*. She could feel the muscle tension in his body. He was deliberately keeping himself under control. His breathing was steady only because he was requiring himself to breathe steadily.

He was being a true cowboy, one with all the cour-tesy and respect that a gentleman traditionally showed a lady. Hadn't she vowed she'd settle for nothing less?

Frankly, she wished the universe hadn't listened to her quite so thoroughly on that point. This man was hers, and they would be together sooner or later, and her body was certainly eager for sooner. With a sigh, she lifted her head and stepped back just a tiny bit, keeping her arms looped around his waist.

"I guess it's too early for fireworks," she said.

The corner of his mouth quirked in that hint of amusement she was coming to love. When the breeze blew her hair forward again, she tried to toss it back with a shake of her head, refusing to let go of Ryan.

He pushed her hair back for her and kept his hands on either side of her face. "I can hardly believe you're real."

"Wanna kiss me again to be sure?"

He laughed at that, a much needed break in the tension. "I know you're real. Amazingly, incredibly real. But today hasn't been. This isn't my real life." He let go of her face.

"But it could be. That's what you came here to decide."

He stepped back, and she let him go. Desire that could not be satisfied wasn't a desirable state to be in. But then he turned away from her—and from the sunset, the mountains, everything. He braced his hands on the fence and looked down at the railing.

As if the man hadn't already stirred up enough emotions in her, she now felt the tender tug of sympathy. There was some pain in the way he bowed his head as well as strength in the set of his jaw. It must be hard for a man's career to be ending when most people were just hitting their strides. The rodeo was unforgiving, and Ryan seemed determined to choose his next step in a purely objective manner. But any man who knew horses and victory and defeat, any man who appreciated music and summer and family, must have a heart.

She hoped he'd listen to his.

"Should I leave my current life and start a new one in

Rust Creek Falls? That's the essential question. I can't drop the commitments I've already made. Being impulsive would hurt too many people. Today was supposed to just be a first step. I only came to see the town and begin evaluating my options."

"That's perfectly logical." She said it with a straight face, the way he had over dinner.

He glanced sideways at her. "You don't think so?"

"I think you've already made up your mind. All this ponderous decision-making isn't necessary, but if it makes you feel better, ponder away."

Her attempts at humor were helping her regain some equilibrium, anyway. She turned around to lean back on the fence, resting her elbows on the top rail and hitching the heel of one boot on the bottom. She let her head drop back far enough so she could look up at the darkening sky.

She managed at least sixty seconds of silence before peeking at Ryan. He'd stopped brooding at the fence, at least, and was watching her. She supposed she bore some resemblance to the ranch dogs who flopped onto their backs when they wanted a belly rub.

"It would have been easier if I'd never kissed you." Judging from the deep bass in his voice, maybe she looked better than she thought.

"Then I'm glad you kissed me."

"Kristen Dalton, you are a serious complication."

"Nope." She pushed off the fence and mirrored his stance, arms crossed over her chest, standing solidly on her own two cowboy-booted feet. "I'm just a big, positive check mark on your balance sheet. You're determined to decide your next step very methodically, I can tell. When you make your official list of pluses and minuses, you'll put me on the plus side in bold letters."

"Kristen."

She waited as he tried to think of the right thing to say, but apparently she'd said something so logical, he couldn't refute it. It was almost as good as making him forget to hold the horse earlier in the day.

"In the meantime, we could stay here, alone, practically invisible to everyone else once darkness falls. Fireworks of one kind or another are bound to happen. That would surely go in the plus column."

He acted like he was giving the idea serious consideration. "Being arrested for public indecency would give me a chance to see the local jail cells firsthand. A well-run police force would go in the plus column."

"I'm sure the cells are lovely, but someone would have to catch us in the act first, and these spruce trees are mighty hard to see through. Did you notice they smell like Christmas?"

"Now that you mention it." He seemed faintly surprised at her words.

"It's the perfect blend for us, summer and Christmas."

Ryan moved to escort her out of their little corner of the world. "I think we need to keep ourselves busy while we wait for the fireworks. Should we head back to the dance floor?"

"You came here to see Rust Creek Falls. I just so happen to have known this town for twenty-five years. I'll give you a tour. You can rack up more check marks in the plus column."

Kristen pointed toward the gate that the bride and groom had used to leave on their honeymoon. "The first step is right this way. You're going to love everything you see."

She glanced up at him just as he said, "I think I already do."

He'd been looking at her, not at the town, when he'd said it.

If she could have blown a kiss to the universe, she would have.

Chapter Four

Ryan was losing his mind—but at least he was losing it while having one of the greatest days of his life with the most enchanting woman he'd ever met. He enjoyed every moment in Kristen's company, every teasing comment, every exuberant laugh, every country-western dance.

But that kiss had been a whole different world. The first taste of her mouth had rocketed into an intense need to make her his, desire going from zero to sixty in one second. It had been primal, almost frightening in its intensity. He was thirty-three years old, yet a kiss, a single kiss while fully clothed, had him rethinking everything he thought he knew about craving a woman's touch.

One particular woman's touch. Kristen Dalton, who somewhere between a waltz and a two-step had made a better life seem possible.

Kristen stopped outside the park and waited for one

lone pickup truck to pass them, then led him across the street. As they walked, he put his arm around her shoulders, left so thankfully bare by her summer dress. She slid her arm around his waist, a move as natural as if they'd been lovers forever. There was a rightness to it.

A rightness? There was that fate nonsense again. When had he ever thought or felt or wondered about the rightness of a casual touch?

Give up the analysis. Just enjoy the rest of the day.

"First stop on your tour. The local junior-senior high school. Go Grizzlies." She beamed at the brick structure, a plain two-story rectangle, government architecture at its most common.

"*The* school? There's only one?"

"There's an elementary school, but this is the one and only high school. It's very important to Rust Creek Falls. Whether you're a teenager or not, this is the hot place to be on a Friday night. It's our number one cure for cabin fever in the winter. When you can't stand seeing solid white out your window, come to the gym for the varsity basketball game. The whole town will be here, not to mention everyone from the opposing team's town. The clash of school colors will dazzle you after months of snow. There's pop and soft pretzels, and you can cheer the players and boo the referee. It'll get you through until spring."

He pretended to consider the building seriously. "It sounds like an item for the minus column. Solid white out your window that gives you cabin fever? Not so great."

"The snow isn't the town's fault, so you can't ding us for that. But to provide a cure for cabin fever?" She spread her hands out to encompass the school. "Definite plus."

It was ludicrous to think that he, Ryan Roarke, with his courtside seats at NBA playoffs, would count it as a *definite plus* to sit on gym bleachers and watch adolescents attempt to shoot hoops. He was accustomed to watching the best athletes in the world. He expected to be entertained by world-class professional cheerleaders. He knew how—

Professional cheerleader. He'd completely forgotten the Laker Girl he'd so recently left. She hadn't entered his thoughts for more than a moment after they'd parted ways, although they'd dated on and off for some time. And yet, had his sister not mentioned this town-wide wedding celebration, he would probably have been with that cheerleader right now, and she with him, simply for the convenience of having an appropriate "plus one" for a yachting weekend that was more about business than relaxation.

He knew other men envied him for never lacking in female companionship, but today—this crazy, emotional day—it seemed more pathetic than prestigious to waste time with a woman who meant nothing to him.

He looked down at Kristen. She was gesturing toward the distant baseball diamond as she told him about more school sporting events, her face radiant even as darkness settled around them. It had been easy for him to come to Montana and forget about a woman in LA, but Ryan knew he'd find it impossible to forget about Kristen when he left Montana. If he could take with him some of her zest for life, he would.

"You must have enjoyed being a student here. Or was it a torturous teenage experience?"

"Ah, another trick question. I want you to think I'm cool, so I should say high school was cool. But I don't want you to think I was too cool, so I should make sure you know I had my moments of angst. Honestly, I was always afraid I didn't fit in."

"You? Not fit in?" The idea was laughable.

"I was pretty insecure at sixteen, but I guess that's normal. Isn't it?"

Something in her voice, a trace of that insecurity, made him look at her more closely.

"Didn't you worry if you fit in?" she persisted.

He had, but it had been assumed by the adults in his life that it was a consequence of his early childhood. He'd been particularly withdrawn his sophomore year, and he'd overheard his parents debating whether or not they should take him to a psychologist. They'd wondered if it was normal teenage angst, as Kristen called it, or damage from being abandoned by his birth mother.

They'd concluded it was just a normal phase, but as he'd eavesdropped on their conversation, he'd concluded the opposite. He could remember the hem of his mother's dress as she'd walked away. No one else had a memory like that. Not his brother, not his sister, not his parents. There had to be something horribly wrong with him.

Thankfully, Kristen had never known that kind of pain. She'd introduced him to her twin on the dance floor. She'd waved at a man she'd told him was one of her brothers, although Ryan had already guessed as much from their resemblance. Kristen had been born into a close family, not adopted after being left behind. She'd been raised with love from the first day of her life.

It was incredible to hear her say that she'd worried

about fitting in. Kristen was outgoing and friendly in a natural way. She had to be welcome everywhere she went. If a woman like Kristen had spent her high school years wondering if she belonged, then maybe his parents had been right. Maybe his teenage years hadn't been anything out of the ordinary.

Kristen was looking up at him, patiently waiting for his answer.

"I worried, too."

But maybe that was normal. It was a radical thought.

She gave him a squeeze. "I told you we had so much in common."

He said nothing, thrown off-kilter by yet another loop on the day's emotional roller coaster, but then Kristen rested her head on his shoulder, and everything seemed to right itself again.

"I've been trying to get some after-school activities going here. The principal said the budget wouldn't allow for another student club. Maybe next semester. Always next semester. Anyway, are you ready for the next stop on your tour? There's a really great donut shop on the next block. It might be worth two pluses."

A teacher. Kristen didn't just live on a ranch and care for horses; she was a teacher. She spoke as if he'd already known it, but he'd missed it somehow—probably while he'd been tracing her curves, gliding his palms over the material of her dress.

He wanted to know more about her. He wasn't so blinded by lust that he'd overlooked her as a person. In fact, every detail about her out of bed contributed to how strongly he wanted her *in* his bed—but currently, his bed was in Los Angeles. Whether or not it should stay there was the question this little tour was supposed to help answer.

Kristen was more interesting to him than the town. He sat on the base of the high school sign and made room for her to sit with him. "What are you going to do if the principal puts you off until 'next semester' again?"

"I'll keep doing what I'm doing. There's always plenty of work at the ranch." She straightened out one leg and studied the toe of her boot. "The last time I interviewed with him, I hit the feed store on the way home. I remember thinking how odd it was to wear my nice professional pumps and carry chicken feed."

"It must be frustrating to have gotten that college degree and then not use it."

It was the wrong thing to say. Kristen stared at him, her blue eyes wide, and then she seemed to crumple a little, sagging against the school sign. "I hadn't thought of it that way. I just thought it would be good to have something to do outside of the ranch. Kayla does some copyediting for the local paper. I kind of envy her for having a little desk in an office in town. But wasting my degree? That sounds terrible."

Ryan wished he could take the words back. As an attorney, he knew that was impossible. They were out there now, on the record. For Kristen, though, he had to try.

"Forget I said that. You belong on that family ranch. You're lucky to be part of something like that."

"No, you made a good point. If I'm not going to use my degree, why did I bother getting it?"

"Pursuing an education is never a waste."

She wrinkled her nose.

He tried again. "Education is its own reward."

His irrepressible Kristen started to smile. "You're trying to make me feel better, aren't you?"

"I truly don't think it's a waste to have gotten an education." As always, her smile was infectious. He felt a little sheepish, but he smiled back. "And yes, I really wish I hadn't said that. I didn't mean to make you sad."

"No apology necessary. You said Montana didn't make you sad, it made you think. You're just making me think."

"And that's a good thing?"

"It's good, but it's not the best thing. The best thing is when you're making it impossible for me to think at all."

With a swish of denim, she stood and turned and then nestled on his lap. Everything he wanted in the world was suddenly in his arms, and it was all Kristen. The weight of her body, the feel of her skin, the smell of her hair and the taste of her mouth overwhelmed his senses. All his worries about normalcy were obliterated. This passion was far outside the boring bounds of normalcy, because the woman in his arms was extraordinary.

Ryan never wanted normal again.

Kristen continued the town tour under strict orders: no kissing.

She and Ryan couldn't seem to master a simple kiss. Outside the school, she'd wanted to be playful when she'd sat in his lap, but once the kissing started, it had gotten serious, fast.

Again.

Hard sidewalks had a way of imposing a limit on how far even consenting adults could go, however, so they'd eventually resumed their little tour, holding hands as they headed up the next street toward Daisy's Donuts.

"This building is one of the oldest ones, built in 1889. The rest of the brick ones on this side of the street are from the years the railroad was built. My mom remembers when this building was a five and dime, but now it's a boring old dentist office. It was built in 1909."

"Did they make you memorize this in school, or do you just have a good memory for that sort of thing?"

An unladylike snort of laughter escaped her. She'd been pulling the wool over Ryan's eyes for a full block of Victorian buildings.

"The only reason I know how old these buildings are is because almost all of them have the year they were built carved in stone. Look up there, at the very top of that building. It must have been a common thing to chisel the year into the keystone or the crenellation or whatever that's called."

"Trickery. Devious residents in this town. I think that has to go in the minus column."

"It's not a minus that a Rust Creek Falls native can read a date that is written in stone. If anything, it proves that the town has intelligent residents."

She stopped in front of the donut shop and faced Ryan. "They serve coffee and bear claws here that count as a plus. They get points for being extra cute, too. Bear claws in the home of the Grizzlies. Bears. Grizzlies. Why aren't you laughing?"

"Do we have any minuses yet? One?"

She stepped closer and wrapped her arms around his waist. "Considering how I want you to come back the first possible moment you can, it's not in my best interest to point out any downsides. You're looking pretty serious. Are you thinking of something negative?"

"Not when I'm looking at you."

She didn't know whether to melt into a puddle or squeeze him fiercely at those words. Her body kind of shivered in a mixture of the two. He broke his own rule with a swift kiss, then resumed their walk.

They didn't have far to go. Now that Kristen saw it through his eyes, the town really was small. At the end of the street, she turned to walk a block along the river that had overflowed its banks two years ago. Tonight, the river was as tame and steady as it had been most of her life. The town might be really small, but it was really perfect.

Kristen tried to imagine what was missing, what kind of thing would count as a minus when Ryan went through the pros and cons to make the decision she was certain his heart had already made.

When she'd moved away, finances had been in her minus column in New York. Ryan wasn't a broke college student, however. He must do very well on the rodeo circuit. His boots and belt were very fine leather. Even the buttons of his shirt were a quality she'd never seen on the shirts her father ordered from the Sears catalog.

Her father had missed her while she'd been at college, of course, and she'd missed him. Maybe family was an issue for Ryan.

"Would moving to Rust Creek Falls bring you closer to your parents, or farther away?"

He slowed his steps. "Much farther away, and you read my mind."

"Missing your parents would be a big minus, then. Will they be surprised if you choose Rust Creek Falls when you settle down?"

"Shocked, but if I decide to do this, they'll support

me. They've always been very goal-oriented people, but their main goal has always been to see their kids happy."

"Even if the pursuit of happiness leads away from home?"

"My brother and sister have already put them through that test. My brother most of all, when he decided to look for his birth mother. If that was what his pursuit of happiness required, then my parents supported him one hundred percent."

"Are you adopted, too?"

"All three of us, each adopted separately. We're not genetically siblings. Closed adoptions. It was a challenge for my brother to locate his birth family."

She felt her lips quirk in a Ryan-like half smile. "You sound like me, giving the answers to the frequently asked questions before anyone asks them. Mine goes, 'We're identical, not fraternal, there were no fertility drugs involved and twins do not run in the family.' Oh—and, 'Yes, I do believe my parents were surprised. Wouldn't you be?'"

He chuckled. "Should I admit that I didn't realize you were identical? In my defense, we only danced past your sister a few times. You are so uniquely you, though. I can't imagine mistaking you for anyone else. Does it happen a lot?"

"Sure. My parents have never been fooled, though."

"Parents are like that."

Kristen swung their hands a little and looked up at the stars. It was fully night and a little chilly, but she felt so content with the world at the moment she didn't mind a thing. "So, your brother found his birth family. Have you looked for your birth mother?"

"No." He rubbed his jaw, and she wondered if it still

hurt where the horse had hit him. "That is—no. I've got no need to."

Why not? The question was on the tip of her tongue, but his *no* had been so curt, she hesitated.

As the breeze from the river teased the ends of her hair, he frowned a bit. "The temperature has dropped. You must be freezing."

Despite the warm day, it usually dropped into the fifties at night, and she was in a halter dress that left a lot of her upper half bare. She'd jumped into her brother's truck to come to the wedding reception, and that was where she'd left her jacket and her phone, darn it.

"I'll be fine." Just to make her out as a liar, her body betrayed her by shivering. "You could put your arm around me."

He did, and they continued along the river, but he was silent and a little edgy beside her.

"This is Main Street." She wanted to lighten up the mood of their little tour. "It's one-stop shopping here for all your municipal needs."

"You've got goose bumps." He let go of her and started unbuttoning his shirt.

"Are you *literally* going to give me the shirt off your back? You can't walk around here undressed. I mean, I've never actually looked up the public indecency laws, but that can't be right. Not that the women of this town would mind a bunch of shirtless cowboys wandering around, but—"

"I'm *literally* wearing two shirts, and you've got none."

Sure enough, when he took off his dress shirt, he had a T-shirt on underneath. A tight, white, body-hugging T-shirt, tucked into his jeans. Good heavens, the universe was pulling out all the stops.

"Ryan..."

When she reached for him, he started dressing her in his shirt, tugging a sleeve over her outstretched hand. His moves were efficient, but it was undeniably sensual to feel his warm shirt on her arms and feel the tickle of his shirt collar on the back of her neck.

"Better?" he asked.

"Thanks." She pulled her long hair free from the collar as he tied the shirttails in a knot at her waist.

His hands lingered for a moment, before he put them on his own hips and squarely faced her. It occurred to her that he could hook his thumbs in his belt loops and yank off a pair of tear-away pants just like that. Not that she'd seen too many male stripper movies.

"I didn't mean to be so curt about my adoption. I'm not curious about my birth mother the way my brother was about his, because I remember her."

In a flash, all the sexual thoughts she'd been entertaining were banked, and concern for him took center stage.

"He was adopted as an infant, but I was almost four. That's still too young to remember much, but what I remember is... It's enough."

And it was enough to make him withdraw from her. The change was subtle, but his stance was tight, controlled. Like he was braced for a fight.

"Did she hurt you?" The idea of Ryan being abused as a toddler was enough to make her sick. All the wedding punch and picnic food churned in her stomach.

It must have showed on her face, because he took her hand again, his grip strong as he threaded his fingers through hers. "As far as anyone could tell, I hadn't been battered in any way. I've been told I was a little underweight, but not significantly malnourished."

"Well, that's good." Such weak words, but she didn't know what else to say. The child he'd been had to be an important part of the man he'd become, but she couldn't pepper him with questions, not like she had over dinner. Not on this topic.

Somewhere on a pop psychology blog, she'd read that men were more comfortable talking when they had something physical to do, so rather than stare at the dark river, she started walking. They turned onto Main Street, silently, together.

Kristen caught her breath at the scene. The street was completely deserted, not one car parked on the edge of the road. The streetlights were soft yellow globes, evenly spaced, drawing the eye down the dark road. The buildings flanked them on either side, standing like timeless brick sentinels in long rows that disappeared into the darkness a few blocks away. Beyond them, the snowcapped mountains marked the horizon, their white peaks lit by the full moon.

"I've never seen it like this," she whispered into the night. "It's like we're the only two people in the entire town. Just you and me."

They left the sidewalk to walk down the center of the deserted street. He must have felt the magic, too. They were the only two people in the world, safe and intimate in the open air. Where better to confide secrets?

As they walked, Ryan began to do just that. "She left me standing on the steps of a church."

"Do you remember her face?"

"I remember the backs of her legs. I remember the hem of her dress as she walked away. She was irritated with me, but I still wanted to follow her. I didn't have anyone else to belong to. The only person I knew in the whole world was walking away."

Kristen held tightly to his hand. He was so tall and athletic, her cowboy, confident, too. It should have been hard to imagine him as a vulnerable preschooler, but the look in his eyes as he remembered that moment touched her heart.

"I'm so sorry. That's a terrible memory."

"It's a useful memory. Without it, I would probably be like my brother, wondering if I had a birth parent out there, and wondering if they would be glad or horrified to hear from me. It's not easy to decide to start that search. In my case, I don't have to go through that. I already know. She didn't want me. She wasn't being noble and giving an accidental baby a chance at a better life. She wasn't torn up inside because she couldn't provide for a child. She just ditched me without any tenderness. Knowing that has saved me from wasting my time and money searching for a woman who wouldn't be glad to hear from me."

Kristen was afraid she'd sob if she spoke, if she could have even thought of something appropriate to say, which she couldn't. She also couldn't stand that remote coolness in his voice. She had to do something.

So she hugged him. She simply wrapped her arms around him and rested her cheek on his chest and hugged him.

His arms came around her immediately, reassuringly. "It's okay, Kristen. It was thirty years ago. Are you crying?"

"Only a little." She sniffed in hard to stop the tears,

determined not to soak the cotton of his T-shirt. "Tell me that your adoptive parents were wonderful."

"My parents were wonderful. They are wonderful still. Why?"

"I just want your story to have a happy ending."

She didn't think he'd found it yet. Then again, they hadn't met before today. She hugged him harder, hoping he could see how much better their lives would be when they could pursue happiness together.

Ryan tried to get his emotions under control. Why in the hell had he shared the worst memory of his life?

He'd come here to see Maggie's new baby. That should have been enough for this trip far from Los Angeles. A pleasant wedding, a Montana-style wedding toast from a paper cup, and he should have been on his way.

Instead, Kristen had waltzed into his arms, and now he never wanted to leave.

He had to. If he didn't fly out tomorrow, a struggling screenwriter whose day in court had come would surely lose his challenge. His material had been stolen by a powerful studio. The man's life's work could go unrecognized and unrecompensed. Ryan was trying to stop a robbery in progress—and that was just Monday's case.

Los Angeles was his life. Today was just pretend, but Kristen's arms wrapped around him were real. Her tears were, too, and he'd unintentionally caused them. He never spoke about his birth mother. He shouldn't have started now. He and Kristen had precious little time left, and he didn't want to spend it making a lovely woman sad.

Her tour had been charming, her list of positive check marks all hopelessly naive and yet there was an undeniable truth that school spirit and homemade pastries were two of life's joys. He wanted the tour to continue.

I want her to show me something that will make me come back to stay. For real.

How could he possibly justify this move? Telling Kristen about his abandonment hadn't helped. It had only reinforced how much he owed to his parents. If he couldn't leave Roarke and Associates because clients needed him, then he absolutely couldn't leave the Roarkes themselves after all they'd done for him.

Convince me anyway, Kristen.

He ran his palm over her hair. She relaxed her grip and looked up at him, her blue eyes bright with unshed tears, her smile outshining them with her effervescent spirit.

Ryan lost his heart.

He wanted to believe something could come of it.

"Let's finish this tour. You were telling me about the wonders of Main Street." He turned to walk toward that faraway white-capped mountain, leaving the last Victorian facades as the buildings became more modern, with spacious stretches of grass between them. "I don't see a year on the keystone of this one. In fact, I don't see a keystone."

"The library. Built in, um…"

"No trickery."

"Well, I went to story hours there as a little girl, so I can guesstimate that the building is roughly twenty-five years old." She gestured to the other side of the street. "I know this one exactly. The community center is brand-spanking-new, built after the flood. The funds came in from an anonymous donor."

Ryan didn't stop her monologue, but he knew all

about the Grace Traub Community Center. Shane's birth father had contributed the money in honor of Shane's deceased birth mother.

"They built it in the perfect spot," she said, drawing him back onto the sidewalk as they continued past the community center. She stopped to point out the two-story town hall across the street, telling him about the monthly town meetings and how accessible he'd find the mayor when he moved here.

Looming at their backs was the church where the day's wedding had taken place, a traditional structure with a steeple that reached for the night stars. Wide, white steps led from the arched double doors down to the sidewalk. He ignored them.

"Living in a town this size is efficient. I'll give you the classic example, one every good Rust Creek Falls resident makes use of eventually, even though we all joke about it. You get your marriage license at the city hall." Kristen turned to look up at the church. "You walk across the street to the church and make your promises in front of the preacher, and then you head to the community center to cut your cake and have your first dance."

A bridal couple would have to pass the exact spot where they stood. Ryan had parked behind the church this afternoon and had entered through a side door. It hadn't been an intentional move to avoid church steps. He never did that—they were only concrete, after all. Tonight, they looked ominous, a ridiculous trick of the mind after an emotional day.

Kristen started up the steps ahead of him, taking them briskly, talking cheerfully. "Having the recep tion at the Fourth of July celebration today was a real departure from tradition."

It had been cold the day his mother left him. The church had been having some kind of Christmas festival, and he'd been given one of those cheap plastic snow globes. He could remember the hard feel of it in his hands as he'd watched his mother walk away.

"I've never seen a patriotic wedding like today's. The red, white and blue thing worked out great, didn't you think?"

Ryan put his boot on the first step and he saw, in his mind's eye, a shattered snow globe. He'd dropped the snow globe after his mother left. He'd forgotten that. For thirty years, he'd forgotten that, until now.

He saw the splattered water darkening the white steps. The shards of plastic. The bits of glitter that weren't as magical when they weren't clustered together. He didn't remember being sad in that moment, only resigned. He'd known before his fourth birthday that nothing good lasted very long.

Kristen's voice came down softly from above him. "Ah, church steps."

Her intuition was amazing to him. From the first moment they'd danced together, she'd been able to read the most subtle change in him.

She came down to the sidewalk. When he kept staring at his boot on the step, she slipped her hand into the bend of his elbow, as if he were escorting her to a formal affair. "Maybe if a man stood on a set of church steps with his bride beside him, it would give him a better memory to wipe that old one away."

She set her foot next to his, the fancy leather scrollwork of her boot obliterating the vision of the shattered snow globe. She was a bold one, this delicate-looking beauty raised in the land of glaciers and grizzlies.

"Maybe it would," he said quietly. "Maybe the ghost of young Ryan Michaels would finally disappear."

He wanted to believe so. Everything good didn't have to end. He'd just handled too many divorces and worked with too many people who were on their third and fourth marriages. In Rust Creek Falls, it seemed possible that two people could stick to one promise. Something good could last.

"I think young Ryan Michaels turned into a good man," Kristen said softly.

He lifted Kristen's hand to press a kiss in her palm. Everything seemed possible today, that the child Ryan Michaels and the man Ryan Roarke weren't so completely separate. That he, Ryan, could even meet the one perfect woman for him.

Kristen climbed the step to stand face-to-face with him. She rested her forehead against his, and he closed his eyes.

"Maybe," she said, "a man and a woman could decide to skip the church steps altogether. They could get their license and say their vows, too, in the town hall."

"But that's not how it's usually done in this town. If the bride had grown up here, she might feel like she missed out on her big day." *If she tied herself down to a man no one knew, a man who was a stranger to the local norms.* "People would talk."

"People would wonder why, but if it made the grown-up version of Ryan Michaels happier not to think about church steps at all, then she'd be happier if she could skip that part, too. They're promising to be a team from that day forward, and if it would make a less stressful wedding day for them as a team, that would be all that mattered."

"Kristen." He hadn't been looking for her; he hadn't thought a woman would ever understand him so well. Yet she'd been here in this tiny town in Montana, and he'd known, somehow, to come and find her today.

Fate. Destiny. Magic. He was ready to believe all of it.

He picked her up off the step and whirled her into the street. She landed lightly on her feet, laughing with him, gesturing toward the Traub Community Center. "Of course, they'd still have a grand reception. Everyone would come, but it would be just the two of them alone on the dance floor for their first dance."

"It wouldn't be a first dance for us." Ryan took her into his arms to waltz once more. In the middle of the street in their own private town, he led her in the elegant steps of the ballroom dance, thighs brushing in the dark as she hummed a country-western tune.

The fireworks were inevitable. The park was only two blocks away, so the fireworks were spectacularly close, their umbrella shapes forming shimmering willow trees over Ryan and Kristen as they continued to waltz, turning around and around on the solid yellow traffic lines that crossed the dark pavement under their boots.

It was just as inevitable that the fireworks would end, their last burst of thunder echoing off the buildings around them. Ryan and Kristen stopped, slightly out of breath from their dance, slightly breathless in their shared laughter. He had to kiss her, and he did, even knowing where that would lead. After long minutes of bliss and need, when the escalating desire made her whimper and he felt the sound in his soul, he broke off the kiss. "Let me take you home."

"Yes." Her fingers tightened in his hair, tugging in a way that was all the sexier because he was sure she hadn't done it consciously. She pressed herself closer to him, soft breasts against hard chest. "No—I mean, yes, but there are too many people at my house. Where are you staying?"

Maggie's.

Impossible. He would never bring a woman to his sister's guest bedroom, anyway, but with a ten-week-old in the house, either Maggie or her husband were up every three hours. Sleep was a precious commodity there, which was why he'd booked himself a hotel by the airport in Kalispell.

Yes. He'd forgotten for a second that he'd booked that hotel after staying with his sister the night before. He'd done it to be kind, wanting to make his predawn flight without waking Maggie and her family in the morning. Kindness was paying off. He could take Kristen to the hotel. They'd have a few hours of bliss, maybe catch an hour of sleep and then…

Damn it. It wouldn't work. He'd rise and pack his things, turn his rental car in at the airport and board the plane to begin ten hours of travel. He couldn't leave Kristen in a hotel room twenty-five miles away from Rust Creek Falls. It failed every test on every level.

The fantasy disappeared in a puff of imaginary smoke. The day was over. This was not his real life, and he couldn't make love to Kristen Dalton as if it were the start of something essential. He was leaving.

"What is it?" she asked. Headlights illuminated her face for a brief second as a car drove through the intersection beyond the church and town hall. Another followed close behind, driving away from the park now that the Fourth of July was over.

He let go of her shirt—his shirt—and walked her back to the sidewalk. "My flight is early out of Kalispell. God knows I don't want to go, but I have to. I've got commitments."

"We've still got tonight."

"To make love?"

"Nothing less."

His blunt question hadn't fazed her. *Nothing less* made him want her more fiercely than ever, but what he wanted was not what was best for her.

"And then what? I'll kiss you goodbye and leave you in a hotel bed by the airport, with no way to get home, and no promise that I'll ever come back."

She winced at that picture. A pickup truck turned onto Main Street and drove past them.

"Kristen, that's not going to happen. You're not the kind of woman who wants a one-night stand, but when I don't know what I'm going to do with my future, I can't promise you anything different."

"Like you said, that's not going to happen." Her soft hand rested on his jaw, so tenderly that it didn't cause him any pain despite taking that hit from the horse earlier. "You've got the heart of a true cowboy."

If today had shown him anything, it was that he wasn't a small-town rancher at all. "A true cowboy? What does that mean?"

"A true cowboy lives by a code that isn't so different from a knight's code of chivalry. You won't make a promise you can't keep. You're telling me that you won't sleep with me tonight because you can't stay the whole night and see me safely home? That's the most caring, romantic thing I've ever heard." She gave his chest a light smack and sighed with regret. "It's sexually frustrating at the moment, but romantic."

Her talk of cowboy hearts would only keep them both in this Montana fantasy. He needed to act like the lawyer he was and cut to the facts.

"We've found something amazing today, Ryan. This isn't going to disappear in the morning."

"But I am."

She flinched. If he'd ever needed proof that lawyers could be bastards, there it was. She withdrew her hand and looked at him with a little frown of reproach. "You don't need to drive that point home. I get it."

A passing car's headlights cast her shadow on the sidewalk and stretched it to the church steps beyond. Ryan didn't trust himself to speak.

"I understand that your job isn't the kind you can just leave on a moment's notice. I know it won't be easy for you to break away for a while, but once you've fulfilled all your commitments, you'll come back. I'll be waiting for you right here in Rust Creek Falls."

Her expression was open and honest and her words were full of promise. It was all too good to be true. Or rather, it was all too good. Nothing good lasted very long. He knew it, but judging by her hopeful blue eyes, she did not.

"I haven't made a decision. You shouldn't wait for me."

She bowed her head briefly, and his heart ached for hurting her.

"I'm sorry," he began, but she cut him off.

"Please don't. I don't want you to say anything that

will make you feel bad while we're apart." She looked over her shoulder at the cars and trucks that drove through the intersection, then nodded to herself a little sadly. "Here's what I think. This magic between you and me isn't going to disappear. I will still want you next week, and next month, and the month after that. You go and take care of whatever you need to take care of, then make your list and tally up your check marks. I have faith in you, Ryan. I'm going to leave now, while our day is still perfect and I can do it without falling apart."

She rose up on her toes and kissed him, hard and quick, on the mouth. "Hurry and come back. I miss you already." She turned and started walking away.

Ryan was so dumbfounded she was out of arm's reach before he called out, "Wait!"

She spun around, hope in her expression.

It was a hope he didn't feel. "I'll drive you to your ranch."

She plastered on a smile that looked almost genuine. "There's no need. At least a dozen people who are going my way will drive past me at the corner and give me a lift. It's a small town, remember? Being able to hitch a ride is a definite check in the plus column."

Then she turned around again, and this time, he let her go.

She'd be better off without some outsider from LA interfering with her secure life and her small-town dreams. Still wearing his shirt, she headed back to the life he'd interrupted today, a life that made her happy.

His gaze settled on the swish of her hem and the backs of her legs. *Woman Walking Away*, that was what he'd title it, if he could capture it in a photograph. He could paint it from memory, if he could stand the pain.

He was no artist. There was no way that losing Kristen after one perfect day could really hurt as much as watching his mother leave him while he'd held a snow globe in his hands. No way—but damn if it didn't feel close.

At the corner by the church, an SUV stopped and Kristen climbed in. She was gone.

A second of childish memory suddenly surfaced. He hadn't dropped that snow globe. He'd thrown it on the ground deliberately with all his three-year-old might, shattering it into a thousand pieces. This new bit of knowledge about Ryan Michaels fit Ryan Roarke. If he had a snow globe now, he'd hurl it at those church steps with all his might, too.

Ryan shoved his empty hands into his pockets and turned to walk in the opposite direction, heading toward the river that would lead him back to the park.

Back to the Porsche.

Back to reality.

Chapter Five

October

"I hate this stupid column."

Kristen let go of one side of the newspaper to flick the offensive page.

"Which one?" Kayla sat behind her on the bed, patiently working a wide-toothed comb through Kristen's hair.

"Rust Creek Ramblings. It's still going on and on about 'the power of the punch' and how many couples fell in love because of that Fourth of July reception. Ouch!"

"Sorry." Kayla was silent for a moment as she tugged a little harder at what must have been a particularly stubborn knot. "Maybe there is something to that poisoned punch theory. Don't you think it's awfully coincidental that people were acting so strangely? I mean, Will Clifton got married that night but didn't even realize it until the next morning. Our own cousin got arrested for dancing in a fountain and then fell in love with the police officer. That's a pretty crazy way to fall in love. Then Levi and Claire—"

"Levi and Claire were already married." Kristen snapped the paper shut and glowered at her sister's reflection in her dresser's mirror.

"Well, they're even more in love now."

If that stupid punch had made everyone realize who their true love was, then why hadn't Ryan come back yet? He'd drunk the punch with her. Kristen tossed the newspaper facedown onto her comforter.

"I need to get the bobby pins." Kayla went into the bathroom they shared in the sprawling log house on the Circle D, the same ranch house they'd lived in all their lives. The bathroom connected their individual bedrooms. It had double sinks and enough counter space for two women to keep all the cosmetics and accessories they could need. Their brothers had dubbed their mini suite "the girls' wing" years ago, and they'd kept away even after the fiercely pink *Keep Out* signs had been outgrown.

Kristen and each of her siblings had inherited land within the Circle D. Her brother Jonah, who had the advantage of being an architect, had designed and built a log cabin on his share, but Kristen and Kayla still lived in the girls' wing of the main ranch house. Owning land was not the same thing as having the money to build a house on the land.

Someday, she'd build her own house. Maybe someday would arrive when Ryan did.

"Okay, let's do this." Kayla returned to toss a card of bobby pins onto the newspaper. She plopped herself down behind Kristen and picked up the comb again.

Kristen moved the bobby pins to read the back page. An ad for next year's rodeo season taunted her. This year's season was already over. June, July and August were the touring months in the northwest for the professional rodeo, summer months that had come and gone.

Where was Ryan?

She wasn't surprised that he hadn't come knocking on her door in July. He'd told her that he had commitments to keep. He'd said it with regret, but people were relying on him. Rodeo riders signed contracts at the beginning of the season, after all, and contracts had to be honored.

The entire month of August, she'd hoped the tour would bring him back her way, close enough to visit her between rodeos. She'd looked up schedules and wondered which towns he was choosing to compete in, but no one named Ryan Michaels appeared in any of the events within a day's drive of Rust Creek Falls. Although she ached to see him again, she hadn't been too worried. The bigger rodeos with the bigger prize money were in the cities farther away. In September, when the season was over, he would come.

Every day in September, she'd dressed with care. Every single day, because every day had been the day Ryan might return.

But now, somehow, it was October.

Without warning, tears stung her eyes, an ambush she couldn't defend against, a sign that she was losing her faith in Ryan. She hated these odd moments where the voice of doubt would suddenly seem to be the voice of reason. *Face the facts: he's not coming back.*

She sniffed the tears back. She would pummel that voice into silence.

"Am I hurting you?" Kayla asked. "I'm so sorry. I'm just trying to get all these tangles out."

"It's okay," Kristen mumbled, too cowardly to admit the truth. Of all the people on the planet, Kayla was the last one who'd chastise her for holding on to her cowboy dream, but Kayla could look at a calendar and see what everyone else saw. Kristen liked to believe that Kayla looked at her with empathy…but that look was getting darned close to pity.

If Kayla looked at her with real pity, that would mean no one, not even Kristen's twin, believed that she'd mattered to Ryan as much as he'd mattered to her.

He's coming back. Even if he was too stubborn to see how many check marks were in the plus column, he wants me. He'll try to talk me into moving to wherever he chose to settle down. He's coming back.

In the meantime, she wasn't being entirely open and honest with Kayla, for the first time in their lives. She was acting, pretending that she wasn't eaten up with worry over Ryan, going entire weeks without mentioning his name, just to avoid that final, hope-killing look of pity.

"This is going to look so good on you." Kayla held up a picture of a beautiful ice skater from a Victorian Christmas card. Kayla's mission was to make Kristen's hair look just like the Victorian ideal of feminine beauty, because Kristen was auditioning for a role in Charles Dickens's *A Christmas Carol*. The play would open Thanksgiving weekend at one of the theaters in

Kalispell, and Kristen fervently hoped it would open with her in the role of Ebenezer Scrooge's former fiancée.

The thought of returning to the stage revived her sagging spirits. There were boards to be trod, greasepaint to be smelled and shows that had to go on. The theater was her passion, and although the principal at the high school wouldn't let her direct an after-school drama club, she wasn't going to give up something she loved any longer.

In July and August and September, as she'd relived every second of her time with Ryan, one moment that had nothing to do with love had kept running through her head. *It must be frustrating to have gotten that college degree and then not use it.* She'd majored in theater because she loved the theater. She had talent. She was trained. And most of all, she missed it. The lack of a theater in Rust Creek Falls might be her own check mark in the minus column, but the fact that the city of Kalispell was within commuting distance was a plus she intended to use.

Today, she was going to pursue something that made her happy. After Kayla finished making her look like a Victorian sweetheart, Kristen was going to drive the forty-five minutes to Kalispell and kill that audition. It was time to get a job doing what she loved.

She had Ryan to thank for inspiring her. She'd thank him in person, when he came to see her. It was October, so now he would come.

"Listen to this."

Kristen set down her half-empty cup and plopped her chin in her hand, prepared to listen to her sister.

"'Sunday, November first. The Power of the Punch has claimed another love match. During the fateful Fourth of July wedding of Braden and Jennifer Traub, Brad Crawford appeared to many to be impervious to the potent properties of the now-infamous punch, but the Rambler asserts that had he not partaken, or more to the point, if his fellow poker players had not partaken of the punch, then he would not have won the piece of property that included his prospective bride.'"

"How can you read that column?" Kristen asked. "It's torture."

Kayla frowned at her over the edge of the newspaper. "It is not. You just don't like it because you're never mentioned in it. You ought to be happy about that."

Of all the things Kristen felt, happiness was not one of them. Oh, sure, she'd been pursuing it. She'd landed that role in the play. She'd even managed to move out of her childhood home.

It wasn't enough.

She pushed her coffee cup away. At least she felt some pride that it was her own coffee cup, and she was sitting at her own kitchen table in her own house. Kayla had stopped in to share her first Sunday morning brunch in Kristen's new home.

Well, it was sort of her new home. Jonah had bought a block of five Victorian homes after the flood. They'd been dirt cheap, because no one else had dared to attempt to rehab century-old houses. Jonah had turned the home on the corner lot into his architectural firm's office. The other four houses were works in progress, and Kristen was going to be part of that progress.

She was proud of her new job in the Christmas play, but the commute from the ranch to Kalispell was over an hour and a half, round trip. The ranch was north of Rust Creek Falls, but Jonah's houses were on the south edge of town, close to the highway to Kalispell. Living here saved her hours and hours of driving every week.

She couldn't pay Jonah much rent. Regional theater was run mostly on donations and volunteers. She was lucky that her role paid anything at all, but it worked out to less than minimum wage when she counted up her hours. Living here was her second job. Instead of rent, she'd agreed to scrape and sand and repaint the interior of the house for Jonah while she lived in it.

Having her own place should have been exciting, and Kristen was certain she'd been performing her role of independent young woman admirably, fooling everyone. No one except Kayla suspected the truth she was masking: she was on the edge of a horrible heartbreak, clinging as best she could to her belief that she and Ryan belonged together. Her sister's empathy had evolved into concern this month. Concern was so very close to pity.

Kayla lowered the paper to peer at her once more. "I finished the rest of the column. It's not horrible, but I think the Rambler might have used the letter *p* just a bit too much, playing off the 'power of the punch.' Was that the part that tortured you?"

Kristen shook her head.

I can't do this. I can't pretend anymore.

"What part bothered you?" Her sister was waiting, no pity in her expression...yet.

"The part that said 'Sunday, November first.'" Kristen choked out her words. "He isn't ever coming back, is he?"

Then she put her head down on the kitchen table and cried.

* * *

The phone wouldn't stop ringing.

In the inner sanctum of Ryan's office, it was only a blinking light on the phone on his desk. Screening calls was his assistant's job, so Ryan could work without interruption. But his assistant was not here, and the incessant noise from the phone in the outer office had broken Ryan's concentration. He answered the damned phone.

"Roarke speaking."

"Roarke speaking here, too."

"Hey, Dad." Ryan tossed his pen onto his desk and sat back in his chair. "What can I do for you?"

"It's November first. You know what that means."

Ryan tried to recall which sporting events were nearby. "It means you're calling me from the PGA tournament at Newport Beach."

"It means it's Sunday. A day of rest. Part of the weekend. What are you doing in the office, son?"

Ryan rubbed his jaw. It had turned slightly black and blue the day after the horse had butted him in Montana. Everyone in LA had assumed he'd been hit by a model's jealous ex. In a nod to his boxing reputation, friends and acquaintances had been equally sure the other guy must look worse. Ryan the Player, everyone's favorite hero. Never would they have guessed he'd been hit by a pure white horse attached to a white-ribboned carriage.

That day had changed him. If he'd skated close to the edge of being a Casanova before Montana, then he'd been a monk ever since. No one noticed; men still clapped him on the back in approval and women competed for his attention in vain. People saw what they wanted to see.

Except his dad.

"You haven't taken a weekend off since when? July?"

Ryan had a feeling his dad knew exactly when. "Somewhere around then. I'm not putting in a full day here. Just a few hours."

"Then meet me at the club. It'll do you good."

Golf was his dad's thing, not Ryan's. Boxing, surfing, those were Ryan's preferred leisure activities. Actually, he hadn't been surfing since July, either. The boxing, though, he'd used like a drug for the past four months, throwing punches until his brain was numb, almost wishing for a hard hit to knock all the thoughts out of his head.

"Humor me. Come hit a bucket of balls with your old man."

Ryan supposed the fresh air would do him good. When he showed up at the club's driving range, he got much more than that.

"Your mother and I have been having some serious discussions about the future of the firm."

Thwack. Damn if his father couldn't make those balls sail. Ryan chose an iron from his golf bag and addressed the ball that had been teed up for him by a trendy automated machine.

"We want to retire earlier than our original timeline."

Ryan ignored the ball and turned to address his father instead. "Have you had some news I should be aware of?"

A week after Ryan's trip to Montana, his father had driven himself to the hospital with chest pain. He'd escaped any permanent damage beyond being chastised by his wife and son for not calling an ambulance, but the doctors had labeled it a wake-up call. It had been one for Ryan, as well. There was no way he could abandon his parents and their law firm for a Montana dream. The whole idea of living in a cowboy town had been a whim, anyway.

Kristen had been real.

Real, and out of his reach.

"I'm as healthy as a horse," his dad said. "But that's the point. I'd like to take my wife around the world while we're healthy enough and young enough to enjoy it. That's always been one of our goals."

Ryan felt the weight of the firm settle on his shoulders as he turned back to the tee. His parents deserved the good life, and to give it to them, Ryan would become the only Roarke in Roarke and Associates. They'd groomed him to take over someday, and he was ready. It didn't matter if that day came now or ten years from now.

I will still want you next month, and the month after that.

Kristen's words were never far from his mind. If Ryan followed in his father's footsteps and retired a few years early, he could move to Montana, guilt-free, in thirty years. That would be swell, if Kristen still wanted him thirty years from now.

Thwack. Ryan sent the ball on a long, hard drive.

His father approved. "Nice hit. We should think about beefing up the Associates part of Roarke and Associates before we retire. We're not trying to burden you any more than you already burden yourself. What do you think about offering partnership to Lori?"

The next ball had been teed up for him. Ryan knocked the holy hell out of it with his nine-iron. "We'd be smart to make Lori a partner whether you retire or not. We'll still need to hire an additional attorney. I'll start the headhunt."

"When? You're already working seven days a week."

Ryan readied himself for another swing, but his father reached across the low wall that partitioned the driving range and placed his hand on Ryan's shoulder.

"Let me tell you another one of my life's goals. I want my children to outlive me. That might make me a selfish old bastard, but I think I deserve to leave this earth without seeing you or Shane or Maggie leave it first. Every parent deserves that, whether they get it or not."

"What the—for God's sake, Dad. What kind of talk is this?"

"You're scaring me, Ryan. No one works as many hours as you've been doing and lives to tell the tale. Whatever demon you're trying to exorcise with work is winning. You need to try something else. Find a healthier way to forget whatever it is you're trying to forget."

Forgetting Montana and its breathtaking scenery, he could do. Forgetting the ideal of living in a small town, forgetting what it was like to belong to a community, all of that he could do. They'd been pipe dreams, Norman Rockwell pictures that were too perfect to be real.

Forgetting Kristen? He couldn't.

He'd been trying to adopt a brotherly attitude toward her. He was watching out for her best interests by staying away. She had a better chance at finding happiness in life and love with a cowboy who'd grown up where she had. She needed a man who understood ranches and horses and that pace of life. It was better for her if he stayed away. He'd learn to deal with it.

"I mean it, Ryan. You're working yourself into an early grave."

Ryan traded his nine-iron for his driver, a better club for beating the crap out of an inanimate object. "This is serious talk."

"It is. Now lighten up." His dad clapped him on the shoulder one last time and stepped back to his own tee. "Go home. Vegetate. Take a pretty girl out to dinner." Under his breath, he added, "Today."

Ryan looked in the direction his father was looking. He recognized the actress, and she recognized him. She changed direction immediately, walking toward him in her white golf skirt like she was walking down a fashion show runway. She had the legs and the attitude to pull it off.

"Ryan Roarke. It's been too long." Her hug enveloped him in perfume. Her civilized cheek kiss landed just a little too close to his ear, suggesting more of a lover's nibble on an earlobe than a meeting of friends. He got the message.

She'd sent him that message before. When word had leaked out that he may have done some work for a Tarantino or a DeNiro, rumors that he would never confirm or deny as part of his professional code, the constant stream of hopeful actresses had become a deluge. That was Hollywood. He wondered what rumor she'd heard this time.

Thwack.

"I've got a secret," she cooed. "I'm doing a screen test tomorrow. Isn't that exciting? It's all hush-hush, but you probably already know it's something for Century Films."

He said nothing. It wasn't necessary.

She placed her finger on her full, lower lip, pretending to be lost in thought. "Come to think of it, you introduced me to the man they've tapped to be the assistant director. He was in our little group when we took that trip to Carmel. Wasn't that a fun weekend?"

Thwack.

"You know, if you wanted to go back, I'm free this coming weekend. Who else was there last time? We could call around and get everyone together again."

"Especially the assistant director."

She perched on the bench that held his gear, crossing one long leg over the other and swinging her foot. "That would be such a boost for me. If you could arrange it, I wouldn't know how to thank you." The low purr of her voice and the come-be-naughty-with-me curve of her smile meant she knew exactly how she'd thank him.

Ryan looked at her, and wished for someone else. "I'm not available this weekend."

She didn't give up easily, but after some pointless banter, she did give up. Ryan had no doubt she'd find some other way to refresh her contacts with the assistant director and anyone else who could give her an inside edge to win the role.

"Not this time, then?"

Not ever.

She left him with another perfumed kiss, too smart to burn any bridges. As she sauntered away, Ryan's father continued working on his golf swing, as if he hadn't paid attention at all to what was happening on his son's side of the partition.

Ryan answered his unspoken question, anyway. "Not my idea of relaxation."

His father only grunted in a neutral way that could have meant anything.

Ryan began working his way through another dozen golf balls in silence. He wasn't interested in relationships that served careers any more than he was interested in the ones that were merely convenient. For the past four months of his life, he hadn't been interested in anything. Not in the golf or surfing that were the hallmarks of Southern California. Not in the endless summer of Los Angeles, and worst of all, not in running Roarke and Associates.

The pursuit of happiness, Ryan Roarke's personal pursuit of happiness, had led him to Montana. He'd fallen in love under the blue sky while looking into Kristen Dalton's blue eyes.

Fallen in love.

Thwack.

He'd fallen in love, and then he'd gone away and stayed away. Although Kristen had smiled and said she wasn't worried, he'd hurt her in those last few moments. If his father thought his son was leading a punishing life, Ryan saw some justice in it. He'd been treating himself badly because he'd treated someone else badly.

He didn't know if Kristen was hurting still. Perhaps she'd moved on.

Perhaps she hadn't.

He had no way to find out, short of making an ass of himself on the phone with his sister. Maggie worked in Rust Creek Falls's one law office for an attorney named Dalton. In a town that size, Dalton had to be related to Kristen somehow. If Kristen had been sad or depressed and told her family it was because Ryan had broken her heart, then Maggie would have heard about it. Kristen obviously hadn't been talking about him.

Brad Crawford, an acquaintance from the flood recovery days, had consulted him about land deeds last month. Ryan had resisted the temptation to ask about Kristen. Brad would have wondered why the heck Ryan Roarke was asking about one of the Dalton girls. Clearly, Rust Creek Falls wasn't buzzing with rumors that Kristen was brokenhearted over the man she'd spent the Fourth of July with, and Ryan would do nothing to stir up gossip where none currently existed.

No news was good news. It meant Kristen was fine without him.

Thwack. As fast as the automated range teed up the balls, he hit them, full force, full swing, full power. *Thwack. Thwack.*

"What's wrong, son?" His father was resting both arms on the wall, all pretense that he was doing anything but worry about his son completely dropped.

I miss her.

"Nothing, Dad."

Ryan needed to see Kristen again, if only to verify for himself that she was doing fine without him. He wanted what was best for her, so he'd have no peace until he was sure she was happy.

"I want to go back. To Montana."

His dad raised one brow, a move Ryan realized he'd adopted himself, long ago. "Your sister and Shane are bringing their families here for Thanksgiving in just a couple of weeks."

"I know. I need to see—I need the change of scene. I'll tie everything up this week and fly out Saturday.

One more document for Crawford came across my desk this week. I'll handle it while I'm there."

His father didn't ask any questions or point out that an overnight courier would be more efficient than an attorney flying to another state.

"Have a good trip, son. Get done what you need to do."

Chapter Six

Date night.

Maggie Roarke Crawford had been looking forward to this all week. She'd even loaded her sweet little Madeline into the car this morning, driven all the way to Kalispell and gotten her hair done for the event. Seven months after having her baby, some of her most chic outfits fit again. Tonight, she felt a little blonder, a little sexier and more than a little ready to paint the town red. She and her husband, Jesse, had hired a babysitter and headed out to the hottest spot in town: the high school gym.

On Friday nights, when it wasn't basketball season, of course, the gym became the town movie theater. Maggie loved it. It was a little like watching a movie in one's living room with extended family, since a sizable portion of the town always showed up. Gossip abounded at the refreshment stand. At the end of the night, the moviegoers all helped stack the chairs.

Tonight's double feature had started with a romance that was replete with tear-worthy moments. Maggie was pretty sure her husband had started out hating it, but midway through, when the emotional scenes on the screen had made her sigh and cling to his hand with both of hers, he'd relaxed and settled in for the duration.

The second show was going to be the opposite, an action-adventure film full of explosions and cars. Maggie felt the need to stock up on chocolate in preparation. Apparently, so did most of the women of Rust Creek Falls, because the line for the concession stand was an almost exclusively female gathering. Everyone was talking about the romantic movie and its handsome leading man.

Her youngest sister-in-law, Natalie Crawford, was behind her in line, gushing about the movie's ending to Ben Dalton's twin nieces. Maggie turned around to join in the conversation.

"Omigosh, wasn't that the most romantic proposal at the end?" Natalie asked. "I think I'd be willing to go through the wringer just to have a proposal like that. Everything turned out all right."

"That proposal happened in the nick of time," said one of the twins. "If he'd done one more jerky thing, I don't think any kind of proposal could have convinced me to marry him."

Maggie wasn't sure which twin was Kristen and which was Kayla—they looked so much alike—but she agreed with the sentiment. "It was lucky for him that all his jerky things were done to save an orphanage. We can forgive a guy who's trying to save children."

"Plus, he had washboard abs," Natalie added with a wink.

"Yes, there's that," Maggie laughed. "Jerks should strive to at least have washboard abs."

Kristen-Kayla, the one who'd been talking, suddenly pressed the back of her hand to her mouth and made a distressed sound. For a second, Maggie thought she'd sneezed or choked, but no, that had been a sob.

"Ohmigosh, Kristen, are you okay?" Natalie asked.

The quiet twin put her arm around her sister's shoulders. "That movie was pretty sad. It had me in tears, too."

Maggie and Natalie and the one who must be Kayla instinctively clustered closer to Kristen, shielding her from public scrutiny.

"Let's scoot out of the way," Maggie suggested. "Here's a napkin."

Although Maggie didn't really know Kristen, there was an unwritten girl code that rallied them all to help. Maggie was just about to suggest they head for the ladies' room when the young woman shook her hair back and straightened her shoulders.

"I'll be fine. Really. I was just thinking that in real life, there's never an orphanage to explain things away, is there?"

Oh, dear. The poor thing had obviously had her heart broken. Maggie sympathized. "I'm afraid when real guys do jerky things, it usually just means they're jerks."

"Is this about the airline pilot?" Natalie asked Kayla, who gave a quick negative shake of her head.

But Kristen did one of those half laugh, half sobs. "It might as well be. I'm starting to think they're all the same. I was dumb enough to believe the pilot when he said he hated to leave. Now I know he was having a grand time seeing his other girlfriends. You'd think I would have wised up, but no. A handsome cowboy comes through town and I actually believe him when he says he hates to leave me, but he must. They always must go, simply must. I even believed that he was going to come back when the rodeo tour was over."

"A rodeo star?" Natalie was clearly dying for more details.

Maggie felt badly for Kristen, who was slowly shredding her napkin.

"I thought a cowboy would be different. He'd love his family more than anything else, and be loyal to his lady. He seemed to be a real gentleman, too."

Natalie frowned. "Yeah, but a rodeo star is a different kind of cowboy."

"He made it sound like this was his final season, because he was looking to settle down here in Rust Creek Falls. I'm such a sucker."

Kayla gave her twin a squeeze. "I would have fallen for the man, too. The stories he told you were so poignant, who wouldn't have?"

Maggie smiled to herself at the sister's show of loyalty. Shane and Ryan had always been loyal to her like that, too.

"He fed you more lies?" Natalie shook her head. "Men are pigs."

Maggie tried to temper that kind of blanket statement. It went against her mind set as an attorney to accept a stereotype as a legitimate argument. "Let's just say if a man acts like a pig, there's almost never a justification. Kristen had it right. They're never protecting a secret orphanage in real life."

"Thanks, guys." Kristen kept tearing the napkin into pieces and crumpling the strips in her palm. "The thing is, I still don't think he lied. If he'd bragged that he owned a fancy sports car, that would be one thing, but what would be the point in telling me he was adopted? He remembered his first mother. She left him when he was three. Just walked away and left him."

That got Maggie's attention. One of her adopted brothers had been abandoned when he was three. What a strange coincidence for this rodeo rider to have been left like that, too.

"I'm sure he made it up to get pity points. What a scum bucket." Natalie gave Kristen a friendly bump, hip to hip. "Did he at least have washboard abs?"

Kristen laughed a little as she dabbed her nose with the crumbled napkin. "He did. I mean, I didn't take his shirt off, but he was rock hard when I hugged him."

This elicited some snickering from Natalie.

"He was a good dancer. Tall. Handsome. Nice voice, nice manners." The hint of a smile lit Kristen's face as she remembered the better traits of her rodeo star. The poor girl was still carrying a torch for this guy. Maggie was glad she had lots of support from a loving sister and from Natalie, too.

Maggie started looking around the gym for her husband, getting ready to graciously bow out of this circle now that the tears were under control. Natalie was settling in for the juicy details, and although Maggie was only a few years older than they were, she was starting to feel like the odd man out as an old married woman. These three were all single and had gone to school together.

Maggie craned her neck a bit, trying to spot her husband. Married women had benefits, and hers was Jesse Crawford.

"Where did you meet him?" Natalie asked. "Is he famous? Would I recognize his name?"

"I don't think so. It's Ryan Michaels. I met him here in town on the Fourth of July."

"The 'power of the punch,' eh?"

Maggie snapped her attention back to Kristen. Her brother was Roarke, not Michaels, but he'd been here for the Fourth of July. A man named Ryan, in town for the Fourth of July, who'd been abandoned at age three? It couldn't be.

"I don't know about the punch. I wish I had an excuse for being so gullible a second time." Kristen's hands doubled into fists. "I believed everything he said. He just about broke my heart with his story. He painted this whole picture about how she left him standing on the steps to a church—just *terrible*. It's over the top, right? I should have seen that, right? At the time, I felt so special that he was telling me something so personal, but it was just a line to make women want to comfort him. It worked."

Dear God, church steps. She was talking about Ryan. Her brother Ryan had broken this sweet girl's heart.

Frantically, Maggie thought back to the Fourth of July. They'd all gone to the wedding together, but Madeline had only been about ten weeks old, and she and Jesse had taken the baby home to nap. They'd all fallen asleep. Later, it had seemed like too much trouble to cart the stroller and diaper bag and the rest back to the park. She'd assumed Ryan had renewed an acquaintance from the flood recovery days, but he must have struck up a flirtation with Kristen. It all made sense, except why on earth had he told this poor girl he was in the rodeo? It was flabbergasting.

Maggie felt physically sick. Ryan had always been a lady-killer, but this wasn't LA, and Kristen wasn't a starlet. How could he? But he had, he clearly had, and now Kristen's spurt of anger was over and tears were welling up in her eyes again.

"The thing is, and please don't think I'm crazy or a complete idiot for thinking this, but the thing is, what if his story was real? He probably has a hard time trusting anyone. Maybe he does want to be with me, but his childhood affected him so that he doesn't believe a woman would love him. Or...oh, I don't know. What if he was injured, and he's been in a hospital this whole time? What do you think?"

I think I'm going to kill my brother.

But first, she needed to give Kristen some immediate advice. "Here's what I think you should do. You should get back in line and buy yourself a serious amount of chocolate, and you should avoid sad movies for a while. The next movie will be all car explosions and no plot. It's perfect." Impulsively, Maggie gave Kristen a hug and whispered in her ear. "Try not to drive yourself crazy with questions that have no answer."

Maggie left to find her husband. She had the rest of date night to salvage. First thing tomorrow morning, she would give Ryan a piece of her mind. Poor Kristen might not be able to get any answers, but Maggie would.

"Get your butt up here. Now. This minute."

"Good morning to you, too, Maggie. Nice of you to call."

Ryan clamped his phone between his shoulder and ear and hoisted his suitcase into the overhead bin. The noise of a couple of hundred people boarding the airplane gave him a certain amount of privacy to talk with Maggie before takeoff. She'd probably hear the background noise and guess where he was, but in the meantime, he could have some fun with her.

"Why would I come see you? Isn't it snowing there? Not to rub it in, but I was golfing with Dad this week. Scratch that. I am definitely rubbing it in."

Ryan took his first-class seat and waved away the flight attendant's offer of a drink. Strangers with backpacks and luggage and kids continued to file past.

"I'm not joking around, Ryan. You have to come up here."

Her tone of voice alarmed him. Ryan tuned out everything but his sister. "What's wrong? Are you at the hospital? Jesse or Madeline sick?"

"You're the sick one. You broke a girl's heart last time you were in Rust Creek Falls, you jerk."

He nearly dropped the phone.

"I was at the movies last night, talking to Kristen Dalton at the concession stand."

The name exploded in his brain. He hadn't heard anyone say her name, not once in all these months. She'd been only his own silent wish, his own secret memory. Hearing his sister speak about her was jarring, a sudden reminder that Kristen wasn't his private fantasy. She was a real woman with friends and family. A woman who lived a normal life and went to movies.

"She was in tears. The movie was sad, and it made her cry, and do you know why? Because you're extra sensitive when your heart's been broken. Kristen Dalton! Oh, Ryan, how could you?"

Kristen crying, brokenhearted—Ryan's own heart stopped beating for a moment. He tightened his grip on the phone.

"She asked you about me?"

"No, she didn't ask me about you. What kind of vain question is that?"

It hadn't been vain. It had been hopeful. He was on this plane because he'd needed to see for himself that Kristen was okay. That she'd moved on. That she was fine without him. *Closure.* He was having too hard of a time in California without it.

But now...

Ryan covered one ear and turned away from the aisle to better hear his sister. This flight connected to Kalispell through Las Vegas, and the passengers who boarded were boisterous, ready for vacation. Ryan concentrated to hear everything his sister said. Every word was crucial.

"If she didn't ask you about me, then how do you know I'm the reason she's heartbroken?" It was far more likely that she'd been dating someone else this fall. Just because Ryan couldn't stand the idea didn't mean it wasn't probable.

"Because I'm standing in line for some Twizzlers and Sno-Caps, and this really pretty woman starts pouring her heart out about a man who was adopted at age three. He's left her behind without a backward glance, that much is obvious to anyone who's listening, but she can't see that, because she's crazy about him. She's clinging to this idea that he's just afraid to believe in love after the way his mother abandoned him on church steps. And this paragon of a man that she's still hoping will come back is named Ryan."

A man that she's still hoping will come back.

The entire purpose of the flight changed in an instant. There was nothing of brotherly concern in his attitude toward Kristen. Screw closure. He wanted Kristen as he'd wanted her from the first: in his arms for a dance and a kiss. By his side for a laugh during a meal. He wanted her in his bed, and yes, he wanted to trust her with his heart.

If she wanted his heart. It had seemed unlikely after all these months, but suddenly, with his sister's words, everything he wanted and needed was possible. Everything could be his, if Kristen still wanted him. They could work out all the rest, somehow.

"You can't leave a girl hanging with her heart on her sleeve like that. She's really crazy about you, you moron. If you think you'll find a better woman down there in LA, you're wrong, but you at least owe it to Kristen to end things cleanly so she can move on."

"I don't want to end things."

"Well, you have to. It's just cruel, letting her carry a torch for you."

Hope was a painful emotion, forcing its way into a heart that hadn't allowed any room for it.

Maggie misinterpreted his silence. Of course, she only saw him as her brother, the player. It wouldn't occur to her that he'd been serious about Kristen. "I mean it, Ryan. If you don't get up here, I'll—I'll—I'll tell Mom."

Her threat cut the tension, and amazingly, Ryan found he could laugh despite the painful hope in his chest. "Don't do anything so drastic. I'm already on my way."

"Good. When you book your flight, let me know, and I'll pick you up at the airport."

"I said I'm already on my way. Listen." He held the phone away from his ear as the flight attendant repeated the announcement, which everyone ignored, about stepping out of the aisle to let others pass during boarding.

"Wait a minute. You'd already decided to come up here? Did Jesse call you last night?"

"I'd already decided last week to see Kristen. I told you I didn't want to end things, but you were too busy chewing me out to hear that."

"Wow. That's... I should get the guest room ready." She sounded a little faint.

"I'm staying at Maverick Manor. Between you, Jesse and the baby, that's three chaperones I don't need while I'm trying to woo a woman."

"Woo her? Not break up with her? Ryan, you can't do this. You can't keep letting her think you're some kind of rodeo star. The fake name, the whole cowboy masquerade—I just can't be a party to that. I'm not going to pretend I don't know you."

The flight attendant stopped directly by his seat and spoke loudly. "Excuse me, sir, but you're going to have to turn off your phone now."

"What are you talking about, Maggie?"

"Sir, I must insist. The doors have been closed."

"Sounds like you have to go," Maggie said. "I'll talk to you when you get here."

"What masquerade, damn it?"

"Sir."

"Kristen Dalton isn't in love with you. She's in love with a cowboy named Ryan Michaels. Hang up before you get kicked off that plane."

Chapter Seven

After ten agonizing hours of travel, Ryan hung up once more after talking to his sister. Numb, he sank onto the foot of the oversize bed in his room at Maverick Manor.

He hadn't done it on purpose. He'd worn cowboy boots and two-stepped to a country-western band, but he'd never said he was a cowboy. He hadn't specifically said he was an attorney from LA, either, but he'd never once talked about rodeos.

When he'd been standing by those church steps with Kristen, he'd accidentally let slip the name that he'd gone by as a preschooler. She'd apparently assumed he was still Michaels. That meant Kristen didn't know he was related to the Maggie Roarke Crawford who worked with her own uncle. She didn't know he was related to celebrity chef Shane Roarke. And she most certainly didn't know he, Ryan, defended contracts for movie studios and recording artists.

He'd wanted it that way. When they'd first met, he'd only said he was Ryan, not Ryan Roarke. He'd wanted to feel what it would be like to be a local.

The locals around here are all cowboys.

Maybe he should have foreseen that, but the locals weren't rodeo stars, damn it. He'd never been to a rodeo in his life. She'd been born and raised on a ranch. How had he fooled her so completely?

Ryan fell back onto the quilt-topped mattress.

He'd just have to level with her immediately. Like ripping off a bandage, he'd have to confess his missteps and mistakes. When he told Kristen that her humble cowboy who'd been considering a move to Rust Creek Falls was actually a high-powered Hollywood attorney who specialized in the entertainment industry, would she still want him?

He stared at the ceiling until the knots of the pine slats blurred into nothing. In their place, he saw the hem of a woman's dress, swishing with every step as she walked away.

The need to rip off a bandage was not a great motivator.

Although Ryan had spent a week rearranging his whole schedule specifically to see Kristen, he found himself stalling now that he was in Rust Creek Falls. He was dying to look into those blue eyes again, to feel her soft palm against his jaw, to run his hand down her soft hair. But first, he had to tell her that everything she thought she knew about him was wrong. She was going to be devastated. His first sight of her could be his last.

And so, after a restless night at the hotel, he spent Sunday morning doing everything except what he'd come to town to do. Instead of asking for directions to the Dalton family ranch, he located Brad Crawford and got his signature on that final piece of paperwork. Instead of knocking on Kristen's door, he stopped by Maggie's house to see the baby, who'd grown so much in four months it was astonishing.

He couldn't avoid the inevitable, but he told himself it was smart to delay it. This mistaken identity had caught him completely by surprise just twenty-four hours ago. He knew how to win a debate and he knew how to persuade a jury. Both of those things required careful preparation, and Ryan was not prepared to rip off any bandages without a plan. He needed time to think, and he needed to avoid Kristen until he was ready.

The hotel was too small for his restless pacing. He considered walking the perimeter of the park while he thought of the right words to say, but Maggie and her family were headed there. She'd become a true Montanan who thought forty degrees was perfectly balmy weather for a Sunday stroll. The park wouldn't provide any solitude.

He could retrace Kristen's tour. Walk along the river in broad daylight. Head up Main Street to that church where he'd said too much—or where he'd said too little. But revisiting the sights seemed too maudlin, too much like a scene from a sappy movie—and too risky. He might run into Kristen unprepared.

He got into the truck he'd rented and drove out of town. The highway led straight to Kalispell, right through the heart of town. Main Street was flanked by the same type of sturdy brick buildings that lined the streets of Rust Creek Falls. There, away from the Crawfords and Daltons, he parked his truck, got out and started walking.

* * *

"Let's try it again from the top of the scene. Old Scrooge and the Ghost of Christmas Past, I want you two to stand a little closer upstage." The assistant director looked over his shoulder toward the back of the theater. "Can we keep the spotlight on Old Scrooge if he moves upstage? Yes? Good."

Kristen stood motionless at center stage. This rehearsal was primarily meant to refine the blocking, deciding where every actor would move during the scene. The lighting director, the stage crew and the prop master needed to know where the actors delivered every line. It was tedious work, but part of being an actress was being patient.

Kristen hated blocking days. She got through them by using them as an acting exercise, in which she had to play the role of Patient Actress. Since Patient Actress would not tap her booted foot impatiently, Kristen stopped. She stuffed her hands in the back pockets of her jeans. They didn't wear costumes for most rehearsals, but Kristen wore a bright blue sweater with her jeans and boots, because her costume was a striking blue gown. She had her hair up in a messy bun to simulate the Victorian style she'd wear during performances. Her hair affected what angle she held her head, even which shadows the different stage lights cast on her face, so it was necessary.

"Belle, switch places with Young Ebenezer. I want Old Scrooge to be looking over his shoulder at you. He'll be seeing your face while you break his heart all over again."

Obediently, Kristen switched places with the actor who was playing Ebenezer in the prime of his life. The assistant director had one key point wrong, however.

"I'm not breaking Ebenezer's heart. He's already decided he loves money more than me. I'm the one who is brokenhearted."

She cut herself short. *I'm the one who is brokenhearted.* Saying those words out loud felt like a personal confession, although no one could know they were true for Kristen as well as Belle, the unwanted fiancée.

The assistant director flipped through the script in his hand, but he didn't stop on any page long enough to read a full line of dialogue. "We're not talking about motivation today. We're talking about lighting."

"Yes, but you want the audience to see Old Scrooge's face," Kristen persisted. "If his shoulder is to that half of the audience, they'll miss his expression. This is the moment where he realizes that letting Belle go was a mistake that ruined the rest of his life."

Again, she fell silent. She knew she was a fool for worrying about Ryan, but she wondered if he was happy now, after choosing a path that didn't include her. Last Friday, she'd said as much during movie night, but it had only earned her those terrible looks of pity from Natalie, Kayla and her uncle's partner, Maggie Crawford.

The actor playing Old Scrooge backed her up. "She's right. I'm the one who has to be devastated, not the younger me. Maybe if we stood this way—" he put his hand on Young Ebenezer's shoulders and the two of them shuffled clockwise for a few steps "—more of the house would be able to see both of our faces. There's a big contrast between what he felt then and how he feels now."

After more discussion, the assistant director left the stage to stand in the audience. He flipped through his script once more. "Okay, let's take it from, uh, Young

Ebenezer's line. 'Have I asked to be released from this promise?'"

Kristen took both of the actor's hands in hers, breathed in deeply to focus herself and then looked up at him with all the sadness of a woman who realizes her love is not returned. To become Belle, Kristen only had to admit to herself that she was unwanted. Ryan was never coming back.

Ebenezer looked at her coldly. "Have I asked to be released from this promise?"

"Not in words, no."

"How, then?"

"In the way you spend all hours in your counting house. In the way your smiles are only bestowed on the scales, when the balance of gold tilts them in your favor. Tell me truly, if you saw me today for the first time, would you make the effort to dance with me at Fezziwig's party? Would you ask your friends for an introduction to a girl who has no dowry?"

He lifted his chin sharply, his nostrils flaring in distaste at her question.

"You see?" She let the tears that welled in her eyes spill down her cheeks. "The man who loved me is only a memory. For his sake, I pray you will be happy upon your chosen path. You no longer want me to walk with you, no matter how much I wish it otherwise. Ebenezer Scrooge, I release you."

She bowed her head, and let go of Ebenezer's stiff hands.

"Okay, that's plenty." The assistant director made his way back to the stage. "That was great, by the way. Just do it twice every weekend from opening night through Christmas, okay?"

Kristen smiled obligingly, back in her role as Patient Actress, and used the cuff of her sweater to dry her cheeks.

"You make my job hard," Ebenezer said. "I'm supposed to look at you like you're as appealing as an empty wallet, but man, I just wanted to go down on my knees and beg you to stay."

"You made my job easy." Old Scrooge patted her on the shoulder with one hand and gave Ebenezer a good-natured shove with the other. "It'll be easy to call this guy out for being a fool. He really is a cold-hearted bastard if he can look in those teary blue eyes and not feel a thing. I was ready to deliver my line with gusto, if that pompous kid hadn't cut us off. When's the real director back again? Tuesday?"

"Thank you, Act Two," the assistant director called out in dismissal. "Act Three beginners, please. Act Three beginners, take your places."

Kristen made her escape into the wing. She couldn't decide if this was the worst role or best role she'd ever taken. The similarity of her situation to Belle's made for difficult rehearsals. The lines she had to speak came too close to her real feelings. She had to relive her dashed hopes over and over.

On the other hand, this role was a piece of cake for her as an actress. She had only to think of Ryan, and very little acting skill was required to give an authentic performance.

The bad news is, I got jilted. The good news is, I got great reviews.

She tried to laugh at her own joke, but the hitch in her breath was more like a sob. She felt a big, ugly cry coming on, nothing like Belle's gentle tears.

"I'm going out for some fresh air," she said to the stage manager. She threw her polka-dotted scarf around her neck and grabbed her red jacket from the folding chair where she'd thrown it three hours ago.

The stage manager checked the large clock over her station in the wings. "You might as well leave for the day. I can tell you right now we'll never make it to the final scene."

Kristen swallowed hard and faked a smile. "Thanks, Sue. See you Tuesday."

She all but ran for the stage door, barely making it outside before Patient Actress and Belle the Fiancée and every other role she'd been playing for the past four months gave way under the crushing weight of being Kristen Dalton, the girl who still wanted Ryan Michaels to come back for her.

The stores and shops of Kalispell were decked out for Christmas. Not one window or door seemed to have escaped the bonds of garland and ribbon. Despite this, Ryan could admire the brick buildings, sturdy brick squares that had withstood a century of Christmas seasons and could probably withstand a century more. He'd survive this Christmas, too. He always did, no matter what bad memories were associated with the holiday.

Ryan tucked his hands deeply in the pockets of his wool overcoat. It was double-breasted and sharply tailored, because he was not a cowboy and not pretending to be one. It was full-length, because he was from Los Angeles and the weather here was flirting with freezing, but it was also open in front because he'd been walking for block after block, building up heat. If the coat flared behind him like a cowboy's duster, he couldn't help it. Let people think what they wanted.

Except Kristen. What she *wanted* to think about him mattered. She wanted a cowboy. He kept running the scenarios in his mind, but no matter how he presented the basic facts, he couldn't imagine her face lighting up in one of her dazzling smiles. *Oh, you're actually living in a megalopolis over one thousand miles away? Fantastic!*

The cold November wind had cleared his mind and cooled his expectations. The truth was, she'd fallen in love with a rodeo rider because that was who she'd wanted to fall in love with. That was not him. He thought she was perfect as she was, a simple ranch girl, born and bred in a small town, but nothing good lasted for long. There was no real chance that he and Kristen could still be a couple after he told her the truth. Her feelings for him would be crushed in an instant, and all the glitter and magic would drain away.

Like a damned shattered snow globe.

He stopped walking, and stood on the cold sidewalk, letting the north wind blow away the childish vision— all gone, bye-bye. He turned on his heel to head back to his SUV. It was time to go face Kristen.

Kristen.

She stood on the sidewalk before him, perhaps twenty yards away, staring into a store window, a beautiful mirage for a man who hadn't realized just how much of a desert his life had become. He drank up the sight of her. How had he survived the deprivation?

She seemed tired, her shoulders low and her expression downcast. When the brisk wind pulled more tendrils loose from her pinned-up hair, she didn't seem to have the energy to turn her collar up.

He knew, somehow, he'd looked just as tired moments ago, before seeing her. He'd denied them both the chance to be happy. She had the right to be furious with him for causing her pain.

"Kristen." Her name was little more than a whisper, the apology he owed her too big for words.

She tucked a wisp of hair behind her ear and turned away, light and graceful in all her moves despite the sadness in her expression. When she turned her back on him and he lost sight of her face, something in him snapped. She had to go; he understood that. Nothing good lasted forever. But he couldn't let her walk away without telling her how grateful he was for the most perfect summer day of his life.

"Kristen!"

She looked over her shoulder. Their gazes met, and her blue eyes opened wide the moment she recognized him.

He took one step toward her, another, and then he realized she was smiling—smiling at *him*—and he was running. She came flying toward him, and he opened his arms wide and swooped her off her feet. Momentum carried them around and around as she laughed.

"You came back, you came back," she said, her arms tight around his neck.

He had her lifted high, so his face was buried in her playful scarf and loose hair for a long, blinding moment of reunion that needed no words. Then she slid down his body, until her cowboy boots touched the ground.

She kept his face in both her hands, smoothing her thumbs across his cheekbones. She was beaming at him, every bit as stunning as he'd remembered, yet ten times more vivid in person than a memory could ever be.

"You look amazing. Even more beautiful than I remembered, and I think of you every day as the most beautiful woman I know." He was babbling. He didn't care.

"I can't believe you're real," she said, exactly what he was feeling. "We never took a photo that day. Neither one of us brought a phone. You can't imagine how much I've wished I just had a picture of you—"

The catch in her voice made him catch her close again, holding her against his chest within the open folds of his coat. "I'm sorry. I'm so very sorry. I shouldn't have stayed away so long."

She nuzzled into the side of his throat. "You must have had a good reason."

Her faith in him was humbling. And misplaced.

You have to tell her the truth.

"I've been working." He rested his cheek on top of her head, regret in every syllable. "In California."

"California?" She picked her head up. Stepped back.

Ryan braced himself. The bandage ripping had begun. He'd known since Maggie's bombshell that it would come down to this. He'd never hated having to do something more.

"No wonder I couldn't find you." She bit her lip and looked up at him apologetically. "I kept checking the Montana papers for event results. Then it occurred to me to look at Wyoming. I might have gotten desperate enough to check out Idaho's results on the web a few times. Pretty bad, huh? But it never occurred to me to look at California."

He had to look away from those trusting blue eyes. "I didn't deserve to have you looking so hard for me."

"Did you come from California all the way back to Montana just to see me?"

"Yes, I did." She deserved to know the truth in this, as well. He wanted her to know he'd suffered, too, although it had been his own fault. "I was going crazy, wondering how you were. I missed you."

Kristen made a quick movement of her hands toward his face, and for a split second, he thought a slap was coming. He deserved a slap. Instead, with two hands in his hair, she pulled him to her, and kissed him. Hard. Hungry.

No memory could wake every cell in his body like this. He was alive, all sensation. The feel of Kristen in his arms, the smell of her skin, the very taste of her, each were their own small miracle. It didn't matter if he deserved her kiss; he was greedy for it and took what she gave him, savoring the connection that made him want to be closer still.

A passing truck honked a horn, whether in criticism or approval didn't matter. It was enough to bring Ryan back to the real world. He lifted his head to study Kristen's face and felt utterly satisfied with how thoroughly kissed her mouth looked and how perfectly pink her cheeks were. She rocked back on her heels—she'd been standing on tiptoe during the entire kiss—and gripped his arms for a moment as she regained her equilibrium.

She looked so feminine, so delicate, but then she smiled like a woman who knew a secret. "Someday, we are going to kiss when we are alone and indoors, somewhere very private, and things are going to burn so far out of control you won't be safe from me any longer."

He could've dropped to his knees on the sidewalk. She was so Kristen, so boldly herself. He wanted her.

Hell, he had her. She wasn't playing coy or shy or mysterious. She was thrilled to see him, as eager to pick up where they'd left off as he was.

But the hell of it was, he couldn't keep her. He wasn't the man she thought he was.

Rip off the bandage.

Not here. Not on a sidewalk in the center of town.

He tried to use humor to ease the sexual tension she'd just ratcheted into high gear. "There's a traditional order to these things. I think you're supposed to buy me a drink first. I passed a bakery not too far back. Maybe they sell coffee."

Her smile only deepened. "They do, but if you're daring enough to cut through the alley with me, there's a diner that serves amazing pie one street over. You'd be indoors with me for the first time, but I think you'll be safe if I have a nice slice of homemade pie competing for my attention."

She led the way through the alley. From behind, she made a colorful picture. Her caramel-colored hair was mostly twisted up. The hem of her red coat cut precisely across her jean-clad rear, and one end of her polka-dotted scarf fluttered among the loose tendrils of escaped hair as she took quick, decisive steps.

Another version of *Woman Walking Away.*

This was what he would see after he told her the truth, then.

He couldn't do it. He couldn't say the words that would shatter her feelings for him all at once. Those feelings were pure and sincere—yes, they were naive, but they were real, and their destruction could leave a permanent scar. For her own sake, he couldn't sit her down in front of a piece of pie and tell her everything she'd loved about him was a lie. It would break her heart.

It would shatter his.

They emerged from the alley onto a street nearly identical to Main, and then into a mom-and-pop restaurant that smelled of wholesome holiday baking. While gingerbread and pumpkin pie were topped with whipped cream for them, Ryan rapidly formed a new plan.

He didn't want to rip off any damned bandage, so he wouldn't. What if he could reveal pieces of the truth bit by bit, and slowly replace the image of Ryan Michaels with the reality of Ryan Roarke? He'd already told her he worked in California when she'd assumed Montana or Wyoming, and she'd accepted that piece of the truth easily enough. What if he could continue to do that this week? If she loved Ryan Michaels this Sunday, might she love Ryan Roarke by next Sunday?

Could she love him so strongly that she'd still want to be part of his life, even if that life had nothing to do with Montana and her cowgirl dreams?

He had one week to find out.

Chapter Eight

The last thing Kristen needed was more sugar. She was already bouncing off the diner's walls with excitement, because Ryan was here.

He's really here.

Just when she'd given up hope, he'd arrived, and gosh, what a reunion. He'd said everything she could have wanted to hear. He'd missed her. He'd come specifically to see her.

Then there was that kiss on the sidewalk. The memory of kissing Ryan and the reality of kissing Ryan were two entirely different things. Every second had been worth a month of missing him. Everything was okay now. Absolutely everything.

She took her gaze off Ryan just long enough to scoop the whipped cream off the top of her pie and eat it all in one bite, sugar be damned, and then she went back to devouring Ryan with her eyes.

Dear God, he looked good. He was dark-haired and dark-eyed, just like she remembered, and his tan hadn't faded despite the November weather. He still had that air about him that set him apart from the other cowboys in town. Something more sophisticated, maybe. A great haircut, a killer overcoat that even looked good hanging on the wall hook next to hers. The sweater he wore with his jeans almost looked like cashmere. If they ever put a rodeo man on the cover of *GQ*, her Ryan would be the perfect model. He had the strong jaw and an expression that didn't look like he laughed easily—but, oh, when he did, the camera must love him.

A camera. She jumped up to retrieve her phone from her coat's pocket and plopped back into the booth across from Ryan.

"I'm not making the same mistakes this time. Say cheese."

He didn't. Or rather, she didn't give him a chance to say cheese, but she got a wonderful shot of that one raised eyebrow and the quirk of his lips when he was going to smile, but hadn't started actually smiling yet.

She hit the symbols on her phone to make Ryan's image her wallpaper, setting it as her lock screen and home screen, both. "Much better. Sometimes, I was afraid I'd imagined you. Fortunately, the whole town seemed to have seen us sitting on that stage, eating barbecue, so I knew I wasn't crazy." Laughing, she looked up to find him watching her with a too-serious expression.

He laid his hand on the table, palm up, and she gave him her phone. He dialed a number, and within seconds, she heard a traditional, classic ring coming from the coat rack across the room. He disconnected the call and set her phone on the table. She felt relieved, knowing they had each other's numbers now.

"Much better," he said, gently echoing her words. "There was no one around me who knew you existed. I think it did make me a little crazy."

She put her hand in his and squeezed hard.

"I should have come sooner." The regret in his voice was painful to hear.

"You were working." She racked her brain for the California rodeos, information she hadn't thought of since freshman year of high school. "Where were you? Redding? Sacramento?"

"Not Northern California. I'm living in Southern California, believe it or not."

She'd been imagining that he was much closer all this time. It made it all the more understandable that he hadn't been able to steal away for a few days.

Southern California had major rodeos, but as a kid she'd known that she'd never be able to travel that far to see one. Kristen hadn't committed that information to memory, not like the events in Montana and Wyoming. Still, there was something about the serious tone the conversation was taking that made her uneasy. She wanted to keep riding the high of simply being in his presence again.

"Of course I believe you." This time, she winked at him. "It explains the tan."

That seemed to be the right thing to say. He relaxed against the back of his seat. She felt so happy she couldn't stay in hers. She got up and scooted into his side of the booth. His arm came around her immediately, and she snuggled against him like they were teenagers.

She couldn't see every nuance of his facial expressions now, but the trade-off was that her hand could rest on his thigh and her head on his shoulder. He was definitely not a teenager, but a man built for work. Thigh and shoulder, both, were hard-muscled. She was going to want to make love with the lights on.

He tapped her nose with one finger. "Is it the gingerbread or the pumpkin pie that's making you blush?" His voice was low, an intimate rumble for her ears only.

"It's you." She hated the blush, but she couldn't stop the direction her thoughts were going. "I should have guessed you were from Southern California. You don't have a farmer's tan like most of the guys around here."

He was silent for a long moment. "Exactly how do you know that?"

"Let's just say I had an opportunity on the Fourth of July to make use of a certain vantage point."

"Damn. I didn't look down your shirt."

"You're a gentleman. I'm not." She ran one finger down the soft sweater that covered his hard chest. "You're a gentleman who is tan all over. I don't suppose you Southern California cowboys go surfing after the chores are done?"

He shifted slightly. "I do surf, actually."

"You do?" The idea of a surfing cowboy was funny. "Do you wear a cowboy hat out on the waves?"

"Never, and that is the truth." With one finger under her chin, he lifted her face for a sweet kiss.

The diner made a good chaperone. The kiss stayed sweet.

It didn't have to stay sweet, not like the last time Ryan had been in town. She had her own place now. She'd never had a one-night stand. She'd never slept with a man on the first date. But last Fourth of July, she would have made an exception. She might even have blamed it on the punch, thanks to all the buzz in town about its having had a chemical effect in some way, but there was no punch in the picture now, and she wanted Ryan in a fiercely physical way.

Sitting beside him in public and eating a slice of pie set her senses on fire. She'd meant what she'd said on the sidewalk. If she got him alone, she'd seduce him.

He was hers. He'd come back to see her, and he'd come a very long way, too. She wasn't going to make the same mistake twice. If he had to leave the next day, she knew for certain she'd miss him whether they slept together or not, so they might as well—

Leave the next day. Those were chilling words.

"You don't have to fly out in the morning again, do you?"

He brushed her hair out of the way. "I arranged a week off work."

"A whole week. That sounds wonderful." It stretched before her like a huge chunk of time. Seven days. Seven nights.

The nights were on her mind. "Where are you staying while you're here?"

"Maverick Manor."

The name of the place triggered her family pride. "My brother designed that place. Jonah. He's an architect."

"It's one of the most striking hotels I've stayed in."

"Isn't it? It was a private house before he worked on it. I've started working for Jonah myself."

She paused, unsure how to proceed. She had no doubt that she'd know exactly what to do with Ryan if she had him alone in her new bedroom. She'd fantasized about the possibilities in detail, but she'd never considered the first step. How did one let a man know he should take her to her home, come inside and stay the night? She'd always had her parents and brothers under her roof before, so this was a new experience.

"You're working for an architect? That's got to be a huge change. I always imagine you working on your family's ranch."

"I still work there, too, four days a week. I couldn't leave my parents shorthanded." She tapped the edge of her pie plate with her fork. "It also gives me a chance to raid the kitchen and eat some of my mother's home cooking after I'm done in the stables."

"Do you mean you moved off your ranch?" He sounded absolutely stunned.

"I'm living in town. Jonah is renovating a block of gorgeous old Victorian houses. I'm living in one of them and working at the same time, a sort of sweat equity. Instead of paying my rent in cash, I'm paying it by doing some of the renovations. Are you going to eat your whipped cream?"

When he slid his plate toward her, she helped herself.

"To be honest, 'renovating' means I varnish stuff. There's lots and lots of varnishing to be done in a vintage Victorian. Lotsa wood in those babies, and Jonah is crazy about keeping every last piece of original trim. It's all curlicue gingerbread and a real pain in the neck. Pretty to look at, but trust me, you don't want to maintain it."

Ryan was listening to every word she said, and judging by that almost-curve of his mouth and the way his eyes were crinkling a bit at the corners, he liked listening to her. Kristen found that to be a total turn-on that had nothing to do with tanned chests and wash-board abs.

"Do you miss living on the ranch?"

"I probably would if I wasn't still showing up for breakfast four days a week. That's just enough to keep me from being so homesick that I want to move back in. I do miss Kayla, but it's fun to have her popping in for some sister time."

"Congratulations, then, on your first home."

Kristen sat sideways in the booth, tucking one leg under her so she could face him more squarely. "Thank you. Not just for saying that, but for being a big part of the reason I made a lot of changes this fall. Do you re-member when we talked about the pursuit of happiness? You said you could be happier, that your work wasn't as rewarding as it had been, and I was so impressed that you were taking action to change things that weren't making you happy."

She hesitated at his slight frown. It probably wasn't realistic to expect him to remember every word they'd said, or even every topic they'd covered throughout the course of that day. She knew every word by heart, but that probably made her look like a lovesick little cow-girl. She wanted him to think of her as so much more.

Still frowning, he reached for one of her wayward curls and wrapped it around his finger. "I remember. Go ahead."

"You inspired me. I realized I was drifting along in a safe routine, but I hadn't stopped to examine what I really wanted. I don't know if you remember that I'd interviewed with the principal—"

"Every word, Kristen. I remember."

Her heart thudded hard, one solid thud, and she knew

it was the sound of a heart falling harder in love. "I decided that just because he'd said no, that didn't mean I had to wait on the ranch for an opportunity to open up. Now I've got my own house, and that was just the beginning."

"That's huge. There's more?"

There was the play, of course. He'd be so proud to know she was using her theater degree. But he was going to be here a full week, and that meant he'd be here on opening night. She was dying to brag about her return to the theater, but this could be a chance to really surprise him on Friday. If she could get him in the audience and then surprise him by appearing on stage, it would be dramatic.

She drew her knee up and hugged it with one arm, still facing him on the bench of the booth. "There might be one or two more things, but you can't expect a woman to divulge every secret at once. I might need to keep a little air of mystery about me."

He raised one eyebrow. "Considering I failed to tell you where I lived, I'm in no position to demand to know all your secrets."

"Here's the important part." She took a deep breath, focused and prepared to deliver her most important line. "You don't need to stay at Maverick Manor this week. I'd like to extend a formal invitation. Mr. Ryan Michaels, would you like to be my first guest in my first home?"

Of all the reactions she might have expected, the way he closed his eyes and turned his face away was not one. Her heart thudded into the silence.

"What's wrong?" she whispered.

The hand he'd rested on the table clenched into a fist. "For one thing, Ryan Michaels is not my name."

"More coffee, you two?"

The owner of the diner had apparently run out of things to do and had come over to chat, interrupting at the worst moment. Ryan needed to explain his name to Kristen. He couldn't sleep with a woman who didn't know his last name, no matter how important she was to him, and he couldn't explain the name confusion if this shop owner didn't leave them alone.

The woman gestured to the phone on the table. "Do you want me to take a picture?" She wiped her free hand on her apron in preparation.

"No, thank you." His curt tone made it clear that she should leave. It would have worked on any server in any city from Los Angeles to London.

Not this woman. She studied him more closely, looking him over. "I haven't seen you in here before. Did you come from the airport? Got a layover tonight?"

This was completely, utterly, not her concern. He glared at her, unwilling to give her a single syllable of *no*, but Kristen let go of the knee she'd been hugging and turned to face her. "He's an old friend of mine, Matilda. We were just catching up. Could you give us just a minute? The pumpkin pie was delicious, by the way."

Matilda kept her eye on Ryan, but she picked up the empty pie plate, took her coffeepot and left. For now.

Ryan had no problem dismissing unnecessary persons, but Kristen accomplished the same thing with a smile. His big-city impatience clashed with her small-town friendliness. He felt like a foreigner once more.

She turned all that sweetness on him. "Was she

standing behind me for long? Did she hear what I said to you? My face is turning ten shades of red now, I can feel it."

"She didn't hear anything."

Kristen had just asked him to spend a week in her home and in her bed. He'd told her she didn't even know his real name, yet she didn't seem hurt or suspicious. He didn't deserve her smile.

"Matilda brought up a good point, though. Did you just fly in today?"

"I landed last night." He hoped his expression was as neutral as he kept it during a trial. He was going to be forced to admit this meeting was a complete accident.

"And you came to Kalispell to find me today, which is…well, not so odd, I guess. Did you stop by the ranch? Maybe Kayla told you I'd be here today."

"No. I just came here because…" There was no hiding the truth in this case. "I had no idea what to say to you when I found you. I came here to walk, basically, and think. Then I planned to head to Rust Creek Falls to find you."

"So it was a total coincidence that you were on the same sidewalk at the same time?"

"It didn't seem so coincidental. I flew in to see you and I was thinking about you when I saw you, but it—"

"—is totally romantic, like you had a sixth sense where I'd be. I've got goose bumps."

Ryan couldn't help it; he had to grin at her relentless optimism. "I was going to say it was totally random."

"Seems more like destiny to me."

That word again. He wasn't ready to claim a belief in destiny, but it seemed better than dwelling on how nervous he'd been to see her again

Kristen, completely at ease with the situation, helped herself to a bite of his gingerbread. "So, is Ryan Michaels like a stage name? You use it professionally?"

Back to the rodeo, then. She was too trusting. He wished he deserved that trust.

"When we met, I only told you my name was Ryan. It was intentional. I didn't want everyone in town to know who I was."

"You said Michaels much later that night, on the church steps."

"I was talking about the three-year-old version of me. Ryan Michaels was my birth name. It changed when I was adopted."

"Oh, of course. I'm sorry, I didn't think of that."

"Don't apologize. Please."

He had to tell her his real name now. It was the obvious thing to say next, but he hesitated. How well did she know everyone in Rust Creek Falls? His sister and cousin lived there. Maggie Roarke, Lissa Roarke. If for some reason Kristen knew their maiden names, then the bandage would be ripped off whether he liked it or not.

If the fates were kind, Kristen would only know his relatives by their married names. Maggie Crawford. Lissa Christensen.

"So what's your real name?" she asked.

He wouldn't have been surprised if his voice cracked like an adolescent. Thankfully, it did not. "My name is Ryan Roarke."

He waited, dreading the next spark of recognition, the inevitable *are you related to...?*

"Roarke," she repeated. "I like it." Then she took a sip of her coffee.

Incredible. Wonderful. He'd dodged the bullet. She didn't know Maggie and Lissa's maiden names.

Thankfully, neither his sister nor cousin had any business on the Dalton's family ranch, and he doubted Kristen had ever needed legal help from Maggie Crawford or hung out in the sheriff's office where Lissa Christensen's photo might have been on the sheriff's desk. His cowgirl wasn't the type to track down everyone's backgrounds—not like the owner of this diner—and for that, he was grateful.

"Ryan Roarke. It's a little catchier than Ryan Michaels, with the two *R*'s. Do a lot of rodeo performers use stage names?"

"I have no idea. Roarke is my real name." He felt the flash of guilt, although he was telling the truth. He *didn't* know if rodeo stars used stage names, although it seemed likely some would.

"It certainly explains why I didn't find you when I typed 'Ryan Michaels rodeo' in my internet search." She put her head back on his shoulder, and Ryan closed his eyes in both guilt and relief.

If she assumed he was still a rodeo star, well…they were getting closer to the truth. Bit by bit. Slow and steady, so that nothing would abruptly shatter beyond repair.

In his mind's eye, he saw the snow globe hit the church steps.

He opened his eyes, took in the sight of Kristen curved against him, the soft leather of the booth's high-backed bench sheltering them both. Nothing harsh. Nothing hard.

Beyond their booth, outside the wide glass panes of the storefront window, snow started falling in slow, fluffy flakes. He had the fleeting thought that he was inside the snow globe.

He hugged Kristen to him tightly. He didn't want anything to break. Not this time.

"That coffee has got to be cold by now." The woman in the apron reappeared, holding her coffeepot above their cooled cups, poised for action if he'd just say the word. "You might as well have it warm."

Ryan curtly nodded his permission.

Too harsh. Too hard.

He mustered up a smile as she poured the hot coffee. "Thank you. Everything here is warm. It's a nice place."

"Well." She produced a fresh spoon from her apron pocket and set it in front of Kristen. "Well, you just stay here and enjoy. It's only going to get colder out there."

"Oh, man," Kristen said in a stage whisper. "Somebody's going to get extra whipped cream from now on."

"I heard you," Matilda said over her shoulder. "You and your old friend just remember that we make wedding cakes here, too."

Chapter Nine

Ryan took her to dinner.

Kristen took him home.

Impatient with the slow burn of sexual tension that had been building all day, Kristen led the way back to Rust Creek Falls in her compact SUV and parallel parked on the street of vintage houses. She waited on the sidewalk while Ryan pulled his rented truck into the next closest spot. Her mind was still processing the incredible fact that today was the day that Ryan Michaels had come back.

No, it was Roarke. Ryan Roarke had come back.

But while her heart and mind kept feeling surprised— *today!*—her body was already well beyond that acceptance phase. Every inch of her craved the intimacy which every smoldering look over a candlelit dinner in Kalispell had promised. They were adults who wanted each other, who'd wanted each other since a waltz in July, and the time had come.

Ryan kept his hands in the pockets of his overcoat as he walked up to her, looking sexy and self-contained. Kristen felt a little shiver of nervous awareness. She might be an adult, but six feet of confident, controlled male wasn't something she invited into her bedroom. Ever. Her past lovers, which numbered exactly two, might as well have never existed, for all that her experience with them had prepared her for a night with this man. Ryan Roarke was in a league of his own.

"Which house is yours?" The bass in his voice struck just the right, delicious note.

She wanted this. Him. Them. So she lifted her chin with a confidence she didn't quite possess and held up her phone, acting as if she weren't dying to get him in the door and naked on the floor. "I'll give you a clue. I told you Jonah was a fanatic about keeping all the original wood. He doesn't feel that way about the electrical wiring. He's completely in love with high tech in his buildings. Ready?"

She punched a code into her phone, and like magic, the second house from the corner lit up. A rainbow of multicolored Christmas lights delineated the elegant lines of its arched front porch. "Isn't it wonderful?"

Ryan shook his head in amusement. "It's not even Thanksgiving yet."

"Less than two weeks away. Come with me. I have to light up the best thing myself."

She slid her phone into her pocket as she led the way up the newly installed wood stairs. Just last week, she'd sealed them against the coming winter weather. Today's flurries were already gone, but she had the satisfaction of knowing the wood had been protected against them.

On the wide porch, Kristen plugged an extension cord into an outlet near the front door. "Ta-da!"

Ryan turned to look at her most treasured garage sale find: a molded plastic Santa that was four feet tall and lit up from the inside by an old-fashioned, sixty-watt light bulb.

"Isn't he great? He should be in the yard, but I'm keeping him on the porch to protect him from the elements. He's the real deal from 1968."

Ryan had gone very quiet beside her, hands still in his pockets.

"He needs a Mrs. Claus, of course. He's half of a pair—you know, the kind where Mr. and Mrs. Claus are leaning forward to kiss each other?"

Ryan stepped behind her, very close.

"It's going to be a challenge to find her, but I've got alerts set on eBay."

Ryan pulled up the bottom edge of her coat and set his hands on her hips, his fingertips grazing her middle as he held her firmly to him. The street was empty, but her winter coat would have made it hard for anyone to see exactly what he was doing.

"Until I find a vintage Mrs. Claus, Santa will just have to blow kisses to the people on the sidewalk, even though I don't have any neighbors yet. Oh, Lord, I'm babbling, aren't I?"

Ryan bent to kiss her neck, nudging her scarf out of the way with his chin, replacing the material's warmth with the warmth of his mouth as he tasted the soft skin under her jaw. As her knees turned to jelly, he slid one hand across her stomach, wrapping his arm around her waist for support.

"My keys," she said, sounding as breathy as a vintage movie star. "Let me just..." She patted her pocket, felt her phone, pulled out her house keys.

Ryan turned her in his arms and kissed her full-on, capturing her gasp in that zero-to-sixty escalation of passion that she didn't want to slow down. He moved them farther away from the row of colored lights, pressing her back against the door's deep framing as he kissed her senseless, or nearly senseless. She kept just enough brain power going to fit the key in the lock and turn it.

She fumbled for the antique iron doorknob but his hand covered hers, his breath hot against her lips, his body hard against hers. "I'm not coming in," he murmured between tastes of her.

"You're—*what*?"

"Not tonight. I'm not coming in." Then he kissed her, hungry, making love to her mouth the way she wanted his body to make love to hers.

"Come in," she gasped. "Now. Please."

With a sharp sound of frustration, he jerked her coat up a little farther. Cold air chased his hot hand as he slid from her belly to her lacy, thin bra. He cupped one whole breast, shaping her softness to the contours of his hand. She melted at his touch, sliding down the frame an inch, grasping with her free hand for an anchor until she clutched his coat's lapel for support.

She tried to say *yes, more, don't stop*, but only whimpered deep in her throat. He stopped caressing her, and they stayed locked in that embrace, not moving, not kissing, just breathing.

"This is a bad idea," he said, panting in a way that made Kristen feel incredibly desirable.

"This is a great idea." She pressed her head back against the framing so that she could look him in the eye. "This is…powerful."

He sharpened his gaze, losing a little of that sexual haze. She knew he remembered using that word when they'd kissed in the summer.

"So come into the house."

"What's between you and me is not going to disappear," he said. "It will be powerful tomorrow, and the day after that, and after that."

Darn the man for using her own summer words against her.

He withdrew his hand and tugged her coat down. He still had her crowded against the door, but she felt that he was creating a deliberate distance all the same.

"If this feeling isn't going to change, then why not tonight?" Her hand jerked his lapel with her plea, a tiny motion that betrayed her huge frustration. They were so, so close.

He kissed her pouting lower lip, soothing her. Placating her.

She didn't want that. She wanted him, so she let go of the doorknob to grab his other lapel and pulled him to her with both fists. Her kiss wasn't soothing. It went from zero to sixty for both of them.

"Because," he said, a long minute later.

It took her a second to realize he was answering her question.

"Not tonight, because you don't know me. Not well enough for this."

"That's crazy. You're all I've thought about for four

months. I didn't believe in love at first sight, until I met you."

After a long moment, Ryan bowed his head. He nodded, even as he turned from her and took a step away, putting real physical distance between them.

She'd put the word out there. *Love.*

Her heart thudded, hard.

"Until a few hours ago, that love at first sight was for a rodeo star named Ryan Michaels. That's not me." His voice sounded harsh. The look in his eyes was…hurt.

So, he must have left the rodeo, something that had been a huge part of his life. He was no longer a rodeo star, and it bothered him. She didn't know how to help a man leave a career behind. To make it worse, she'd called him by the wrong name today, a name that reminded him of the worst time of his life. That, at least, she could fix.

"Your last name doesn't change my feelings. Ryan Michaels grew into the man Ryan Roarke is. You've been you all along."

He looked at her across three feet of porch planking as if he were looking at a woman who was far out of his reach. "Trust me on this. You should know me better before we make love. I do mean make love, because as powerful and crazy as this is, it's real. It would gut me if we made love and you came to regret it."

But there is a chance you might.

The implication was clear. So was Ryan's expression, his stance. Everything about him as he warned her off seemed straightforward and sincere.

What could she learn about him that would possibly cause her to regret having slept with him? She didn't regret sleeping with her college sweetheart, even though the relationship hadn't lasted. Then there was Captain Two-Timer—

She regretted that one. Ryan was right; there were a few possibilities that would be showstoppers for her.

"Okay, then. In the interest of avoiding any future regret, can I ask you a few questions?"

"Yes."

"Are you married?"

Surprise flickered across his face. "No."

"Involved with another woman? Is there another woman in another small town who thinks you are coming back for her?"

"No. I'm not using you to cheat on anyone else. It goes without saying that I'd never cheat on you."

"It goes without saying." She still felt like a fool for not having realized the truth about her pilot sooner. "But it's still better to have that one laid out as a ground rule."

"It sounds like there's a man out there, somewhere, who'd be better off not crossing your path again. Or mine." He crossed the gap he'd put between them, and brushed a few loose strands of hair away from her cheek. His fingers were cool in the night air. "No other women. An easy promise, one I've been keeping since the day I met you."

She shivered at his touch and his words, and let her eyes close.

Kiss me, kiss me.

He put his hand back in his pocket. "Did you have any other questions?"

She opened her eyes, disappointed. What else could cause her to regret sleeping with Ryan Roarke, whom she'd dreamed about for months, who'd traveled the length of the country just to see her again? "Do you have a disease?"

"Fair question. No. Do you?"

"Oh, you mean…no, not those kind of diseases. I mean, I've got nothing, uh, contagious. That wasn't what I was asking—but we should be asking, of course, I just wasn't, and…" She could beg him to make love to her without blushing, but everything else seemed to make her cheeks burn.

She took a deeper breath. "I meant, are you dying of any disease? Am I going to regret making love to you when I find out you have an inoperable brain tumor or something? Not that I wouldn't still care for you, though. If our time is short, I'd want to make love to you all the more, really."

"I see." His lips twitched into that almost-curve. "Nothing that I know of."

"Don't laugh at me. It would be horrible. Those are my least favorite movies. You can't drag me into a theater to watch heartbreak like that."

She was glad to see his sense of humor returning, anyway, his expression relaxing into a smile, although he maintained his stiff posture, hands in his pockets. As his chuckle made his breath puff out in little white clouds, it occurred to her that he might be cold. They'd had some flurries today, and he was used to the weather in Southern California, not at the Canadian border.

"We could go inside to talk. It's pretty cold out here. I promise not to seduce you."

"I can't make the same promise. Every minute we talk makes you more appealing."

She wrinkled her nose. "What turned you on? The talk about diseases or my sorry history of being cheated on?"

"It was the way you made yourself blush, and the way your past experience makes me feel so protective of your heart."

Thud. The man could stop her heart with his words.

She threw up her hands in frustration. "You know, Ryan, if you're going to talk like that, you have to take me to bed."

He smiled a bit, but he had those sad eyes again. "Let's give it a little time. Are there any other showstoppers you'd like to ask before I admit that I'm freezing and say good-night?"

"Showstoppers. That's exactly the word I was thinking. We're so alike." She looked around at her Christmas lights and her plastic Santa. "I'm drawing a blank here. I can't imagine what you're afraid I'll find out about you. Unless…"

"Unless?"

"You don't have any sexual fetishes I should know about? You're not into, like, Roman orgy reenactments or anything?"

Ryan crossed his arms over his chest and leaned one shoulder against the wall. "I'm not that cold, after all. Let's discuss this. Roman orgies are out, then? What other sexual fetishes are off the table? Or on?"

Kristen crossed her arms over her chest and leaned against the wall, too. "Describe yours for me, and I'll decide."

She'd managed to keep a straight face, but Ryan just about doubled over with sudden laughter. She was laughing, too, when he kissed her softly, then stepped back before she could test his willpower with a more passionate kiss. "On that note, I better leave. I'm already not going to be able to sleep tonight."

"Will I see you tomorrow?"

"What's the earliest possible time I can pick you up?"

It was so lovely to be with a man who was as eager to see her as she was to see him. "Actually, I have to work tomorrow at the Circle D. I'll be there by six."

"In the morning?"

"Of course. Why don't you come? You could check out our horses. I've got one who's an absolute nightmare to get trailered. You must know tons of good tricks about transporting animals."

Ryan's smile faded.

"Or maybe that's a really dumb idea. I'm sorry, I forgot this is your vacation. You probably don't want to muck out a stall on vacation."

He rubbed his jaw, then nodded as if he'd come to a decision. "The Circle D is a part of who you are. I'd like to see it. I'll pick you up and we can drive to the ranch together."

"Actually, if we showed up in the same rig before sunrise, my family might jump to some conclusions about how we'd spent the night. I wouldn't mind doing the time if I'd done the crime, so to speak, but why don't you just meet me there? Anytime after six will be fine."

"All right. I'm looking forward to seeing a genuine cowgirl in her natural habitat."

"Whatever you say, cowboy."

Ryan's smile didn't touch those sad eyes as he left without risking another kiss.

A *cowboy*.

Ryan threw his coat on the log bed of his hotel room. Throwing a well-tailored length of blended wool was a completely unsatisfying outlet for his frustration. A punching bag or a sparring session in the boxing ring would be better. Instead, he had to prepare to spend tomorrow with a bunch of horses.

He didn't know squat about horses, but Kristen was going to expect him to give her advice. She'd talked about love at first sight tonight, but she'd meant love at the first sight of a cowboy.

He was no horse whisperer, but his brother-in-law was. Ryan called Jesse.

Maggie answered, of course. Being both a lawyer and his sister, she was doubly direct.

"Did you straighten things out with Kristen?"

Ryan yanked off one boot. "I'm working on it, Maggie. Let me talk to Jesse."

"Working on it? You didn't tell her the truth?"

"We're getting there. She knows I live in Southern California now. She knows my name is Roarke."

"Roarke the rodeo star? Or Roarke the attorney?"

"Let me talk to Jesse."

"You've got to tell her. The longer you let this go on, the more hurt she's going to be when she finds out the truth."

He yanked off the other boot. "I never told her I was a rodeo star."

"But you're letting her believe it. She's going to hate you for that when she finds out the truth."

She's going to hate you...

He couldn't stand the thought. He hated the very words. God, he wanted only for her to love him.

"Ryan?"

He set the boot down carefully, lining it up neatly beside the rough-hewn leg of the rustic chair.

"Ask Jesse to call me when he gets a chance." His

voice sounded calm. His hand was steady when he tapped the button to end the call.

She's going to hate you...

He dropped his head in his hands and gave in to the shudder that racked his body.

Tonight, she'd said she loved him—or, at least, that she believed it was possible to have fallen in love with him at first sight. She didn't seem to resent him for being gone for months, and so far, she wasn't upset that at least two of her assumptions about him had been wrong. A name and a home state, those she could forgive—because she loved him?

Love should be unchangeable. He should be able to tell Kristen everything: Ryan Michaels, Ryan Roarke, cowboy, attorney. None of it should matter, but he had an old Christmas memory that proved otherwise.

Love was not unconditional, no matter what fairy tales others believed. A mother could decide she didn't love a little boy anymore. Nothing good lasted forever. He had to be careful with Kristen, and handle the possibility that she loved him with care.

He had a good plan. Kristen had pieced together one picture of him, and he was going to replace the wrong pieces, one at a time. Some day, Kristen might think his skills in a courtroom were impressive, but tomorrow, he'd be in a stable. He didn't want to look like an ass. When the phone rang, he knew what he had to do.

"Jesse. I've got a hypothetical situation for you. It's six in the morning, and you walk into a stable full of horses. What's the first thing you do?"

Chapter Ten

Ryan entered the stables with trepidation.

His brother-in-law had said the first thing he did was walk the entire length of the barn, once through. "You can get a feel right away if the horses as a group are calm. Then I look for any one horse who seems out of sorts."

According to Jesse, every barn had its own feed and care routine, so Ryan should follow Kristen's lead and respect the routine of the Circle D—as if Ryan might have a different routine in mind.

"You don't need special training to dump feed into a bucket or skim loose hay out of a water trough," Jesse had said.

"If she asks me to do anything more complex than that, what's your advice for a man who last touched a horse at eighth-grade summer camp?"

Jesse had laughed. "Generally speaking, horses are

patient creatures. They'll put up with a lot when they know you're trying."

"Generally speaking?"

"Good luck."

Ryan's first step into the barn startled a cat that bolted across his path and headed up a pile of hay bales to the safety of the rafters.

"I know how you feel," Ryan said under his breath. He wished he could dodge potential danger as effectively, but helping Kristen with her morning chores was a minefield he had to negotiate. He'd considered changing their plans. He could pick her up once she'd returned to her house and take her out for a nice lunch. Dinner and a movie. But he couldn't sleep in the plush bedding at Maverick Manor knowing Kristen was working hard in the cold November dawn. It offended some sense of chivalry or manhood deep down, concepts that were probably outdated, but he felt them nonetheless.

His first sight of Kristen Dalton in her natural element forced him to be more honest with himself. She looked like his most cherished Montana fantasy come true. This wasn't about helping a damsel in distress; this was about spending every possible moment with this woman, period. Full stop. If Kristen wanted to be with him, he wanted to be with her, wherever, whenever and doing whatever.

Her back was to him as she hung a pitchfork on a wall hook. Despite the barn's temperature being nearly the same as outside, Kristen wore only a faded pink sweatshirt and blue jeans. Her glorious hair, something that could easily become a fetish of his, hung in one long braid down her back, bouncing with each step as she pushed a wheelbarrow away from him, heading for the open door at the opposite end of the barn.

"Just cool your jets, tough guy. I'll get to you in a minute."

Ryan stopped in surprise, until a black horse stuck its head out of the stall she'd just passed and snorted at her, shaking its mane impatiently. Kristen continued out the wide door without stopping.

Ryan slowly walked down the center aisle of the barn, absorbing the feel of the place. It was spacious and organized, and smelled equally of animals and hay. Most of the stalls were empty, so he assumed they normally held the horses that he'd seen milling about in a fenced-in grassy area adjacent to the barn. As Ryan reached the door through which Kristen had taken her wheelbarrow, the black horse and three others stuck their massive heads over their half doors and looked at him with knowing, dark eyes.

He wondered if he should have brought carrots or some other bribe. He held his palm up to the brown beauty closest to him. "Sorry, I've got nothing."

The horse snuffled his palm, anyway. He petted its nose, the softness as surprising now as it had been in eighth grade. Ryan moved to the next stall and repeated the greeting with the next horse. He could see what Jesse had meant about being able to get a feel for the horses' attitude. Ryan could tell these animals were content and cared for. It didn't take a lifetime of ranch experience to recognize good health and a friendly disposition.

The black horse across the aisle bit at his door's latch and bobbed his head in a demanding way. The name plate over his stall identified him as Zorro. "Everyone's patient except you, son. You need to work on your attitude. You heard Kristen. Don't rush the woman."

"That's right, Zorro. I hope you're paying attention." Kristen's voice had a laugh in it. She let go of her empty wheelbarrow and came toward Ryan with her arms open for a hug, but she stopped short. "You look too nice. I'll get you all dirty."

Ryan took the final step toward her and scooped her against him. "You look fantastic."

"Oh, yes. Like a mucker of stalls."

"The braid and boots thing is definitely working for me." He lingered for a few dangerous seconds longer than he should have as he kissed the happy curve of her mouth, and set her down again.

"If braids and boots are your fetish, you'll be in heaven here in Rust Creek Falls. Put it in your plus column."

He couldn't resist touching the fine bones of her face, trailing his fingers over her cheekbone and along her jawline. Such delicate features for a woman as strong as she was. "The braid and boots only turn me on when your pretty face is part of the package."

Her gaze flickered over his shoulder. "I told you that you'd be in heaven. There are two women in Rust Creek Falls who meet your criteria."

Ryan turned to see a duplicate of Kristen walking toward them. It was disconcerting for a second, like seeing a special effect from a movie, although he'd known she had an identical twin. On the Fourth of July, they'd passed her sister a few times on the dance floor, but there'd been clear differences in their clothing and hair and the way they moved. Now, in jeans and boots and the braid he supposed was practical for working in a barn, they were startlingly identical.

"You must be Kayla," he said, extending his hand.

She dropped her gaze but took his hand, then looked up at him again with a shy duck of her chin. She was so unlike Kristen in her actions Ryan doubted he'd ever be fooled for more than a second.

"And you must be Ryan Michaels." Her voice was quiet in the cavernous barn.

Kristen jumped in. "It's Ryan Roarke, actually. My mistake. That's why I couldn't find him in any rodeo results."

"Roarke?" Kayla looked at him more directly. "Are you related to Lissa Roarke, then?"

Ryan released her hand, but not before she must have felt his little jolt of surprise. She knew maiden names, obviously. This was an unexpected mine that needed to be carefully defused.

"Lissa who?" Kristen asked.

"Lissa Christensen," her sister explained patiently. "The sheriff's wife. She was Lissa Roarke when she came here from New York and wrote that blog about the flood, remember?"

"Oh." Kristen turned to him and made a little gesture toward her sister. "If it has to do with writing or newspapers, she's into it. English major."

Ryan smiled, ignoring his racing heart. "Lissa is my cousin. She grew up in New York, though, while I was in…"

"California," Kristen finished for him, and she turned to her sister. "He's from California."

Ryan knew instinctively that Kristen was anxious to prove that she knew him well, although she hadn't made the connection with Lissa.

"Is that why you were here for the Fourth of July, then?" Kristen asked, phrasing her question like her sister. "You were visiting Lissa? That makes so much sense."

"Lissa was in New York because Gage was on duty for the whole holiday weekend." Ryan hadn't lied about his intention that day in the park, and he wasn't going to start now. "I came to look into relocating to Rust Creek Falls, remember?"

Kristen's expression brightened. "But now I know how you heard of Rust Creek Falls in the first place. A cousin has to go in the plus column. Being far from your parents is a bigger minus, but at least you'll have some family in town."

She was still so certain that the plus column would win. Whether or not Lissa lived in town didn't change the fact that the full responsibility for Roarke and Associates was being laid on his shoulders by his parents' impending retirement. Once he explained the situation fully, he hoped Kristen would understand. The dream he'd toyed with in July about living here couldn't become a reality. They'd have to be a long-distance couple, or she'd have to move to LA.

The black horse chose that moment to remind them all that he was not where he wanted to be.

"Okay, Zorro. Chill out. Let me check your feet before I turn you out." With efficient movements and a grace that Ryan was certain could only come from a lifetime of working with horses, Kristen put a halter on the black horse and led him out of his stall, then tied him to a railing in the aisle with some kind of knot that Ryan had probably failed at tying back in his scouting days. She grabbed a small tool from a bucket that hung on the wall, and crouched down to lift the massive animal's front hoof. With a series of soothing "good boys," she started working on Zorro's hoof.

Kayla picked up the handles of the wheelbarrow. "I'll be mucking stalls if you need me."

"I'll help." Ryan was confident he could master a pitchfork faster than the two-step, and he'd mastered that in less than one verse of a country-western song.

"You'll ruin your clothes," Kayla said. "That overcoat is just too nice for chores."

"It's all I brought on this trip. It can be cleaned."

Kristen looked up from her crouch on the floor. "Just put on another coat. I think Eli left that one here." She pointed with her pick to a beige canvas coat that hung on a wall with a cluster of leather straps and ropes.

Ryan hung his long overcoat in its place. The battered canvas coat was the same temperature as the crisp November air that filled the barn from the open doors. He'd barely shrugged into it when gentle Kayla took another tool out of the bucket and lobbed it not so gently at Ryan. He caught it by the wood handle, thankfully, because the rest of it looked like a loop made from a metal saw.

"Zorro has sensitive feet. If you brush him at the same time, he won't be so fussy for Kristen." She took the wheelbarrow and headed down the aisle to an empty stall.

Ryan thought the tool in his hand looked more likely to torture than soothe. He walked up to the horse, struck anew at just how large the beast was. He scraped the teeth of the metal loop lightly along Zorro's side. The horse didn't object, so he did it again, a little more firmly.

Kristen moved to the other front hoof, so Ryan kept running the brush along the horse, resting his free hand on the horse's neck as he worked, appreciating the heat and power contained in the muscles under the black coat. Although Zorro's hair had seemed to be too short to be brushed, the shades of black varied after each stroke as the nap of the hair reflected light at a new angle. Ryan kept the brush moving in a methodical pattern over the black gloss.

"I can see why he finds this soothing." Immediately, Ryan realized he'd said something that revealed this was a new experience for him. *Too soon, don't shatter—* but he couldn't cover the mistake without lying, and he couldn't lie to Kristen.

"Zorro's one of those that really love it. Of course, Snoopy over there really hates it. You know how it is. What works with one horse has the opposite effect on another." She moved to another hoof. "Good boy. You boys like to keep us guessing, don't you, Zorro?"

Ryan relaxed again. The sky outside the double doors began to lighten with the coming dawn. Incredibly, despite his blunder, Kristen assumed he knew horses. Then again, growing up on a ranch in Montana, maybe a person who *didn't* know horses was as foreign to her as an alien from a UFO.

He chose his words with care. "Kristen, I never told you I was in the rodeo. What makes you think I am?"

She stood up, finished with that hoof, and looked at him over Zorro's back. She rested her arm on the horse as she talked, like one would lean on a piece of furniture. She was completely comfortable around an animal that weighed one thousand pounds. Her unconscious confidence was sexy.

"Every once in a while, someone at the picnic would recognize you. I knew right away that you couldn't be just another hand making the rounds of the ranches, looking for work. You carry yourself like you are used to being in charge. Besides, and please don't think I'm materialistic or anything, you don't dress like the average ranch hand. You must be doing something that's a little more lucrative than a standard cowboy paycheck. I put two and two together."

She disappeared again, crouching down to pick up the last hoof.

Ryan kept brushing. It had been that simple, then. For a woman who only knew cowboys, there was only one kind of cowboy who would get recognized at the town picnic.

"Have you ever *not* dated a cowboy?"

The scraping sounds stopped for a moment.

"Once."

The scraping started again.

"He was from the city."

She said the word *city* like it was a curse. She referred to Kalispell as a city, with its population of how many? Twenty thousand? Los Angeles was a city of fifteen or sixteen million. If she thought a place like Kalispell was too big, she'd hate Ryan Roarke's reality.

"He was based in Denver."

A bigger city, then, but still small compared to Ryan's.

"A pilot."

The bitterness in that simple word snapped his attention from his own sorry worries back to Kristen. Bitterness was rare from her, but he'd heard it once before, during last night's conversation on the porch. Her one experience with a non-cowboy had been a bad one.

Ryan worked his way around to her side of the horse, brushing as he went, staying calm. "This was the guy who didn't understand that some things go without saying."

In her crouched position, her head was bowed, and her hands went still. "He was in the shower, getting ready to go back to work after his layover. His phone was right next to me on the nightstand. The screen lit up that he'd gotten a text, with a little preview of the message. There was this tiny thumbnail photo of a topless girl, and the first line said, See you at five. The current time was in big numbers, 10:16. That will be stuck in my brain for a long time."

Zorro threw his head up, objecting to the stroke of the brush. Ryan stopped until the first wave of jealousy and anger passed, then he crouched down next to Kristen.

"I told him off, of course," she said. "He put on his uniform and left me in the hotel. Seven hours after we'd been in bed together, I knew he was back in Denver, having sex with her. Breaking up with me didn't hurt him for half a day. I'm sure I was just some dumb cowgirl from Montana to him. Another variety to add to his menu."

Ryan kept his fury at the unknown pilot under control, mindful of his tone of voice around the horse. "I know that type. He'll never be faithful to anyone, ever, and it doesn't matter how wonderful the woman is."

It was rare for Kristen not to look him in the eye, but she toyed with the pick in her hand for a moment, then ran her hand down Zorro's leg, soothing the horse to soothe herself.

"Believe me, Kristen. It wasn't that you weren't a good enough girlfriend. The fault is all his."

She nodded. "I get that. I do. It's just that I'm ashamed of myself for believing his lies. I should have been able to see through them. I saw him every other week, and never questioned what he did or who he did it with between those times. He looked me right in the eye and lied to me, over and over, trip after trip."

She's going to hate you when she finds out the truth.

He couldn't tell her about himself today. He couldn't risk it. At that moment, he wanted, more than anything else in the world, to be a cowboy for Kristen, so she'd never doubt her own judgment again.

"I made a promise to myself," she said. "No more city slickers. I wished for a cowboy, and now here you are."

With regret, with tenderness, Ryan kissed her cheek. He hadn't lied, but he hadn't told her the complete truth. He stayed crouched beside her, wanting to tell her something true. "It goes without saying, I am with you and only you."

"I know. Cowboys get it."

"No. *I* get it. It's got nothing to do with cowboys, and everything to do with you. Because you're such an amazing person, there's no room in my head or my heart for another woman."

The wheelbarrow came to a halt beside them. Kayla crouched down. "What is it? Does Zorro have a cracked hoof again?"

Kristen barely glanced at her sister, but apparently, the look was enough between identical twins.

"Never mind." Kayla stood and pushed the wheelbarrow away.

Ryan stood and resumed his brushing, hoping the motion would help him center himself and bring back that calm feeling.

It didn't. It couldn't, because he hadn't clarified anything with Kristen except his desire for her, and she had to have known that already.

Kristen finished with whatever she'd been doing to the horse's feet and started loving on the horse, petting his nose and telling him sweet nothings. "You are being spoiled today, aren't you? Don't get any ideas about leaving me for Ryan. You can't run off to join the rodeo with him. No fame and fortune for you."

"Kristen."

He couldn't do this. He couldn't let her go on believing he was a rodeo star.

Don't risk it. Don't let it shatter.

He couldn't rip the bandage off, but he had to make one point perfectly clear. "My name won't ever be in your newspaper for winning a rodeo event. There will be no tour and no fame and glory. If that's what you're looking for in a relationship, I can't offer it to you."

She left the horse's side to walk up to him in that unhurried way ranchers seemed to move, but he didn't reach for her, nor she for him. They stood in the open door of the barn, the sunrise coloring the sky beyond them, the cold air between them.

"I didn't ask you to." Her blue-eyed gaze was unwavering. "It sounds like you haven't had a great love life in the past, either. Instead of a two-timing pilot, I'm guessing there's a woman who was more interested in getting close to fame than in getting close to you. Probably a lot of women over the years."

Every relationship. Some very intelligent women, some very talented, all of them beautiful and all of them, every single one, hoping to improve her Hollywood clout and connections. The up-and-coming actresses, the aging actresses, the models who wanted to be actresses. The pressure was constant in Hollywood; the game of who knew whom was crucial to landing parts. He didn't blame them, but he was weary. Kristen's complete lack of interest in Hollywood added to her small town appeal.

"It's a career hazard. I've dated women like that too often."

"Was this what you were afraid I'd regret? That I would be sorry I'd slept with you if you weren't going to be on the rodeo tour next season? Because that would be insulting to me, and it would hurt to think you knew me so little. I realize you're used to women who want to travel with a celebrity, but I'm not that kind of woman."

"I know you're not." She was fresh-faced, makeup free, a naturally beautiful woman against the backdrop of a beautiful part of the country. Her braid had fallen forward and was lying over one breast. He wanted her fiercely. "You are too much a part of this ranch and this town to want to waste your life on the road."

"Well, that sounds nicer than saying I'm a homebody, I guess." Her smile was as irrepressible as the growing sunrise. Ryan wanted to hold her close and feel that warmth.

Reading his mind, she stepped into his willing arms and laid her head on his shoulder. He caught her close and kissed her hair, the corner of her eye, the bridge of her nose. She relaxed under his touch, the change in her muscle tension as obvious as Zorro's had been.

"I'm so glad you're here. After this week, will you be gone long?"

"I'm spending Thanksgiving with my parents. After that…"

He didn't know. He hadn't thought beyond this week, beyond satisfying that burning need he'd had to see Kristen once more, just once more. Standing in this barn, the differences in their lives were more obvious to him than ever.

So was his need to be with her. One week with her would not be enough.

"It may be a while, but…" He shook his head at his own idiocy. He wasn't kidding anyone, least of all himself. "I don't think I can go without you very long. I'll come back."

"I knew that last July." She shushed the impatient Zorro, then turned her sunny smile on Ryan once more. "But it's nice that you know it now, too. Four months was a long time for you to realize you should come back to the place you said makes you feel at peace. I hated knowing you were out there somewhere, not at peace."

"Montana doesn't give me peace. You do."

The sound of a very loud, very human yawn startled them both. Kayla was behind them, stretching her arms overhead as she sat on an overturned barrel. "I hate to bother you two, but if we could turn out these last four horses and clean the stalls…" She yawned again.

Kristen frowned a little. "Another late night? You've been tired a lot lately."

"I'm fine. I'm just trying to live without coffee."

Kristen looked horrified. "No coffee? Why would you do that?"

Kayla ducked her head, shy once more. "Caffeine is supposed to be bad for you. I read this blog that made me want to try going without it. Just for a little while."

"Sis, I love you, but that's nuts. Maybe you should get some breakfast. Ryan's here. He'll help me finish up."

Kayla left after a few more protests. Kristen picked up a pitchfork and sifted through the hay in Zorro's empty stall, coming up with a clump of manure and tossing it into the wheelbarrow. "Why don't you turn out the rest of the horses while I get started on the dirty work?"

Ryan took one look at the ropes and knots and bridles hanging on the wall and took the pitchfork out of Kristen's hands. "I'm sure your horses would rather say good morning to you." He was also certain he'd make a fool of himself trying to put a bridle on a horse for the first time. A pitchfork took no skill, only muscle, and that, thankfully, he had.

Kristen slipped a leather bridle around the brown horse's head, reaching up to guide its ears under a strap, all while keeping her gaze on Ryan. "We can get breakfast afterward."

Ryan stopped in midscoop. Here was another obstacle he hadn't planned on negotiating. If he met her parents, there would be the inevitable getting-to-know-you questions. He tossed the manure into the wheelbarrow. "I hadn't planned on meeting your parents this morning."

Before he could add an acceptable excuse, Kristen jumped in. "Oh, I didn't mean breakfast at the house.

It was too late last night to call and tell them you'd be here this morning. I know my mom. She'd kill me if I walked into the kitchen with you while she was in her bathrobe."

Kristen led Zorro and the brown horse around the wheelbarrow, stopping in front of him and tossing her braid back over her shoulder with a graceful movement of her head and shoulder. "My house in town is always an option."

Her hands were full and so were his, but their mouths met with a hunger that had nothing to do with breakfast.

"Wow. You weren't kidding about the braids and boots, were you?"

"Your house is not a safe option." He stepped back. "How about that donut shop from our tour?"

"Bear claws and coffee. Sounds perfect."

"Go Grizzlies."

"Spoken like a true Rust Creek Falls native."

He had no answer for that, either, as Kristen led the two horses out of the barn.

He wasn't a native, and no matter how content he felt in Montana, he couldn't leave his parents and their practice. It was clear that Kristen belonged here with her family just as strongly. He couldn't pull this sweet cowgirl out of Montana, and he couldn't hide from his responsibilities in California, either.

He jabbed the pitchfork into the hay. He'd be lucky to get away from work one weekend every few months. Her two-timing pilot had been able to spend more time with her than Ryan could. How long would he and Kristen keep these tender emotions and this burning attraction going? Through how many lonely months of separation between the occasional three-day weekend?

He dumped more waste into the wheelbarrow.

Nothing good lasted forever.

It couldn't be done.

Ryan stared at his laptop in defeat. The firm's calendar was no more flexible than a judge's gavel. There was no way Ryan could squeeze in a return visit to Montana between Thanksgiving and Christmas. When he left Kristen at the end of the week, he'd be leaving her until February, at the very earliest.

I'm in love with you, Kristen. I'll miss Thanksgiving, Christmas and New Year's, but I can make it back by Groundhog Day, and Memorial Day three months after that. Is that the relationship with a cowboy you've always dreamed of?

His reality sucked. He needed to tell her all of it, before someone else burst their private bubble. If he kept taking Kristen on dates in Rust Creek Falls, it was inevitable they'd run into Brad Crawford or Lissa or, God forbid, Maggie.

Disaster had been narrowly avoided this morning. After they'd mucked the last stalls and washed up, they'd headed for the donut shop. As Ryan had rounded the corner in his rented rig, the local term for any kind of vehicle, the sheriff's rig had been parked squarely in front of the donut shop. There was no way Lissa's husband, Sheriff Gage Christensen, wouldn't have sat with them. There was no way he wouldn't have asked Ryan how LA was treating him, and God knew what else. But the sheriff's truck had pulled out of its park ing space just as they were pulling in, and Ryan had dodged yet another bullet.

After breakfast, he'd had the inspired idea to order sandwiches to go. A picnic at the actual waterfall that Rust Creek Falls had been named after had given him time alone with Kristen. He hadn't had to fear being unmasked at any moment by a friendly townsperson who might remember him from the flood cleanup. They'd seen no other humans on their afternoon hike. No grizzlies, either, and the placid but alarmingly large moose they'd spotted had been completely uninterested in meeting the new guy in town.

There'd been no dinner date.

Alone with his laptop was not how he'd hoped to end the night, but Kristen was at her mystery job in Kalispell. She'd given him one clue. Her job would help her become outrageously overqualified in the high school principal's eyes. Ryan had pretended not to guess the obvious, that she was teaching a night course.

He loved Kristen's determination. She'd win that teaching job sooner or later. Kristen as a cowgirl, home renovator and schoolteacher was an adorable combination. Kristen was perfect as she was, where she was. He couldn't ruin her life with his selfish desire to have her waiting for him in his beachfront high-rise at the end of his fourteen-hour days.

Sometimes the pursuit of happiness ended in a dead end.

It didn't have to end immediately, at least. Once she knew who he was and the limits of what he could offer, she might choose to be his long-distance lover. It couldn't last forever, but a few months of anticipating insanely heavenly weekends was as good as his life was going to get.

But if she said no when she found out how little he really had to offer her, he wouldn't be able to stop her walking away sooner rather than later.

One thing was inescapable: sooner or later, it was going to hurt like hell.

Chapter Eleven

"We never did go horseback riding yesterday. He wanted to go back out to the falls again. He thinks our falls are as pretty as Glacier National Park."

"Which you went to on Tuesday?"

"Right."

Kristen whispered the details of her week to her sister as they stood in the wings of the theater. Tonight was the final dress rehearsal, which meant she had to press down the hoop skirts of her blue Victorian gown to get close enough to her sister to whisper.

"And?" Kayla whispered. "Are you sleeping with him?"

"It was rated R, not X. But it was romantic, just the two of us." Kristen wriggled a little with the happiness of the memory. The motion added to her joy, because it was fun to make her skirt sway side to side.

"It's been just the two of you all the time. Awfully

private." Kayla was wearing regular clothes, all black from head to toe, the standard uniform of a stagehand. She had volunteered to serve as the prop master for half of the schedule.

"We don't always go off alone. You went to lunch with us today."

Ryan had driven her to Kalispell for buffalo burgers and sinful fries. It had been his suggestion to invite Kayla. Kristen had sworn Kayla to secrecy, though. She couldn't tell Ryan about tonight's dress rehearsal, only that she'd give Kristen a ride home after work.

"I want him all to myself. Kayla, I'm so happy when I'm with him. If he asked me to marry him today, I'd say yes."

"Silence on stage," the director called from his seat in the third row.

Kristen tried not to giggle like a disobedient child. She looked at Kayla, her partner in the crime of whispering, but Kayla was absentmindedly trailing her fingers over a bit of the black velvet trim on Kristen's gown, looking so sad that Kristen immediately felt sad, too. What had she said to put that look on her sister's face?

Marriage. It dawned on Kristen that she'd been taking giant steps since this summer, moving out, finding work, expanding her horizons. Most of all, falling in love. Maybe Kayla was feeling excluded.

Before Kristen could give her sister a squeeze and whisper that she shouldn't worry, that nothing could change the bond they shared as identical twins, Kayla yawned. She looked so tired. Come to think of it, she'd been sort of sad and tired for a while now, long before Ryan came back to town.

Without thinking further, Kristen put her hand on her sister's forehead.

"What are you doing?" Kayla whispered, jerking away in surprise.

"Do you feel okay? You seem kind of down."

"I'm fine."

"Maybe we should get you a chair."

"Really, I'm fine. I'm just a little…"

"A little what?"

Kayla squared her shoulders, and pulled Kristen deeper into the wings. "I'm worried about you. Everything seems pretty sudden with Ryan."

"I've known him for months."

"You've known *of* him for months, but you've really only known him for days. Are you sure you're in love with Ryan Roarke, or are you in love with the idea that this cowboy has come to town who fits your image of the perfect man?"

Suddenly, Kristen felt like she was the one who needed the chair. Hearing Kayla whisper doubts after she'd finally met Ryan was a horrible turn of events. She wanted her sister to say Ryan was wonderful. She wanted her sister to say that, having met him, she understood now why Kristen had kept such faith in him for all these months.

"Don't look like that," Kayla whispered. "I just want you to be sure you're paying attention to the real man, not the idea of being in love with a man. I don't want you to be hurt again."

Understanding dawned. "He's nothing like that stupid pilot. Ryan's like us. He worked with us in the stables twice this week. Didn't you think he loved all our twin stories over lunch today? He understands loyalty, and family, and—and love." But she hesitated over the last word, because Ryan hadn't said he loved her.

Really, she hadn't said she loved him, either. They hadn't talked about their future as a couple, only that he loved being with her and would come back as soon as he could. Maybe Kayla was right. Maybe she hadn't been paying enough attention to the real man.

The theater was plunged into darkness, her cue to take her place center stage before the lights went up on her big scene. It was time for Belle to make things perfectly clear with Ebenezer. Then she'd walk away and leave him alone in a spotlight as artificial snow began to fall.

Kristen picked up her fur muff and hurried to her mark. Belle needed to have a lot of courage to be so frank with Ebenezer about their relationship.

A little shiver ran down Kristen's back.

It's just a touch of stage fright.

But it wasn't. She couldn't stay in her happy fog much longer. She needed some of Belle's courage to ask Ryan exactly where their relationship stood. Tomorrow.

Kristen took her spot and waited for the curtain to rise. There was nothing to fear. She knew her part and she trusted her crew.

She had nothing to fear tomorrow, either. Ryan was no Ebenezer. Ryan would never place his career before her. In real life, she wouldn't be walking out of the spotlight and into his past.

"Oh, my gosh. It's my Mrs. Claus."

Kristen squeezed Ryan's hand in excitement, pulling him to a stop in front of the thrift shop. They'd had lunch in Kalispell again, and were window-shopping in the quaint part of town, the part that included Depot Park and the theater. Tonight was opening night. So thrilling—but so was finding Mrs. Claus.

"Do you think she's the right size? I don't think she's four feet. She might be the three-foot version. They made that in 1970. I've got the 1968 Santa. He's bigger."

"Maybe your Santa likes his women petite. I do."

Kristen bumped him with her shoulder, and he smiled his not-quite-a-smile.

Pay attention to the real man.

Her sister's words had been haunting Kristen all day. She looked at Ryan more closely as they stood outside the window. Its entire display was of Santas. Large ones, small ones, ugly atrocities from dime stores, all were mixed in with porcelain antiques. It was a dizzying array of red suits and white beards, but Ryan had already turned his back on it. That half smile said it all: he wasn't comfortable.

"Do dolls creep you out?" Kristen had gone to college with a girl who had a genuine phobia about dolls. To this day, Kristen felt bad about teasing her before she'd realized just how real the girl's aversion had been.

"Dolls?" Ryan looked at her with that brow raised in surprise. "Hardly. Did you want to watch a horror movie tonight or something?"

It was her turn to laugh uncomfortably. "No, I've got something else planned." His ticket to tonight's show was burning a hole in her pocket. She pointed at the store window, stretching the blue crochet of her mitten with her index finger. "So, it's Santa Claus, then. You don't care for Santa?"

He was about to say no, she knew it, but then he shook his head and looked at her like she was an unusual creature of some sort. "You really pick up on the strangest things. You're right. I don't care for Santa. I'm not a big fan of Christmas in general."

She remembered his words from the summer. "You said once if anyone could make Christmas better, it would be me."

"The decorations definitely look better when you're in front of them." His words were light and teasing, but Kristen knew she wasn't imagining the guarded look in his eyes.

"I thought you meant I'd make a good thing better, but you meant make a bad thing tolerable, didn't you?" She should have been paying attention. Tonight's play had scene after scene that included carolers and Christmas trees. "Just how averse are you to Christmas?"

Ryan turned to look at the street, with its red bells and green garland stretched between stores and giant candy canes tied to every pole. Then he looked back to the window full of Santas. "Most of this is fine. I hadn't really made the distinction, but you're right. It's Santa that particularly bothers me."

His attention was all on her. For once, it made her uncomfortable.

She tried for a nonchalant shrug.

"I don't believe in aggravating old injuries. You told me once about the church steps, and I think it's smart to just avoid them. There's a side entrance to the church, so why stand on the steps when you don't have to?"

Why go to a Christmas play when you don't have to?

She wouldn't give him the ticket. It was so disappointing, but really, she wouldn't make him do something unpleasant for the sake of her pride. She'd wanted him to see her onstage, but he'd love her just the same if he avoided a play that made him cringe.

He hasn't said he loves you. Pay attention.

Fine. Then he'd care for her just the same whether he saw her onstage or not.

She loved him, though, and she was concerned for his comfort. "Avoiding church steps or whatever else is unpleasant is simple enough, but avoiding Santa Claus... I don't think it's possible. December must be torture for you."

The sting of tears caught her by surprise. Disappointment, concern, love for a man who was leaving two days from now, her uncertain future—all of it added up. She puffed out a little breath and blinked back the tears quickly.

Not quickly enough. Ryan pulled her protectively into the alcove by the window. "Is that a showstopper? I didn't think that would make a woman consider walking away." The stiffness with which he asked the question was a sure sign that this was not a passing curiosity. This question mattered.

A woman walking away. Pay attention.

"What if you have children someday? Would you raise them without Santa?"

He was silent for an eternity.

She felt awful, keeping him by this window full of Santas. "We can keep walking. We don't even have to talk about this."

To her surprise, he enveloped her in a hug. "It's okay. I've never dated a woman who made me think about having children."

She hugged him back, grateful once more that he was leaving the rodeo forever. It sounded like a rotten life.

He let go of her and cleared his throat a little, a man prepared to make a formal statement. "I think children deserve to believe in the magic of it all."

Kristen let out the breath she'd been holding. If she'd had time to think up a right answer, that would have been it.

"I'd handle it." To her relief, Ryan winked at her. "You'll notice I'm standing in front of this window without going crazy at the moment. I didn't run screaming from the Santa on your porch. I'm a grown man, I can control my feelings. If I was with a child who wanted to sit in Santa's lap, I could stand in that line at the mall for as long as it took. Does that answer your question?"

She smiled and nodded and pretended she wasn't choked up by those tears once more. Poor Ryan. Her Ryan. The one she was paying attention to.

She started walking toward Depot Park and her theater. Ryan fell in step beside her, and she reached out to hold his hand, blue mitten to his black leather driving glove. Only one event in his childhood could have given him such an aversion to Christmas. "Did you see Santa before or after your birth mother walked away?"

He whistled softly. "Has anyone ever suggested the law to you as a career? You're so fearless in your questioning. I can just see you with a witness on the stand."

That surprised her, in a good way. She swung their hands a little bit. "I like that image. It makes me sound tough. Much more flattering than what my brothers would say. They say I'm like a bull in a china shop, always jumping in without thinking."

"No, it's an insightful question. Childhood memories are tricky, though."

"You were three, right? I'm trying to come up with a memory from when I was three. I don't think I have any."

"I was almost four, but I still only remember a couple of moments."

They'd come to an intersection with a traffic signal. Ryan pushed the button, and out of habit, Kristen shifted from foot to foot to stay warm while they waited for the signal to walk. She'd been doing that since she was a little girl.

"When I was three, my sister and I were taken to a preschool here in Kalispell once a week while my mother did the big shopping. I really only know that because my mom has pointed out the preschool to me and told me about it."

"The big shopping?"

"You know, the weekly grocery stock-up. My brothers went through boxes of cereal, so she bought them by the gross."

The light turned green, and they continued walking hand in hand, like grown-ups.

"Anyway, I suspect the preschool was a way for her to get her shopping done without hauling around two three-year-olds, but she insists that it was to improve our social skills. If you think about it, it would be easy for twins on a ranch to grow up without ever seeing other children their age. I don't remember the preschool at all, or at least I thought I didn't, but I remember this toy kitchen. It was made of wood, but it had a stove and sink, and the knobs were blue. I asked my mom once what happened to it, who had we given it away to, and she said we never had a toy kitchen. It had been at this preschool."

She slowed her steps, concentrating on that memory, and Ryan slowed down with her.

"That's it. I can't remember the classroom or any of the other kids or what the teacher looked like. I remember blue kitchen knobs. Isn't that weird?"

"I'm told that's normal. Below a certain age, you might remember something like the candles on a birthday cake, but you wouldn't remember the whole day, like who was at the party or what gifts you got. Just an image of a flaming cake."

"You were told that?"

"Part of the adoption process included counseling for my parents as well as me. I don't remember that, either, but to this day, my parents recommend it to other adopting parents. When I was old enough to ask questions, they always seemed to know what to expect. I asked about the church steps when I was in middle school. Before that, they weren't sure I had any memory of my birth mother at all."

His adoptive parents must have cared about their new son very much to have prepared themselves to answer all his questions in the future. She'd like to meet them some day.

"Is that all you remember? Church steps and the backs of her legs and the hem of her skirt?"

"It's like one of those six-second videos that you see on the internet. I'm looking down at my shoes, and I'm standing on cement steps. I know it's a church, and it's some kind of Christmas festival, because I'm holding a snow globe. It's brand-new to me, like I've just gotten this snow globe, and my shoes hurt, and my mother..."

He trailed off into silence.

"I'm sorry," Kristen said. "I shouldn't have asked you to relive that."

He looked almost surprised at her apology. "It's okay. I was just replaying that scene, and you were right. I would have said that Santa wasn't part of it, but he was. That snow globe had a little plastic Mr. and Mrs. Claus in it, puckered up for a kiss and bending toward each other with their eyes closed."

"Oh, no. Like the one on my porch?"

"It's a common scene. I dropped the snow globe when she walked away. There was water and glitter splattered everywhere, and those red figures were lying there in the open air, still straining toward each other, still trying to connect. They never get to kiss, do they?"

They reached the park, which was really just an open square. Soon, it would be filled with cocoa stands and craft stalls for the official start of the holiday season. Right now, in the sunny-cold afternoon, it was a still-green square by the railroad tracks, empty except for the plain evergreen in the center that awaited its holiday finery.

Kristen stopped walking and turned to face Ryan. "Why didn't you tell me? I would have retired Mr. Claus. I would have at least shut up about my quest for Mrs. Claus."

"Unnecessary, remember? I can handle it."

She felt the tears sting her eyes. "Right. Because you're a big, tough man and you can control your feelings."

"Is that so bad?"

She stepped into him, her boots fitting between his as she clutched his lapel in her mittens and looked up at him through lashes that were wet with tears. "I'm so very sorry. I'm sorry that Ryan Michaels had to learn to control feelings like those. And I'm sorry that Ryan Roarke has a girlfriend who is too curious. I shouldn't have been so nosy."

"Don't be sorry. I want you to know me." He lifted her chin with his leather-gloved hand and kissed away a tear. "You are so special because you want to know me. It's a gift to be with a woman who asks such real questions. Most women just want—"

He cut himself off abruptly.

"Women just want what?"

Long moments ticked by. At first, she was horrified that she'd brought up some other terrible memory, but when he wouldn't quite meet her gaze, she looked at him harder. What did women want from him?

"Oh, my gosh," she blurted. "You're blushing, aren't you?"

"Of course not."

"You are." She slapped the lapel of his overcoat with her palm. "That's what women want from you, huh? I guess I'm not very unique."

They both began to laugh, and it felt wonderful to be with him, laughing by an evergreen on a sunny day in the park.

"Kristen." Ryan pulled her to him. "You are the most perfect you. Never has a woman touched my heart the way you do."

Her heart soared at those words, and she looked up at him through lashes that were still dotted with tears. "With you, I'm crying one minute and laughing the next. I think that definitely means I love you."

"Are you sure you can love a man who is more of a Scrooge than a Santa?"

If only he knew. "Scrooge had his reasons for hating Christmas, and so do you. I'd have to have a heart of stone to hold it against either one of you. I've always had a soft spot for Scrooge."

"I've always liked Scrooge, too." His eyes narrowed the tiniest bit, and then he straightened and looked around the square. Red bells, candy canes, the tree awaiting its decorations—he looked critically at them all. "I've always thought I hated Christmas, but I don't. None of this bothers me. I watch at least one version of Scrooge every year."

"You do?" The ticket in her pocket might be a sweet surprise, after all.

"I do. I don't hate everything about Christmas."

"Just Santa?" she asked, wanting to be sure.

"Yeah, I'm not so crazy about him, but now I've pinpointed why. Thank you. I told you those questions were good ones."

"Being like Scrooge could be a good thing. He changes at the end of the play and ends up as the biggest Christmas fan of them all."

"That may be a bit ambitious, but I'll work on it."

"The day after Thanksgiving, there's a big parade through town that ends right here. The mayor lights the tree, and it stays lit all month. When you come back, I'm going to bring you here and kiss you until you have a great Christmas memory to start building on."

His smile dimmed a little at her words, but that was probably because a great Christmas was a new concept for him. "I told you when we met that if anyone could make Christmas better, it would be you."

She looped her arms around his neck. "And when I find my 1968 Mrs. Claus, I'm going to put her on the porch with her little mouth pushed right up to Santa's. It's too sad that they never make that connection. Mine are going to get to kiss all winter long."

He'd said her questions were like a gift to him, but she had something better to give: a promise. So while he was still chuckling, she spoke very seriously. "And, Ryan Roarke, whether it is Christmas or the Fourth of July or spring or autumn, I will never, ever walk away from you."

Kristen loved him.

Him, Ryan Roarke, who had once been Ryan Michaels, and who bore all the complications that came with his history. Miraculously, he'd come to Montana and found the one woman who had taken the time to get to know him inside and out, and she loved him.

They'd spent all week sharing their histories, their feelings, their desires. She knew nothing about the cars he owned or the clients he helped, but she knew his heart. She loved him, the real him, not an idealized image of a cowboy or a rodeo star. He could tell her about his law practice now, and it wouldn't change anything she loved about him, because she'd fallen in love without knowing about his Hollywood connections or his bank account. When he explained that he couldn't make it back in December, that there'd be no kiss by the town's tree, she'd be disappointed, but she'd still love him in January.

"Speaking of Scrooge," she said, "there's something you don't know about me. Close your eyes."

He closed them obediently. He heard the rustle of her bright red coat as she unbuttoned it. His own coat was unbuttoned despite the temperatures staying in the thirties. In only one week, his body had learned to tolerate the cold far better. If he lived in Montana, it would take no time to adjust.

"Now let me turn you so you're facing this way."

If only he could live in Montana. He couldn't let his parents down, but he needed to find a way to see Kristen more often. December was impossible, but perhaps he could fly Kristen to Los Angeles, if she could juggle her ranch, her renovations and her teaching job. She'd never want to live in LA, but she might find a visit interesting.

"Okay, open your eyes."

Kristen was beaming at him as she held a ticket in her mittened hand.

He took the ticket. "*A Christmas Carol*? We were just talking about it. You had this in your pocket the whole time?"

"I did, but I wasn't going to give it to you if it would make you sad. You have no idea how relieved I am to hear you say you like Scrooge. Tonight is opening night, right here at this theater." She gestured toward the sprawling brick building she'd turned him to face, a renovated train depot, by the looks of it.

She seemed overly excited about attending a local play, but he was game. "Great. We'll go. You've got the other ticket?"

"That's the surprise. You know that job I've been working at every day? This is where I've been."

His brain made a feeble effort to tie a teacher into the theater. She tutored children in the cast, perhaps. Dread started building, knotting his gut. He tried to connect a cowgirl to the theater, grasping at straws. Perhaps there were live animals in the play, and she wrangled them. But his heart knew what was coming, what came next.

What always came next, with every woman.

"After I met you, I knew that it was time to get serious about my passion, my career, my life. Everything. Because of you, I'm pursuing a little happiness here in this theater. I don't need a ticket, because I'll be onstage."

No. Don't say it, don't break it.

"I'm an actress!"

Good God. He staggered back a step. How could he have thought it would be any different with this woman?

He crumpled her ticket into his fist and shoved his hands in his pockets. "You knew. All along, you knew."

Her smile didn't falter, but the little wrinkle between her brows betrayed her concern at his reaction. She wasn't a good enough actress to hide her concern.

"I knew? Well, yes, I auditioned in October."

"An actress." He looked at her beloved face—yes, beloved, damn it—and felt like a fool.

"You knew I was an actress."

He couldn't speak he was so disgusted.

Her smile was completely gone now, as she so earnestly tried to make him believe this was a good thing. "You were the one who encouraged me to use my degree. You were the one who inspired me not to take no for an answer."

"From a principal. So you could teach."

"So I could create a drama club. I majored in theater, Ryan. I'd love to direct a play at the school. I love the theater."

"Of course you do."

She blinked at his mocking tone and even pulled that

trick with the tears again. He wanted to applaud her performance, shout *Brava!* for the way she'd so thoroughly performed her part this week, but he couldn't go that far. Not yet. Not while she looked like the innocent ranch girl of his dreams. Once she made it to Hollywood—and he had no doubt that a woman with her exquisite features could get noticed there—she'd be Botoxed for no reason, her lips augmented and her hair dyed blond, and then, when she didn't look so much like Kristen, he'd be able to harden his heart completely.

Right now, it hurt like hell.

"Well done, Kristen. Well played. A word of caution, though. You almost gave away your game at the beginning of the week. You accepted the fact that my name was Roarke too easily. You should have played it a little less cool that I was from California. You were supposed to think I was a rodeo star, remember? There are no cattle operations in LA."

"But… Bakersfield. Salinas." She sounded faint. Bewildered. Still beautiful.

He couldn't bear to look at her. For a week, he'd been denying himself the pleasure of her body, wanting her to know who he really was before he made love to her.

He had to laugh at his own naïveté. "I must've thrown you off by refusing to share your bed, but you compensated brilliantly. All those long talks, all that tender concern. It was a novelty to me, I admit. What were you hoping for, Kristen? Was I supposed to go to your little play tonight and be so besotted that I'd run to Scorsese and sing your praises? What are you earning at this theater, equity minimum? Did you think I'd negotiate a top contract for you?"

She'd deserve it. The way she was pressing her little mittens to her temples in confusion, the way her hair tangled with her polka-dot scarf and the November breeze pinkened her cheeks—oh, yeah. She was playing her role to perfection. He could get her top dollar.

"It backfired," he informed her coldly. "The sex would have been fine. No hard feelings. But to make me believe in love and family and goddamned Santa Claus? I just feel like a sucker. No one does favors for people who treat them like suckers."

Kristen held her palms out in a helpless gesture. The gentle shake of her head was just enough to make fat tears drop from her lashes to her cheeks.

"Who *are* you?" she whispered, the plea in her voice sounding so real his heart squeezed hard in his chest.

"Did you really think I was a cowboy? The rodeo star of your dreams? Please."

Finally, she dropped the innocent shock and moved on to something else, something angry. The stomp of her booted foot and the clenching of her fists were perfect touches. "Stop this. Stop. You're being hurtful, and I don't know why. You're from Los Angeles and you were never in the rodeo? What on earth do you do?"

"I'm an attorney." He crossed his arms over his chest, closing his jacket against the cold. "An attorney in the entertainment industry, and a damned successful one, as you well know."

"An attorney."

"A simple thing to search for on the internet. I honor my confidentiality agreements, but Hollywood studios do not, when they want to stir up publicity. My role in the Century Films controversy became common knowledge. How convenient for actresses who are ready to take their careers to the next level."

"I searched Ryan Michaels, the rodeo rider. You lied to me."

"I never claimed to be in the rodeo."

"But you knew I thought so. All week, you've been lying to me. You let me spill my heart out—oh! When I told you about that lying, cheating pilot, you should have told me you were just like him. Just toying with me while you were in town. Just playing a game until it was time to fly off to some other life."

And she hated him for it, judging by the look on her face. He steeled himself against the pain. Maggie had predicted it, but Maggie hadn't known that Kristen had been playing him for a fool all along. This was just an act.

Kristen took in a shuddering breath. "Were you lying from the beginning, even in the summer? Were you really considering moving to Rust Creek Falls? Did you care for me even a little?"

He'd be damned before he told Kristen any more about his feelings. She didn't need to know that his parents' need for him to take over the firm had ended his dream to move here, either. But as he looked into her blue eyes, wide with hurt and bright with tears, some piece of Ryan wanted to hold her and soothe her and reassure her.

He squelched the impulse. "I'm not the actor here, Kristen. You are."

Let her make of that what she wanted.

The cold air had dried the tears on her cheeks. "You shouldn't play with people's lives. You shouldn't have hurt mine. I only loved you."

Ryan hated himself for how badly he wished that were true.

"I think we've covered everything sufficiently," he said. "There's no need for a dramatic ending. You'll forgive me if I don't wish you luck in your acting career. Goodbye, Kristen."

She closed her eyes, a moment of misery, and started to turn away. But she only began the motion with her shoulders before she stopped herself and leveled her gaze on him once more. She said nothing, did nothing.

He raised one brow. "Go on. Your theater awaits. I've got nothing left to say."

"You're waiting for me to walk away. I made you a promise before I handed you that ticket. I told you I would never walk away from you. I'm standing right here, Ryan. If you want to leave me, if you want this to end, then you are going to have to be the one who walks. I won't do that to you. Not even now."

Now that you've broken everything.

Nothing good lasted forever. Finding out that Kristen's love had been a lie was really nothing more than he'd expected. Actresses were always ambitious, after all.

Ryan turned on his heel and began walking away. He shoved his hands in his coat pockets and felt the ticket. Without missing a step, he pulled the crumpled ticket from his pocket and dropped it onto the sidewalk.

I'm not this good of an actress.

Kristen could hardly hold herself together. Her hands were shaking as she tried to button the tight cuffs of her Victorian costume.

"Do you need help?" Kayla stopped to put down the bowl and spoon Scrooge would be using to eat his gruel.

In her shapeless black clothes, with her headset on her head, Kayla looked ready to make sure all the props made it onstage throughout the performance.

"Oh, Kayla. I'm so glad to see you. I had the most awful day with Ryan."

"Hold that thought. One second."

Kayla dashed off to one of the toilet stalls in the women's dressing area, cutting Kristen short just when she'd been about to spill all her misery.

She shouldn't give in to the misery, anyway. She should get through the show before she let her feelings out, because once she started crying, she was afraid she'd never stop.

She managed the buttons on her cuff, then the other cuff. Still, her sister stayed in the bathroom. Kayla hadn't been herself for weeks now, and Kristen was worried sick about her. She couldn't handle any more bad news, not on top of Ryan's betrayal.

Ryan. She couldn't stop thinking about him for a second. How could she have been so deceived? A Hollywood attorney, playing at being a cowboy. They'd never actually done any riding or training of the horses this week, she realized suddenly. That had been by design. *His* design.

But, dear God, the horses had loved him, and so had she.

He'd lied to her.

He'd left her.

She pressed her hand to her mouth, physically trying to hold her sobs in. She couldn't do this. She couldn't go out on that stage and say her heartbreaking lines while her heart was truly breaking.

"We've got a full house." The stage manager's voice came over the little speaker that was kept backstage. "Two minutes to curtain."

She was about to find out whether or not she could. The show must go on.

Chapter Twelve

Kristen's tears didn't wait for their cue.

From the wings, where she hovered anxiously near Kayla's prop station, she watched the first scenes of the play. The little boy playing the youngest version of Ebenezer was doing a good job. Too good for Kristen's state of mind.

The little boy had no one to love him, no place to spend the Christmas holiday. His classroom was barren. One by one, every other student left with a mother or father. The teacher gave him a book to read and threw one measly piece of coal into the stove, then walked out. Alone, rejected, unwanted, the boy huddled at his wood desk.

In the dark cocoón of the wings, Kristen's tears fell. If young Ebenezer had just dropped a snow globe on the floor...

Poor Ryan. He'd been even younger than this boy

when he'd been left alone in the world. Thank goodness he'd been adopted, but despite thirty years of being a Roarke, Ryan was still the little boy who'd learned to be so careful with his heart. Kristen had thought she could prove to him that her love was unbreakable, as solid and real as the love his adoptive parents had given him, but he wouldn't give her the chance.

Maybe a man who'd spent thirty years avoiding pain, a man who'd only very carefully chosen to return the love of those immediate family members who'd spent years loving him first, maybe that man would never change.

She would never know.

The tears started anew, and Kristen knew she would have to repair her stage makeup. Quickly. The Christmas party scene at the jovial Fezziwig home was about to begin.

While the stage was blacked out, the stagehands rushed antique toys onto the set, setting them under the tree. Kayla rolled a rocking horse onto the stage, then she zipped back to the wings with her arms full of schoolbooks from the classroom scene. She placed them in their assigned spot at her station, then she put her hand on her stomach and gave herself a pat.

Kristen's sobs hiccupped to an abrupt stop. That pat was the kind of thing a pregnant woman did to her growing belly.

Kayla was pregnant.

No. They were sisters. Twins. Kayla would never keep such a secret from her. She wasn't even dating anyone. But the months of fatigue, the nausea, even the decision to give up caffeine...

The lights onstage came up, bright white to make the

colorful party set pop. The audience applauded the set design before the first line of dialogue could be spoken, and Kristen watched her sister smile and take her hand away from her stomach to applaud, too. The white lights bounced off her black clothes, and Kristen wanted to cry all over again. Her sister had a definite baby bump. The first secret Kayla had ever kept from her was one of the most important ones of all.

It didn't seem possible that two people Kristen loved had so completely hidden their real selves from her. From Ryan's livelihood to Kayla's new life, Kristen had been oblivious to it all, a trusting, blind fool. Like the character of Belle, she only wanted to go back to the way things had been.

Belle was brave, though. When the man she loved changed, Belle faced the truth. In the face of Ryan's betrayal, Kristen had no choice but to do the same.

With a swirl of blue velvet, she hurried back to the makeup station, suddenly thankful for the chance to play Belle tonight. For the length of a few pages of script, Kristen would get to be brave.

And then, when the lights went out and the audience left, she would fall apart.

The Ghost of Christmas Past showed no mercy.

Old Scrooge wanted to enjoy the happiest memory of his life, but the figure in white and flame dragged him away as the curtain came down, obliterating the sight of Fezziwig's party and the lively dancing.

Ryan shifted his weight as he leaned against the very back wall of the theater. The happiest memory of his life was a dance, too. A waltz in the middle of an empty road. A sky lit by fireworks, a woman's voice humming the melody that guided them. Destiny.

The bitterness threatened to choke him. Her perfection had been an act, just as her performance tonight would be. Ryan had decided to buy a ticket at the last minute. He didn't bother taking his seat, because he'd be leaving soon. He only wanted to see Kristen onstage before he caught the last flight out. He needed to witness all her fake glory as an actress. When the happier memories swamped him, as they already had while he'd gone back to his hotel and packed, he wanted to be able to recall her on the stage, pursuing the career that she'd hoped he would boost.

The Ghost of Christmas Past pointed to the center of the dark stage. Scrooge begged her not to show him the inevitable, but of course he had to turn toward center stage, as well.

In contrast to the full set of the Christmas party, this scene opened on a simple park bench lit by a single spotlight. Standing in the center of the circle of light was Kristen, absolutely breathtaking in her winter velvet gown. Snow gently fell all around her.

Ryan heard a hiss of breath and realized it was his own. Kristen looked like a figurine in a snow globe. He'd come for a memory. He didn't want this one.

A young man in top hat and tails entered the circle of light. Kristen looked at Ebenezer with such longing, such regret, that Ryan was taken aback. With talent to match her looks, the sky would have been the limit if he'd wanted to launch her career.

Eventually the words of the play penetrated his thoughts. "Tell me truly, if you saw me today for the first time, would you make the effort to dance with me at Fezziwig's party?"

Yes. A waltz or a two-step, a wooden floor or asphalt, anything at all to feel her in his arms one more time.

"The man who loved me is only a memory. For his sake, I pray you will be happy upon your chosen path. You no longer want me to walk with you, no matter how much I wish it otherwise."

For God's sake, he couldn't stand here and listen to this. Either she was a world-class actress stuck in an obscure regional theater in a tiny town, or her heart was truly breaking as she spoke her lines. Either way, it was her misfortune. She was the one who'd been planning on using him. She'd said everything he wanted to hear in exchange for her shot at Hollywood.

Impatiently, Ryan picked up his coat and gloves and headed for the exit. The usher stopped him at the door. Ryan would have to wait until the end of the scene to open the door into the bright lobby. From the corner of his eye, he saw the hem of Kristen's long skirt as she walked out of the spotlight and was swallowed by the darkness.

"Go after her, you fool," Old Scrooge cried.

The usher held up his finger. One minute more.

Old Scrooge implored his younger self with an urgency born of grief. "Do you not see her caring heart? Lift your eyes from that cursed gold ring. Go after her! It's not too late for you."

But it was too late. The Ghost's flame was extinguished, the scene went dark, the audience erupted into applause and Ryan got the hell out of there.

An hour later, as he settled into his seat on the evening's only flight out of Kalispell, the voice of the pilot came over the speakers. "Ladies and gentleman, this is Captain Toomer speaking. Along with the rest of your Denver-based crew, we'd like to welcome you aboard Flight 89."

Ryan dropped his head back against the seat. A crew out of Denver. What were the odds? He could be leaving the woman who'd lied to him by taking a flight piloted by the man who'd cheated on her. Given destiny's warped timing, the odds were good.

The pilot who had *allegedly* cheated on her. Kristen could have invented the entire story to manipulate Ryan's emotions. That story had made her look good, really. She was the one who knew how to be faithful. She'd implied that the experience had negatively colored her opinion of men from big cities. Men like him.

Ryan lifted his head, a sudden jolt of adrenaline making him alert. She'd said she didn't like men from big cities. If her goal had been to attract Ryan, why would she say she avoided men like him? If her goal was to move to Los Angeles, why would she insist she didn't want to leave her hometown?

You fool...do you not see her caring heart?

It had been a trick. She'd used reverse psychology, saying she wanted the opposite of her goal to make herself seem all the more innocent. That had to have been it. She'd hidden her ambition, so he'd let down his guard. Ryan rested his head back once more, settling in for the first leg of his journey home.

You fool...

That had to be the explanation, because if it wasn't, then he'd just shattered something priceless.

* * *

"Another scotch, son?"

"Sure." Ryan turned with the decanter in his hand, ready to fill his father's glass.

His father had no glass. He merely stood on his own patio, his swimming pool sparkling in the sun beyond him, and slipped his hands into the pockets of his slacks.

"Ah. You meant, am I having another scotch?" Ryan tried not to sound too bitter as he laughed. Leave it to Dad to make his point so subtly. "Last I checked, I was over twenty-one, and I'm not driving anywhere."

Thanksgiving dinner was over at the Roarke home, but no one was leaving. Shane and a noticeably pregnant Gianna had flown in from Thunder Canyon, so they were spending the holiday weekend in one of the guest suites of their parents' home. Maggie and Jesse and baby Madeline had flown in from Rust Creek Falls and were staying for the weekend, too. Ryan was staying, as well, although he lived in the city. He wasn't going to leave this mini family reunion to spend the night alone in his exclusive, sterile penthouse. He didn't need more of his own company.

The sliding glass doors were open, and the sounds of football on TV spilled onto the patio. Sometime in the third quarter, the kitchen would be raided for a second piece of pumpkin pie or the first cold turkey sandwich of the weekend. Every year, he looked forward to that as much as he looked forward to the formal, hot dinner earlier in the day. This year, he'd also looked forward to finding relief from the loneliness that had been crippling him in the week since he'd left Kristen. Surely, surrounded by the family he trusted, Ryan's heart would be eased.

Instead, he was the seventh wheel. His parents, Christa and Gavin, were one couple. Shane and Gianna, another. Maggie and Jessie. That left Ryan feeling the absence of Kristen Dalton more acutely than ever. Thankfully, his father kept excellent scotch.

Shane joined them, carrying baby Madeline, practicing for his own impending fatherhood. "I can't get over the weather here. You forget how warm winter can be. It's already snowed at the resort. The ski bunnies are thrilled, but it means the main color we're going to see from now until Easter is white, white and more white."

"Go to one of the local high school's basketball games. There'll be lots of color."

Shane and his father both looked at him in surprise. Ryan shrugged, unwilling to explain where he'd gotten that advice.

Kristen's solution for a winter white-out had been so enthusiastic. Practical, too. Despite her secret agenda, he had to acknowledge that she really knew Rust Creek Falls inside and out. There'd been nothing fake about that tour. She'd had him seriously imagining himself trading in his penthouse for a luxury log home somewhere on the outskirts of town.

Which wouldn't have helped her get noticed in Hollywood.

Ryan stared into his scotch. Kristen must have known who he was that first day, of course. He'd been sitting with Maggie in the church during the wedding. Surely people knew Maggie was related to Shane Roarke, celebrity chef. It would have been a simple thing for Kristen to connect Roarkes with LA and show business.

Of course, she'd pretended not to know Maggie's maiden name later, but Kristen was a very good actress. She must have seen them together and realized that Ryan could be her chance to get out.

Then why had she invited him to come in? Had he moved to Rust Creek Falls, her plans would have been thwarted, yet that's exactly what she'd tried to get him to do.

The attorney side of him, which he'd once thought was his only side, picked another hole in his story. When, on that first day, could Kristen have seen him with Maggie? Kristen hadn't been at the church. Maggie hadn't been at the park.

Ryan set the scotch down, untouched.

"Are you in or not?" Shane asked, holding up a dollar bill.

"What?" Ryan couldn't think straight. His loneliness was rapidly morphing into a sick sort of dread. He may have screwed up. He may have made the biggest mistake of his life.

"Are you putting a dollar down on the Cowboys this year or not?"

"Sure." Ryan had been betting on the Dallas Cowboys to win the Thanksgiving football game since childhood, when losing a dollar had meant financial pain for the two brothers. "I don't have any cash on me. Spot me."

Shane sighed as if being asked for a dollar were a terrible imposition. "Here. Hold the baby."

Madeline let herself be handed from one uncle to the other without fussing. A series of mundane little family events followed. Shane took his wallet out of his back pocket as Maggie and Jesse joined them on the porch. When Maggie held her hands out for her daughter, Madeline stoutly refused the offer and clung to Ryan's neck.

There was laughter and Maggie pretended to be out-raged at Madeline's preference for her uncle. Through it all, Ryan managed to stay on his feet and act sane. Inside, he was losing his mind.

Everything that had happened at the wedding had been real. Kristen hadn't been lying on the Fourth of July.

Ryan walked away from his family, carrying Madeline around the edge of the kidney-shaped pool to a lounge chair. He sat and stretched his legs out on the cushions. Madeline stretched herself out on his chest.

Away from the noise of his family, Ryan called upon his analytical side. Even if Kristen had started flirting with him innocently in July, this month had been a different story. On that late flight out of Montana, Ryan had decided it was entirely too coincidental for Kristen to have run into Maggie at the movies. She must have arranged it. Then she'd pulled off a performance as a lovesick woman that had been realistic enough to fool his sister into calling him back to Rust Creek Falls. He'd already been on his way, but Kristen hadn't known that. She'd had to use Maggie to be sure he returned.

The baby fussed a little, burrowing herself into a more comfortable sprawl on his chest. He patted the baby's back absently and stared at the blue water of the pool as she fell asleep. In the bright light of day, the scenario that had made sense on a midnight flight was full of holes so big, it didn't take an attorney to find them.

There was no movie theater in Rust Creek Falls. Movies were only shown on a certain Fridays in the gym. Most of the town turned out for the basketball games, Kristen had said, and he was sure that was true for the movies, as well. It was quite possible that Kristen and

Maggie had run into each other there without any nefarious plotting on Kristen's part. Ryan only knew a handful of people in town, yet he hadn't been able to take Kristen to a donut shop without running into Lissa's husband, the sheriff.

For the rest of his theory to work, Kristen had to have known not just that he was a Roarke, but that Maggie Crawford was, too. The biggest proof of Kristen's innocence was her sister. Kayla was Kristen's twin, her confidante, her biggest cheerleader. If Kristen had hatched a plan to hitch herself to Ryan for a Hollywood career, her twin would have known about it. Instead, when she'd learned that his last name was Roarke, her surprise had been genuine. *Are you related to Lissa Roarke, then?* Kayla was no actress. She and Kristen hadn't known he was a Roarke until he'd told them in the barn.

Case dismissed. Kristen was innocent, and he was a fool.

He'd shattered a snow globe once again. A thousand flakes of glitter and a hundred drops of water couldn't be put back together. Once upon a time, Christa Roarke had come and replaced the birth mother he'd lost. This time, no woman could replace Kristen Dalton. She was the only one he wanted. The only one he'd ever want.

Baby Madeline snuggled her soft head under his chin. Even a bachelor like Ryan knew that sleeping babies should not be messed with. His infant niece had him pinned to the chair when he wanted to pace restlessly. He wanted to hit a punching bag until he was too tired to think, but there'd be no escaping today. Ryan closed his eyes, remembering Kristen as he'd seen her last, a vision in Victorian blue, standing in a snow globe of a spotlight.

He had to try to fix this. He couldn't live the rest of his life alone like a bitter old Scrooge, angry at himself for not going after the woman with the caring heart. If putting a snow globe back together was impossible, then...

Then he'd be grateful that people weren't snow globes. He was going to fix this.

The baby wriggled. Ryan spread his hand across her back to calm her. Holding a baby, he realized, was even more soothing than brushing a horse. If he could win Kristen back, he'd give her all the horses she wanted, and as many babies as she desired.

Having babies meant getting married. It meant living together in one house as one family. He couldn't commute from Montana to LA and be a good husband and father. Ryan knew, without a doubt, that he'd want to raise his family in Rust Creek Falls, if he could find a way to make it happen. Unfortunately, he was a lawyer, not a cowboy, and there was barely enough legal work in Rust Creek Falls to keep Maggie busy four days a week.

Kalispell wasn't too far, and the town was easily four times the size of Rust Creek Falls. If he practiced law there, he'd never make as much money as he did here in LA, but he could make a good living. If he could win Kristen back, if he could fix the damage he'd caused, then he would never have to get on a plane and leave her behind again.

There was one thing he couldn't do if he moved to Montana. He couldn't run his parents' firm for them.

The sense of obligation was familiar. He wanted his parents to be happy. He wanted to help them out any way he could, but when any way meant he couldn't have a life with Kristen...

This was the point where he always got stuck, the point where he would give up and do something mind-numbingly physical. Not today. The baby breathed evenly, her little rib cage expanding gently under his hand, forcing him to stay still. Forcing him to find a solution.

He didn't have one.

The sound of his mother's laughter carried over the pool water. Ryan opened his eyes and took in the scene. Parents, siblings, their spouses. More babies on the way. His family. His foundation.

He didn't have a solution, but he did have a family. He hadn't trusted Kristen's love—a crucial mistake. But in many ways he hadn't trusted in his family's love, either. He'd once told Kristen that he knew his parents wanted him to be as happy as Shane and Maggie, but he'd been afraid to put it to the test.

It was time he stopped silently taking on problems alone. Tonight, over pumpkin pie and turkey sandwiches, he'd rely on the family he trusted to decide the future of Roarke and Associates together.

Then he'd get on the first plane back to Montana. Would a permanent move to Rust Creek Falls be enough to convince Kristen to give him a second chance? He'd shattered that snow globe in such a spectacularly awful way that he wanted something equally spectacular to prove he'd never lose his faith in her again. He needed some way to demonstrate that he would never again be the cold-hearted bastard he'd been when he'd left her.

Madeline's tiny fist gripped his shirt as she slept. He kissed the top of her head. Kristen's words came back to him. *What if you have children someday? Would you raise them without Santa?*

Ryan ran the tip of his finger over the dimples in the back of Madeline's hand. "You deserve a chance to believe in the magic, little one. For you, I could tolerate Santa."

The germ of an idea started to form.

Carefully, he got to his feet and carried his niece over to the family. "Maggie. Shane. I need your help. Who do you know in the mayor's office in Kalispell?"

Chapter Thirteen

There was no performance on the day after Thanksgiving.

Kristen should have been thankful for the respite. Tonight, she wouldn't have to relive the horrible feeling of losing the man she loved. Instead, she had to play a role that seemed even more daunting. She had to ride on a float in a Christmas parade, smiling and waving and throwing candy and generally acting like she was in a happy holiday mood.

The entire cast of *A Christmas Carol* was assembled on a flatbed truck that had been turned into a float. Kristen wore her full costume. In addition to the corset and hoops, the heavy skirt and tight bodice, she carried a faux fur muff and wore modern long johns under her dress, because tonight, the snowfall was real.

They waited at one end of Main Street near a high school band, a motorcycle club and a cluster of rodeo riders whose horses were dressed to the nines in silver saddles and fancy tack. Kristen looked away from the rodeo riders.

The last float featured Santa Claus himself, who would join the mayor in lighting the Christmas tree in Depot Park.

Santa Claus. The symbol of everything magical and wonderful about the holidays for her was a symbol of misery for Ryan. Was it any wonder that a man who didn't believe in Santa couldn't believe that her love was real, either?

It took every bit of acting skill she had to look happy through the entire parade. Two miles had never crawled by so slowly, but her ordeal wasn't over yet. Because of their picturesque costumes, the cast had been asked to wait by the Christmas tree until Santa's float arrived. When Santa lit the tree, the cast would add charm and holiday spirit to the town's official photos. They would be posted on websites and spread around social media. The exposure would have been nice if Kristen was trying to get jobs outside her hometown, but no matter what Ryan Roarke thought, she wasn't. The only things she'd get out of this photo session were frozen toes.

She stamped her feet and clutched her hands more tightly together inside her muff. The cast had been on the first float. Santa was on the last.

"Okay, let's have everyone line up now, half on each side of the tree." The Kalispell newspaper photographer also doubled as the wedding photographer for most of the couples in town, so he was pretty quick about getting everyone posed, ready and waiting.

Hurry, Santa. I want to go home. It's been at least five hours since I last cried. I'm overdue.

At last, the float with Santa's cardboard and plywood sleigh arrived. Kristen plastered on her smile when the cameras started to flash.

Santa dismounted his float with ease, moving in a way that was far more sprightly than his white beard would indicate he was capable of. This year's Santa was as tall as he was wide. He worked his way through the crowd, passing out candy canes to the children, who jumped excitedly at the sight of him. With every "ho, ho, ho," the children squealed in delight. Kristen's stiff smile relaxed into something more genuine, as well.

"Ho, ho, ho. Merry Christmas."

Kristen jerked her gaze away from the children to study Santa instead.

"Merry Christmas," Santa called again.

He sounded like Ryan.

Her mind was playing tricks on her. Ryan was in LA, where he belonged. Her sister had made some polite small talk with Lissa Christensen the day after Kristen and Ryan's fight, and Lissa had said that her cousin had left a day early, probably to put out a fire at his law firm.

Kristen knew he'd only wanted to get away from her as quickly as he could. He'd been so full of self-righteous anger—all of it directed so unfairly at her—that he'd wanted to put a thousand miles between them.

Kayla had also broken the mortifying news to her that if Lissa was Ryan's cousin, that meant Maggie Crawford was Ryan's sister. Apparently, she was Maggie *Roarke* Crawford. When Kristen remembered that meltdown at the movies, she didn't know how she'd ever look Maggie in the eye again.

"Smile, please. Keep smiling." The photographer

hadn't stopped snapping yet. Kristen obediently forced her face into a semblance of happiness.

"Ho, ho, ho."

Honestly, that man sounded just like Ryan. Impossible—even if Ryan had returned to town to visit his sister or cousin, he would never, ever be caught dead in a Santa suit.

With his sack of candy canes now empty, Santa walked to the tree and shook the mayor's hand. The switch was thrown, the lights came to life and the crowd went wild. So did the camera flashes.

Santa chose to stand right between the only two women, Kristen and the actress playing Mrs. Cratchit. It could have been Kristen's imagination, but Santa seemed to give her an extra warm squeeze. Was Mrs. Cratchit feeling such a strong arm around her waist?

"Ryan…?"

This man didn't seem to be angry at her at all. Considering how furious Ryan had been just days ago, it couldn't be him. Then again, Santa was an important role. Santa could never get angry in front of children—and Ryan would never ruin Christmas for a child, despite its having been ruined for him.

But Ryan also had no earthly reason to ever wear a Santa suit. Whoever this year's Santa was, it couldn't be the man who'd so recently broken her heart. It was pitiful that she missed Ryan badly enough to imagine it was him.

At last, the ceremony was over, the photographer was satisfied, and the cast was free to return to the theater to remove their costumes. Santa offered Kristen his arm as she headed across the green to the theater, and they each smiled and returned waves from the children and adults they passed.

They entered the theater through the stage door, which led almost directly to the black curtains of the wings. Santa looked all around, turning in a full three-sixty. "Are there any children here? No? Good. I'd hate to confuse the little kids."

He pulled off his hat with one hand and his white beard with the other, and turned to kiss Kristen, hard.

She hadn't seen his face, but it didn't matter. She recognized his kiss.

"Ryan." She murmured his name against his lips, but before she could begin to ask him the questions his presence raised, he spoke.

"I'm so sorry. Please forgive me for being a stubborn, pigheaded jerk."

"But..." She shook her head at his padded costume, just one more mystifying piece of the puzzle that was Ryan. "Why?"

"Because I hurt you. I jumped to all the wrong conclusions, and I refused to listen to you when you told me the truth. I don't deserve it, but please forgive me."

"I meant, why are you Santa Claus? This is like your worst nightmare."

"Not even close. Losing you is my worst nightmare."

Most of the actors had made their way back to the dressing rooms, but Ryan pulled her deeper into the wings, where the black curtains muffled their voices and gave them a sense of privacy.

"I'm wearing this suit so you'll know that I mean it when I promise you that I won't make the same mistakes twice."

"You won't assume I'm some kind of gold-digging, movie star wannabe?"

Well, that had rolled off her tongue a little too easily. She'd had a week to relive every painful word he'd said to her, though.

He dropped his head for a moment, chagrined, then looked at her again with such tenderness in his expression, it took her breath away. "For starters, yes. That kind of mistake. I'm so sorry. Do you know why I assumed the worst? Because those were the only type of women I'd known. They were the only type of women I dated, because they couldn't hurt me. They didn't matter. If they walked away, nothing inside me would shatter."

He touched her face with one hand, tentatively cupping her cheek, then stroking his thumb over her cheekbone. "But you, Kristen, you matter."

"Oh, Ryan." Kristen turned her face into his hand.

"I didn't know how to handle that. You are this wonderful, remarkable, beautiful woman who somehow fell into my hands, but I didn't know how to hold you. I was so afraid I'd lose something good, that I was paralyzed. I did nothing. That was a mistake, too.

"I was afraid to lie to you and afraid to tell you the truth at the same time. I told myself you couldn't handle too many corrections all at once, but the only real truth was that I was petrified I'd lose the best thing in my life. That's you. That will always be you.

"I learned when I was young that nothing good lasts forever, but I don't think that's true any longer, not after meeting you. I believe forever is possible, a good forever, as long as I can spend it with you. I'm wearing this Santa suit because I'm not going to avoid the good things in life anymore. I hope that, someday, you'll love me again. I hope that you'll trust me not to make the same mistakes again."

Kristen swallowed past the lump in her throat. Just seeing his face again, just being touched by him again, made her happier than she could have believed possible just a short time ago. She pressed her hand to heart, feeling out of breath from the emotions.

"If you can't forgive me tonight, I understand," Ryan said. "I screwed up badly, but I'll be here tomorrow. And next week. Next year. You promised me you'd never walk away from me, and I'm here to make the same promise back. I'm staying. Right here in Montana, right here with you, until you believe me when I say I love you."

"Oh, Ryan." Kristen tried to throw her arms around his neck, but his red suit's padding was completely in the way. Her hoops pushed gracefully behind her when she got close to him, but his stuffed belly stayed stuffed.

Ryan unbuttoned the coat and tossed it on a folding chair. Underneath, he was wearing a fitted black T-shirt with the baggy red velvet pants. He pulled her into his arms and held her against his strong chest almost as tightly as she'd dreamed for the past lonely week.

"I don't want you to settle for a Scrooge when you want a Santa," Ryan whispered. "I don't want you to settle for a lawyer when you want a cowboy."

"I don't want a lawyer or a cowboy. I want a Ryan."

"Michaels or Roarke?"

"Both, as long as he's happy with me."

"He couldn't be anything else with you in his life, and that's the whole truth."

Kristen kissed him almost as passionately as she knew she'd be kissing him tonight. In her house. Finally.

The cast of the play had begun filtering back out of the dressing rooms. A man in street clothes whistled at their embrace. Kristen tried to brazen it out, giving the crew a nonchalant shrug of one shoulder as she broke off the kiss she'd initiated. She smoothed her gown into place over her hoops.

"Some things go without saying, but this needs to be said. I love you, Kristen Dalton. It's been seven days since I've held you, and I never want to go seven days without holding you again."

Ryan dropped to one knee in front of her, and Kristen thought her heart stopped. Cast, crew, costume— all were forgotten as she focused on Ryan.

He patted his oversize pants pockets and got a little of that deer-in-the-headlights look, but then he slid on his knee to the discarded Santa coat and dug through it until he came up with a gray velvet box. The theater people gathered around them began to buzz with excitement.

"I wanted to wear the Santa suit to show you how precious you are to me." He opened the gray box and held it up. The diamond ring inside sparkled with every color of every Christmas light ever strung on a cozy house for two. "This is the other way I want to show you how precious you are to me. I love you with all my heart, Kristen Dalton. I will never deserve you, but I'm not going to let that stop me from being happy with you. Will you marry me?"

The photographer by the town Christmas tree was tireless in his effort to capture the happiness of the newly engaged couple.

Kristen had changed into her street clothes, including a chic white jacket with faux-fur trim and the most flattering nipped-in waist. She'd bought it this week in a futile attempt to use retail therapy to soothe her heartbreak, but now she was thrilled to have something fabulous to wear for her engagement photos. Ryan was looking handsome and sexy and cute all at once. That was possible when the fine tailoring of a man's coat contrasted with the bright red Santa's hat he wore.

"Wassail!" One of the street vendors came up to their little cluster of friends and family. "It's on the house. Wassail to toast the happy couple."

Kayla was standing next to Kristen, so Kristen took the chance to offer her some sisterly advice. As surreptitiously as she could, she gestured toward her sister's thickening middle. "If I were you, I'd pass on the mystery punch this time."

Kayla colored. "I don't know what you mean."

"I know your secret. I want you to be as happy as I am. We've got to talk."

"Soon. Don't worry about me right now. This is your special night."

On Kristen's other side, Ryan scrutinized the two cups he held. "Do you suppose this is safe to drink? They still haven't solved the case of the Power of the Punch."

"I was just saying the same thing to Kayla. You and I have so much in common."

"On the other hand, we just got engaged. Who cares if the wassail is a little too strong?" He grinned at her, looking more carefree than she'd ever seen him look.

"It is a very old Christmas tradition." She took one of the cups from him.

"You know, Christmas is rapidly becoming my favorite time of the year. If I'm going to be a changed man like Scrooge, I believe I need to fully support all the traditions."

Kristen tapped her cup to his. "In that case, down the hatch."

"In that case, Merry Christmas to the future Mrs. Roarke." They drank to their own happiness, and kissed under the lights of the tree.

"From now on," Kristen sighed, "I'm always going to love wassail-flavored kisses."

"From now on," Ryan said, "I'm always going to love you."

* * * * *

Look for
MERRY CHRISTMAS, BABY MAVERICK!
by Brenda Harlen

On sale December 2015

MILLS & BOON®

Cherish™

EXPERIENCE THE ULTIMATE RUSH OF FALLING IN LOVE

A sneak peek at next month's titles...

In stores from 20th November 2015:

- **Her Mistletoe Cowboy** – Marie Ferrarella *and*
  Proposal at the Winter Ball – Jessica Gilmore
- **The Best Man & The Wedding Planner**
  – Teresa Carpenter *and*
  Merry Christmas, Baby Maverick!
  – Brenda Harlen

In stores from 4th December 2015:

- **Carter Bravo's Christmas Bride** – Christine Rimmer
  and **Bodyguard...to Bridegroom?** – Nikki Logan
- **A Princess Under the Mistletoe** – Leanne Banks
  and **Christmas Kisses with Her Boss** – Nina Milne

Available at WHSmith, Tesco, Asda, Eason, Amazon and Apple

Just can't wait?
Buy our books online a month before they hit the shops!
visit www.millsandboon.co.uk

These books are also available in eBook format!